Awards Received for book one and two of this ballet trilogy
84 Ribbons & When The Music Stops

2014 Moonbeam Book Award

Hollywood Book Festival

Beach Book Festival

New York Book Festival

Eric Hoffer

Los Angeles Book Festival

The San Francisco Book Festival

Great Northwest Book Festival

Feathered Quill

Eric Hoffer

Eric Hoffer, Montaigne Medal

Reader's Views Reviewers Choice

Great Northwest Book Festival

London Book Festival

San Francisco Book Festival

Beach Book Festival

Hollywood Book Festival

Other Accolades for 84 Ribbons

Indie Excellence Awards—finalist, Book Interior Design—Fiction and Young Adult Fiction

Dance Spirit Magazine 'Pick of the Month' for April 2014.

YA ForeSight, ForeWord Magazine. 84 Ribbons selected for showcase article. One of five young adult novels showcased for Spring 2014 in *The Risky Business of Growing Up.*

Praises for Paddy Eger's When the Music Stops

★★★★★ A Great Sequel. I really enjoyed this book and would recommend it to those who love the world of dance or love to read about the world of dance.
—**Sandra K. Stiles**, (Teacher, Reviewer)

★★★★ ...a beautifully written sequel to the enchanting first book, 84 Ribbons. ...The array of characters are complex, well developed, and the writing flows gracefully across the pages, easily captivating readers.
—**Stacie Theis** (Beach Bound Books)

Eger's characters are entirely believable, the pace of the story is perfect, alternating in an almost ballet-like way between poses and bourrés, and the questions in Marta's heart are resolved beautifully.
—**Katie Johnson**, Author of *Red Flags for Elementary Teachers*

[The story] provides a wry look at ballet, while the beauty and passion of Marta's dancing demonstrates why people want to learn the craft.
—**Clare O'Beara**, *(Fresh Review)*

Author Paddy Eger has created a wonderful story for readers who love ballet and the dance. Part love story and part coming-of-age, readers will enjoy the story as the characters learn to overcome tragedy.
—**Kristi Bernard**, (Reviewer)

I would describe this book as gentle. It has a heart-warming theme of family and neighbors and friends all looking out for one another. But it still has a lot of depth.
—**Trish**, (Reviewer)

I found When the Music Stops-Dance On to be an easy to read standalone novel, though it did inspire me to put 84 Ribbons on my reading list. The characters are realistic and believable, especially for the times. [late 1950s]
—**Arianna Violante**, *(Reader's Views)*

Praises for Paddy Eger's 84 Ribbons

Author Paddy Eger realistically portrays the daily life of a professional ballet dancer in this wonderful coming of age novel. The setting of 1950's America adds to the appeal of the story.

—**Cheryl Schubert** (Librarian)

It's a realistic look into the struggle of making it dancing professionally, including the pain, blood, sweat, and tears required, as well as the devotion to perfection. Marta doesn't have an easy ride at the Intermountain Ballet Company, but she's determined to prove herself and succeed. ...it's more than just a ballet book.

—**Leeanna Chetsko** (Net Galley Reviewer)

I loved this short book's quiet, deceptively simple voice; its strong sense of time and place (Billings, Montana in 1957); and the timelessness of its topics and themes, which include moving away from home, making friends and enemies, and dealing with first love, loneliness, temptations, and career decisions. It is squeaky clean in terms of language and content yet also candid about things like eating disorders.

—**Hope Baugh** (Librarian)

As a former bunhead who grew up in Washington, I thought this book was both credible and enjoyable.

—**Amy Anderson** (Librarian)

...Overall, this book was a pleasant surprise. It is the best ballet book I have read in a long, long time and I'm excited to see that Paddy Eger has a follow up planned as I'm keen to see what happens next.

—**Trish Hartigan** (Net Galley Reviewer)

I could see the whole thing unfold in front of me like a movie. ...I will continue to think about this story for a good while, it's just one of those books. ...Thank you, thank you, for the opportunity to read this beautiful story!

—**Holly Harkins** (Net Galley Reviewer)

Praises for Paddy Eger's 84 Ribbons

This was a very good coming of age story that follows Marta Selbryth as she attempts to follow her dream of becoming a professional ballerina.

—**Courtney Brooks** (Net Galley Reviewer)

I really enjoyed this book. It reminded me of Laurie Halse Anderson's "Wintergirls" in a great way. ...I loved how ballet provided the framework, but how the characters really took over. ...We'll be ordering a copy for multiple collections.

—**Stephanie Nicora** (Net Galley Reviewer)

This was a great look into the world of ballet. This would be entertaining for readers of all ages from teen to adult.

—**Jessica Rockhey** (Librarian)

84 Ribbons *is a real story for young adult ballet fans. It's not one of those melodramas all about some hot boy.* ...This was one of the better YA theatre/sport oriented books I've read. ...If you liked the Drina books by Jean Estoril or Girl in Motion by Miriam Wenger-Landis; then I'd also recommend this book to you.

—**Sonya Heaney** (Net Galley Reviewer)

Letters to Follow

A Dancer's Adventure

Paddy Eger

Tendril Press
AURORA, COLORADO

Letters to Follow—A Dancer's Adventure

Copyright © 2017 Paddy Eger. All Rights Reserved.
www.PaddyEger.com

Published by Tendril Press™
www.tendrilpress.com
Denver, CO
303.696.9227

This book is a work of fiction. Names, characters, places, and incidents are either products of the author's imagination or are used fictitiously. Any resemblance to actual events, locations, or persons, living or deceased, is entirely coincidental.

All images, logos, quotes, and trademarks included in this book are subject to use according to trademark and copyright laws of the United States of America.

No part of this publication may be reproduced, stored in a retrieval system, or transmitted in any form or by any means, electronic, mechanical, photocopying, or otherwise, without the prior written permission of Tendril Press and Paddy Eger. The material in this book is furnished for informational use only and is subject to change without notice. Tendril Press assumes no responsibility for any errors or inaccuracies that may appear in the documents contained in this book.

ISBN 978-0-9858933-9-2

Library of Congress Control Number: 2016949025

First Publishing: February 14, 2017
Printed in the United States of America

Author Photo by: Yuen Lui
www.YuenLuiStudio.com
Lynnwood, WA
425.771.3423

Cover Design by Karin Hoffman
Cover Images © shutterstock.com

Interior Images
Tour in auto a Parigi—© Giuseppe Porzani – stock.adobe.com
vecchia cartolina postale vintage—© Giuseppe Porzani – stock.adobe.com
Vintage Memo Book Open to Blank Pages—© Mark Carrel - stock.adobe.com
note paper piece label vintage grunge tape—© picsfive - stock.adobe.com

Art Direction, Book Design and Cover Design
© 2013. All Rights Reserved by
A. J. Business Design & Publishing Center Inc.
www.AJImagesinc.com — 303•696•9227
Info@AJImagesInc.com

This paper meets the requirements of ANSI/NISO Z39.48-1992 (Permanence of Paper).

Dedicated to the traveling spirit in all dancers and readers.

The dance is strong magic. The dance is a spirit.
It turns the body to liquid steel. It makes it vibrate like a guitar.
The body can fly without wings. It can sing without voice.
…The dance is life.

—Pearl Primus

Author Notes

Writing *is* an adventure that I look forward to stepping into daily. When the story moves on to become a novel, it involves a lot of assistance for me and many thanks to a long list of supporters.

Ideas and Research:

While the story came from my imagination, many details settled in from reading novels set in France, scanning travel guides and pouring over maps and visiting my local Sno-Isle Library System. I enjoyed every hour of my time. In fact, at times I got lost in research.

David Behrendt generously shared his 1960's student trip to Europe, helping me ground my characters and details from that time period. My French-speaking friends, Denise Bertrand and Lucile Marshall, corrected language errors, but any remaining errors are my own. And the kind people at Aurora Stamps and the American Philatelic Society helped with post cards and stamps in use in 1959.

Winners of my name-a-character drawings at book events named Lucia, Artemesia, Cheryl, and Vera Dei. Thank you for sharing your suggestions. Each character became a unique and important part of this, my third book in the ballet-themed trilogy.

A Note about Music, Choreography, Ballet Terms and Tour Map:

I watched many hours of musical scores and recorded dancing via YouTube to inspire my descriptions of the dances performed throughout the novel. In the back of the book I've provided a Glossary of Ballet Terms.

To enhance your reading pleasure, I invite you to visit my website paddyeger.com for a list of YouTube channels that share ballet music and dances mentioned in the novel.

Also, check the pages after the novel for a map. It shows many of the stops for the dance troupe and for Lynne's adventure after the tour ends.

Editing:

We often think that writing the book is the end of the path. In fact, it is the middle component. After we write, we edit, looking for ways to enhance the story, eliminate glitches, and check conventions and punctuation to smooth things out for our readers.

My critique groups helped me dig out interesting details. Then my editor, Linda Lane, polished my pages and Karin Hoffman, my publisher and creative designer finished the pages so they became print-ready for release to you. The e-book versions were prepared by Julie Mattern, an amazing web person. (As usual, any remaining errors are mine alone.)

Letters to Follow

Lynne stormed into the dressing room and threw her ballet slippers into her locker. "That woman! She never stops yelling at me!"

"Maybe you deserve it. I mean, you're late a lot and…"

Lynne swung around. "Mind your own business, Suzette."

"I'm just trying to be helpful."

"Back off!" Lynne glared at the saccharine smile. "You couldn't help an old lady open a cereal box."

The dressing room fell silent. The first-year as well as the seasoned dancers watched the two women elevate their dislike to the level of a boxing match. All they needed were padded gloves.

Madame Cosper hobbled into the dressing room. "What's the ruckus?"

The dancers turned away, pretending to ignore Madame's glare.

"Well?" Madame looked around, pointing her cane at a new dancer. "Tell me!"

"It's Lynne and Suzette," she said.

"Is that true, Lynne? Suzette? If so, you need to settle down." Madame looked around the dressing room, shook her head, and left.

Suzette packed her dance tote and sashayed from the room. Lynne watched her leave, then leaned against her open locker, ignoring the dancers looking her way. Since Marta left the company, she'd become Madame's new whipping girl. True, she did come in late; she lived far out of town, and January's snowy roads required caution. True, she didn't back down when Madame corrected her, but Madame was often wrong. True, she'd pushed Madame to accept the little girls she taught as replacement dancers in the Nutcracker, but they'd performed well. Might be time to make a change—if she could last four more months to the end of the season.

Lynne exited the building and found Jer, a fellow dancer, pressed against the building with his face buried in his winter coat. He shook his head. "That was you and Suzette, right? We heard you down the hall in the guys' dressing room."

"I know. Suzette gets to me. It's as if she knows when I'm vulnerable, like now. And Madame." Lynne paused. "I can't watch her pouting red lips and not think of how she forced Marta to leave."

"Not true, Lynne. Marta left because of her injury. The way you antagonize Madame during practices— I don't know why she doesn't fire you."

A smirk edged onto Lynne's lips. She raised one eyebrow. "Because I know about her skeletons, her after hours' indiscretions."

Jer grabbed Lynne's arm. "What are you talking about?"

"I'm not sharing. Let's get out of here. The auto repair shop closes in ten minutes."

ஒ

Jer dropped her off at Al's Auto and headed to his girlfriend's apartment. Several workers followed Lynne with their gaze as she entered the shop. She avoided eye contact and attention, even from the cute grease monkeys looking up from the pits where they worked under the cars.

Al, a burly, bald guy, wiped his greasy hands on a stained rag. He smiled, then shook his head. "Honey, I've got bad news. Your Chevy is ready for the junk yard."

Lynne rolled her eyes. "Know a place that almost gives away cars?"

Al chewed on his lip. "No, but my cousin's got a used car lot south of here, east off 27th. I told him you'd be stopping in real soon. He'll make you a good deal."

Lynne nodded as she pulled out her checkbook. "What do I owe you?"

Al walked to his desk and cranked out her charges on his adding machine. "Forty even."

She shook her head as she wrote out the check. "Guess I don't eat the rest of this month."

As she drove back to her aunt's place by Lake Elmo, she wondered if she should apply for a car loan one more time. She certainly couldn't ask her folks for money with her dad recovering from his heart attack.

She pulled into Aunt Vivian's driveway and turned off the engine, too tired to move. Her aunt approached and knocked on the window. "Plan to stop over for dinner tonight. I have exciting news!"

There goes my chance to sit and pout, she thought. At least I'll get a decent meal.

They sat down to a pork chop dinner followed by warm apple pie. Vivian laid down her fork. "I'm selling this property. I know I've talked about it since you first rented the garage apartment, but my sister purchased a duplex in Baltimore and wants me to take the second half. It's walking distance to downtown and has a small backyard where we can raise vegetables."

"That's great, Aunt Vivian."

"I already have a buyer."

Lynne choked on her mouthful of pie. "You do?"

"Yes. It's a lovely family of four. I'll head out the end of June. That gives you plenty of time to find a new place to live. I'll miss you and watching the little dancer girls, but I miss my sister more. You understand, don't you?"

"Of course." She did understand, but she preferred to keep as much distance as possible from her family to avoid working in the family-owned hardware store. But where would she find another inexpensive place to live?

Maybe she'd board at Mrs. Belvern's like Marta had done. That would frost Carol, the six-year college student and resident grouch.

"It's exciting news, right, Lynne?"

"Sounds perfect. I'll miss having you here and pestering you for last minute food. Your sister's lucky. I wish I had a sister. Sure would make my life more fun. Brothers can be such a pain!"

She climbed the stairs to her garage apartment, unlocked the door, and tossed her purse and dance bag on the floor. She dropped into her favorite chair and closed her eyes without bothering to turn on the lights. "What's happening today? My first day back, Madame jumps down my throat, the car repair empties my bank account, and now my aunt is moving." She sighed. "Why am I talking to myself?"

The next day as she changed clothes to head off on her lunch break, Lynne saw a note taped to her locker:

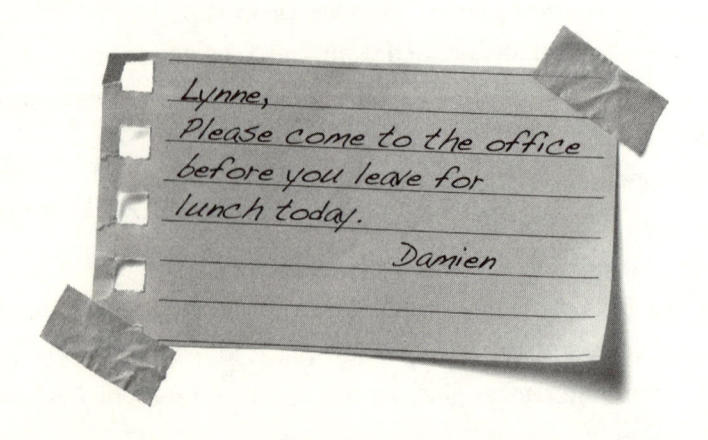

> Lynne,
> Please come to the office before you leave for lunch today.
> Damien

Now what had she done? It was only her second day back. Why was she summoned upstairs to the director's office?

She knocked. Damien, the dance master, called out, "Enter."

A quick glance around the room relaxed her; Madame Cosper wasn't lurking in the shadows, ready to pounce on her for being away or voicing her latest complaints.

Damien looked up as she entered. "How's your father?"

"Better. For a while we thought we'd lose him, but he's going to be alright. Thanks for asking and for allowing time for me to go home to be with my family."

"Of course. If you want or need help getting caught up on the choreography, let me know. I'll make time to work with you."

"No need. I've not been granted solos or back-up roles in *Coppélia*."

"That's part of why I wanted to speak with you." Damien's smile faded. "We need to discuss your attitude. Your interactions with other dancers lack professionalism. You're an extraordinary dancer, but you're stalling your own career."

She curled her hands into fists and avoided Damien's stare, afraid her intended comeback might stir up problems.

"You want to dance with us, don't you?"

"I guess." She swallowed hard and wiped away a tear.

"That's not good enough." Damien stood and paced behind the desk. "We need a hundred-and-ten percent from you." He paused. "Yes, I know about you and Suzette. Everyone does."

Lynne's face heated; she squirmed. "I'll work on my attitude."

"Good. Now take your break."

She could think of nothing to say, so she nodded and backed out of the office.

Suddenly, she needed to get away. She grabbed her coat and the packed lunch her aunt made and headed to her car.

She turned on the heater and stared straight ahead, seeing nothing beyond her dirty, frost-covered windshield. The fact that Damien knew she was out of control concerned her. She needed to pull herself together and ignore Suzette.

By the time her car heater kicked in and her windshield cleared, it was time to head back into the building. She left her uneaten lunch on the seat.

In the practice room, Suzette turned her direction. Her smirk sent a chill down Lynne's spine. Suzette stepped from her usual place at the *barre* to stand in Lynne's spot. Lynne clenched her fists and lifted her chin. Even though she seethed inside, she nonchalantly moved to the only space left, the longer *barre* behind Patrice, the principal dancer of the company. No one wanted to stand behind her and invite comparisons.

Lynne straightened her wrap and smoothed back her hair as she settled into first position.

Patrice turned toward her. "How's your father?"

"Better. Thanks for asking."

"If I can help in any way, please let me know." Patrice twisted her neck side to side as she spoke. "Five years ago my father suffered a similar emergency, but he didn't survive."

"I'm sorry," Lynne said. "How's your mother handling things?"

"She died last year. I miss my parents every day."

"That must be hard."

Patrice nodded and turned away to prepare for afternoon warm-ups.

When Damien entered the practice room, the dancers settled and began their afternoon. Lynne turned her attention to her *demi-pliés*. With each bend of her knees she repeated under her breath, "I can do this. Suzette is a stupid bug." By the time she'd progressed to the steady beat of *battements*, her mood improved. Thinking of Suzette as a bug did the trick, especially when she imagined antennae growing from her head and barbs sprouting from her legs. She smiled. If Suzette saw the bug Lynne pictured, the stupid girl would explode with anger.

Rehearsals for the *Coppélia* intensified; performances began in two short weeks. She moved with the other *corps* dancers from one rehearsal room to another, tracking the soloists to learn the choreography to become a back-up dancer. For her the task was meaningless beyond learning steps for future seasons. Even so, by four o'clock she felt as exhausted and lost as if she'd missed a month rather than a few days.

ઝ

When she returned home, she sat in her car, staring at nothing. Once again her aunt rushed out her back door and hurried toward her. "Your mother called. I told her you got back safely and were attending rehearsals. She wants you to call."

"Thanks. I'll call when I go inside."

Lynne called home, reported in, and learned her father's health continued to improve.

"When will you be home again?" her mother asked.

"I'll try to get home in June unless I accept a summer job teaching ballet like I did last summer. You could visit me in Billings. You'd enjoy the open spaces of Montana."

Her mother's answer didn't surprise her: "It's hard to travel that far. Your brothers can't run the business without us, but we'll think about it."

Always her brothers, the favorite children, even though they were grown-ups and should function independent of their parents. And why couldn't the two able-bodied, unemployed brothers run a hardware store? They lived close by and could lend a hand on weekends if they were needed. Men.

After the phone call, Lynne stood in front of her open refrigerator, yawning. She threw out the oozing slice of Christmas pie, the wilted head of lettuce, and the wax-paper-wrapped leftovers she'd ignored on her race to catch the train home to Trenton. She picked up two heels of Wonder Bread, spread on creamy peanut butter, and added two sliced baby dill pickles. Cutting her sandwich in half, she stared at her concoction. Was she hungry? It didn't matter. She needed to eat *something*, so she stood by the sink and nibbled the sandwich while she made a list for later.

She set her dirty plate next to the sink and grabbed the sweaty leotards and tights out of her dance tote. When hot water had filled the sink, she dumped in a handful of Ivory Snow and swirled the water until bubbles frothed on the surface. Washing dance wear provided think time. As she squeezed the soap and water through her clothes, she thought about being back home. Thank goodness her dad survived his heart attack. At forty-three he was too young to die. Of course, her eighteen-year-old dance friend Bartley was also too young to die, but nothing saved her.

Lynne knew she should have called her best dance friend, Marta, or sent her a note; but she'd rushed to get back to Jersey to comfort her mother and see her dad maybe for the last time. Marta had come to Billings for the holiday to visit Steve, her steady boyfriend, so she probably hadn't noticed that Lynne was gone.

Thinking of Marta brought back her conversation with Damien. Had dancing for the Intermountain Ballet Company lost its glamour? With her two ballet friends no longer around to share their free time, could she date enough guys to keep herself distracted?

She rinsed and rolled her dance clothes in a bath towel, then hung them on the shower rod to dry. Trying to forget everything, she sighed and slumped in her chair; but her thoughts wouldn't stop cycling. A hot shower might settle her mind.

The steaming water cascaded over her head and shoulders, washing away thoughts of her time on the train as well as today's sweat. Muscles in her chest tightened, then released. A hollow space expanded inside her; her breathing became ragged. She grabbed the wall of the shower. Her knees flexed as if she carried a thousand pounds. Tears tumbled down her cheeks while she relived the moment she first saw her mom's face, tight with fear of losing her husband. Why now? She'd not cried once when she was in Jersey.

Wrapped in her flannel pajamas, heavy chenille robe, and fuzzy slippers, she scanned her apartment for something to distract her until bedtime. Settling down at her small dining table, she gazed around the room. What did she want to write? Nothing. She took a blank-faced postcard out of her purse. Might as well get this over with.

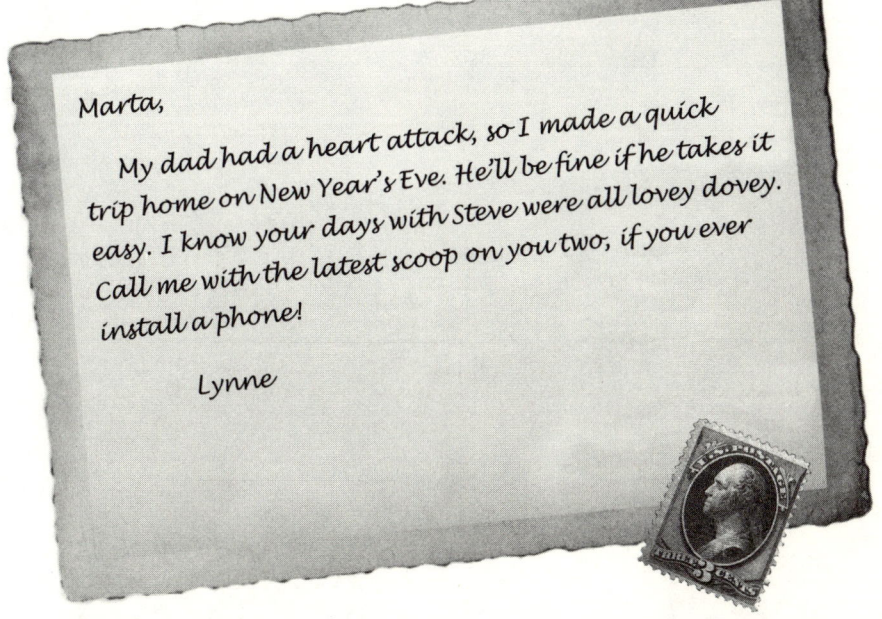

> Marta,
>
> My dad had a heart attack, so I made a quick trip home on New Year's Eve. He'll be fine if he takes it easy. I know your days with Steve were all lovey dovey. Call me with the latest scoop on you two, if you ever install a phone!
>
> Lynne

After she added a three-cent postage stamp and stuck the card inside her purse, she sorted her pile of dirty clothes to handle tomorrow, then stopped and stared at her clock. It was already seven. The grocery stores were closed. She'd also forgotten she'd promised to help Aunt Vivian carry packed boxes to the garage tonight. After all her aunt had done to support her, she should have remembered and at least called her to apologize. It looked like a PB and J without bread would be her breakfast *and* lunch tomorrow.

2

At eight the next morning, Lynne walked through the snow to her aunt's back door and knocked. Vivian appeared in her bathrobe with a frilly apron over it. "Did you call home yesterday?"

"I did. They're all fine." Lynne shifted from foot to foot. "I was wondering if you could spare two pieces of bread so I could make toast this morning? My fridge is as empty as my wallet."

Vivian smiled. "Certainly, but why don't you come in. I'm fixing French toast, and I'd love your company. Everything tastes better when it's shared."

Eating with her aunt gave her a much needed boost. She admired the way Vivian found the bright side in every situation. In addition, she always asked about Lynne and the ballet company and her boyfriends. She even purchased a season ticket to the ballet and brought Lynne small gifts after performances: a bouquet of daisies, a biography of Anna Pavlova, and, Lynne's favorite, homemade cookies.

Last season she'd convinced Lynne and Marta to teach ballet to four young girls from her church's afterschool program. Thanks to an emergency, they danced in local *Nutcracker* performances, which entitled them to scholarships for the Arinna Darnivilla Ballet Academy. Lynne avoided mentioning how she'd manipulated Madame Cosper to arrange for the girls to dance. Vivian, like Marta, would never approve of her tactics. It had worked. No one got hurt, so why not help the little girls get scholarships?

As Lynne stood to leave, she remembered the boxes she was supposed to help move. "I'm sorry about not helping you last night."

Vivian took Lynne's hands in hers and smiled. "If it had been earth-shakingly important, I'd have knocked on your door. As it turned out, I spent two hours on the phone with my sister. By then it was too late to start moving boxes."

◈

Later that week, as Lynne exited morning class, Damien called to her, "Meet me upstairs."

She caught a glimpse of Suzette's smug grin but pretended she hadn't seen it, focusing instead on what she'd possibly done *this* time.

Damien closed the office door and invited her to sit. "I want to congratulate your effort to avoid encounters with Suzette. I've watched her try to upset you and you've ignored her, probably more than I could in your shoes."

Lynne tightened her lips and nodded, holding back all the things she wanted to say about Suzette's taunting.

"Now, on to why I wanted to see you. An opportunity has arisen. The hospital is conducting an injury prevention seminar for athletes. We're invited to send representatives. Would you be interested in representing the *corps de ballet*?"

Lynne smiled. "Of course. Thanks for asking me."

"Great. I'll let you know the details once the physicians confirm the schedule." He checked his watch. "It's your lunch break, so enjoy your downtime. I'll let Madame know we've spoken. I've already shared your improved effort. Keep up the good work."

Lynne nodded. "I plan to. And thanks again for thinking of me for the seminar."

As she opened the office door, a surprised Suzette almost tumbled inside. She caught herself and stood, then brushed back her hair.

"Hello, Suzette," Damien said. "I'm glad you're here. I need to speak with you."

Lynne walked around Suzette, noticing her usually smug expression fade as she entered the office. Lynne closed the door with a quiet click and smiled. Looked like Suzette might get a taste of her own medicine, Damien style.

This past week, Damien and Madame had complimented her dancing. Maybe biting her tongue and offering to join the injury prevention team would help others to see her in a positive role. If not, she'd need to consider a bigger change.

As she packed to leave that afternoon, a small notice on the bulletin board caught her attention:

Dance Journal Classified Ads

Summer Opportunities:
American Dancers Tour in France
Hiring: First & Second Year Corps Dancers
Dates: June 23 through September 20
For: French summer festival performances
Classical and original choreography
Wages plus travel, room, and board
Application Deadline: February 12, 1959
Include: Ballet dance history and ballet company letter of recommendation
Mail to Americans Dance in Paris Tour
c/o Cheryl Menkins
12346 Tolt Ave.
Buffalo, New York
Details by return mail for invited dancers.

Hmm, she thought. A change of scenery could be good. She looked around. No one was watching, so she pulled down the ad, folded it, and tucked it into the top of her leotard.

"You not allowed to do that," a voice down the hallway called out.

Lynne turned and rolled her eyes. "What can't I do, Suzette?"

"Take notices off the board without permission."

Lynne shook her head as she walked away. "So sue me."

༄

After a grueling day at the ballet company, Lynne hurried to the grocery store and grabbed a cart. Thank heavens she found the ten dollar bill her aunt gave her for Christmas. Now she could fill her empty shelves.

As she wheeled the cart down the canned food aisle, she saw Suzette picking up and putting down can after can. If her shelves hadn't been achingly bare, she'd have left and come back tomorrow rather than encounter her aisle after aisle.

She pretended she didn't see her as she placed canned peas, green beans, and tomato soup in her cart. But Suzette saw her and shoved her cart into the middle of the aisle so she couldn't pass.

"Those canned vegetables contain lots of salt. Could make you retain water and gain *more* weight."

Lynne stared at her, deciding whether she could ignore her or not. This wasn't the ballet company. Why should she walk away? "What's your problem?"

Suzette posed with her chin lifted and her lips curled into a snarl. "I don't have a problem. I watch what I eat."

"Huh. You could have fooled me. I thought maybe something you ate made your tongue wag about things that are none of your business."

Suzette opened her mouth like a baby bird, then huffed away, turning back to look at Lynne several times before she disappeared around the corner into the next aisle.

Lynne grabbed bread, peanut butter, bananas, apples, and a pound of hamburger just as the grocery lights dimmed and a voice announced the store was closing in seven minutes. As she hurried to check out, she saw Suzette strolling down an aisle as though she had hours instead of minutes to make her purchases. Typical. A cute blonde with big blue eyes, she got away with a lot. If only she'd catch the chickenpox or get laryngitis, practices at the ballet company would be much easier.

The drive back to Lake Elmo forced Lynne to focus on the weather. The snow that melted earlier in the day had frozen into a treacherous sheet of ice. Could be a great evening to go skating on Lake Elmo if she had skates. Instead, she sat at a stop light, waiting to turn right.

Just then, a pick-up truck blew through the intersection, fishtailed, and slammed into her car. Lynne flopped hard from side to side, then back to upright. She screamed and covered her head with her arms as metal scraped against metal.

3

Total silence surrounded her, followed by bits of metal clattering onto the ice-covered street.

Lynne opened her eyes. She lay pressed against the driver's door, her left arm crushed against her body, her legs immobile as though they were wrapped together.

The front of the truck had bent her hood into an inverted "V" and sent a pillar of steam spewing from her radiator. The right side of her car rested against the light post on the corner of the sidewalk. Just then, the light post groaned and crashed onto her car.

Suddenly, two people stood at her window, peering in, shouting, and banging on the broken windshield. "Are you alright? Do you need help?"

She opened her mouth. No sound came out. She thought she nodded.

Her neck and shoulders throbbed. Pain shot through her back and knees. She felt the same nausea as last summer when she was teaching and fell off the elevated stage.

A patrol car with a flashing red light arrived. Two men set out road flares before walking toward her. "Stay where you are, Miss. We've called an ambulance."

She closed her eyes.

One police officer stayed with her until she entered the ambulance. After a slow ride along the icy streets, they rushed her gurney into the hospital and parked her in the emergency hallway. Just last year, she'd been here in January, watching Marta lying in the same location with her ankle injury. Hopefully, tonight's diagnosis would be less severe.

A nurse stopped to check on her and added a second blanket. "Sorry for the delay. Had a head-on collision on the highway. We should get to you very soon."

Lynne nodded, then winced from the movement and closed her eyes.

Half an hour later, they wheeled her for x-rays, then into an emergency cubicle. A tall, thin man entered with her chart. "Good evening. I'm Doctor Henderson. Sorry you had to wait so long. How are you feeling?"

"Stiff and sore."

"That's understandable. From what I've read, you got hit hard." He held x-ray film up to the overhead light and nodded. "No problems with your left elbow." He looked at a second X-ray. "How's your neck?"

"It hurts when I move."

"That's from the whiplash." He paused and studied another film. "I don't see any breaks in either leg, just swelling and misalignment in your knees. Do they ever pop?"

"Only when I walk up stairs."

Dr. Henderson nodded. "You have what we call adolescent anterior knee problems. Your accident tonight aggravated the condition. I suggest you ice and rest as much as you can. Now, let's find out where you're feeling the most pain."

His hands moved along her legs. She winced when he touched the area around her left kneecap.

"The patella is inflamed and shifts a bit. Use anti-inflammatory medication and wrap both knees with ace bandages for added support."

"I'm a dancer. When can I return to normal activity?"

"A couple of weeks. Over the next month, avoid sudden and repetitive motions, climbing stairs, or jumping. Make an appointment with your doctor next week. After a round of physical therapy sessions, he'll determine when you can resume dancing."

She frowned. Dancing *was* filled with repetitive movements and jumping. It appeared she'd miss part or all of *Coppélia* and maybe the following ballet preparations and performances. That meant no salary, which made paying her bills impossible. Why did the truck that hit her car need to be in such a hurry?

As she talked herself out of feeling sorry for herself, Vivian arrived to take her home. Fitting Lynne into her two-door car would look funny if seen in a comedy. However, being wrapped in ace bandages and getting stiffer by the minute didn't provide any chuckles. She maneuvered into the passenger seat, tipped her head back, and closed her eyes.

"Do you have a headache? How's your neck?"

Lynne took a jagged breath. "I hurt all over. Even my eyeballs ache."

"I want you to stay at my place tonight so I can keep an eye on you. I'll get whatever you need from your apartment and tuck you into the guest room."

Lynne shivered from the cold as well as from reliving the last seconds before the truck slammed into her. "Thanks. Did you see my car?"

Vivian laughed. "Yes. It's mangled. Thank goodness you weren't seriously injured."

By the next morning, Lynne felt stiff as a two-by-four. Turning her head hurt; moving from one side to the other hurt. Vivian handed her two pills from her prescription.

"You should rest as much as possible today."

"I need to call the ballet company at nine o'clock," Lynne said.

"Let me. I'll explain what happened The doctor said to give yourself a few days of total rest and two weeks before resuming your normal life."

Normal life. Is that what she had? She didn't feel normal. She'd miss all of *Coppélia* and chances for solos or back-ups in *Sylvia*. At least she hadn't broken any bones, although feeling totally stiff was almost as bad.

⁕

The third day, Damien called to check on her, suggesting she go to the company's physical therapist. "We'll pay for five sessions; I hope your insurance will cover the rest. You'll need a release from both your doctor and the physical therapist and absolutely no *pointe* work until well after they release you to dance."

"May I come in to watch the choreography?"

"Of course, but just to watch. Doctor's orders."

⁕

Five days of doctor-enforced lounging felt like five weeks. No wonder Marta became restless and grumpy while wearing a cast for several months.

On day four Lynne inched her way up the stairs to her apartment and shuffled from the bed to the bathroom to the fridge. Much as she loved her aunt, having her hover every few minutes wore thin.

Each morning, Vivian drove her to therapy sessions, then to watch rehearsals. Her back and leg cramped; her knees remained swollen and tender to her touch. She executed gentle *pliés* and tried bending to each side, but each movement felt as if she wore a Santa suit pillow around her middle.

By the time the four-hour afternoon sessions with the dancers ended, she felt limp as a ballet slipper. Jer drove her home; she'd eat dinner with Vivian, then return to her apartment to walk through the day's choreography before she dropped into bed. The longer she waited to return to classes, the harder it would be to execute the choreography she'd observed.

At the end of the second week of watching, she knew she needed to begin full days. She called Mrs. B., Marta's boarding house landlady, and asked about hiring her cousin to drive her to therapy and classes.

"Greg would be glad to help," Mrs. B. said. "He works night shift at the refinery, but earning extra money will be appreciated. He's planning to get married next fall."

Since Vivian allowed her to stop paying rent until she returned to dancing, she'd be able to pay Greg and buy basic food over the next month. She winced. Her budget was tighter than her pointe shoes.

The insurance company assured her they were working as fast as possible in processing her claim, but gave no indication she'd be able to buy a new car any time soon. "New" in her case meant 1950 or older with high mileage and a ratty interior.

The full-scale physical movement of dancing exhausted Lynne even though she wrapped her knees with ace bandages. Since adding four dancers, the company danced a series of seven annual ballets instead of last year's five. More dancers meant more competition for solos. Between her earlier absence and her current injury, her chance to advance to soloist wouldn't happen any time soon.

Suzette strolled past her and sat on an adjacent bench, watching Lynne secure her ace bandages. "Looks like you'll soon be joining your washed-up friend, Marta."

Lynne glared at Suzette's Cheshire cat smile. She turned away, pretending to look for something from her locker, knowing she'd blurt out something she'd regret if she continued their staring match.

"Guess this means you'll not be considered for solos or back-up roles. You might as well go home and stay there."

Lynne bit her lip, packed up her tote, and walked past her as though she didn't exist. How did the others not see how mean and vindictive Suzette could be? One of these days, she'd make a mistake and someone who could do something about what she said would hear her—just not today.

꼬

Day after day, Lynne worried about the continuing pain that traveled from her knees into her lower spine. She'd followed her doctor's orders, gone to therapy, and iced as instructed. Still, she experienced pain and cramped muscles even after taking her medication. The doctor assured her the healing was progressing as expected. Tell that to my knees, she thought.

Early February dragged along with no letup in snowfall and bitter winds. As she sat in her apartment, sorting bills from other papers, she spotted the ad she'd taken from the company bulletin board: the summer dance troupe in France.

She reread the information and checked the calendar. If she planned to apply, she'd need to fill out the forms, give them to Madame and Damien, and get them mailed in five days. With her injury and problems with Suzette, would they consider recommending her? Her application might prove to Damien and Madame that she still wanted to dance. Besides, it would be exciting to travel to France and get paid to do it.

She listed her dance experiences and wrote a letter requesting a recommendation from Madame and Damien. After several attempts, she finalized both, woke her aunt to use her typewriter, then carried her information to the ballet company the next morning. "What have I got to lose?" she thought.

꼬

The first athlete injury meeting began the next evening in the hospital conference room. Damien, Madame, Patrice as principal dancer, and Lynne joined local high school and college coaches to hear from the doctors and therapists. Lynne took pages of notes. The following day, she joined Madame, Damien, and Patrice in the ballet company office. Their decision was unanimous; several specialists would be invited to talk and work with the dancers.

Madame spoke with unexpected energy. "Damien and I are considering quarterly meetings for our dancers: foot care and exams, as well as conditioning and rehabilitation, with half-yearly consults on nutrition. We'll take two hours once each quarter. Dancers with private issues may sign up for private consults. For general meetings we'll expect all dancers to attend. Once meetings end, dancers will be dismissed for the day."

"These meetings will become a regular part of every season," Damien said, "if the dancers actively participate. We're lucky to have physicians and other specialists offering support. Dancer health and fitness is vital. It's an important part of who we are as a company."

After the meeting, Patrice sat with Lynne to plan. "I'll work with the eight soloists and coordinate with you. I wish we'd had this support when I joined the corps. It would have helped me protect my feet."

"Therapy is helping me get back," Lynne said.

"So I've seen. Let me know if any dancers resist attending. I'll speak with them. You *do* know I'm thinking of Suzette, don't you?"

"I do."

The next day, Lynne called the corps dancers together to share information. She'd arranged a grouping of chairs and stood waiting for the dancers to settle in. Before she spoke a single word, Suzette stood to address the group.

She crossed her arms and lifted her chin as she spoke. "I don't see why the rest of us need to attend just because *you're* not taking care of yourself. Besides, I prefer to handle my issues privately rather than with you gawking at me."

Lynne's eyebrows lifted. She turned to Suzette and smiled. "Interesting. So you have problems? Why not get assistance free of charge and get paid to attend?"

"They're paying us to come to the meetings?" one dancer asked.

"Almost. The meetings will be held during our contracted day, so it's like being paid," Lynne said.

A first-year dancer spoke up. "We'll be taking time from practices. How can we afford less rehearsal time?"

"Work harder," said a voice from the back of the room.

The *corps* dancers turned to see Patrice standing inside the practice room door. She surveyed the assembled dancers with a furrowed brow. "It's important that we open ourselves to changes that will improve our health and performances."

The dancer who questioned the meetings sank down and said nothing further.

"Damien and Madame are one hundred per cent behind this." Patrice said. "We need to protect our bodies and be open to discussing our problems. Suzette, there is no intention of sharing your personal matters with the group. The meetings are planned to give you resources. How you use them will be up to you. When—"

"I don't see why we need to listen to Lynne," Suzette said. "Who selected her to be our representative anyway?"

"Damien and Madame. Do you have a problem with Lynne?"

Suzette scanned the group. Most dancers turned away. Those who kept eye contact with her said nothing. Lynne saw Jer's smile. At least one person supported her. Maybe more would follow.

4

Lynne heard nothing from Madame or Damien about her request for a recommendation to the dance troupe. Were they too busy with the upcoming performance of *Sylvia*? Maybe they'd gotten a good laugh, then tossed it out as preposterous. At least she'd tried.

Dinners with her aunt became bright spots in her week. She came home so tired she'd settle for her old stand-by, a peanut butter and jelly sandwich, rather than cook. However, her aunt's hot meals and light conversation were the perfect unwind and prelude to a relaxing evening and an early bedtime.

"I always wanted to be a ballerina," Vivian confided. "I was so excited when your mother called and told me you were coming here to dance."

"Why didn't you tell me? You know I live and breathe dancing. That's why this injury is so frustrating."

"You were always so busy, but you don't have to ask me twice. How's the latest ballet coming along?"

"*Sylvia* is a romantic story with a mishmash of female archers, forest creatures, shepherds, and Greek gods. You'll recognize the music, but don't look for me as a huntress with a fake bow. I'm only in the corps."

"You sound snippy tonight. What's going on?"

Lynne carried their dishes to the sink. "I'm fine. Just irritated about Suzette and my injury and my application. It's like I'm invisible, same as when I'm back in Trenton."

Vivian joined her at the sink and nudged her to one side. "I wish I knew what to tell you. Sounds like you need to figure out how to handle your setbacks."

"Maybe, but right now I can't show my skills, so I can't prove myself."

The only person who noticed her frustration was Suzette, and that meant trouble with a capital 'S.' She was like a jack-in-the-box that kept popping up when least expected.

Late the following afternoon, Suzette pranced around the dressing room, sharing views on her huntress solo. Lynne gritted her teeth as she listened to her chatter.

"So I said to Patrice, don't you think the turn toward your partner would look more romantic if you stopped short and stared into his eyes? I certainly..." She stopped and turned toward Lynne. "Oh, Lynne. I forgot you aren't with us for those rehearsals. Maybe next performance you'll get *something*."

When none of the dancers in the dressing room reacted, Suzette continued her critique. "Anyway, I suggested that Patrice..." She looked up, stopped again, and busied herself rearranging her locker as Patrice walked past.

The dancers scurried back to packing up but kept watch as Patrice stuffed her towel into her dance tote and left the dressing room. "Night, everyone. You too, Suzette."

Tittering circled the room. Suzette slammed her locker and huffed into the showers. All eyes turned to Lynne, who shrugged and left. Score one for me, she thought.

Lynne stared at her funny Valentine from Marta. She'd not added a single personal word. Maybe she was still upset about their ongoing argument over her use of diet pills. That wasn't something Lynne planned to downplay with her best friend, even across hundreds of miles.

She placed the card in a small basket on her dresser, stopped, and pulled out the last postcard Marta sent. She chuckled to herself about the crazy fish with bubble words. She'd miss Marta if their friendship shifted from confidants to acquaintances who sent sterile holiday cards.

The phone rang as she stepped from her shower. The voice on the other end started speaking without introduction.

"Hey, Lynne, it's Donald. Just calling to let you know we can resume dating. I got a divorce last month, so I'm a free man. I'm—"

She soundlessly hung up the phone. She was not about to resume dating Mr. Oh-So-Wrong. He made sitting at home alone feel exciting.

∽

Rehearsals filled the next week, followed by opening night, which ended abruptly. During Act III, Lynne stood ready to enter and felt a tug on her silvery sash. When she whipped her head around, Suzette was smiling. As Lynne stepped onto the stage, her sash slipped to the floor. She stepped on it. Her foot slid. She leaned forward to catch herself, bumping into the dancer ahead of her, causing that dancer to knock over the statue of Bacchus.

The line of dancers entering behind them tumbled like dominoes in the tangle of bodies sprawled on the floor. Dancers entering at stage right slowed and stared. The audience gasped. The orchestra stopped playing. Stage hands hurried to remove the statue and reposition nearby urns. The audience sat in silence.

Lynne swallowed down her anger as she tossed her sash aside. Someone had tampered with her costume, and she knew the culprit. Who would Madame and Damien blame? Her? The costume shop secured all sashes before hanging the costumes on the rack and tacking on the dancers' names.

The curtain closed as the dancers repositioned themselves. When it reopened, the orchestra resumed playing the score, the dancers entered, and the scene continued without incident. The final act ended, the audience applauded, and the principal dancers bowed. There were no curtain calls. Audience members exited with murmured conversations instead of their usual animated dawdling along the aisles.

The dancers stood on the stage, in costume, waiting for Madame and Damien. There was no point in exiting until after the coming lecture. Tonight's foul-up would be addressed immediately and linger in conversations for weeks to come.

Madame and Damien ignored the dancers for several minutes while they spoke with the dressers and stage crew. Lynne watched their heads nodding and their hands gesturing with occasional bursts of argued words. Madame left without glancing toward the dancers.

Damien approached them. "We're not sure what happened tonight, but this was a first-class disaster. If you know *anything* about it, please tell me. We'd prefer you not discuss this outside the company; we want to understand the cause and how to prevent such disasters in the future. I suggest everyone but the principal dancers skip the patrons after-party function. We'll make your excuses."

The dancers quietly moved off stage to change and pack up for the evening. Thank heavens the newspaper reviewer at their dress rehearsal wrote a lively article, buzzing about their superb dancing. After tonight someone would contact the paper and suggest the arts columnist revisit an upcoming performance. So much for adding new patrons.

The dressing room filled with whispered speculation. Lynne watched them glance her direction through her mirror. Only two people knew the cause of the fiasco. Should she tell Madame and Damien what she suspected? Would anyone believe her after her earlier problems?

She stole a glance at Suzette. Tonight she sat removing her make-up, unusually quiet for a change. Should she confront her tonight or wait until they were alone? She felt sure if she cornered Suzette, she'd spin the details and shift blame away from herself. Best to wait and see.

༄

The dancers heard no more about the incident. Instead, Damien walked them through subtle changes in their entrances and exits and asked the seamstresses to adjust the sashes on the *Sylvia* costumes.

The remainder of the performances were sparsely attended. The local reviewer made an unexpected appearance, then wrote positive comments about the principal dancers and the orchestra's performances. Lynne guessed that *Sylvia* would be buried in their repertoire for several years before it would be danced again.

Toward the end of February, Lynne was called into the office. She stood watching Madame, who ignored her and continued to sign checks. What Intermountain Ballet Company rule had she broken or stretched this time that annoyed Madame? She'd performed without complaining and avoided Suzette. Maybe they had pieced together the reason for the disastrous performance of *Sylvia*; maybe Suzette had pointed an accusing finger at her. Whatever it was, she'd know very soon.

Damien entered. Madame set aside the last of the checks, then waved a paper under Lynne's nose. "We received your letter earlier this month. It surprised us, considering how your career is stalled. You expect us to recommend you for dancing in Europe this summer?"

"Yes, Madame." Lynne stared straight ahead, trying to bury her surprise that Madame would even discuss this with her after the *Sylvia* fiasco.

"Why should we recommend you? You've found difficulty following directions since last fall. True, you've made changes recently, but do you think dancing elsewhere would prove valuable?"

Lynne clenched her teeth and wanted to ask if she'd even considered writing a letter. Instead she said, "A change might have been good."

"We agree," Madame said as she handed her a full page letter written on Intermountain Ballet stationary.

Lynne read the first part of the letter. She looked up at Madame. So she *had* proven herself and... Her shoulders drooped. "This supports my application, but the deadline passed around Valentine's Day. Also, it isn't signed."

"We know, but we think this experience will give you perspective," Madame said. "I've spoken with Cheryl Menkins, the coordinator. I've ask her to hold one space open until she must make her final selections on April first. That gives you time to prove your changes are sincere and ongoing."

Damien reached for the letter Lynne held. "If we see a continued positive shift in your attitude, we'll sign and mail our recommendation to Cheryl. If not, the next four months of our season might be your last with the company, especially if we discover you were involved in creating the *Sylvia* disaster. Is that clear?"

Lynne blinked and looked around the room before she answered. "I've done what you asked of me. What additional changes do you expect?"

The furrow between Madame's eyebrows deepened. "You know what we need. I doubt you can sustain a change. However, if you want to be considered for this summer program abroad, I suggest you give it your best effort."

Lynne nodded and curtsied, feeling a gigantic weight press her toward the floor. She resisted surrendering to her impulse to stomp her feet and shout.

Madame walked her to the door. "Remember, we fill our roster by late August. Since the European tour doesn't end until mid-September, at most you'll receive a partial contract for next year."

Lynne's intended reply dried up in her mouth. She nodded, swallowed hard, and curtsied.

"You're obstinate at times, but you could represent our company well if you maintain a positive attitude. Now, hurry along. Afternoon rehearsals begin any minute."

Lynne exited the office, stunned at how her application to the tour clarified her future with the company. Leaning against the wall to catch her breath, she overheard Madame's voice.

"Well, Damien? Did we make the correct decision?"

"Absolutely! Lynne could have remained distracted over her father's illness and her injury, but she didn't. Giving her the task of liaison to the injury committee was a wise move, Anna. She's taken her role seriously. Working with another group and a different instructor might improve her focus. If not, we'll need to seriously consider whether or not we want to renew her contract."

"I'd be glad if she were gone for awhile," Madame said. "Rehearsals would be calmer, and my blood pressure would surely drop."

Lynne covered her mouth to stifle her gasp. A strange knot tightened inside her. Were the doors on her career sliding closed? Might Madame ditch her? Could Suzette's plan be working? What about her lifelong dream to become a principal dancer? Maybe if the touring company accepted her, she wouldn't care if she returned to Billings.

She tiptoed down the hall and descended the stairs. In the small rehearsal hall, she shook out her legs, and stared straight ahead, waiting to lose herself in the music.

At the end of the day, Lynne remained distracted by her conversation with Madame and Damien. She heard her phone ringing and raced up the still-icy stairs to unlock the door. The buzz of a disconnect hummed in her ear. *Just my luck*, she thought. She'd hoped Marta might be calling her; she missed their time talking.

The phone rang again. It was Mr. Oh-So-Wrong, her dating disaster from last August.

"Hey, Lynne. I called just now and the other night, but it sounded like someone picked up and then hung up. Thought I'd call back in case something was wrong with your phone. Lots has changed since we spoke a few months ago."

She closed her eyes and exhaled. "Really, Donald? I'm very busy. I don't have time to date right now."

"Hmm. I see," he said. "Well, give me a call when you're free. We had a lot of fun together. Remember?" He made a smooching sound, then hung up.

A shiver wiggled down her spine. *Anything*, even a toothache, was better than dating Mr. Oh-So-Wrong.

When she opened the fridge to check on her choices her dinner, she found half a can of tuna, wilted celery, a tomato, lettuce, pickles, and Wonder bread. Looked like a tuna salad with a plain piece of bread. That would be quick, but it also gave her more time than she wanted to agonize over her future. Why couldn't life be filled with puppies and ice cream instead of unending decisions? What was so special about growing up anyway?

5

Daily rehearsals made escape from Suzette difficult. The more Lynne moved away from her, the more she stepped into her space.

One morning as Lynne stepped to the *barre*, Suzette crowded in front of her. "Excuse me. I was standing here yesterday. I need to continue using that space."

"And why is that, Suzette?"

"My eye doctor said I need to face away from the brightness of the winter sky. It has something to do with my pupils. I can ask Madame to get involved if you wish."

Lynne bit her lip. Her fingernails gouged into her palms. She backed away. The image of Suzette as a bug flashed through her mind. She smiled. Soon her tormentor would be too hairy and fuzzy to waddle across the floor, much less exercise at the *barre*.

∽

That evening as she mended her tights, the phone rang.

"Hey, it's Marta. I'm sorry to hear about your dad. How's he feeling?"

"He's better, thanks for asking. He needs to rest, but they say he'll make a full recovery if he follows orders. I was afraid we'd lose him."

"I understand how that feels," Marta said. "I was seven when my dad died. I'm glad yours will recover."

"Me, too." Lynne drifted away from the conversation for a moment, thinking about her dad. "So tell me about you and Steve. Did you have a great time together in the mountains?"

The line went quiet. "He offered me a ring. I refused. He asked about the diet pills and got furious when he discovered I still used them occasionally. He—"

"Marta? I thought you stopped taking them!"

"Not yet, but I've thrown my last pills away. I'm trying to handle my stress without them." She paused. "It's harder than I thought."

Lynne sighed. "You can do it. Get more sleep and eat better food. Those pills will ruin your life if you don't ditch them."

"I know, but I feel so listless without them. And now that Steve and I are taking a break, I—"

"Marta! Listen to me. Stop...taking...them. Promise me!"

Another long pause. "I promise. Maybe when I—"

Lynne tapped on the phone. "No maybe. Just stop! Look. I need to go. My aunt is having guests, and I promised to help. Call me evenings. I'm glad you've finally gotten a phone. What's your number?"

"I'm still using my mom's, but mine's being installed soon. I miss you, Lynne."

Lynne stared at the now-silent phone. Why had she made an excuse to hang up? Marta was her best friend. Maybe it was because of all the craziness in her own life. She knew Marta needed the conversation to be about herself and Steve since they'd reached another impasse. Would they *ever* get their lives on the same page?

Talking about her dad, her aunt's move, and her situation in the ballet company wouldn't help Marta or herself, if she was honest about it. She shook her head as if to clear away further thoughts.

When she finished repairing her tights, she tossed them into her dance tote with a clean leotard and looked around her apartment. Soon, she'd be moving. In the meantime, she needed to take her own advice: get extra sleep and eat better food. Thank heavens she'd never succumbed to taking diet pills.

~

The afternoon practice of *Swan Lake* ended early. Lynne dialed for Greg to drive her home, then waited outside for him to arrive.

As they headed toward Lake Elmo, she asked him about Mrs. B.

"She's fine. I see her at church and family gatherings. Why do you ask?"

Why did she ask? "Just curious. Mind if we stop by her boarding house?"

"No problem." He smiled. "We might land an invite to dinner."

Mrs. B. wrapped each of them in a bear hug as soon as they stepped into the common room. "I'm so glad to see both of you. I'll set places for you at the dinner table. It will just take a minute." As she bustled away, the front door opened and Carol walked in.

Lynne and Carol stared at each other. Lynne smiled; Carol raced up the stairs with one look back, as if to confirm that Lynne was real and standing in the boarding house, *her* boarding house.

Dinner conversation circled the table, jumping over Carol, who kept her head down while she ate. Shorty and James talked of their work. Faith, the new tenant, asked how Lynne knew everyone.

"My best friend lived here. We were both dancers at the Intermountain Ballet Company. Marta got injured and returned home to recover. I haven't seen her since Christmas."

"I love the ballet," Faith said. "Wish I could afford to go. What's your next performance?"

"*Swan Lake*. I have guest tickets and no guests. I'll give you and Mrs. B. my tickets."

Both ladies thanked Lynne profusely, and the boarders scattered to their various pursuits when the meal was over. That left Lynne in the kitchen to chat with Mrs. B. while they did the dinner dishes.

"It's so nice to see you again," Mrs. B. said. "How is everything at the ballet company?"

"Fine." She paused. "No, it's not. It's been a challenge since my car accident. I've tried to distract myself, but with no car I can't get around. I haven't reached Steve to check on his job hunting."

"He called here a few weeks ago to ask if I'd spoken to Marta. I haven't since the Christmas evening at his parents' house. Those two have such a hard time getting their lives on the same track."

Greg leaned into the kitchen. "Lynne? We need to go. I've got to get ready for work."

Once she returned, she called Steve's parents' home, hoping to get caught up. "Not much to tell," Steve said when he finally answered. "I have a lead in Portland, Oregon, so I'd be near her. I hope it comes through. You probably heard I offered her an engagement ring, which she rejected."

"I heard. It's worth the effort to mend whatever's broken. You two have something special."

"I'm not sure anymore, Lynne. It's up to her... I...let me know what you hear from her, okay?"

"Sure. Good luck finding a job."

Swan Lake rehearsals progressed well. The dancers knew the music and much of the standard choreography from their years before joining the company. Now, with their first performance coming soon, they refined their movements and practiced the ballet company's personal stamp on the choreography.

Damien clapped his hands. The music and dancers stopped. "Act I, the palace celebration looks good. Soloists, watch your spacing. Suzette, you're crowding out Martin. Jer, you need to stagger more as Benno, the tutor, after he drinks too much. That will contrast to his sudden sobering to lead the hunting party.

"Let's revisit Act II for the rest of the afternoon. The real drama begins here, kids. Patrice's Odette has passion and dignity. You other swans must add feathery arms in your cygnet dances. Right now, your timing is off. We need perfect unison, like your *Serenade* performances.

"Backstage, leave ample room for Jer's quick changes back and forth from the tutor to the magician. Okay, from the top of Act II."

When the last class of the day ended, Suzette stepped in front of Lynne with her hands on her hips. "I haven't see your name on the list of soloists. Given up, have you?"

"No," Lynne said as she put on her broadest smile, "I'm letting you have a chance at the parts."

Suzette glared at her. "Humpf. Like I need *you* to step aside. Next week you'll see my name on the first cast. Maybe you can be my back-up." She waltzed away toward the dressing room.

That evening Lynne practiced *Swan Lake* until sweat poured down her body. Thanks to Mrs. B.'s generosity, she had access to the boarding house basement. It felt good to return to the space she'd shared with Marta, even though her friend was long gone. She didn't even mind nosey, annoying Carol interrupting with complaints that her music disturbed her evenings, two floors above.

༨

The *Swan Lake* performances received rave reviews. Lynne danced with the dignity Damien requested. She watched performances from backstage when possible and helped Jer with his quick changes. She had to admit Suzette rose to the occasion and danced her best. Any chance of Suzette's dismissal faded, but Lynne smiled. She still saw her as a hairy bug.

When she got home after the last Saturday performance, she brought in the mail and stopped in to see her aunt, who was busy making cakes for the church bazaar. "A man stopped in this afternoon. He said something about settling on your damaged car. He wants you to call him."

She rushed to her apartment and made the call. Five minutes later, she hung up and plopped down into her comfy chair. She'd get money for her old car, but only enough for another old car. If she skipped buying a car, she'd have money for the trip to Europe—if it was approved. But then she'd be stranded, forced to catch rides, or keep using Greg as a driver. Why did her life get tangled at every turn?

All evening she paced her apartment, weighing her choices. Standing in a long, hot shower, she made her decision: she needed to be independent. She'd take the money and find a car. What that car might look like would be anyone's guess.

༄

Three days later, Lynne drove her "new" car to rehearsals. She purposely parked a block away, knowing the guy dancers would laugh when they saw it.

Two of them saw her locking it as they passed. She braced herself when she entered the dance company building. Sure enough, cat calls and snide comments followed her along the hallway to the women's dressing room. She ignored them. If she could ignore Suzette, she could ignore anything.

During their morning break, a group of guys sauntered over to her and handed her a ski mask.

"What's this for?"

"It's to wear when you drive your *new* car," Jer said. "That way, no one will know who you are."

Lynne smiled and put on the mask. "Thanks, guys. I didn't know you cared." She did a fashion show turn. "How do I look?"

All the guys except Jer laughed and walked away. He stood watching her. "I told them you'd handle their jibes."

She removed the mask and shrugged. "What choice did I have? That's all I could afford."

Jer laughed. "It's a turquoise Nash Rambler. Where did you even find it?"

"Al's Auto. He took it in as payment from an old lady for repairs on her new car. I got it cheap. It gets good mileage, has new tires, and it runs. Plus, it fits in small parking places. I wanted to save every penny if I have the chance to...."

"Chance to what?"

"Nothing," she said. "I might be taking a trip. I'll know soon." She put the ski mask on top of her head but didn't pull it down over her face. "Want to go for a ride later?" She smiled and walked away before he answered.

6

She stood watching the latest snow storm cover the sidewalk and street in front of the ballet building. Even in daylight, it glittered like pixie dust before the breeze picked it up and blew in into the nearest drift.

Today, April Fool's day, she felt as stormy inside as the weather looked outside. What would Madame and Damien decide?

Butterflies stirred inside her as she waited outside the ballet office after rehearsals to speak with Damien. She wiped her sweaty hands on her leotards and brushed back her hair for the tenth time in the last few minutes. "Come on, come on," she muttered.

Suzette ambled past. Lynne closed her eyes, hoping Suzette would pass by in silence.

"So-o-o-o." Suzette stretched out the word to a long slur. "You're in trouble again, I see. I don't know why they don't fire you. If I ran the company, I..."

The office door opened. Madame Cosper stared at the two young women. "Is there something you want, girls?"

Suzette curtsied and flipped her hair off her shoulders. "I was on my way to a fitting when Lynne tossed off one of her rude comments."

Lynne gasped. She looked from Suzette to Madame and back to Suzette. When she felt Madame eyeing her, she straightened and shrugged.

Madame Cosper shook her head and walked toward the stairway.

Seconds later, Suzette circled back to where Lynne waited. She pursed her lips as she thrust her face inches from Lynne's face. "Bye, bye, Lynne, dear."

Before Lynne could reply, Damien opened the door. "Lynne? Shall we talk?"

She took several deep breaths, stepped inside, and stood before the desk.

Damien smiled. "Don't worry; we heard the entire exchange. These walls are paper thin." He rubbed his hands together and gestured for Lynne to take a seat. "So, today we're making the final decision about the summer troupe in Europe. How do you feel the past few weeks have gone?"

She shrugged. "Pretty well. I've paid more attention to my actions. It's a struggle dealing with one of the dancers. Otherwise, I'm refocused."

Damien paced the small office. "Anna and I agree. We think joining Cheryl's troupe might be good for you."

Lynne nodded, afraid if she spoke, she'd awaken from her dream. It had to be a dream, didn't it?

"I'm prepared to offer you extra practice sessions for the choreography you'll be expected to know. I'm also hoping you will be my emissary to the group and co-teach portions of my new ballet I'm sharing with Cheryl."

"Me? You want *me* to teach *your* ballet?"

"Right. Now, take the contract home and read it carefully. We'll call Cheryl tomorrow if you accept the position. You've made impressive changes, Lynne. I'm positive you'll handle any challenge on tour."

"Thanks." That was all she could spit out.

"Of course, I'll expect you to maintain focus on our regular sessions, as well."

She nodded. Her body began to quiver as she struggled to keep from jumping up and down like a five-year-old. She smiled and curtsied. "I appreciate your confidence in me. I'll do my best to represent this company and your choreography."

She hurried out onto the sidewalk and gave a whoop. Finally! Things in her life were changing for the better!

∽

Lynne read and reread the contract. The group performed three or more days a week, twice on many days, with rehearsals twice a week. Their one day off also served as a travel day. Such an intense schedule didn't leave much time for rest and recovery.

Curiosity sent her to the Billings library and a giant desktop atlas. She searched out every stop on their tour: Paris, Chartres, Versailles, Rouen, Orléans, Angers, Tours, Bourges, Lyon, Dijon, Metz, and Reims. They'd cover much of northern and central France before ending in Frankfurt, Germany, at an invitation-only festival. Wait until she told Marta. First things first, however.

Back at her apartment, Lynne brought her checkbook up to date; she had $79.93. She groaned aloud. If she saved every penny of her wages between now and June, she'd barely have enough money to pay for the ship to Europe. Totally doable if she didn't have to pay off her doctor bills, move from her garage apartment, buy additional *pointe* shoes, or eat another meal.

Maybe her family would lend her the money. She hated asking, but how else could she guarantee she'd survive until June? Surely they would understand that she'd pay them back as soon as possible.

She placed a collect call home.

"So, Lynnie, what do you need?" her dad asked. "Is your car in the shop again?"

"My old lady car is fine, Dad. Why do you think I need something?"

"Honey, you were just here, and you talked with Mom recently."

Lynne hesitated. "You're right. Could you loan me seventy-five dollars until September?"

"That's a lot of money for us right now. What do you need it for?"

"I have the chance to dance in Europe this summer." Lynne waited. The silence on the phone dragged on and on. "Dad?"

"I'm sorry, but I can't swing it. Maybe you can quit eating out or stop buying new clothes for a while."

"I'm not doing either one of those things. Could you spare fifty?"

"Sorry, Lynnie, I can't. Maybe in July when local weekend builders put on new decks or rebuild their fences."

Lynne nodded toward the phone. "Okay. Thanks anyway. Is Mom there? I'd like to say hello."

"No. She's at bridge. I'll tell her you called."

For the rest of the evening, she paced, rummaging her brain for ideas on how she'd locate enough money to get herself to France.

The next afternoon she sat outside the ballet company office, waiting to speak with Damien after he finished a phone call. She hated to disappoint him and turn down the summer invitation; but she saw no way she could afford to travel home, let alone all the way to France.

Damien opened the door and invited her in. "I assume you read the contract?"

She rotated her shoulders and nodded. "I want to accept the offer, but I can't afford the cost of getting there."

"I'd be willing to loan you money if need be, so go ahead and accept the position. I want you to experience this opportunity."

Tears filled her eyes. "Thanks." She wiped her face and swallowed hard. "I'd be proud to represent the Intermountain Ballet Company."

Damien dialed Cheryl and handed the phone to Lynne. "She'll be excited to know you're joining the group."

Once the call ended, Damien smiled. "This is a fantastic opportunity. How do you feel?"

"I want to laugh and cry or dance and shout. Thank you again."

Damien smiled. "Now, you need a partner for the *pas de deux*. It means extra rehearsals without pay, but the guy you select will get a head start on choreography. Is there someone you'd like to ask? I can't force anyone to help you."

She smiled. "I think I know just the guy."

Lynne sat across from Jer in the Bison Café. He'd joined the company the same season she had. When she'd invited him to lunch, her treat, he'd accepted; but the longer they sat talking about the weather and their food, the more suspiciously he eyed her.

"Okay. What's up? I feel a favor coming on. Is it about your car?"

"It's much better or worse, depending on how you answer." Lynne laughed and explained the situation. "Now I'll need to work after hours with Damien to brush up on choreography I can't do without a guy."

"So, you're asking me to help you, and you thought a free lunch would seal the deal?"

"I hoped it would help. I estimate it will take anywhere from two to four weeks after hours. I know you and what's-her-name spend late afternoons and weekends together. I realize this favor will take more than a burger to seal our deal."

Jer shook his head. "Her name is Hannah, H-a-n-n-a-h. Why does that not click in your head?"

"Okay, Hannah. Anyway, I'd hoped she'd let me borrow you for a few days. It will give you a head start on new choreography."

Jer scrunched up his mouth and frowned. "She won't be happy. We'd planned a couple of weekend trips before she heads home the end of May, but I'd like to do this."

"What if I bought her something or give you money?"

"Since when do you have money to spare?"

Lynne shrugged. "I'll stop eating." She reached across the booth and covered Jer's hands with hers. "Please?"

"When do you need to start?"

A tingle of excitement slid through her. "Whenever you can arrange it. Damien will make time weekday evenings between five and seven and Saturday mornings from seven to ten."

"This must be a big deal if Damien is committed to helping you."

"It is, Jer. Know that I'll owe you forever."

He checked the time. "We need to get back. I'll talk with Hannah and call you tonight."

All afternoon Lynne kept her focus on the choreography but made quick glances toward Jer. She left for home without stopping to change clothes and paced her apartment like a caged animal. Being broke made life complicated. Nothing she owned had much value; she hoped Hannah wanted something attainable.

The phone rang. She swallowed hard as she picked up the receiver.

"Hannah's okay with everything. All she wants are your guest tickets to the rest of the season—plus, an invitation for two to the May celebration."

"Okay. Anything else? Maybe my kidney or my right arm? How am I going to get her an invitation to the patron function? We're barely invited ourselves."

"That's it. Once I can promise those tickets are hers, she promises to be a good sport about you monopolizing my time."

"And what do you want, Jer? My pug-nosed Nash? I'd gladly give it to you."

Jer laughed. "No one wants that car. I'm still wondering why you bought it."

"It was all I could afford. It drives well and fits into small spaces. What do you *really* want, Jer?"

He sighed. "I'll settle for learning new choreography. It might help me impress Damien and speed up my goal to be named a soloist."

It was settled. Lynne gave away her tickets to the rest of the season. Now, she'd need to buy Mrs. B. and Faith tickets. Luckily Damien gave her two tickets plus passes to future patron functions. Jer began after-hour rehearsals the following week.

The practice room felt a bit strange without the usual hubbub of sweaty bodies, quiet chatter, and stop and start music. In a moment of extreme generosity, Damien covered half of Jer's time. "This opportunity is important for the three of us," Damien said. "Giving away a few dollars and a couple patron tickets are a small price compared to how much the Intermountain Ballet Company will gain. Now, let's get started."

Jer was a perfect choice. He supported her on every lift, held her with patience during prolonged fish dives, and partnered for waltz steps like they'd been dancing together for years instead of off-and-on across two seasons.

Next, Damien shared his newest choreography. "As you both know, I'm enthralled by Gershwin. I've completed my interpretation of *An American in Paris*, and Lynne will be taking it with her when she joins the troupe in France. That means you, Jer, will have a first look at it. For now, let's keep the details under your hat since we'll not introduce it locally until next fall."

Several mornings later, before Damien excused the dancers for their midday break, he called them together. "I have an exciting announcement. Lynne's joining Americans in Paris, a summer dance troupe that travels to festivals around France. Congratulations, Lynne!"

All the dancers, except Suzette, clapped and rushed forward to hug her or pat her on the back.

Lynne smiled and curtsied.

"How was *she* chosen?" Suzette asked.

"I applied and was accepted."

Suzette pursed her lips and crossed her arms. "I saw her take the ad off the bulletin board so the rest of us couldn't apply."

"What do you mean?" Patrice said. "I saw it hanging up there a few days before the deadline."

"Well, I saw her take it."

Lynne crossed her arms and tilted her head as she stared at Suzette. "I didn't *take* it—I borrowed it. I put it back in time for anybody else who wanted to apply."

The silence in the practice room hung in the air for several seconds until Jer spoke up. "I'm proud of Lynne, and I wish her a fantastic tour."

Clapping resumed as dancers stepped forward to congratulate her again before they headed to their lunch break. Suzette stared at Lynne from a distance, then turned and walked off as if she had somewhere important to go and she was running late.

༄

A few evenings later as Lynne sat watching *I Love Lucy* on her fuzzy black and white television, the phone rang. It was her mother.

"Lynnie. How are you? I haven't talked with you for weeks. Vivian tells me you're going to France. How did that happen?"

"Didn't Dad tell you? I talked to him a couple weeks ago."

"He didn't mention it. You'll have to forgive him, Lynnie. He's still not quite himself yet after that awful heart attack."

Lynne explained the situation. "Whether or not I go depends on having money to get me there. Damien will loan me money, but...you don't have a hundred dollars socked away, do you?"

"No, but your Uncle Leo might lend it to you. He's always liked you. Let me call him."

When the phone rang again, she was tempted to ignore it. She changed her mind, hoping to hear Marta or Jer on the line.

"How's my favorite niece?"

"Uncle Leo?"

"I hear you want to go to France. Sounds like a great adventure. Tell me what's going on."

Lynne explained and heard excitement build in her uncle's voice. "I'm looking for an adventure myself. How about I go with you? I could pay for the ship. After you got done dancing, we could drive around for a few weeks. Might even buy a car over there. I hear that's the cheapest way to get around. I have a new BMW, so I could give you the car I bought, if you need one."

An answer formed in her head but didn't reach her mouth.

"Lynnie? Are you there? What do you say? It could be fun."

"Wow. That sounds perfect! Thanks, Uncle Leo."

After she hung up, she danced around the apartment, then raced to tell Vivian her good news.

"Are you sure about this? You know how Leo is." Vivian frowned. "What if he changes his mind?"

"My dance mentor, Damien, will loan me the money. It looks like I've got what I need to make the trip. Plus, now I'll bring home a new car!"

7

The next morning Lynne strolled in early to speak with Damien and Madame. Wait until she told them that she'd found a way to fund her trip. That should prove she'd taken responsibility and made changes on her own.

She expected pats on the back. Instead she faced two scowls. "I thought you'd be excited that I found a way to do this on my own."

"I admire your ingenuity," Damien said, "but saving your spot for an additional month creates a problem."

"It's another example of you not putting our ballet company first," Madame said. "Did you think we'd welcome you back whenever you returned? This is a business. It requires a full complement of dancers."

She felt as if someone had slapped her. Why did this not occur to *her*? She wanted to pace and think about it, but that was not possible while she stood in front of the company directors.

"Well?" Madame said as she stared at Lynne then turned to Damien.

Lynne straightened and looked from Madame to Damien. "I didn't think through the problem this created for you. I apologize. I love this company. I want to dance here. Once I return, I'll accept whatever you give me, even if it means starting over."

Damien looked toward Madame before he spoke. "Let Anna and I talk about this situation. We'll get back to you by the end of the week."

Lynne curtsied and left. A knot forming inside her threatened to take over the rest of her day. How did she get so out of step with the company? What would she do in October if they didn't allow her to return? Worse yet, what if they convinced Cheryl to drop her from the summer troupe?

༄

Three days later, Lynne again stood in front of the directors. Over the past days she'd not been able to sleep or eat. Despite her best efforts, she'd felt wooden and off the beat.

"Madame and I want you to make the trip to France," Damien said. "I promised Cheryl my ballet. I can't leave her in the lurch. That means you'll still make the trip."

Lynne sighed.

He continued. "When you return, you'll need to audition. If your dancing remains strong and continues to meet our standards, we'll offer you a partial contract in the *corps de ballet*. What you do with it depends on you, understand?"

"I do, and thank you." Lynne steadied herself, curtsied, and walked quickly from the office. Once she reached the women's dressing room, she allowed herself to collapse on a bench. Hopefully, she'd not used up her lifetime of luck; she'd need it for the rest of the season as well as to survive the hectic summer.

༄

The end-of-the-year gala and May reception drew a huge crowd. Lynne changed out of her costume and 'mingled' as ordered, but as the crowd of benefactors and local attendees thinned out, she stepped into a small side room and flopped down on the couch to rub her aching feet.

A tall, handsome, twenty-something man walked toward her with a glass of champagne. He smiled. "May I join you?"

She scooted to one end of the couch and curled her battered feet under her taffeta skirt. He sat down, finished his drink, and set it on a nearby table. He leaned forward, folding his hands between his knees. "Tired?"

She nodded.

"Do you come to these shindigs often?" he said.

"All the time."

"This is my first. Are they always this crowded?"

"Yes, but the ballet company needs these events so benefactors can visit with cast members and one another before they open their wallets to fund another year of ballet."

A grin spread across his face. "Tell me more."

She liked his smile. "You'd not be drinking that tasty bubbly if some rich rancher hadn't donated it. Probably would have had to settle for beer."

He nodded. "Do you prefer beer?"

"That's all I can afford. How about you?"

He hesitated. "I'm the son of the rich rancher who bought the champagne."

Lynne lowered her head, shielded her eyes, and took in a slow breath before she met his gaze. "Sorry. My tongue gets away from me sometimes."

"That's okay. Actually, I prefer beer—out of a bottle."

She cleared her throat and smiled. "On behalf of the Intermountain Ballet Company, we thank your family for donating the champagne and supporting our company."

"We? Are you a musician, a dancer, or what?"

"I'm a dancer who hopes you'll accept her apology."

"You know what? I didn't hear a thing." He paused. "Would you like to join me for that beer or a coffee?"

"Maybe. Are you married or anything?"

The man pulled back; his eyebrows knitted together. "No anything. I don't even have a parking ticket."

Lynne bit her lip to contain the smile that bubbled up inside her. "That's good because Billings doesn't hand out parking tickets."

The man laughed. "I know." He reached his hand toward her. "I'm Noel Elijah. And you're?" He scanned her left hand, "Miss...?"

"Lynne Meadows, a lowly *corps* dancer. You probably want to offer that beer or a glass of champagne to a soloist."

"I'm asking *you*, Miss Lynne Meadows. Ready for a quick getaway?"

She nodded. He offered her his hand and pulled her to standing. She put on her shoes and looked around. Across the room she noticed Madame's disapproving glare. She gambled by sharing a smile and a wave as they exited.

Lynne took side glances toward Noel as they walked to the cafe down the street. She liked the way his chestnut-colored hair curled around his ears and turned up against his shirt collar. His cowlicks caused it to spike out in several places. Under the sidewalk lamps, his eyes smiled and danced.

He reached for her hand. She felt his calluses against her fingertips. "So tell me about Lynne Meadows, *corps* dancer."

"I'm from Jersey, have four brothers, and love to dance. I've accepted a contract to tour in France this summer. Then I'm staying on to chauffeur my uncle through Europe for a month."

"That sounds like fun. Have you ever been to Europe?"

The warmth of Noel's hand distracted her. "Europe? Ah, no. That's part of the reason I applied. Otherwise, I'd never make the trip."

"Why's that?"

"Money and time. Dancers don't earn a lot. Besides, when I'm off in June and July, I must work to afford an apartment the rest of the year."

The hostess at the coffee shop seated them in a small booth, took their drink order, and told them a waitress would be by to take their food orders.

Lynne looked around as they settled in, then smiled. "Let's talk about Noel."

He kept her hand in his as he spoke. "I'm born and raised in Billings, and now I help my father manage our seven-thousand-acre ranch southeast of town. We run cattle three hundred and sixty-four days a year, but I always take off my birthday."

"When's your birthday?"

"Christmas Eve. That's why my name is Noel. The ranch hands like to get my goat by calling me No-elle, but I'm used to that. My Father fought my mother on the name. Since she did all the birthin', she won."

Lynne shook her head. "Your family sounds like mine. Everything has a reason."

"Really? Tell me more about your family."

"First, I need to confess. I ordered a soda because I'm thirsty and... I'm not old enough to drink a beer. I should have told you so you could've chosen an older dancer."

He squeezed her hand. "I'm fine here with you. So tell me about your family."

"I have lots of relations in Jersey. I miss Spot, my dog who died last year. My dad is recovering from a heart attack, but he'll be fine. I have no boyfriends, no parking tickets, and no place to live when I return the end of summer."

"Are you looking to change that dating status?"

Lynne toyed with the straw in her Green River soda. "I hadn't thought much about it lately. Since I leave town in a couple weeks, I'm cleaning house, so to speak." She smiled. "I might be interested in a few last-minute dates."

"I'm glad to hear that."

She glanced at the clock on the wall. Had more than an hour passed since they arrived? Noel placed his napkin on the table and pulled out his wallet. She pushed down the tingly feeling that circled inside her. She didn't want the evening to end just yet.

"Let me drive you home so we can discuss the details of a few last-minute dates."

"Sounds good. If I'm lucky, someone will steal my old-lady car and save me driving it to the junkyard."

He gave her a strange look but didn't ask about the car as they walked back to the theatre parking lot.

Lynne slid into the passenger seat of his red Chrysler convertible and leaned against the pomegranate-red leather seat. "Now this is a great car."

"Are you a car buff?"

"No," she answered. "But I do appreciate nice cars. My uncle plans to give me the car we buy in Europe. I'm hoping it's as nice as this."

༄

When they reached her apartment at Lake Elmo, Noel turned off the engine and turned to face her. "Thanks for a brief, yet lovely evening. How about I call you before you leave? We could continue our talk and get to know each other."

"Sounds nice." She scribbled her number onto a scrap of paper, smiled, and handed it to him. "Thanks for driving me home."

Once inside her apartment, she watched him back out of the driveway. Thinking about him replaced her tiredness with a calm she wasn't accustomed to feeling at the end of a date. Either she'd sleep like a rock tonight or she wouldn't sleep at all. Regardless, she couldn't erase the smile on her face.

The next afternoon, a bouquet of daisies and wildflowers tied with a blue bandana greeted Lynne as she returned from cleaning out her locker at the ballet company. She smiled. What were the odds she'd meet a seriously nice guy just as she planned to pack up and leave town? Wait until she told Marta. That should get a good laugh from her.

Lynne plucked the card from the bouquet.

Dear Lynne,

Thanks for making that ballet celebration a special event for me. Here I thought I'd be in and out in a cowpoke's minute, and then I saw you. Thanks for the conversation. I haven't enjoyed myself that much in months.

I'll call you and hope there'll be time for you to join me on a ride around the ranch. You can wear the kerchief like a real cowgirl.

Sincerely,
Noel

She walked around her apartment, looking for the perfect place to display her bouquet. She settled on the dresser in front of the mirror; the reflection doubled the flowers' abundance. Sitting in her overstuffed chair and smiling, she thought she'd better appreciate these since she'd not receive any once she left for Europe unless she bought them for herself.

The next day she returned home and found a dozen roses beside her front door. Noel again? She read the new card:

> Dear Lynne,
>
> Must be out of town for a few days. Didn't want you to think I'd forgotten my promise to take you riding.
>
> I'll call when I get back. Hang onto that bandana!
>
> Noel

She found a larger vase and merged the flowers into a huge arrangement, then sat down to enjoy them. Time to call Marta.

Their conversation was brief. Marta was preparing her summer class schedules and had a meeting starting any minute.

Marta laughed. "Two bouquets in one week? Sounds like Noel's interested."

"Or else he has partial ownership in a flower shop. Wish I'd met him months ago. He'd have saved me all the drama from other guys I dated."

"Keep me posted. He sounds like a huge step in the right direction."

❧

Two days later, Noel hadn't called. Maybe he'd changed his mind and saying he was going out of town was his way of stepping away. His loss.

Day five. She edited the bouquet, removing the wild flowers, which had faded like her hope of his ever calling.

❧

Lynne grabbed the bag of groceries from the trunk of her car and started up her stairs. Her phone was ringing as she struggled to unlock the door without dropping her purchases. By the time she got inside, the ringing stopped. Drat! If it was Noel, she'd missed his call. What if he didn't call… The phone rang again. She grabbed it.

"Hi, Darlin'. Sorry to take so long to get back to you. I know you're busy, but do you have time for that ride I promised you?"

She did a little twirl, then settled herself. "I might."

"Can you fit it in tomorrow?"

She curled herself up in the cord as she pushed down her excitement. "How's two o'clock?"

"Perfect. We'll ride into the hills and picnic on Moonrise Point."

"Can you guarantee I'll see the moon?" She heard herself getting all girly and flirty.

He laughed. "I can if you stay overnight."

"Whoa, cowboy. You're getting ahead of yourself."

"We can do something else if you'd rather. I'll let you set the pace. It should be obvious to you what I want."

She closed her eyes, picturing him at the celebration event. "What do you want, cowboy?"

"To make your 'A+' list of suitors."

She smiled at the phone, wishing he stood in front of her. "I don't have an 'A+', or a 'B', or even an 'X' list."

"Fair enough. Let's start one. I'll be first. Now that we have that settled, I'll pick you up at two."

She hung up the phone and squealed like a little girl.

∽

As soon as she returned from working with Damien the next day, she fussed over her hair, braiding and unbraiding it, brushing it into a ponytail and adding the blue bandana Noel had sent with the first bouquet. Which pair of slacks to wear? If she kept seeing him, she'd need to buy a pair of jeans. Right now she was broke, so her gray slacks would have to do.

Last night she'd painted her fingernails and toenails, changing the color three times before deciding on bright red. When she heard him drive up, she looked for her sandals but settled for slip-ons rather than keep him waiting.

She opened her apartment door just as he started to knock, catching his hand in mid-air.

"Hi, ready to go?"

She grabbed a sweater, locked the door, followed him out, and stepped up into his truck, a ten-year old Chevy that showed hard use.

"No convertible today?"

"Nope. We'll be driving along ranch roads. It's my grandfather's old homestead. He devoted his life to turning the open land into a working ranch. We have a lot to maintain and upgrade—the land, the crops, and the livestock—to honor his legacy."

"Did you ever think about going to college?"

"I did. I have my bachelor's in agriculture and my master's in business management."

"Wow. I'm impressed. I have a degree in long hours, sore feet, and putting my foot in my mouth."

"I'd add gracefulness and a fascinating personality."

Their banter continued as they drove south across the Yellowstone River and into the hills. Twenty minutes later, they turned off onto a wide dirt road that wound through stands of trees, past open fields, and in and out of grassy hillocks.

"When will be reach your family's property?"

"It started back where we turned onto the dirt road."

"What? That's a mile behind us."

"We need lots of grazing land for our animals."

They stopped at a large log home with a wraparound porch. Rocking chairs and wooden benches reminded her of the homes she saw on westerns like *Gunsmoke*.

She stepped from the truck and looked down. "I've discovered a greeting from one of your critters."

Noel laughed. "Lynne, Lynne, Lynne. What are you wearing on your feet? Don't you own any real shoes?"

"These are real. I'm glad I found them rather than the sandals I planned to wear."

He carried her to the porch and plunked her down in a rocker. He hurried inside and returned with a wash basin, a towel, white socks, and a pair of well-worn cowboy boots. "These look to be about your size. I'll buy you a new pair of princess shoes, and you'll need boots before you come back again."

She felt a tingle of contentment when he said 'again.'

Before their picnic, she fed the pigs, gathered eggs, milked a cow, and help saddle the horses for their ride. She brushed the dust from her slacks. If she was going to be a ranch hand, she'd *definitely* need jeans.

Once they reached the ridge, Noel spread a blanket under a large oak and placed their picnic basket on one edge. He sat down and patted a spot beside him. "Join me."

She surveyed the vast prairie stretching below her. "Quite a view. Do you ever get tired of it?"

"Never. It reminds me of the pioneers who crossed here more than a hundred years ago. Off to the west, you can still follow their wagon tracks. I've thought of building a bunkhouse and camping area for city kids to preserve this for future generations. We'd invite groups to stay a week and get back to the old ways: sleeping under the stars, eating from a chuck wagon, and learning about pioneer life. The local historical society wants to get involved."

"Who are you? A rancher, a ballet patron, or a historian?"

Noel smiled. "Can't a fella be more than one thing?"

"I guess, but I've never met one. I've been hard pressed to meet a gentleman, let alone one who had dreams beyond next week."

"You've been shopping in the wrong department."

They sat in silence under the wide canopy of the giant oak, watching dragonflies flit through the withered grasses.

He stretched and leaned back on his elbows. "I love the open spaces, the blue sky and," he paused, "having time to get to know you. Up to now my dad, the ranch hands, and Cook have made my life near perfect."

"What about your mother?"

He looked away. "She left when I was five. Decided she missed the parties and society life back east."

"How could she leave you? Doesn't she call or come to see you?"

"Let's talk about you. How did a Jersey girl end up in Billings?"

She laughed. "Luck. I had a string of auditions and offers. Like a lot of college kids, I chose the one furthest from home."

"So you had family problems?"

"No." Lynne paused. "My family loves its boys. My brothers can do no wrong."

"That explains a lot." He reached out and covered her hand with his. "Whatever the reason you became who you are, I like what I see."

Her face heated up as Noel looked at her. "Me, too."

∽

The rest of the afternoon they rode around the property, crossing dry riverbeds, investigating small canyons, and trotting up and down hills. As the sun dipped behind the neighboring hills, they stopped on a knoll to rest the horses.

"I'm so glad you agreed to come. Considering that you're a city girl, I'm surprised by how well you ride."

"My experience is limited to a pony ride at a carnival when I was five. I've never been on a full-size horse before today."

Noel broke out laughing. "My dear Lynne, you should have told me. I'll apologize now for tomorrow. Promise you'll not be too mad at me?"

"Why?"

He turned their horses toward the ranch house and slowed their ride to a walk. "Just promise to forgive me, okay?"

8

The next morning Lynne started to stretch. Spasms gripped her legs and lower back. Now she knew why Noel apologized. Silly girl. She'd agreed to forgive him *yesterday*.

She scooted to the edge of her bed, then worked herself to standing, wincing with every tiny movement. How could she feel so stiff and sore when all she did was ride a horse?

The phone rang. She hobbled to answer it. When she lifted the receiver, she heard a quiet laugh. "Noel? It has to be you."

"Yep. I'm guessing you're feeling pretty sore about now."

"Good guess."

"Sorry, darlin'. You rode so well, I assumed… Are you mad?"

"No, just sore. Thank heavens I've no need to dance for a couple days. I can barely stand, let alone put one foot in front of the other."

His chuckling continued. "Is there anything I can do?"

"I think you've done enough, and stop laughing."

"Ah, Lynne. How about I bring an early dinner around five? What sounds good?"

"Burgers and vanilla shakes. I'm not a salad kind of girl unless forced."

"It's set then. I'll bring it over since you won't be able to navigate those steps or drive until tomorrow. Keep moving. You'll loosen up."

After a long, hot shower, she attempted to get dress. Her legs refused to bend, so she slipped on her ancient chenille robe.

Over the next hours, she walked around her apartment, bending her knees and twisting her back. Near five o'clock, she tried dressing again, but she still couldn't.

When she heard a knock at her door, she opened it and saw him waving a white handkerchief like a flag of surrender and holding out a bag that smelled of burgers and fries.

She smiled. "It's okay. Come in."

He kissed her cheek as he stepped into her apartment and looked around. "This is cozy. Just enough space for one." He pointed to the table. "Shall we sit here?"

"You sit. I've decided to stand. What can I do to walk again? I have special rehearsals coming up."

He pulled a tube of Ben-Gay from his pocket. "Use this where it hurts. Mostly, you need to give your muscles time. I won't offer you a massage where you need it most, but I can rub your shoulders." He moved behind her and gently kneaded her stiff muscles.

"Oh. That feels wonderful," she said as she rotated her neck.

His hands stopped moving. He stepped back. "I just remembered something. I need to get to the feed store before it closes at six." He plucked his hat from the table and shot out the door. "Enjoy your dinner. I'll call you."

Lynne hobbled to the door in time to see the tail lights of his car as he sped from the driveway. Why did he leave like his hair was on fire? She hoped it wasn't something she said. Maybe he sensed his massage felt too good for this early in their relationship.

The rest of the evening she waited for his call. The same on Friday, Saturday, and Sunday. Late Monday morning, he called and wanted to stop in for a few minutes.

Over the past two days, she'd regained her mobility. This morning she stood at her kitchen counter in second position and executed some *demi-pliés*. Luckily, she had a few hours before she had to dance. She remembered how upset Madame had been with Marta for her hiking fall and then for breaking a bone in her foot. Any mention of her stiffness was a bad idea. If Suzette realized she was not up to par, she'd point it out to everyone.

Lynne smiled as she stood in a hot shower and formulated a prank to pull on Noel. Later, when she heard him turn off his car engine, she hurried onto the landing outside her door. Then she grimaced and inched down her steps His face looked pained as he watched her move as slow as a snail.

Stopping near the bottom, she leaped toward him, wrapped her legs around his waist, and grabbed him around his neck. His eyes opened wide. He staggered backward.

"I'm better!" She smiled.

His face looked confused as he peeled her off his body. "I see that."

She stepped back. "I'm sorry. I guess that wasn't as funny as I thought."

He shrugged, then smiled. "Payback, right?" He took her hands, pulled her to sit next to him on the bottom step, and turned to face her. "We need to talk."

Her insides contracted. She swallowed down the words that waited to rush from her mouth. *So, here it comes. Another relationship ending because she'd acted too crazy.* She pulled in her lips and looked down at their clasped hands.

"About the last time I was here. I shouldn't have left so abruptly."

She nodded, waiting for him to continue.

"I met a young woman in college; we fell in love. Over the years we did everything together: study, eat meals, walk to class, and... We'd planned to be married this coming fall. Then last December, she quit school, emptied out her apartment, and left town without a word."

Lynne squeezed his hand but remained silent.

"I like you a lot, Lynne, but I'm still working through being deserted by the women in my life. The other day when I was massaging your shoulders, I felt like we were moving too fast. I needed to step back and slow things down, especially since you're leaving town soon. Does that make sense?"

She kissed his cheek. "Thanks for telling me. I totally understand."

"But Lynne, I want to see you again. Maybe jeep around the ranch or go to dinner?"

"Sounds like fun." She nodded and patted his hand.

He kissed her cheek and stood. Reaching into his car, he tossed her a small package. "I got this for you to remember our first horse ride," he said. "I'll call you tomorrow."

After he left, she sat by the window in her apartment, fingering the gift, a narrow, leather-corded string tie. The slide on the tie was a horse. He'd called it their *first* ride. Maybe there'd be more. And maybe he was right. They were moving fast. Tomorrow, she'd be calm and not scare him with her crazy impulses. He deserved her best behavior.

ॐ

The next day, they drove to a small bluff near the steep hill that abutted the ranch property and overlooked the vast plain.

"The cows look like brown dots spread over the area. How many are there?" she asked.

Noel tipped his Stetson forward to shield his eyes and scanned the plain. "Three thousand head. Wish you were going to be here in late summer. Roundup is something special. You could have helped."

She nodded, wishing the same thing. Being with Noel created a warm spot inside her she hadn't known before. More than ever, she planned to return to Billings, dance position or not.

Back home that afternoon, she smiled as she turned over a post card with the photo of cowboy boots, rope, and Stetson. Perfect!

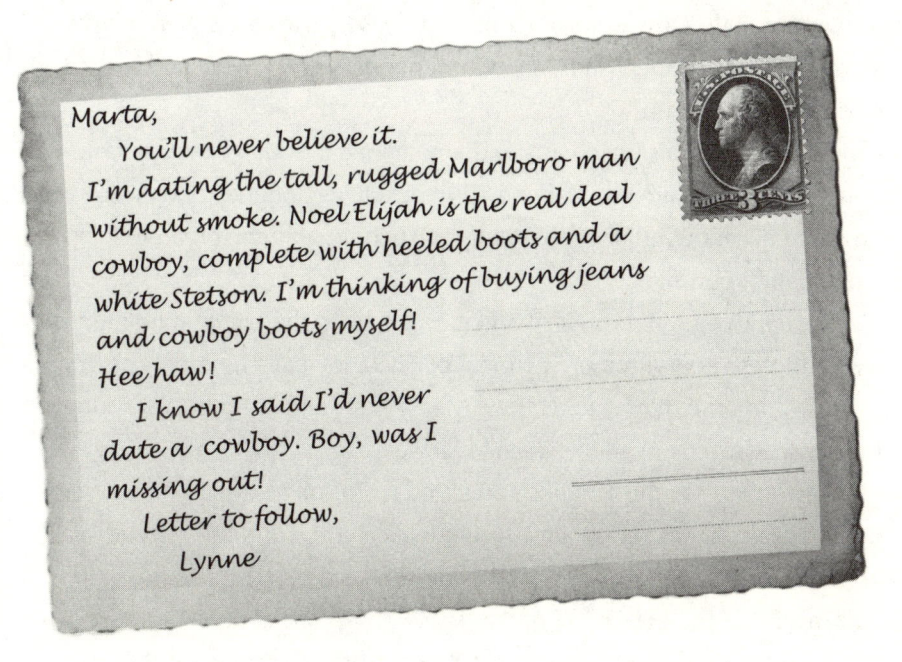

> Marta,
> You'll never believe it. I'm dating the tall, rugged Marlboro man without smoke. Noel Elijah is the real deal cowboy, complete with heeled boots and a white Stetson. I'm thinking of buying jeans and cowboy boots myself!
> Hee haw!
> I know I said I'd never date a cowboy. Boy, was I missing out!
> Letter to follow,
> Lynne

A quiet tap on her door startled her. She hadn't changed out of her tattered shorts and snug T-shirt. Throwing on her chenille robe and tugging the belt around her waist, she navigated piles of clothes and boxes and opened the door. Her eyes sprang open in surprise. "Hey! I wasn't expecting you."

He kissed her cheek. "I was in the neighborhood and wanted to ask if you'd drive to Laurel with me. We could have dinner. I'd have you back before dawn."

"Now that's a long dinner." She looked down at her robe and ran her hand through her hair.

"Take your time." He eyed the piles of boxes that filled her apartment. "I'll wait in the car. Come down when you're ready."

She raced to the shower, then toweled off and combed her hair into a high ponytail. Pawing through both suitcases, she found her favorite shirtwaist dress, added perfume behind her ears and knees, and rushed out of the apartment.

Noel checked his watch as she opened the car door. "That was fast."

"What can I say? I'm starving." Lynne bit her tongue to keep from finishing her thought aloud: starving for such an attractive man to keep calling and courting.

They enjoyed dinner in a small café. She liked the fact that he didn't try to impress her with a pricey meal or his fancy car. The more she got to know him, the more she realized Marta was right; she'd been looking for guy friendships in all the wrong places.

They drove into the foothills and found a pull-off to watch the sun set behind the western mountains. Lynne leaned toward Noel. He slid his arm around her, pulling her snugly against his side.

"This is the perfect way to end a day. Thanks," she said.

He smiled and kissed her hair. "My pleasure. You do know I'll miss you while you're gone. Do you have an address so I can write to you?"

She turned to look at him. "You'll *write* to me?"

"Of course. The question is, will you write back or will you leave town and forget all about me?"

She started laughing. "I was thinking the same about you, wondering if I'd be out of sight and out of your mind."

He started the car and shook his head. "Not a chance."

At the top of the stairs to her apartment, she paused. "Thanks again. Do you want to come in for a few minutes?"

"Yes and no. I promised you could set the pace of our dating, but…"

Lynne pulled on his hands as she opened her door. "But what? I invited you in."

"I know. Let's say good night out here."

༄

After her final goodbyes to Vivian the next afternoon, Lynne sat on her two suitcases beside the base of the stairs to her apartment. It had been a small but serviceable home. Both Bartley and Marta had enjoyed spending time here with her. Was it easier to leave knowing her aunt was also leaving, or did that make it harder? As she pondered her own question, Noel arrived in his pick-up.

She smiled when he stepped from his truck and tipped his hat. "I see you're ready to go." He hoisted her bags into the bed. "Do you have bags upstairs?"

"Nope. We're only allowed two. Besides, I can raid my closet back home or buy what I need in Europe. Doesn't that sound amazing?" Lynne stretched her arms wide and looked skyward. "When *I* arrive in Europe!"

"Now don't get too excited and forget to come back. You did promise me you'd return to Billings. I'm holding you to that."

She smiled and kissed his cheek. "I'll be back. You're holding my lovely turquoise Nash hostage. Plus, I can't let you build that camp without a female voice in decisions." She stopped. "I'm sorry. I didn't mean… I'm certain your mother would have had good ideas if she'd hung around."

He looked away. "Let's not discuss that today, okay?"

On the drive to the depot, they joked and laughed, listening to the radio until Bing Crosby began singing "Now Is the Hour". She closed her eyes and listened to the lyrics about leaving. She swallowed hard and turned off the radio as they pulled into a depot parking space.

They sat in silence for several moments. Noel held her hand, then gave it a gentle squeeze. "I'll check in your luggage."

While they waited in the depot, they held hands and watched passengers arrive, embrace, and wait too. Did they feel as conflicted as she did about leaving?

A low rumbling shook the building. People gathered their belongings as the train slowed, its wheels scraping against the rails as it gave an exhausted swoosh. Passengers headed onto the landing.

"Now boarding," the PA system announcer said, "Train to Great Falls, Minot, Minneapolis, Chicago, and all points east. All aboard."

Noel drew her to her feet and into a bear hug. "Take care of yourself. Write often and come back."

Her throat clogged; she couldn't speak, so she nodded and backed away to board the train.

Tears streamed down her face. She took her seat and stared out the window at Noel standing on the landing. He smiled and tipped his hat. She waved.

The train started moving, pulling her away from Billings and from him. This deep churning, this clawing in her throat, must be how Marta felt when she left last year. How horrible.

༄

The prairie stretched along both sides of the tracks. By midday tomorrow, she'd change trains in Chicago and be headed for Philadelphia. Maybe it was a bad idea to visit Bartley's mother, but she'd discussed it with Marta and had promised to stop. It was the least she could do. She'd had plenty of time to figure out what to say to her. But for now, she'd avoid thinking about it and write a letter instead.

Dear Marta,

I'm on the train heading east. Too late to turn back now. So many changes lately: spending hours learning new choreography, Vivian moving, meeting and dating Noel. I enjoy his company more than I thought I would. (sigh)

Visiting Bartley's mom makes me nervous. I'll keep you posted.

Lynne

As she tucked the letter into her purse, she pulled out a small, wrapped package. Noel must have shoved it in when she was kissing him. She opened the wrapping. Tears threatened as she read the inscription in the tiny journal:

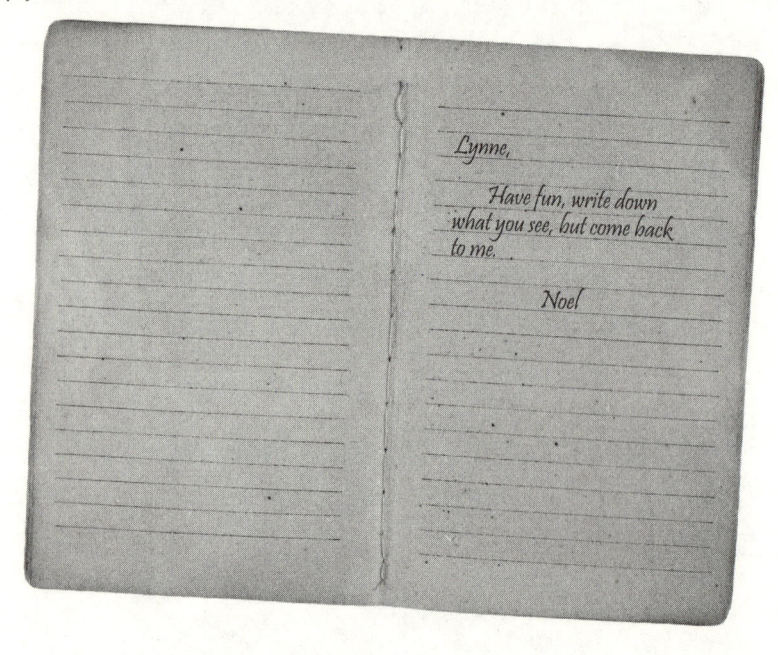

> Lynne,
>
> Have fun, write down what you see, but come back to me.
>
> Noel

9

Lynne hurried into the Philadelphia train station to beat the rush for the ladies lounge. She shoved her luggage under a sink, took a sponge bath, and dried using the scratchy tan paper towels from the dispenser. After adjusting her pony tail, she pressed down as many wrinkles as possible to make her pin-striped shirtwaist dress look presentable.

She checked her watch, grabbed her bags, and hurried out into the humid Philadelphia heat, so different from what she'd left in Billings. She yawned and looked around for the ride Mrs. Timmons promised. Only a limo waited at the curb. The driver stood next to the idling car.

"Miss Meadows?"

She nodded, stepped into the car, and inhaled the aroma of polished leather. The interior was dark as night: black seats, black carpet, dark wood paneling, and tinted windows. So this was how Bartley traveled.

As the limo pulled away from the curb, the driver said, "I trust you had a pleasant journey."

"Yes, thank you." If she'd had this comfort on the train, it might have been pleasant.

"We'll arrive at the Timmons residence in about twelve minutes. Please help yourself to any drinks in the bar."

"Thanks." She craned her neck to view Philadelphia's skyscrapers.

They reminded her of New York City, but weren't packed so tightly together.

The Timmons home sat on the crest of a hill, surrounded by a massive, manicured lawn, an unexpected greenness in the summer heat. Gardeners worked in the flower beds as the limo entered a circular drive and stopped. The driver opened her door just as the wide front entry also opened. A woman in a gray maid's uniform smiled. "Welcome, Miss Meadows. Please follow me."

"Thank you." Lynne stepped into a two-story foyer. Sunlight streamed in through tall windows and bounced off the gigantic chandelier, creating starburst patterns along the marble floor. What a lovely, gigantic waste of space, she thought.

The maid stood waiting as she looked around. They proceeded down a wide hallway into another sun-filled room.

"Mrs. Belfors-Timmons will be down shortly. Please make yourself comfortable. Help yourself to the breakfast buffet. If you need anything, please let me know."

"Thanks," Lynne said. By her count she'd said "thanks" more times this morning than she'd said it over several months back in Billings.

Groupings of sofas and chairs divided the large room into eating and conversation areas. Vases of yellow and blue iris decorated every table, including the two breakfast buffets with silver tray covers that gleamed in the sunlight.

She peeked beneath each hot tray dome: scrambled eggs, French toast, hash browns, bacon and sausage rolls, and crêpes with a berry sauce. A covered plate of croissants, a bowl of mixed fresh fruit, and three kinds of juice sat next to glasses, a short stack of plates, a coffee pot, and porcelain cups.

She wondered if she should wait in case others might arrive until she noticed the table had one chair. No need to wait. She took a small serving of fruit, a crêpe with berry sauce, and a spoonful of scrambled eggs.

While she ate, the only sounds she heard were her fork scraping across her plate and herself swallowing. The quiet sent a shiver down her spine. Even though she hadn't eaten since leaving Billings, the overabundance of rich food and her reason for visiting dulled her appetite. She set her plate to one side and walked to the windows.

The sunroom faced a large patio with a swimming pool beyond. Flowering bushes and trees provided shade on one side while allowing sun worshippers ample space to stretch out on chaise lounges in another area. Why didn't Bartley ever talk about her home and the beautiful pool and patio?

A door opened. Lynne turned as a tall, thin woman in a pale green linen suit entered. With her bronze skin and her styled blonde hair, she looked like a mature version of Bartley.

"Miss Meadows? Welcome. I'm Mrs. Belfors-Timmons. I hope your train trip was pleasant." She nodded but didn't extend her hand.

Lynne had reached out her hand but quickly withdrew it. "Yes, thank you. I appreciate your invitation to stop on my way east. Your home is lovely."

Mrs. Belfors-Timmons blinked several times. "Thank you. It's comfortable. Shall we sit?" She indicated a chintz sofa. "You can tell me about your upcoming trip to Paris. It's truly a beautiful city. Lots of amazing shopping."

Shopping? That's what you want to talk about? Well, Mrs. Timmons, you're not getting your way. I couldn't care less about shopping, she thought. Instead, she shared her dance plans with Bartley's mother, noticing the way her eyes traveled around the room, as if she had more important things on her mind.

"I also wanted to stop because I have something for you." She reached into her purse, took out a small velvet pouch, and handed it to Mrs. Timmons. "Bartley gave this to me for my birthday."

Mrs. Timmons tipped out the contents of the bag in her hand. She exhaled deeply. "I remember this. Bartley called and asked me to find or have a silversmith make a circle pin of three ballerinas for you."

Lynne nodded. "Bartley, Marta, and I called ourselves the three musketeer dancers. We supported one another and spent much of our free time together. I think Bartley would want you to have it...now that...now that she's gone."

Mrs. Timmons' body sank down as she stared at the pin.

"Bartley was a wonderful friend and a graceful dancer. This will remind you of her dancing in Billings."

"Thank you," Mrs. Timmons said as she closed her fingers over the pin and sighed. She straightened and lifted her chin. "Let me step away for a moment. I want to share photos of Bartley with you."

Turning the pages of the albums, they laughed at the four-year-old Bartley posing with a pout on her face, smiled at the photos of Bartley winning first place trophies in ballet contests, and cried when they turned to the obituary.

Mrs. Timmons closed the last album and rested her hands on the cover. "What did Bartley tell you about her family?"

"She missed you when she moved to Montana. She appreciated the opportunities you provided for her and said she wanted to make you proud. Everyone who saw her dance fell in love with her."

"I thought she decided to dance far from home because she wanted to get away from us. I feel guilty we didn't make plans to watch her dance in Billings or San Francisco. Our schedules were so busy, and the time slipped away. Then it was too late."

Lynne pulled her elbows against her sides to hold herself taut and to keep from crying or blurting out Bartley's comments about her family ignoring her. She cleared her throat before she answered. "She knew you thought about her and wanted to come visit."

"Did she say that? I mean, we wanted to come... Did she blame me for the diet pills? I didn't know she watched me take them. I only used them for a few years when I needed a boost."

Lynne swallowed the truth as she knew it. That's exactly what Bartley said about the pills. "Bartley made a mistake. She didn't realize the pills were addictive." She paused. "She didn't blame you. She loved you."

Mrs. Timmons reached out and squeezed Lynne's hands. "Thank you." The room remained quiet until Mrs. Timmons stood. "I know you need to catch a train, but please give me a moment." She rushed from the room again.

Lynne fidgeted and looked around, waiting for whatever came next. She moved to the windows and studied the view. All this property for two now-childless people. Noel could build his camp for kids several times over if he had even a small portion of their wealth. Noel. She missed him so much.

Mrs. Timmons reappeared, holding a small jewelry box. "Sorry to take so long. I had to dig through several boxes in Bartley's room." She handed the box to Lynne. "Please take this. Inside are silly little things, but they were her special treasures. Share them with Marta and anyone else you wish. I know you'll understand their meaning to Bartley."

Lynne opened the box and stared. Inside were several cheap, plastic charms, the ones bought in gumball-type machines. An ache sliced through her heart.

"I know they're silly, but every time we went into a shop where they had those awful plastic globes, she begged a penny. She hoped to win a pink or blue hard plastic dancer. All she ever got were tiny rings, cowboys, or animals."

Lynne nodded, unable to respond.

"When she packed to move to Billings, Bartley came to me in tears. She asked about her plastic charms. I told her I'd tossed them into my bedroom trash can. She raced into my room and picked them out, shouting that I didn't understand. She said she made a wish every time she turned the knob that she'd become a ballerina. You probably understand her wishes and dreams."

Lynne wiped her eyes as she stood to leave. "I do, and thank you for giving these charms to me. I'll share them with Marta."

The late afternoon commuter train pulled out of Philadelphia's Penn Station at four. Lynne dragged her two bags along the aisle and plopped down in a window seat. Thank heavens it was only thirty miles to her childhood home.

It was obvious Mrs. Timmons missed Bartley, so there was no way she could share Bartley's loneliness or how she emulated her mother's use of diet pills. Those conversations wouldn't bring Bartley back. Hopefully, her omissions honored Bartley's memory and showed respect for Mrs. Belfors-Timmons.

Lynne closed her eyes as the train picked up speed. Every muscle in her body ached from holding herself taut. Bartley's mother acted like any grieving parent Lynne had ever heard about, but something was missing. Maybe it was their lack of closeness over the past years. Maybe it was Bartley's fault since she'd moved so far from home. *Maybe I need to keep my family connections open*, she thought; *I'd hate to feel the void in my family that I sensed with Bartley's mother.*

Marta had the right idea when she went home to recover from her injury. She'd found a new life even though she didn't yet realize it. Lynne marveled that she could see her friend's future before Marta did. By the time she returned from Europe, she might be ready to make a change herself, settle down, date one guy, and look to her own future, especially if she continued to dance in Billings.

She pulled two postcards of Philadelphia from her purse and started writing.

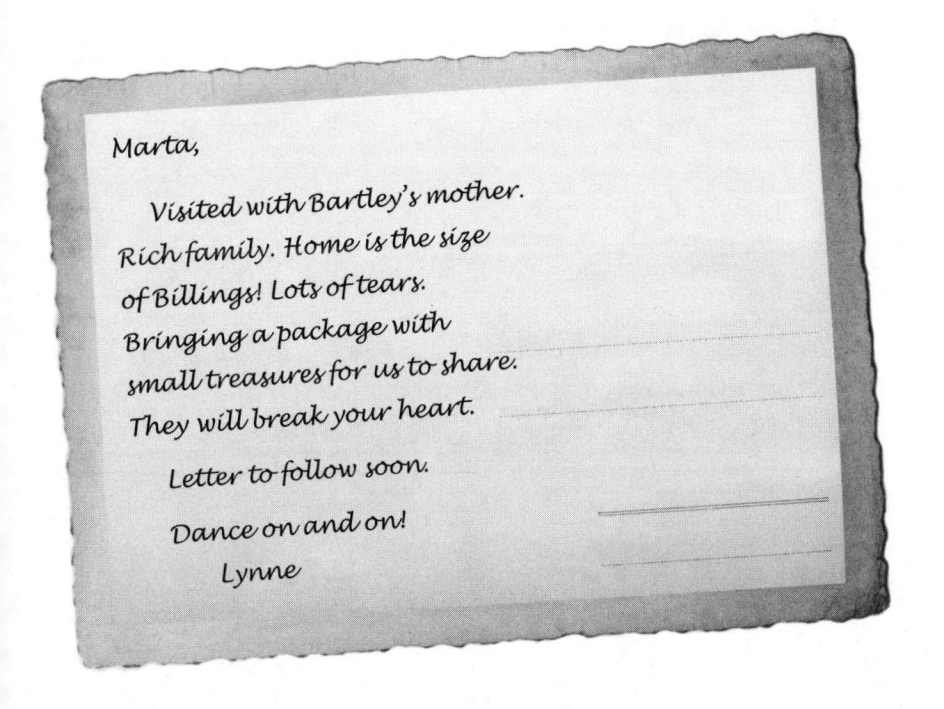

> Marta,
>
> Visited with Bartley's mother. Rich family. Home is the size of Billings! Lots of tears. Bringing a package with small treasures for us to share. They will break your heart.
>
> Letter to follow soon.
>
> Dance on and on!
>
> Lynne

Noel,

   Thinking of you.
   Thought about your camp plan. Maybe ask your rich friends to help create a fund or a foundation that helps kids.
   Hope you miss me as much as I miss you.

      Lynne

10

One hour later, Lynne exited the train in Trenton, New Jersey. She called home, then enjoyed the warm breeze that fluttered her skirt as she sat on her suitcases, waiting for her father. He honked and waved when he pulled up in his clunky Chevy truck. She struggled to hoist her bags into the truck bed, hopped in, and gave her dad a peck on the cheek. "Hi, Dad. Thanks for picking me up."

"It's good to see you, Lynnie."

She watched him navigate the downtown roadways. He drove as well as he'd done before his heart problem. That was a good sign. "How are you feeling?" she asked.

"Better. I'm working part time. Your cousin Bill is taking the rest of my shift. My biggest challenge is convincing your mom that it's okay for me to drink a Pabst while I watch baseball."

"The doctor approved your drinking beer?"

"Not really, but I can't let Leo drink alone, can I? Not very hospitable." Her dad paused. "You should know we've given Leo your room. Since he's paying for your trip around Europe, we thought he deserved special treatment while he's visiting this month."

"Doesn't he *always* get special treatment?"

"Be fair, Lynnie. He's more excited than you are about traveling. He's anxious for you to finish your dance lessons and get on the road."

She closed her eyes as a shiver of frustration zigzagged through her brain. "Dad, they're not lessons; they're practices and performances. And why aren't my brothers helping in the store? They're out of work, aren't they?"

"Yes, but the boys need a break before they start looking for real jobs in the fall."

Always her brothers, the boys. They could do no wrong. It also appeared they'd do no work to help their dad. "Couldn't they help in the store until they find jobs?"

"They've got college degrees. I wouldn't expect them to sell nails and tape measures." He smiled and patted her hand. "But when you decide you're done dancing, you could come home, find a husband, take a bookkeeping class at the community college, and work for me."

"Dancing *is* my career. I don't plan to give it up after only two years." After all her years dancing, he'd yet to understand her career choice. "So where am I sleeping?"

"On the couch in the den. Your mom will make it up as soon as her bridge group leaves. Leo's friends are coming by at ten-thirty tomorrow for a good-bye brunch. You'll need to be up early to help fix the food. She's so excited about Leo's visit. You'd think he was her baby brother."

"But he's almost twenty years older than Mom and retired from the jewelry shop. Can't he stay in a hotel?"

"Yeah. But your mom has a soft spot for Leo. Besides, he's giving you the car after you finish driving around. I'd think you'd be grateful."

She had jumped at the chance to drive him around Europe, but Uncle Leo was fickle. As a car salesman, Fuller Brush associate, and carpet seller, he'd made and lost money faster than she could change pointe shoes. And if he was in I'm-the-center-of-attention mode, their days together might feel especially long.

When they arrived at her family home, she noticed that nothing had changed except the flower pots on the back porch held primroses instead of weeds. Mom had started to spruce things up, but it looked like she'd run out of time before she got to the main flower beds. Lynne followed her dad into the kitchen and left her luggage in the back hallway. Then she straightened her shoulders, stepped into the living room, and smiled. "Hello, everyone."

The bridge ladies looked up and smiled or waved their greetings. Her mother laid down her cards and hurried to give her a hug. "Welcome home, dear. Leftovers are in the fridge if you're hungry. Leo said to tell you he'd see you tomorrow. He's gone out with old neighborhood friends and told me he won't be back until late." She returned to her bridge table and resumed playing.

Lynne watched the ladies for a few seconds before retreating to the kitchen, where her dad sat drinking a beer. He'd already dialed a buddy to talk baseball. She walked out the back door, crossed the lawn, and sat in her childhood swing. Rocking back and forth soothed her. Why had she thought she'd receive a different reception? One where she and her parents sat down together to talk? A time when "the brothers" or Leo didn't soak up the energy in the family? She pushed herself out of the swing to walk around her old neighborhood.

As she passed her friend's home, she saw people sitting around a small bonfire in their side yard. She cut across their lawn and shouted, "Hey! Got room for one more?"

"Lynne!" Her best high-school friend's mother, Mrs. Gale, rushed to grab her in a bear hug. "Nice to see you. When did you get back?"

"Earlier today. I'm on my way to Europe to dance for the summer and then tour for a month."

Over the next hour, the group plied her about her life. With the mention of Bartley, they shared her sadness; Suzette and Madame Cosper brought up witchy people they knew. They liked Noel, sight unseen. By the time she headed home, she realized how lucky she was to have the chance to dance and travel. Both promised a lifetime of memories.

The next morning, Lynne and her mom completed preparations for the brunch, then sat at the breakfast table, looking through the S&H Green Stamps Catalog.

"You could get a new card table now and save up for matching chairs," Lynne said.

The front door opened. Uncle Leo sauntered in. "Mornin', everyone," he said as he loosened his tie and removed his sports jacket. "What a lovely morning. Ready to begin our adventure, Lynnie?"

So much for coming in late, she thought. "We'll need to leave here by two o'clock."

He checked his watch. "I have just enough time for a catnap before I spruce up for the party." He started for Lynne's bedroom, then backtracked. "I brought in the mail. Left it on the table. I see Lynnie's girl friend, Noelle, sent her a letter."

Lynne's mouth dropped open. Noel wrote. Warmth surge through her as she grabbed the mail and took her letter outside to the swing. Her fingers trembled as she ripped into the envelope.

Letters to Follow

> June 6, 1959
>
> Dear Lynne,
>
> Where to start? Maybe the moment you mentioned the champagne my family provided for the celebration? Probably the highlight of my week, maybe my month. You know you captivate me, don't you? That hasn't happened since college. I think I can see you blushing while pretending to ignore my comment, right?
>
> I enjoyed our dates on the ranch and around town. I wish we'd had more time together before you danced out of Billings. Just know you haven't heard or seen the last of me. Stay safe but have fun.
>
> Thinking of you,
> Noel

Lynne brushed away tears. She felt as if Noel stood beside her, pushing back his cowboy hat and grinning. He was so sweet, but it was too late to turn back now. Too many promises made to too many people. Her future as a dancer depended on proving herself a valued member of the Paris troupe. Yesterday and today, one thing became crystal clear: no way would she return to Trenton and become the family bookkeeper.

She tucked Noel's letter away for safekeeping and hurried back inside to make phone calls before changing clothes for the brunch and the train to New York. She'd start with her Aunt Vivian. Since she was leaving Billings shortly, she wanted to remind her to forward mail to Mrs. B's boarding house.

Next, she called Marta. "Your letter writing hasn't improved yet, I see."

"Lynne?" Marta said. "I wrote to you early last week."

"Well, it didn't arrive. Now I'll never get it. That's why I'm calling you. I wanted to check on all the drama in your life, so spill."

Marta laughed. "Steve and I had a long talk. We've reconciled. I accepted the engagement ring and told him I'd move to Portland as soon as everything at the dance studio settled. You know, you could have mentioned he'd taken a job there. It would have saved me a lot of agonizing."

"I know, but I didn't want to influence your decision. For once I kept my opinion to myself."

"Anyway, the summer dance sessions begin soon. The loan to buy the building from Lindsay is in the works, thanks to the women in my exercise class and the fact Mom is selling our family home."

"Any regrets about selling the house?"

Marta didn't answer for a moment. "Not regrets so much as relief. I feel like my life is shifting. I have control. Thanks for all your pushing and shoving as well as your listening to me moan and groan. I'll miss you, knowing you are so far away. If you think of it, bring the programs from where you dance. I'll use them to inspire my dancers to work harder. Have fun and be safe."

Finally, she dialed Noel. Always save the best for last, her mother had taught her.

"Darlin'? How are you?" Noel's voice sounded smooth and steady. "Did you get my letter?"

"I did. Thanks for writing. How's everything at the ranch?"

He laughed. "Fine, except I miss you."

"Ah..." She sighed. "Could you...would you...I mean...how's the ranch?"

"You just asked me that. Are you okay?"

"I guess I'm tired." She shook her head and closed her eyes at her fib. She should tell him how she felt. She'd have all summer to rethink and even retract what she said if she changed her mind. She swallowed slowly. Here goes, she thought.

"Noel...thanks for all the nice things you wrote. I, I'm, ah, I feel the same way about you." She paused. "I'll miss you."

Noel chuckled. "I'll miss you, too, darlin'. Take care."

As Lynne hung up, she pictured herself standing in front of Noel, smiling, him brushing the wisps of hair off her face and kissing her. Could she hold on to picturing his face close to hers over the next three months? She'd certainly try.

♾

Uncle Leo made his entrance to the brunch dressed like 1940s movie star Clarke Gable and smelling like a men's department store cologne counter. The forty-plus-year-old women at the brunch who'd focused on hearing about Lynne's dance career suddenly turned their attention his way. Some batted their eyelashes while their husbands stood back with their hands in their pockets.

How could she have forgotten the show Leo created when he came to town? If he carried on like this on their trip, she might live to regret her decision.

She watched for a few minutes, then backed away into the kitchen, where her mother was assembling extra trays of food. "Lynnie, why aren't you in with our guests?"

"Leo is handling everything and everyone without me. I didn't remember him being such a ladies' man."

"Leo?" Her mother laughed. "Honey, he's always loved the ladies. That's why he's been married and divorced four... no, five times."

§

The brunch was a huge success. Everyone ate, drank, and chatted. After the last guest left, Leo flopped down in her dad's TV-viewing chair. "Lovely brunch, Sis. It was great seeing my friends, but many of them are looking old."

"Leo, you and the rest of them *are* old," Lynne's mother said. "Just because you color your hair doesn't mean you aren't their age."

Lynne laughed. "You color your hair? Really? Do you use that *Grecian Formula 44* stuff?"

Leo smiled. "Yep. The ladies like dark hair they can tousle when we're, you know." He winked and turned on the baseball game.

Lynne's mom laughed as she gathered up used dishes from the living room. "My brother is such a ball of energy. Sometimes I envy his carefree life. I've always wanted to travel."

Hm-m. Would her mother consider traveling with Leo in her place? True, she'd miss out on seeing extra sights and getting a new car, but it meant she could return to Billings a month early. Noel wouldn't mind; neither would she.

She trailed her mother into the kitchen. "Since Dad's feeling better, maybe *you* should drive Leo and see the sights."

Her mother stared out the window over the kitchen sink and sighed. "I'd love to, but I can't. Your father needs me. He's not fully recovered. I go in every day to check on him and help at the store. Last year's recession hit us hard; we can't afford to hire permanent help right now." Her mother sighed again. "You go. Have fun. When you come back, maybe you'll be ready to stay here and help out."

"We've had this discussion before. I have a job in Billings. I plan to go back there as soon as I return."

"But, Lynnie, we need you. Couldn't you dance closer to home or teach classes for Gail? She says you're always welcome."

Lynne pulled in her lips to keep from responding. How could her mom, the woman who'd driven her to years of dance classes and attended numerous recitals, not realize ballet *was* her career? Maybe most parents were like this. Bartley's mother certainly was.

But Marta's mom understood, possibly because she worked in a dance studio.

Was she overreacting? No. If she even hinted she'd leave the Intermountain Ballet Company, her parents would expect her to come home to help out.

11

Lynne stared up at the *SS United States*, the massive ship tethered to the pier in ropes that hung like spider webs. Her gaze rose to where the ship widened and tiny portholes poked through its black hull. She sighed, wondering if others felt small as ants beside the gigantic wall of metal with deck piled on top of deck, reaching toward the sky.

The congestion on the New York City dock grew as hundreds of passengers with thousands of pieces of luggage stood waiting to board. Well-wishers joined them, talking, laughing, and turning the ordinary wooden dock into a celebration.

Tickets were checked, and the throng surged toward the gangplank. Uniformed crew members loaded passenger belongings on carts and followed them up the ramp.

As they boarded the ship, excitement seeped into her pores.

Leo guided her to the left. "Follow the cabin steward to your cabin. After you stow your belongings, meet me." He handed her a paper with his cabin information: Deck A Room 240. "We'll grab a place at the railing. They serve free champagne when leaving port."

She expected she'd have a room with walk-around space and a large window. Instead, she stepped into a tiny room with a tiny porthole and two narrow bunks. So much for having space to breathe.

The steward handed her the key and stood waiting.

"Thank you," she said.

The young man continued to wait.

Lynne looked at him. "What?"

He rolled his eyes and left.

Lynne tossed her bags on a bunk and stepped to the porthole. She stooped and pressed her face against the glass. Traces of the bright June sky behind nearby buildings and blue harbor water did not create a magnificent view.

Minutes later, she walked through the crowded passageways and up several decks in search of Leo's cabin. He opened the door just as she knocked. "Ah, Lynnie. How are your accommodations?"

"Small, but fine; I'm small." She stepped inside and looked around. "Is this a suite?"

"No, this is first-class. The luxury suites are too pricey. They're often filled with movie stars and people who want to be left alone. Traveling in first class, I'll meet people who want to talk while they drink and dance and play cards. Sometimes we make plans to meet up after we dock."

She nodded as she scanned his room with such a huge walk-around space she could do cartwheels and not bump the double bed. A large window showcased the New York skyline like it might appear on a billboard. From his window, the harbor water appeared far below. Hm-m, she thought. So this was how it was to be. He was paying, so she guessed he got to choose.

He rubbed his hands together. "Let's sit by the window." He pointed to the two modern chairs tucked against a small table. "Check out the gift basket. Nice, huh? I always grab the tin of peanuts. You want anything?"

She shook her head. She didn't remember seeing a basket or a table in her tiny cabin.

He opened the can, letting the mouthwatering aroma escape, and popped a handful of salty nuts into his mouth. "So, Lynnie, what do you think? Nice digs, huh? Sailing is the only way to travel."

She nodded. Changing her mind, she took an apple from the basket.

He continued to munch handfuls of peanuts. "Once we land, I'll hit a few museums and walk around a couple castles. Mostly, I like to meet the people, especially in England; I understand most of what they say. It's a life-of-Riley time."

"A what time?"

He chuckled. "A casual time, no cares, no worries, no one pushing you to punch in or get a project done before next week."

Chimes sounded. A man's voice announced, "All visitors aboard the ship are asked to disembark. All ashore who are going ashore. I repeat, all visitors are asked to disembark."

They hurried upstairs to stand along the dockside railing. The horns blared. Passengers and dot-size people on the dock waved. Toy-like tugs far below nudged the massive *SS United States* into the Hudson River. They were intent on leaving the enclosed waters around Manhattan, the Statue of Liberty, and Staten Island behind.

She inhaled deeply, closed her eyes, and smiled. With all that had happened, how had she garnered this spectacular opportunity? She vowed to make each moment count.

꼭

After shipboard drills and welcomes, passengers spread in all directions. Leo walked her around the common areas on the tourist deck: lounges, dining hall, movie theatre, small ballroom, TV-viewing room, library, card rooms, beauty salon, clothing boutique, small cafes, and casual seating areas.

"It's a floating city," Lynne said.

"Yep." He checked his watch. "Nothing to do but sit back and be waited on." He checked his watch again.

"Do you need to be someplace?"

"Sort of. I've signed up to play cards in a private card room." He patted her arm and backed away. "My deck is mostly off-limits to you, but I'll call you. We'll eat together tonight. After that, I'll be dining in first class. Remember to dress up for dinner. See you at seven-thirty on the port side entrance to your dining room."

She looked around. How would she find her cabin? As she moved through the passageway, she noticed discreet signage. Arrows pointed to the various amenities and cabin decks. As she descended to her room, she noticed the passageways, like the rooms, became smaller. At least she had a bed. Now she needed to learn what 'port' meant.

Unpacking took five minutes. Did she have a roommate? Maybe she'd luck out and have the cabin to herself. For now, she'd wander around the tourist-class shops and outside on the deck. When she wanted to get away from the crowds, she could always head to her quiet little room with its little bed and take a little nap.

The New York City skyline had disappeared; even the sea gulls that wheeled above the ship had turned back toward land. In every direction was the Atlantic Ocean.

Deck chairs with cushions and blankets lined the exterior walkways. Passengers sat talking, reading, sleeping, or playing cards. The space between them and the railing held shuffleboard courts, ping-pong tables and badminton nets.

When they were boarding, she noticed most of the travelers brought on trunks of clothing while she had just two suitcases. With so many passengers, maybe no one would observe that she wore the same outfits day after day. Thank heavens she'd brought two dressy tops for dinner at Leo's insistence.

She heard music and laughter above her and started up the stairs to investigate. As she stepped onto the landing, a steward stepped forward. "May I see your key, please?"

"My key? Why?"

"Your key shows me your level of access. Without your key to verify your access, I must ask you to return below."

When she returned to her deck and moved toward her cabin, she heard shrieks of laughter. Was that noise coming from her cabin?

She opened the door and thought she'd stepped into a junior high sleepover. Two girls were cackling and shoving each other off both beds, messing up her space in the process.

When they spotted her, they smiled and settled to slow bouncing.

How old were these two? They dressed like they were well out of their teens, but their mannerisms suggested they were much younger. Could be a long five days!

"Hi," said one of the girls. "We're the Katies. Who are you?"

"I'm Lynne." She sat on her bed, so the girl bouncing on it leaped across to the other bed. "So you both are named Katie?"

They giggled and poked each other. "I told you she'd say that. We hoped a cute guy was bunking in here. But you look okay."

The taller Katie stepped off the bed and reached out to shake Lynne's hand. "I'm your cabin mate, Katie Kay."

Lynne forced a smile. "Mind if I use the bathroom to get ready for dinner?"

"Go ahead," Katie Kay said. "Just shove my stuff out of your way."

"Do you want to sit with us for dinner?" the other Katie said. "You could be our chaperone." Both girls laughed.

Chaperone? How old did they think she was? "I have plans, but thanks." The giggling and poking resumed as Lynne unpacked her dinner clothes and stepped into the bathroom to freshen up.

Guests in tourist class lined the passageways, waiting to be seated. Leo was right. She needed the black silk skirt and fussy white blouse. Passengers dressed as formally as they did for attending the opera or ballet.

She and Leo were seated with six others, ranging from teens to grandparents. Lynne heard the Katies across the room and felt grateful to be seated far away from them.

The meals were served by waiters in white jackets. Each carried two dome-covered plates at a time, uncovered them in front of the guests, and stepped away to retrieve two more. The personal service continued until the entire table received their dinner: roast beef, brown gravy with mushrooms, mixed vegetables, garlic mashed potatoes, and Parkerhouse rolls. Mom would have loved being waited on like a rich lady, she thought with a sigh.

Leo directed the table conversation, recounting his travel adventures as well as his "fascinating moments selling jewelry." He appeared to enjoy every smile, every nod, every appreciative comment about his exciting life. For the love of goodness, she thought; since when did *he* lead an exciting life?

Dessert arrived on rolling carts: yellow cake with chocolate gouache, brownies with cream cheese frosting, or tropical fruit cups. Lynne splurged. One gooey brownie never bothered her waistline in the past.

As they left the dining room, Leo grinned. "I need to talk with you later, say around nine-thirty. Think you'll be in your cabin?"

She tried to read his expression. "I'll make sure I am."

"I'll call you." He waved and walked off whistling.

Was his cheeriness a good sign, or was Leo scheming? She'd know after nine-thirty.

12

Leo's call invited Lynne to meet him outside the Sapphire Room, the small ballroom on the tourist deck. Sounds of music and voices greeted her arrival. A small band playing current hits reminded her of her favorite Billings radio station.

Her uncle walked up, a wide smile spreading across his lips. "This is my surprise for you, my dear."

She looked around. "You're taking me dancing?"

"No. I thought you'd want a keep up your practicing, so I saved money on your cabin and rented this small ballroom."

"You're kidding."

"I never kid where money is concerned. It's yours from six to nine every morning. Your cabin steward will unlock the space when you ring for him. You'll be sharing it with another dancer. What do you think?"

Her eyes widened as she peered around the space. "It's perfect. Thank you!" She hugged him. Her recent snarly attitude slid away. "What made you think of this?"

He shrugged. "I know how religious you are about rehearsing. Don't worry about tipping the steward; I'll see that he gets a generous 'thank you' in his pocket. Now, I'm off to the casino." He kissed her cheek and walked away, whistling again.

She stepped into the room. A small stage took up the center of the far wall, flanked by windows facing the promenade deck and a bar on the interior wall. Overhead fixtures lit up the room, and a glittery ball circling near the ceiling cast bright streams of light on the polished wooden floor. She smiled to herself. Maybe Uncle Leo wasn't uncaring after all.

༄

Her alarm woke her at five-fifteen; she called the cabin steward. When she arrived at the ballroom, the steward pointed to a placard in the corridor. "Each morning, a notice will be placed here to let others know this space is reserved from six to nine. Move the tables and chairs as you wish. I'll return to lock up at nine." He bowed slightly and left.

She walked around the room and peeked out the windows toward the deck. Many passengers strolled by; early risers sat bundled in blankets in deck chairs, facing the ocean. Using a dining chair as a *barre*, she executed several *pliés*.

The corridor door opened. A petite, young woman entered. "Hi, I'm Lucia. I'm sharing this room with you for the next few days."

Lynne walked toward the girl and extended her hand. "I'm Lynne. Are you part of the Americans Dance in Paris troupe?"

"Yes. You too?"

Lynne nodded. Her appreciation for her uncle's generosity grew.

"Isn't it exciting to be going to France to dance?"

"I never dreamed I'd do that. I'm so glad to have someone to practice with."

It wasn't often that Lynne towered over another dancer, but with Lucia she did. The bronze-complexioned young woman kicked off her sandals, slipped on ballet slippers, and pulled a chair up next to Lynne's. "Guess we're back to basics? I haven't tried *barre* work with a chair for years."

Between the two of them, they knew the choreography to almost every piece they played. Focusing on the waltzes, they ran through their solos until the steward returned to lock the room.

Afterward, they sat together in a lounge area. "Tell me about yourself, Lynne."

"Not much to tell. I'm plain old Lynne from Jersey. Not certain where I got my blue eyes. My mom calls me sarcastic. I call it my way to hold my own against my brothers, who teased me incessantly."

"I'm envious, even for brothers," Lucia said. "I'm an only child, so I'm considered spoiled. After our tour ends, I'm spending a year in Florence with my grandparents to take art and ballet classes. Then I'll spend next summer in Stockholm before I head home to New York."

"Will your dance company hold a position open that long?"

Lucia nodded. "I have a year's leave. How about you?"

Lynne shrugged. "My future's up in the air, for the time being."

The girls ate dinner together, then joined several hundred other guests in the movie theatre to watch the new animated *Sleeping Beauty*.

Lynne stretched as she and Lucia strolled along the inner passageway before heading to bed. "I loved the cartoon."

"So did I," Lucia said, "but I prefer the ballet. Tchaikovsky's music excites me more than Disney songs."

"I agree. Tchaikovsky inspires every inch of my body to move."

Lucia yawned and checked her watch. "It's eleven-thirty. If I don't get some sleep, you'll see my grumpy mood tomorrow." She reached up to hug Lynne. "I'm so glad we have each other."

Lynne returned to her cabin, changed into her night clothes, and flopped onto her bed. The quietness enveloped her. Having Lucia as a dance friend was an unexpected gift. Tomorrow they'd continue working together, assuring they'd arrive in Paris well-prepared.

When the cabin door opened much later, she heard the two Katies enter, giggling and bumping into things until they turned on the overhead light. The clock read one-thirty. Lynne covered her head with a pillow and turned away from their chatter. The next moment, it seemed, the phone rang, announcing her five-fifteen wake-up call.

"What's that noise?" Katie mumbled.

Lynne sat up. "Go back to sleep." She felt off balance as she stood.

"I can't sleep with alarms ringing and people chattering." Within a few seconds, however, she had drifted off and didn't stir as Lynne left the room.

She remained sluggish as they rehearsed *The Nutcracker* and *Sleeping Beauty* selections and moved on to their solos. Maybe she needed more sleep or quieter roommates.

"I love the way you dance your *Firebird* solo," Lucia said. "My only suggestion is to extend your body along diagonals, toward the audience, especially on your ending." She demonstrated, then restarted Lynne's recording.

Lynne repeated the section, adding longer reaches with her arms.

"Much better. Now, hold the ending a fraction longer."

Lynne suggested Lucia quicken her toe picks *en pointe* and smooth out her head positions. "Remember, the *Swan Lake* cygnets' dance must be exact, especially if you dance it as part of an ensemble."

The girls ignored the smattering of passengers peering in through the promenade deck windows. As long as they didn't tap on the windows or step into the room, they didn't interrupt the dancers.

After they cleaned up, they shared breakfast at a small dining room table. When Lynne stood, she swayed and grabbed the nearest chair to steady herself. She straightened slowly. "I think I'm getting the flu. I'm going back to bed and try to sleep."

Lucia guided her uneven steps. "Maybe it's not the flu. Maybe you're seasick. The ship is swaying a lot today."

When they opened Lynne's cabin door, the two Katies were dancing on both beds and swinging long strips of black licorice like wands. Whenever they stuck out their blackened tongues, they broke into giggling fits.

Lynne grabbed the door jamb as her stomach roiled. Her head ached as if she'd completed a dozen *chaîné* turns without spotting her desired destination.

A chime sounded. An announcement followed on the ship's PA system. "Your attention please. We're entering heavy seas. If you feel dizzy, nauseous, or unstable, you may be experiencing mild motion sickness. Until the symptoms pass, we suggest you avoid eating. Do not read or lie down. It's best to get fresh air and focus your eyes on the horizon."

Lynne stared at her roommates, then turned toward Lucia. "I can't take their craziness right now."

Lucia pulled her into the corridor and closed the door. "Come with me. You'll never get any peace and quiet in there."

Lynne felt too dizzy to object to being dragged up stairs and down a passageway. She entered Lucia's room and plopped down in the chair. Chair? Lucia had a chair! Her friend's cabin was the size of hers, but with only one bed.

"Oh-h." Lynne grabbed the arm of the chair and closed her eyes. When the sensation passed, she let out a long, slow breath. "Thanks for bringing me here. The quiet helps. The two Katies spend all their time talking about dreamy boys and clothes, painting their nails, and eating snacks."

"Stay as long as you like," Lucia said. "I'll grab a book from the ship's library and come back to keep you company."

For the next several hours, Lynne focused on thinking of anything but herself. She and Lucia talked, and she dozed upright in the chair. At lunchtime, she opted to walk along the deck to focus on the horizon. By dinner she felt better, but skipped going to eat, just in case.

Lucia returned from dinner carrying two fluffy dinner rolls and a bottle of soda water. "The steward suggested this. I hope it helps."

As Lynne ate the rolls in Lucia's cabin, an announcement came on the PA system. "Would the following passengers please contact their cabin stewards as soon as possible: Thomas Kent, Mary Linstrom, Lynne Meadows, Joyce Sythe, and Alice Dever."

Lynne stiffened. Had something happened to Leo? She picked up the phone and dialed. The steward answered after one ring.

"This is Lynne Meadows. I was asked to call you. Is something wrong?"

"Just a moment." the line went quiet. "Mr. Leo Turner requested we contact you. He hasn't been able to locate you. Shall I connect you to his room?"

"Yes, please." She let the phone ring a dozen times, then hung up.

She returned to her own cabin and fell into a deep sleep until her phone rang at midnight. It was Leo checking up on her. At least he hadn't forgotten about her.

After moving cautiously during their morning practice, Lynne returned to her cabin, where she found Katie waking up.

"Hey, roomie," Katie said. "Where have you been? An old guy kept calling yesterday, asking about you."

"He's my uncle. I spent the day with a friend I'll be dancing with this summer."

"Dancing? Sounds like fun. Katie and I are spending our summer hitchhiking. This ship will be our last chance to have someone cook for us and give us a comfy bed."

"Why's that? Where are you going?"

"Wherever we feel like. We'll stay in hostels, then head out early each morning to hitch as far as we can."

"Is it safe to hitchhike?"

"Safe as at home. We do need to stop early so we can get a bed in the hostel. Otherwise we'll be sleeping out under the stars or in the rain or in a barn with cows." Katie snorted a laugh.

"Your parents let you do this?"

"This is our second trip to Europe. We did it last year after we graduated from high school. It was a blast!"

"Hm-m." she looked at Katy with a different eye. The girls were close to her age. Next to their plans, her summer looked tame. Thank heaven she didn't need to hitch rides or find hostels each evening. Traveling with the dance troupe and with Leo had definite advantages.

໒ຉ

The next morning Lynne shared Damien's recording of Gershwin's *An American in Paris*. "He's choreographed the opening seven minutes. We dance the first two and a half minutes, sharing *pirouettes* and fussy *piqué* turns. Next, comes the *adagio* with fluid, swimming movements and elongated arms. The guys take over with leaps and turns while we pose and catch our breaths before we resume dancing."

"My favorite music is the middle," Lucia said. "The strings make the *adagio* feel romantic. That's how I picture Paris."

Lynne smiled. "I know. Let's start there and build up to the beginning section. All the city sounds, the honking, and the bustling music takes every ounce of our energy."

After a light lunch, the girls strolled the deck, then returned to Lucia's room to rummage through their dance bags to decide what clothing they could share once their Paris performances began.

"I love your colorful skirt, Lucia. I wish mine had so much detail. Where did you get it?"

"My mother decorated it. She loves to sew. But I like your skirt too. It's such a unique design."

Lynne laughed. "I bought it at a flea market. The lady who sold it to me called it batik. She printed it using wax. I doubt the detailed patterns will ever catch on."

When the girls returned from a break on the deck, Lucia's phone message button was flashing. She frowned as she listened to the message. "A guy named Simon—the ship's activity director—wants to meet with us as soon as possible." After her call to him, she appeared confused. "We're to meet him at the Sapphire Room in ten minutes."

"I hope they aren't taking away the room. We've done what they asked, haven't we? Do you think people complained?"

The girls watched a tall, thirty-something man wearing a nametag and carrying a clipboard approach. "I'm Simon. You must be the dancers." He looked at his clipboard. "Lucia and Lynne?"

They nodded.

He unlocked the ballroom door and invited them to join him at a table. "Thank you for meeting me. As you've probably noticed, passengers have discovered you. Many say they've gotten up early to watch you practice. More than a handful have asked if you'd consider performing."

Lynne stared at Simon. "You want us to *perform*? We don't have proper costumes or professional recordings, and we're only preparing excerpts from various ballets."

"I understand, but people like what they see. I'd hoped to talk you into performing in here for a few minutes, say at two tomorrow afternoon? Share your warm-ups, dance a couple of selections, and talk about yourselves." He smiled. "I'm authorized to pay you fifty dollars."

"Wow! That's great!" Lucia said.

Simon nodded. "I'd love to place you on tomorrow's schedule of ship events. What do you say, ladies?"

13

The girls looked at each other, raising eyebrows and shrugging. They nodded and smiled at the same time.

"Fantastic!" Simon handed each of them his business card. "Here's my personal phone number. Once you've made a plan, contact me. Remember, we're not expecting anything different from what you've been doing. We'll just open the doors and let passengers come in and sit down. They'll appreciate whatever you decide to do."

"We'll get back to you before dinner." Lynne looked to Lucia for agreement.

"Fantastic! Ask your steward to track me down. I'm glad you can do this on short notice."

The girls waited until Simon had disappeared down the corridor before they spoke. Lynne turned to Lucia and smiled. "What do you think?"

Lucia pulled in her lips and shrugged, then let out a long, slow puff of air. "I'm in shock." She looked around and signaled for Lynne to follow her into an alcove, where she starting jumping up and down. "Wow! We're performing daily stuff, and we'll each get twenty-five dollars!"

"I know! We're making our own program, performing what we want, and getting paid. Maybe I should pinch myself. Is this a dream?"

The girls sat in Lucia's stateroom, planning their presentation. They'd perform *Serenade*, their solos, and the "Garland Waltz" if Simon located a hula hoop and cut it in half for them.

They practiced introducing themselves, wrote up their plan, and gave it to the steward in exchange for the severed hula hoop. Then they set to work decorating the half circles with the scarves they'd brought. By the time they'd finished, it was time to dress for dinner.

Lynne called Leo's stateroom and left a message about their event. "... So, Uncle Leo, you don't need to get up early. Get your beauty sleep and attend our performance tomorrow at two."

***

The girls requested a dinner table for two and ended up in a cozy booth. "I like this," Lucia said.

Their dinners arrived: chicken with broccoli and rice served with a Waldorf salad and a golden croissant.

"Yum." Lynne broke her croissant open and slathered butter inside. "Guess they're preparing us for French breads. It's not long now!"

After dinner, they skipped the movie, *Some Like It Hot,* and walked to the fantail glass dome enclosure to sit in deep lounge chairs and look at the stars.

"This trip is more exciting than I ever expected," Lucia said. "First, I met you. Now we're creating our own dance program and watching the stars while we sail to France." She gasped. "Did you see that shooting star? Did you make a wish?"

Lynne smiled. "I did. If Noel could be here with me, this would be perfect."

***

Day Four's activity schedule lay under the cabin door when Lynne woke up.

2:00-2:30 Sapphire Room Special Event
Meet Lynne and Lucia.
Join us for a Sneak Peek as two American dancers prepare for a summer tour in and around Paris.

***

She slid the copy into her suitcase as proof of their performance. Wait until she told Marta and Noel. She should get a copy for Madame and Damien. This opportunity was truly a gift, plus they got paid half a week's salary for thirty minutes of their time.

The girls met as usual to practice. Once again they noticed passengers looking in. Lynne smiled toward them. "I feel like we're in a fish bowl."

Lucia changed the recording from warm-ups to the music of *Serenade*. "We may be experiencing our crowds right now."

"That's okay. We'll get in an extra practice time and get paid. Can't beat that combination."

A shower and breakfast followed their practice. The rest of the morning dragged on the way it did when the Intermountain Ballet traveled and prepared for performances. Lynne didn't expect more than a handful of guests: Simon, the AV person, and Leo, if he broke away from his socializing.

At one-thirty, their event was announced. The dancers met Simon and the AV person in the ballroom. By one-forty-five, all was ready. At one-fifty, three people wandered in and sat down.

Lynne's enthusiasm dipped as she adjusted her tights and double checked her hair. Suddenly, a flurry of muffled conversations filtered in from the hallway. Passengers chatted and found places to sit. By two o'clock, when Simon stood to introduce them, the Sapphire Ballroom was standing room only.

"Ladies and gentlemen, welcome. It's fantastic to see this room filled with so many guests. It's my pleasure to introduce Lynne and Lucia, two professional American dancers we're lucky to have sailing with us. These young women were selected to join an elite group called Americans Dancing in Paris, directed by Cheryl Menkins of New York.

"Our young dancers have agreed to share part of their warm-ups, dance a bit, and answer questions at the end. Please sit back and relax. Our European-bound ship, the *SS United States,* is proud to introduce Lucia and Lynne."

Lucia took the microphone. "Thank you, Simon. Lynne and I love ballet and appreciate your coming here today. We began warm-ups before you arrived. Back home in our dance companies, we take more than thirty minutes to warm our muscles so we are able to dance more smoothly and avoid injury."

She continued to explain *pliés, rond de jambs,* and other exercises as Lynne demonstrated. She also introduced their first dance selection.

"When George Balanchine wrote the choreography for Tchaikovsky's *Serenade,* he called it pure dance. It doesn't have a story like *Sleeping Beauty,* but it creates a mood. Usually, it's performed by a complement of a dozen or more dancers. Today, we'll share the opening moments with you. We suggest you watch our arms and our feet for the subtle movements Balanchine created."

Lucia and Lynne took time to tie their pink wrap skirts over their pink leotards; then they stood motionless. As the music began, they moved their arms and heads slowly, in unison, quickly opening their feet to first position. The slow pace of the choreography emphasized their subtle yet precise movements.

As the music ended and the dancers bowed and straightened, the audience sat silent for several seconds. Suddenly, applause burst forth; many in the audience stood and clapped. Lucia and Lynne gave each other side glances, smiled, and bowed again.

Each girl presented her solo, followed by their character dances from *The Nutcracker;* Lynne danced the Chinese and Lucia the Arabian dance. They quickly added long skirts for the "Garland Waltz" from *Sleeping Beauty* and used the scarf-decorated hula-hoop as garlands. Both girls entered with *balancés*, then graceful *arabesques* before they crossed and re-crossed the floor to a waltz rhythm followed by *tour jetés* and *balancés* in perfect unison.

The audience responded again with enthusiastic applause.

Lynne's energy and pride surged. They'd prepared and organized a brief program the passengers enjoyed. Simon treated them as valued professionals. It had been a long time since she'd felt valued as a dancer.

After several bows, Simon asked for questions, which he repeated so everyone heard each question clearly.

"How long have you danced, Lynne?"

"Since I started elementary school. Lucia started when she was four."

"Lucia, do you have favorite music and choreography?"

"I love Tchaikovsky's music and Balanchine's choreography." Lucia looked toward Lynne. "What are your favorites?"

"I also like Tchaikovsky. My favorite choreography is from Damien Black, my ballet master. He writes a lot using Gershwin."

"When will you become a premier dancer, Lynne?"

She hesitated before answering. "I'm a second year dancer. In my company they require another year of dancing in the *corps* before I'll be considered as a permanent soloist."

"How long do you work on learning a piece of choreography, Lucia?"

"That's hard to answer," Lucia said. "We often learn a piece in a couple of weeks. A full ballet takes a month or longer. We work in overlapping rehearsals, so we move from one studio to another to learn various sections of the choreography."

"And my favorite question: Lynne, do those pink ballet shoes hurt when you go up on your toes?"

Lynne laughed. "Yes, *pointe* shoes make your toes ache, but you get accustomed to it. Our feet have blisters and bunions, but it's a price we are willing to pay to dance."

"Thank you for..." Simon began, then stopped. "I see one last hand madly waving. What's your question?"

A young man standing in the back shouted, "Will one of you go out with me tonight?"

The audience and dancers broke out laughing. Clapping and hoots filled the room.

Simon shook his head and held up his hand. "I'm not going to let these dancers answer that. You'll need to ask them in private. Thanks for coming, everyone. Remember tonight is our last dinner aboard ship. The chef is preparing a special meal, so please come looking your finest."

By two-forty-five, the last of the passengers left the ballroom. Only the dancers, Simon, and Leo remained. Simon smiled as he handed Lucia and Lynne envelopes.

"Lovely program, ladies. I'm confident the entire troupe's performances will be wonderful if they are anything like the two of you. I'd like to invite you and one guest each to join us tonight in the first-class dining room for the Captain's Farewell dinner and Showcase Event. It's a formal affair that begins at eight o'clock. I'll need the name of your guest as soon as possible to seat you at the captain's table."

Lynne turned to Leo. "Would you like to join me?"

Leo bowed. "I'd be honored."

"I'm traveling alone," Lucia said, "but I'll be there. Thanks, Simon."

The girls stood watching Simon and Leo walk away. Lucia opened her envelope and gasped. "Lynne, Simon didn't give us twenty-five dollars."

Lynne frowned. "That's what he promised." She ripped her envelope open and leaned against the passageway as she stared at a fifty-dollar bill. "Oh my good gracious!"

ღ

The Captain's Dinner was an extravagant affair with several courses accompanied by professional singers and musicians during and after the meal. As the evening ended, Leo kissed Lynne's cheek. "I'll try to call you before we leave the ship. In case I don't, I'll see you as promised, in Paris, at your apartment building."

Lynne nodded and watched him walk away.

Simon stepped forward and asked the girls to stay a minute. "I wanted to once again tell you how impressed I was with your dancing today. People are stopping me to say how much they enjoyed your program. That said, if you young ladies plan to return to the states by ship, the cruise line is prepared to offer you two options. If you will lead morning exercise or ballet classes, we can reduce your return fare, or we'll provide an upgrade. How does that sound?"

"Amazing. But we're not returning together," Lucia said.

"It doesn't matter. Just call the number on my business card and ask for the events coordinator. I'll leave your names with the office staff." Simon shook hands with both girls. "I've enjoyed meeting and working with you. Fantastic dancing, ladies. Have a wonderful tour!"

"Thank you for the surprising gift of fifty dollars each," Lynne said. "We'd have danced for free."

Simon laughed as he turned to leave. "Spend it in good health and call when you know your plans to head home."

Lynne stood frozen in place. "Did I hear right? We could travel home for less money or in a better tourist cabin?"

"Seems that way. Simon's card may be a gold mine of opportunity."

As Lynne and Lucia walked from the dining room, a woman approached them. "My name is Pamela Ulman. I'm a reporter for *Ex Pat*, a monthly newspaper for ex-patriots from the U.S. and Canada living in France. May I have a few minutes of your time. I promise to be brief."

The three met in a quiet corner of the lounge, where Pamela confirmed their personal details and collected information about their summer dance schedule. "I'll post this information in my July and August columns so ex-pats and tourists will be able to find you as you travel. I'll also make certain the wire services in the states gets the information. That way your hometown papers can pick up and share your story."

Lynne let the impact of the article wash over her. Wait until she wrote to Marta and Noel. Maybe she should send a note to Madame and Damien. Yes, that's what she'd do tonight before she packed. The ship would mail the letters home for no charge.

As Lucia and Lynne walked back toward their rooms, they made plans to meet the next morning and exit the ship together. "The steward told me the Le Havre train station is a ten-minute taxi ride," Lucia said. "We have two hours to catch the train; then it's three hours to Paris. I can hardly wait."

Lynne stopped short as she entered her stateroom. The two Katies stood waiting for her. Each handed her tonight's dinner menu, asking for her autograph. "We didn't know you were a celebrity," Katie Kay said.

"I'm not. I'm a *corps* dancer, not a soloist."

"But you danced so well," the second Katie said. "We loved watching you. Sorry we acted so juvenile in the cabin."

"It's okay. Being eighteen myself, I get it."

"You're *our* age? Wow. You seem older, like you know where your life is heading. That must feel good."

Lynne smiled. "Yes, it must."

After the Katies left, Lynne sat down to write letters. Simon had given her a handful of the leftover event schedules, so she used the blank backs as stationery.

> Marta,
>
> Getting ready to pack up to disembark tomorrow. Great experience except for getting seasick. Passengers love to play dress-up. Their clothes put our costumes to shame. So glad I bought my fru-fru outfit for dinner. I'm getting sick of seeing myself wear it even though it is beautiful.
>
> As you can see, I danced with one of my American dance troupe members. You'd love Lucia. She's smart, friendly, and a great dancer. The ship even paid us $50 EACH!
>
> Tomorrow my adventure begins. We take the train to PARIS! I hope the dancing doesn't wear me too thin IN PARIS!!
>
> Write often,
> Love,
> Lynne

Noel,

You'll never know how surprised we were when they asked us to dance. We had fun planning our brief event. I get how you like to lay out things in your life. See, I'm changing—a little.

I miss you tons. Wish you were here. You'd have to give up your jeans and Stetson. These people are New York fashionable!

Please write often. I'll do my best to write back and send picture postcards.

I look at the stars each night and think of you.

Lynne

Madame and Damien,

I had the opportunity to dance on the ship with another troupe dancer. Our audience enjoyed each selection we shared. Thank you for giving me this opportunity. I'll do my best to make you proud.

Sincerely,
Lynne

14

The train from Le Havre to Paris passed through fields of green, tasseled grasses and herds of cattle lounging along the Seine River. While Lucia napped, Lynne enjoyed her first glimpses of small villages with stone cathedrals and narrow streets. She was in France! The hard work of learning and polishing choreography was about to pay off.

As the train slowed, her stomach did flip flops reminiscent of her seasickness on the ship. She exhaled as they stepped off the train. "Paris, here we come!"

They followed signs up the stairs and outside to enter a hubbub of city activity: taxis, street vendors, and buses. At an information kiosk, both girls got directions to their housing. Lynne prayed the attendant fully understood their requests and that Métro Line 13 took her to her apartment.

She thought of Leo, off on his own. They should have planned some way to check in with each other over the next two months. He'd traveled before, so he'd be fine. She hoped she would too.

Lucia hugged her, jolting her back to their parting. "I wish we were staying in the same place. Guess I'll see you tomorrow." She backed away, waved, then disappeared along the crowded sidewalk.

Lynne descended to her subway. When the train arrived, she followed the crush of strangers through the door and watched them scurry for seats. The people around her sat or stood, read, dozed, or stared straight ahead. She stayed near a door so she wouldn't miss her stop. The car rattled back and forth, screeched to a stop in station after station, then continued down the tracks as if in a hurry to a special destination.

She exited with the wall of people toward a bank of elevators. It appeared that catching the elevator could take a long time. How many stairs could there be to get to the street? She decided to find out.

Sweat trickled down her arms and back as she moved up the steep, seemingly endless steps. Her legs trembled with exhaustion; stagnant air irritated her lungs. Only her short, white gloves kept her hands from slipping off her luggage handles. No wonder people waited for an elevator.

Sunlight. Finally! The sidewalks were crowded with people heading in all directions. She spotted a tourist kiosk and handed the man a slip of paper. "I'm looking for this address."

He shook his head. "*Non.* Two more stops on Métro Line 13."

"Could I walk there?"

He looked at her two bags. "*Oui*, but with bags is not advised."

She returned to the subway and boarded the train. At her stop, she moved with the crowd and waited for an elevator to whisk her to street level. The late afternoon sun beat down hotter than any stage lighting. She stopped to rest in the shadow cast by a tall, thin building.

Four blocks later, along a noisy street of wall-to-wall stone buildings, she located Le Palais Pension-Appartement, her summer home. The building looked old and neglected. It's single star on the plaque by the entry wasn't reassuring since it had space for more stars.

As she walked up to the entry, her foot slid to one side on the second step. She looked down. A familiar, nasty smell reached her nostrils. The replacement princess shoes Noel bought for her were officially christened with French dog poop. "Welcome to Paris," she mumbled to herself.

She scraped off her shoe, then rang the buzzer. No answer. She rang again. Still no answer, so she removed her shoes and stepped inside.

The entry showed signs of heavy use. Oriental rugs lay between two lumpy-looking, thread-bare sofas covered with cigarette burns. Battered trunks served as side tables. Overflowing ashtrays reeked of stale tobacco. Used drinking glasses and crumb-filled plates lay in piles on every flat surface.

The walls and wainscoting needed a fresh coat of paint, as did the high ceiling. The cobwebbed chandelier high above the cracked marble floor had three of a dozen bulbs lit.

She knocked on the door marked *Madame Zelb: Concierge.* "Hello?"

A tall, dark-haired woman her mother's age with fire-engine red lipstick appeared at the door. *"Bonjour. Puis-je vous aider?"*

Lynne tried to decide what she'd said. Madame Zelb waited. Lynne handed her the rental information she'd been sent. *"Je voudrais…"*

The woman nodded. *"Vous êtes le danceur américain, oui?"*

"Yes, I mean *oui*. I'm Lynne Meadows."

Madame Zelb picked up a lit cigarette from inside her apartment, took down a key, and beckoned for her to follow. *"Viens avec moi."* She stopped and pointed to Lynne's bare feet. *"Tsk, tsk, Mademoiselle. Où sont vos chaussures? Vous devez porter des chaussures!"*

"Avec dans porch?" Lynne said, struggling to recall any remnant of vocabulary from her unsuccessful high school French class.

The concierge rolled her eyes and took a puff of her cigarette. *"Mais non."* She hurried to the elevator and inserted the key. Nothing happened. She tried again. The antiquated lift groaned to life. Madame opened the gate and stepped into the bird cage-like enclosure.

Lynne tried to follow, but she and her bags would not fit.

"Non, non." The woman shooed her out and waved toward the stairs. *"Vous devez porter voc sacs dans les escaliers."*

Lynne grabbed a few words: *vous* was you. 'Port-something' sounded like it might mean 'carry.' The elevator began to clunk its way upward.

The open stairway circled its shaft. She watched Madame; the woman ignored her.

Rattle. Crunch. Grinding gears sent shivers down Lynne's spine. The complaining car stopped two feet short of the second floor landing. She set down her suitcases and waited as Madame attempted to restart it. Nothing happened.

Madame opened the gate and reached her hand toward Lynne. *"Donnez-moi un coup de main. Vite! Vite!"*

Suddenly, the contraption shuddered and began to creep downward. Lynne yanked the woman's arm and fell backward. Madame landed on top of her with her lit cigarette pressed against Lynne's skirt. The smell of singed cotton rose in the air.

Madame rolled onto the floor, stood, and dusted herself off. Lynne sat on the cold marble floor, staring at the hole in her skirt.

"You burned my best shirtwaist dress!"

Madame shrugged and signaled for Lynne to follow her on up the stairs. Up, up, up the winding stairs they climbed. Floor three, floor four, and around the landing. Where was 4B, on the roof?

On the next landing Madame walked to a door marked "B," inserted a key into the lock, and turned the knob. *"Allo?"* she shouted. *"Allo?"*

Lynne heard scurrying. A door somewhere inside slammed. A muffled voice called out through the partially open apartment door, *"Madame, Oui? Tu as besoin de quelque chose?"*

"Oui, Mademoiselle," Madame said. *"Voici votre locataire."*

Lynne pieced together what few words she could. She guessed the conversation was about her arrival rather than the faulty elevator.

The tall, willowy, twenty-something woman who opened the door wore only a bath towel. "You are Lynne, yes? I'm Kitsy."

Lynne nodded as Madame handed her the room key and left. Kitsy stepped back to let her enter. She looked down at Lynne's bare feet and the hole in her skirt. *"Vous apprenez à regarder où vous marchez."*

"I think she said something about watching where I walk," Lynne thought as she gazed around the space. The narrow room had the tallest walls she'd ever seen in an apartment, at least fifteen feet high. Two mismatched chairs at a tiny dining table and a small sofa filled the sitting area. A rustling sound came from inside a partially open inner door. She waited and watched, but no one appeared.

On the other side of the apartment, she saw a corner with a half-size refrigerator and open shelves above a dish-filled sink. If she had a tape measure, she'd confirm her suspicion that this apartment would easily fit into her old garage apartment twice. She let out a slow breath. What had she gotten herself into?

A young man appeared from the partially open doorway. He buttoned his shirt, slid his feet into sandals, kissed Kitsy, and left.

From the kitchen side of the apartment, a young woman stepped through a curtain. She smiled. "I'm Arty. You must be Lynne."

Lynne nodded, feeling like she'd stepped into the hidden camera TV program where any minute someone would come forward and say, "Smile, you're on *Candid Camera*!" Everyone would laugh at the joke they'd played on you. But this was no joke.

"Glad to meet you," Arty said as she opened the curtain, revealing a daybed, a dresser, and one side table. "This used to be the living room, you know. Since I got here first, I claimed the daybed. That leaves the trundle for you, but we can trade off." She pointed to a narrow door. "We'll need to share the closet. Our hostess, Kitsy, has the only bedroom. The bathroom is down the hall."

Lynne's eyes widened as she set down her bags. "You're kidding, right? Down the hall?"

"I'm not kidding. We share it with three other tenants, you know. It's easier to go down to the third floor bathroom since there are only two renters living there right now. Oh, and be sure you lock the door and put the chair under the doorknob unless you want company while you're in there."

"Company? You mean the door doesn't lock?"

"Sometimes it does."

"Hm-m. O-kay, I guess. How long have you been here?"

"Two days. My parents and I came over the end of May and toured. They left for home early yesterday. I'll be glad to have someone who speaks English, you know. I only speak a little French, so conversations with Kitsy are difficult. I can rattle on, you know, but I'll let you unpack. We'll have plenty of time to talk after you get settled."

Getting settled took five minutes. Arty had saved half the closet and the two top drawers in the dresser for Lynne. The suitcases became a bedside table once she stacked them and covered them with one of her bath towels. She sat down on her open trundle bed and closed her eyes. Home sweet home was more like home crowded home. They'd be traveling much of the time, so maybe it wouldn't matter.

Lynne watched Arty curl up on the daybed. "So what's with this being on the fifth floor?"

"In Europe the ground floor is not called the first floor," Arty said. "They start numbering floors *above* the ground floor, you know. What we call the second floor is their first floor and so on."

Lynne shook her head. "I'll have to remember to always ask for ground or first floor rooms when we're touring and when I'm on the road with my uncle."

"You're staying after? Where do you plan to go?"

"We're driving around France, Spain, and Portugal, then back through Italy, the Alps, Germany, and Holland."

Arty opened a bottle of lemonade that sat on her bedside table and invited Lynne to share it. "Might as well sit up on the daybed, you know. It's more comfy, I'm guessing."

"Have you located our practice rooms?" Lynne asked.

"Yesterday. It's about a six-block walk. I met Cheryl. She's American and seems nice enough. She let me stay and do *barre* work while she finished paperwork. Everyone is due in tomorrow, you know."

Lynne sipped the lemonade and made a face. "Guess there's no ice?"

Arty shook her head. "There's barely a refrigerator, but it'll be fun shopping for fresh bread and cheese, you know."

She leaned toward Lynne and whispered, "If you want to keep your personal stuff safe, don't leave any of it out. Kitsy plucked my blouse off the clothes line and wore it without asking. She's frustrating, but at least our room is free, you know."

Lynne smiled but shuddered at the thought of listening to Arty say 'you know' every few seconds. Maybe this was a test of her patience.

Arty walked Lynne downstairs to the common areas. "The entry is a mess, so this will surprise you." She opened a pair of tall sliding doors to reveal a large dining area.

Unlike the entry area, the dining room was spotless. A half-dozen small, square, linen-covered tables were organized into a large rectangle. Two buffet tables stood empty except for vases of sunflowers and coffee carafes with mugs stacked nearby.

"The room is set for dinner. At breakfast all the tables are separated. The first and second floors are bed and breakfast rooms, you know. The third and fourth floors are long term tenants. We eat breakfast together. Dinner is only for tenants and is served family-style at eight."

"That's later than I'm used to back home."

"It's a European thing. You'll get used to it. I found a small shop where we can buy snacks and lunch food to take to class, you know. We can stop there later."

"Sounds good. I doubt I can make it until eight o'clock. I haven't eaten since I left the ship early this morning. But first, I need a shower. Oh, is there a laundry room?"

"Yes and no. It's reserved for the manager's use. Kitsy has one of those cable lines she reels out from her bedroom window. Using it is a problem. She's a Follies dancer, you know, so she works late and sleeps late. If I were you, I'd hang clothes out in the afternoon and bring them in before bedtime."

"What's a follies dancer?"

"The *Follies Bergeré* has a chorus line of sexy dancers with scanty costumes and big, feathered head pieces. She rehearses in the late afternoon, then works past midnight."

"How did you learn about everything so quickly?" Lynne asked.

"From Bert, a young Brit student who's lived here for two years, you know. He sat with me at breakfast this morning. He's offered to give us tours around Paris if we'll go out with him in the evenings. I hinted that we *might* be interested in day trips."

Lynne nodded. "Sounds like a good deal. So why is the entry such a mess while the dining area is spotless?"

"Bert says the owner tries to avoid extra government fees. Weekdays, the breakfast room is never cleaned up until after government office hours, in case an inspector stops in to check on things. He thinks she's decided to ignore the entry since so many people come and go all hours of the day and night.

"One tenant, Renny, works as a sous chef a couple blocks away. I hear the food there is inexpensive and tasty. Bert shared the area with me yesterday, so now I can show you. I think he has a crush on Kitsy and sees me, us now, as a way to get close to her since she's not here for meals, you know."

They headed outside. Lynne struggled to get oriented. One direction were food markets, cafes, and laundry; the other way she saw shops and touristy sites.

"We have one shelf in the fridge, so we'll need to shop every day like Parisians do," Arty said. "Kitsy must not like to shop or cook. She pilfered my groceries yesterday. You probably noticed she doesn't like to do dishes, so don't expect to find clean plates."

"What's she getting out of having us stay in her apartment?"

Bert told me she gets paid for the days we stay with her, you know. Bert thinks once we start to travel, she'll probably take another roommate to save money."

They stopped in a *backeri* to buy two buns. Across the street they entered a small park, a *jardin*, where they sat in the shade to eat and people-watch.

"How did you get the name Arty?"

"My given name is Artemesia, you know. I was named for the sixteenth century artist who painted with Michelangelo. My mom fell in love with her paintings as well as her name. If I ever become a famous ballerina, I'll use my full name. Until then, I'll stay Arty."

The girls watched people scurry along the park paths. Lynne yawned, moved to the coolness of the lawn, and dozed until Arty nudged her. "Dinner is served in fifteen minutes. I'll be curious to hear what you think after you meet the tenants."

15

Lynne sat at dinner with Arty. She hoped her sweat and grime wasn't obvious to others and no one detected any disgusting smell arising from her.

"*Allo,* Bert," Arty said as a short, young man with black-rimmed glasses joined their table. "May I introduce Lynne? She's in my troupe."

He bowed. "My pleasure, I'm sure."

When Lynne extended her hand, he held it long enough to kiss it. She smiled but wished she could wipe the slobbery residue on her skirt. Hopefully, the kissing business ended after their introductions.

"I'm so glad you've arrived. I'll enjoy the pleasure of escorting two lovely women."

Just then, two young girls pushed through a swinging door, carrying platters and bowls of food, which they placed down the middle of the long, rectangular table arrangement. Slices of roast beef surrounded by small potatoes covered a huge platter, accompanied by a bowl of green beans and one of glazed carrots.

Lynne reached for the closest platter to take a small portion. Arty placed her hand on Lynne's and shook her head. Lynne looked around. Every diner sat waiting for something. She didn't understand, but she joined them in waiting.

Madame Zelb entered the dining area, wearing a lavish fringed shawl over a black dress. Her hair was swept up into a meticulous chignon. She smiled toward everyone as she took her place at the head of the table. When she nodded, everyone began passing the food, eating, talking, and ignoring Arty, Bert, and Lynne.

Interesting, Lynne thought.

Bert began a long-winded discussion of Paris culture and history that didn't invite participation; so Lynne ate, nodded, and kept an eye on the rest of the people seated at the table. Madame carried on a discussion in rapid-fire French that contained few words she could understand.

"Isn't that correct, Lynne?"

Bert was speaking to her. Arty nodded. Lynne grimaced. "I guess."

"Don't you find it strange when many European museums own artifacts from other countries? Why, even in Britain we have statues from Italy and mummies from Egypt."

Lynne nodded and turned back to her primary interest, eating. She gave Madame credit for serving delicious food. As she took a final bite of beans, she noticed the servers returning with a large plate of cheeses. Shortly they brought in a tray of fresh fruit, followed by small cups of something with a burnt crust. Lynne shook her head; she guessed Madame couldn't get everything cooked perfectly.

Bert rubbed his hands together, "Ah, *crème brûlée*. My favorite dessert!" He picked up his spoon and dipped into the crusty, burnt topping, pulling up a spoonful of custard.

Lynne watched him, then tasted hers. The velvety, smooth custard in the ramekin tasted of rich vanilla. Her sigh matched Bert's. It tasted marvelous. If all their meals were this rich, she'd need to watch her portions or she'd return home half a dozen sizes larger.

After dinner, the roommates walked back to the park and sat under a large tree to cool down before heading upstairs to the humid apartment.

"What do you think of the Le Palais and Bert?"

"The place is more a collection of contradictions than a palace. The entry is messy, but the dining room is tidy. There's a questionable elevator and strange rooms, yet amazing food. All the tenants except Bert are... standoffish."

"They are. Bert said most French people collect a close group of friends and have no interest in including new people. We don't speak French or are only visiting for a short time, so we're on our own."

"Maybe that's why so many people think the French are rude."

"Could be," Arty said. "I know Bert's a pain in the *derrière*, and he's not even French. He means well, I think. If we work together, we can beg off going out nights, you know. Once we start dancing every day, the last thing on my list is roaming around bars and lounges until dawn. I don't know how he can be a night owl and attend day classes."

☙

Lynne assembled her clothing, towel, and shampoo, and accepted the two coins Arty offered for the shower's water heater.

"These looks like nickels," Arty said, "but they're not. They're half a *franc*. An American dollar buys five *francs*. Your shower will cost about ten cents if you use one coin. Not bad, huh?"

"Wait until I tell Marta! We could live here like royalty on a dancer's salary."

Arty frowned. "Only if you got paid your American salary."

☙

The shared bathroom was enormous with wide open space between the claw foot bathtub-shower and the two toilets, one without a seat. Why they needed two toilets confused her. Who'd share the bathroom when they were using the toilet or tub? And why would anybody use a toilet with no seat? She'd ask Arty about that.

The antique shower apparatus reminded her of Girl Scout camp. The massive porcelain bathtub-shower had tall pipes that climbed half way up the wall before they disappeared. Faucets and a shower-wand hung head high on the pipes. A shower curtain dangled from an oval metal bar suspended from four sturdy supports that reached into the ceiling. She shuddered as she moved the shower curtain aside; metal scraping against metal set her teeth on edge.

She inserted both coins into the coin slot, turned on the water, and set her shampoo on the tiny shelf next to the bathtub. She stopped. She'd forgotten her soap and toiletries bag, so she hurried back to get them.

When she returned, she put the chair under the doorknob and smiled to herself for remembering. Steam was spitting from the shower wand. Ah, just what she needed. A long, hot, shower like those on the ship.

The wand proved a bit unwieldy, twisting around itself like an unruly Slinky. But once she stepped into the tub and felt the hot water soothe her tired muscles, that didn't matter. Had it only been a few hours since she'd struggled up and down the Métro stairs with her luggage? It felt more like a week had passed.

As she lathered her shampoo, she yelped. The water turned cold. She twisted the faucet handles right then left, but the water remained cold. "Great," she muttered to herself, "the water heater's broken. I can't leave this shampoo in my hair!"

Lynne turned off the water, hung up the shower wand, and squeezed shampoo out of her hair, planning to finish washing it in the apartment kitchen sink. But as she was about to step from the tub, the bathroom lights went out.

The tub was in total darkness, and she was dripping wet. She waved her arms around and screamed. Grabbing the shower curtain as she slipped, she landed in the tub with a thud. The curtain cascaded around her, rings and all.

"Think, Lynne, think," she said aloud. "How can you get help? You're naked!" A strangling feeling began in her stomach and threatened to leave her body in another scream. She bit her lip and shivered.

She stood and felt around. When her hands touched the faucets, she got her bearings. Edging to the long side of the tub, she dragged the shower curtain with her. After easing herself out of the tub, she got down on all fours and crawled through the blackness.

She batted the air with her outstretched arm. Where was her towel?

Her hand touched a wall, then the toilet without the seat. She pulled her hand back and crawled on.

Crash!

She dislodged the chair from under the doorknob, but now she knew her location in the room. As she reached up the wall for the light switch someone pushed the door open. The light came on.

Lynne screamed. The sudden brightness blinded her. She covered her body with her hands and the rumpled shower curtain.

Someone muttered in French as *he* let the door close behind him.

A guy! How mortifying!

With the overhead light now on, she grabbed her towel from the hook on the wall and jammed the chair back under the door knob. As she dried herself, she scanned the room. It looked like a battle had taken place: puddles on the floor, the shower curtain in a heap nearby. Her tidy pile of clothes now soaking wet in one of the puddles. Tears filled her eyes, but laughter erupted. Or was it hysteria? She wished a hole would open so she could crawl inside.

A commotion filled the hallway. Someone banged on the door, yelling in French.

She recognized Madame Zelb's voice. "It's Lynne. Give me a minute." She wound her towel around herself and pulled the chair from under the doorknob. "I'm fine, I'm—."

Madame rushed in, saw the mess, and waved her arms toward the shower. *"Mon Dieu! Qu'avez-vous fait? Pourquoi avez-vous détruit ma salle de bain? Vous aurez à payer pour cela!"*

Lynne had no clue what she said, but her loud rantings delivered a clear message.

Arty appeared, followed by a young man wearing a food-spattered chef's jacket. The man said something that calmed Madame down. She left, waving her arms and shaking her head.

Arty sized up the young man and smiled with one raised eyebrow. Then she turned toward the mess in the bathroom. "You've been busy in here." She touched Lynne's foamy hair. "E-e-ew!"

Lynne grabbed up her lotions and toiletries, handing them to Arty. "Take these. Bring me two towels and then guard the door while I clean up this mess."

Arty returned with towels, which the young man took and then squatted down. *"Parlez-vous français?"* He smiled at Lynne as he began to mop up the water.

She secured her towel more tightly. "No Frawn-say. Sorry." Arty shook her head and walked away.

When the young man finished wiping the floor, he smiled, bowed slightly, handed her the soaking towels, and left.

Once she heard an apartment door close, she scurried to Kitsy's apartment and knocked. "Arty. Let me in. Hurry!"

Arty opened the door. By the time Lynne finished her shower story, Arty doubled over with laughter. "Oh, my gosh. That's the worst possible shower you'll ever take. I should have warned you, or maybe you need a training session, you know. We'll call it European Bathrooms 101."

Arty explained that both the light switch and the hot water tank were on timers. "It's best to reset the light as you step into the shower. As for the hot water, you need to either put in more money or start washing before the water heats up so you have enough at the end to rinse before your time runs out."

"I thought I had a kind roommate, not a prankster!"

Arty started to reply but stopped. "You're teasing me, right?"

"Partially. But in the future I want you to promise you'll clue me in." She swiped one of Arty's towels as she walked to the kitchen area. "Now I'm off to rinse the shampoo out my hair in the kitchen sink, just like back home in Jersey."

Lynne rubbed her hair dry and watched Arty flipping pages of a magazine. "Who was the guy who came to my rescue?"

"Renny, the sous chef. He's the only guy on this floor. Kinda cute, huh? Bert says the other two apartments are occupied by a bank teller and a hermit. Few people see either of them."

Arty turned back to her magazine, so Lynne decided to write to Marta and clear up things Marta didn't realize needed clearing up.

> *June 22, 1959*
>
> Dear Marta,
>
> Time to confess. Since you'll have time to get angry before I hear from you, maybe you'll also have time to forgive me.
>
> No, I didn't do anything illegal or tell off Madame Cosper. I had a bad car accident last January. (I'm fine now!) It was an icy night; totaled my lovely hunk of junk. Got a worse car as a replacement.
>
> I injured my leg and my arm enough that I missed weeks of classes and performances and I

> needed therapy. I had too much time to think about myself while I was healing, but I still made it to France.
>
> I understand how you felt when you broke your ankle. I hope I was sympathetic enough back then that you'll forgive me for not telling you about my accident earlier. You were all messed up about Steve and your life, so we weren't really talking much. I felt alone and know I should have shared that with you, my best friend.
>
> I miss you and I miss Noel. He's my version of your Steve! I hope he's there when I return from my adventure.
>
> Love,
> Lynne

When Arty's alarm sounded at 6:30 the next morning, Lynne struggled to wake up. The trundle bed was surprisingly comfortable, low to the ground, and, except for needing to rollout onto the floor before she could stand, she felt rested.

They'd need half an hour to get ready, twenty minutes for breakfast, ten minutes to buy lunch foods, and thirty minutes to reach the ballet practice rooms. They dressed quietly, picked up their dance totes, and exited the apartment, hoping their movements didn't disturb Kitsy.

As Lynne left the bathroom, she passed the man from last night.

"Bonjour, mademoiselle. Se vais?" he said.

"Yes?" Lynne hoped she'd said the right thing. She definitely needed a phrase book.

He followed her down the stairs as he buttoned his chef's jacket. *"Est-ce un meilleur matin pour vous, mademoiselle?"*

She pretended he wasn't there.

He hurried passed her and called back over his shoulder. *"J'ai aimé votre costume de bain la nuit dernière."*

Arty chuckled as she passed Lynne on the stairs. "From that luscious smile on his face, I'm thinking you made a favorable impression with our sous chef last night. You may want to learn French so you'll know what he says to you."

Lynne caught up with Arty. "Why? What did he say?"

Bert joined them on the next landing. "What happened last night?"

"Nothing you need to know," Lynne said, then grabbed Bert's arm. "Wait. Do you know what that guy said?"

Bert smiled and pursed his lips. "Something about your birthday costume in the bathroom last night. You simply *must* tell me the whole story, or I'll be forced to create my own version. I have a vivid imagination!"

16

Arty checked her watch. "We need to hurry if we're going to get to the studio on time."

The early June morning shimmered with the promise of a hot day. Long shafts of light peeked around the tall buildings, warming the sidewalks. Their walk to the dance studio carried them along a quiet street where many Parisians sat at sidewalk cafes, drinking their coffee. Others walked briskly along as if an important destination awaited their arrival.

Within five minutes the quiet gave way to the hustle, bustle, and noise of a large city: trucks idling in traffic lanes, drivers unloading their crates and boxes, taxi and car horns honking, and hands gesturing at the snarls. Paris was awake.

～

The beige stone building in the middle of the crowded block wore a coat of soot. Depressions in the four stone steps to the entry showed decades of wear deep enough to hold water if it ever rained in Paris in June.

A paper sign attached to the entry plaque read: Americans Dance in Paris. The sign, plus the cacophony of music flowing from four floors of open windows, welcomed Lynne like a friendly hug.

Outside 401, dancers in leotards sat against the wall or stood stretching. Lynne felt a wave of relief when hearing their chatter in English. After her first day of unsuccessful attempts to string together semi-intelligent French phrases, she could relax.

Just then, arms surrounded her from behind. Lucia held her in a tight hug. "You're here! Thank heavens."

Lynne laughed. "It's been a long day since I left you." She reached out to pull Arty into the tangle of arms. "This is Arty, my roommate. Arty, this is Lucia, my shipboard dance partner. You two and I are my new three musketeer dancers. How's your apartment, Lucia? Is it nearby?"

"It's three Métro stops away. I'm staying with a retired dancer. She has three noisy grandkids, two dogs, and a chatty husband. I hardly need to say a word. How about you?"

Arty tapped Lynne's arm and pointed toward a practice room door. "Look."

The girls stopped talking and stared as a tall, thirty-something woman stepped into the hall. She smiled. "Welcome, everyone. Come in."

Cheryl Menkins was taller than any dancer in the room, including the guys. Her long, brown hair was drawn back in a high ponytail and held in place with a rubber band. She wore black leotards, a black knee-length wrap skirt, and ballet slippers. Her dark brown eyes skimmed the assembled dancers she invited to sit on the polished wooden floor.

Lynne thought she saw a gentleness as Cheryl met each dancer eye-to-eye when she checked off their names and local contact information. When she finished, she gracefully sank to the floor to join them. So *not* like Madame Cosper.

"Again, welcome, everyone. At my studio back home in New York, I'm called Madame Menkins. Here, I hope you'll call me Cheryl. I trust you've had a pleasant journey so far. I've directed these European summer troupes for the past two years. I speak French, so I can interpret for you if needed. My French assistant, Jean Paul, will join us later. He's in charge of our practice and travel schedules, as well as our finances, so please hold any questions related to those topics for him.

"As dancers ending your first or second year in your local *corps de ballet*, you are about to experience a hectic yet enthralling summer. Let's start by introducing yourselves and where you dance in the U.S."

The dancers ranged from California to Maine and Oregon to Florida with no two from the same dance company. Of the twenty-four present, eight were guys. That meant limited performances of *pas de deux,* partner dances.

"As you can see, we've scored a great practice room. The dance studio that rents this space is on holiday, so it's ours for the length of our stay. The only requests they made are that we sweep, close the windows, and lock the doors each evening. We're allowed to stay until nine, but we'll only stay that late if we have kinks in our program. If you arrive on time, nine each morning, we'll finish by five. While the French take a two-hour lunch, we'll take a one-hour American lunch break around one o'clock."

"May we eat in here?" a guy asked.

"I'd rather you didn't. There's a lovely garden down the street. Since it's summer and bound to get super hot in here, I suggest you get out and enjoy fresh air during our lunch break. There are small cafes nearby, but eat light because our rehearsals will be intense. Also, no alcohol unless you are legal at home."

"Is the drinking fountain water safe?"

"Of course it is. We're not in the backwoods, kids; we're in Paris. The taste of the water might not be to your liking. You could buy *eau mineral,* which is mineral water, or *eau gazeuse,* carbonated water. I suggest *l'eau du robinet* which is tap water. Paris gets hot in the summer, so you'll need to stay hydrated.

"On tour we'll provide your morning and evening meals, but you may need to use part of your weekly stipend for lunches. Any housing concerns?"

"The apartment where I'm staying is the size of my bedroom back home," one dancer said. "Three people are sharing it. Is there any way I can move?"

Cheryl smiled. "I'm afraid not. You'll need to make do or pay for a place on your own. We'll be traveling much of the summer, so think of your apartment or boarding house assignment as a place to sleep and stow your two suitcases. If you encounter serious problems, however, let me know; we'll locate a safe place for you. Any other housing questions?"

"My apartment is fine," another dancer said, "but the bathroom and toilet are down the hall."

Cheryl nodded. "Raise you hand if your bathroom is shared and down the hall or down or up a floor."

All hands went up. The complaining dancer looked around and grimaced but said nothing more.

"It's common in older buildings to share bath and toilet facilities. Many of them date back to the last century. When you return home, I imagine you'll appreciate your living accommodations more than when you left."

Cheryl stood and handed out a paper. "I've compiled a list of important phone numbers and addresses: the post where you can call home and mail cards or letters, the American Embassy office where your general delivery mail is held, bank and money exchange information, and Métro details.

"Each day we'll start with a brief meeting. We have lots to rehearse, plus new choreography to learn, so we'll squeeze as much dancing as possible out of every minute we're together. That said, let's get started."

Every dancer moved to place their left hand on the *barre* in first position with their back muscles pulled taut. The warm-up proceeded as it would back home: *pliés, battements,* and *rond de jambs,* actions to warm every muscle group from the toes up. The universality of the movements comforted Lynne. So far, so good, she thought.

During the morning, she eyed her competition. Since each dancer had completed at least one year as a *corps* dancer, they possessed similar background knowledge, which should even out everyone's skill level.

The troupe reviewed and refined the choreography from *The Nutcracker* waltzes and character dances, followed by the "Sleeping Beauty Waltz" and *pas de deux.* True, each dancer knew the selections, but each ballet company used adaptations, requiring adjustments in steps, arms, and body positions. Luckily, the choreography Lynne had danced in Billings followed the original and Cheryl's notations closely.

Any changes Cheryl requested were minor. The fact that she called them "requests" impressed Lynne. Bartley's similar experience in San Francisco explained why she proclaimed her happiness in California. Too bad she didn't live long enough to enjoy her good fortune.

Lynne perked up her energy by walking in small circles between sections of choreography. The coolness of nine in the morning disappeared by early afternoon when sunshine blasted through the open windows. The clock read twelve-fifteen. Only forty-five minutes until break. Lynne daydreamed about her favorite lunch: a chicken sandwich, crunchy dill pickles, a crisp apple, and a chocolate chip cookie. She'd even settle for a cupboard-is-bare peanut butter and jelly sandwich if she could find one.

The afternoon session began with Cheryl discussing the sharing of partners. "We need to stay totally flexible since I anticipate we'll have injuries. Work together. Be patient. Get comfortable with as many partners as time allows."

Lynne's favorite partner so far was Wallace, a tall red-head from Nebraska. His strong hands reassured her as she completed turns. Unfortunately, he squeezed her midriff like a tube of toothpaste when he lifted her to his shoulder.

During a break, she took him aside. "I appreciate your strength, but you're squeezing me in half. Let's practice a lift or two right now."

Wallace looked horrified. "Did I hurt you? I didn't mean to. I got lost in the music and didn't want to drop you."

"Relax. You won't drop me, but I can't dance if I have bruised ribs."

They practiced several lifts. He relaxed his hands while still supporting her and eased her to standing.

"Nice work, everyone!" Cheryl clapped her hands. "Thank you for staying focused amid the heat. Women, please remain for *Serenade* rehearsal. Guys, you're excused until tomorrow at nine o'clock. We'll provide lunch tomorrow."

The women completed several *Serenade* run-throughs. By the time they ended, they were soaking wet, and their feet felt as if they were on fire. On the way home, Lynne and Arty stopped at the *pharmacie* down the block to buy a wash basin and Epsom salts.

Neither girl spoke until they reached Le Palais. With the elevator a non-option, they made their way up the marble stairs and collapsed on the daybed in their corner of the apartment.

"Cheryl has so much energy," Lynne said.

"Yes," Arty said, "and I'm learning so much already. I'm thinking about working on my French. I love being in Europe, you know. I'd like to become Cheryl's assistant."

"Right now, all I want is a shower, clean clothes, and a snack."

Arty rummaged through her stash of food. "Dang! All that's left are empty food wrappers and butter. I think Kitsy ate our snacks. Want to go out and find something?"

Lynne moaned. "Are you sure there's nothing to eat?"

Arty opened the refrigerator. "Just a half-eaten plate of pasta."

Lynne sat up. "I'll take it! Dinner is two hours away. Eight o'clock is a long wait after a day of tough rehearsals. Tomorrow, we need to buy snacks on the way home."

The girls shared the pasta, then dozed until time to clean up for dinner. Afterward, they looked over the information and schedule Cheryl handed out.

"The post office is near the dance studio," Arty said. "We can use our lunch breaks to make calls and mail letters. The American Embassy office is across town. We'll need to grab mail on our days off or after class."

"Did you locate a money exchange?"

"Not yet." Arty yawned. "Might be a good thing we didn't go shopping beyond the *pharmacie*. All I have left are traveler's checks. Small shops won't even look at them."

17

Day two with the dance troupe began like day one, with brief questions and answers followed by warm-ups and work on the *pas de deux* performance pieces.

Lunch was a shared meal in a small room next to the main practice room. Cheryl's assistant, Jean Paul, brought in salads and moderately cold drinks, then fielded finance and travel questions.

He also shared their schedule. "Mondays are usually your day off. Keep your schedules with you; there'll be updates. We'll travel by train and local-area private buses. Props and audio equipment are limited to what fits into a small truck that will meet us in each town. You'll need to pack and tote your own bags. That way, if we run into truck problems, you'll be able to perform with the clothing you're carrying."

Cheryl nodded. "Since you brought ample clothing and footwear, I doubt you'll need the amazing dance shop across town. But..." Cheryl made a slow turn. "I bought this strappy-topped leotard there. It's a style I've not seen before. Feels good on hot days."

The young women chuckled. Lynne knew she and Arty would make the trek. What dancer could resist an entire shop dedicated to dancing and dancers?

"How long are our performances?" one dancer asked.

"In past years our share of programs ran to forty minutes. We'll be joined by local dancers and musicians, making each program about ninety minutes. Performance stages vary in size and location; most are indoors. Small villages are a challenge, so be prepared to dance on pavement once or twice."

"What about the solos?"

"We'll hold auditions like you do back home and create groups A & B to showcase a variety of dances. You'll dance more solos over the next three months than you ever dreamed possible. That should increase your skills and value to your dance companies when you return to the states."

Lynne and Arty had already discussed the strain of their performance schedule and how they'd stay healthy. Lynne wondered whether Madame Cosper approved her joining the troupe to challenge her patience and skill or maybe to show her what continuous, hard work meant. She vowed to handle whatever danced into view.

୨

"Nice, everyone," Cheryl said. "Since we have *The Nutcracker* and *Sleeping Beauty* choreography handled, we'll move on the 'Garland waltz.' Guys can stand aside since you don't enter until the fifth minute. Girls, organize yourselves, eight per side. Enter on diagonals with eight counts of *balancés* before the *arabesque*. Sway to create flowing arms as your lines cross and as you circle. Finish with *bourrés, jetés,* and *arabesques*. Ready? Begin."

After half a dozen run-throughs, the ladies rested while the men worked on their leaps and final movements. Next, they combined the sections. Practice on their ten-minute waltz, with solos added, lasted all afternoon.

Cheryl applauded as she lifted the needle from the record. "You've all worked hard today. We'll create performance groups, but those groups will change as people have emergencies. *Please*, stay healthy. Wear sensible shoes to avoid ankle injuries when you're walking along the cobblestone streets in many areas of Paris."

"Don't you mean *arrondissements* instead of areas?" one dancer said with a sly smile.

Cheryl laughed. "Exactly." She checked the clock, opened a calendar, and tsked. "Today's Wednesday, June twenty-fourth. That gives us less than eight days to work our magic. Dress rehearsals begin on the third of July, and I want us to wow our guests. They're regional and local arts reporters as well as directors of dance academies. We want to spread the word about our project. For now, go home, get some rest, visit the dance shop, or whatever. See you back here tomorrow at nine."

Lynne and Arty headed for Printemps, a large department store in Paris. They wandered from floor to floor, checking out merchandise as they looked for thermoses.

"I give up. Where should we look?" Arty said as they stepped into the elevator.

The elevator operator snickered. Lynne jabbed Arty in the ribs and whispered, "This guy understands English. Ask him for help."

Arty moved next to him and smiled. "Excuse me, sir. Where can we buy a thermos?"

The operator stared at her, then laughed. "You know I zsepeak Anglish, yes?"

"Yes. Help us, *sil vous plais*."

"Of course," he said. "Go to the *pharmicae*, and you will find."

"Merci. And buying Métro tokens?"

"Stop at a *tabac* shop."

Arty surprised the man by kissing his cheek as she thanked him. His face registered a warm smile when he opened the elevator door.

Lynne chuckled. "I can't believe you kissed him. What if he got angry?"

Arty stopped took her arm. "How many guys get angry when you give them a kiss? Besides, I wanted to thank him for speaking English, you know."

"Well, I have a plan to avoid kissing scenes," Lynne said. "Next time I'm going to ask Cheryl or Jean Paul or Bert to write out what we need and where we need to get it. That seems like an easier—and safer—way to handle things."

Arty didn't respond, so Lynne changed the subject. "What do you think of our troupe?"

"Besides us, of course, I like Tu and Lucia," Arty said. "They're easy to talk with. Their solos look amazing. My favorite dancer is Vera Dei. She has fire in her movements. She's part Romany, you know. When we go to Versailles, she says she'll take us to visit the caravans."

"Rom what? Caravans? What are you talking about?"

"You'll see. Now, stop talking about the girls and move on to the guys. I like Karl, Jando, and Wallace They are amazing to watch, especially Wallace, you know. He leaps so high and is a great partner. I'd like to get to know him personally."

Lynne laughed. "You'll have more than two months to do that. He acts shy, so you may need to thank him with kisses like you did the elevator operator."

They entered the apartment laughing, stopped, then gasped. A hurricane of clothing covered the living area. "Have we been robbed?" Arty asked as she stepped inside.

"I can't tell," Lynne said.

Just then Kitsy stepped into the room from her bedroom. Both Arty's and Lynne's eyes widened; their mouths dropped open.

"You're wearing my skirt!" Arty shouted.

"And that's my best blouse," Lynne said. "Did you make this mess?"

Kitsy shrugged, began chattering in French, then changed to English. "I needed zumzing to wear. I share *my* apart-mont with you. I not think you mind."

Lynne stood with her hands on her hips, glaring at Kitsy. "I mind. Besides, you're getting paid to let us stay here. Now, take off my blouse and give Arty back her skirt."

Kitsy started removing the borrowed clothes until Lynne gasped. "Wait! Stop! You're not wearing underwear."

"I never wear the underwear," Kitsy said. "You want back, *oui*?"

Both Arty and Lynne nodded. Kitsy resumed disrobing. She kicked at the clothes as she'd dropped them to the floor, then sauntered into her bedroom and slammed her door.

Lynne collected her clothes and tossed unfamiliar items to Arty. By the time they'd finished sorting, Kitsy left the apartment, saying nothing as she walked out wearing a wrinkled skirt and a stained blouse.

Lynne shook her head. "Can you believe she wore our things without underwear? I'm washing all my clothes, in case she tried on everything."

The girls looked at each other and began laughing. "Good idea," Arty said. "I guess we need to lock our clothes in our suitcases. I wonder how long she planned to pretend she didn't speak English."

It was dark by the time they'd hung everything to dry on makeshift lines strung across their sleeping area. Lynne flounced down on her trundle bed. "At least it's summer, so they'll dry quickly if we squeezed enough water out of them. I don't want drips in my face all night."

∽

The next two days of practices progressed smoothly. By Saturday noon, every dancer showed signs of exhaustion. Cheryl used the afternoon to share their solos and group them to create the best variety of dances for their performances. If all went well, Group A women would dance their solos one day and Group B the next. The male dancers would be exhausted since they were expected to dance their solos and all partner dances every day. Sometimes being a girl was a better deal, Lynne thought.

Cheryl critiqued each solo, made suggestions, and assigned groups. The friends Arty, Lucia, Tu, Vera Dei, and Lynne belonged to Group A, along with three other girls they'd yet to befriend. The remaining dancers formed Group B. Lynne silently toasted Group A, hoping everyone stayed healthy. Dancing with friends was always a plus.

൙

The apartment was messy but quiet when Arty and Lynne returned. The kitchen sink was invisible under the pile of dirty dishes.

Lynne took their dance clothes to the bathroom sink to wash them while Arty cleared a corner of the counter to whip up a quick salad for their weekend dinner.

When Lynne returned, Arty asked, "Did you eat the food we bought yesterday?"

"No. Why?" Lynne said.

"It's all gone. Kitsy is a menace!" She checked her watch, "It's too late to shop. Everything's closed, you know. Do you have any leftover lunch?"

"No, I ate everything." Lynne flopped down on Arty's bed. "Guess we'll need to lock up our food as well as our clothes." Lynne reached for her purse, pulled out a handful of French coins, and counted them. "I've got enough for a bowl of soup. How about you?"

"About the same. Let's go find something cheap. I'm starving."

The dancers walked to the corner cafe and sat people-watching while they ate chilled tomato soup and French bread. As they finished, the young sous chef who lived on their floor walked past, backtracked, and stopped at their table.

"Bonsoir," he said. "*Vous êtes la jeune dame de la salle de bains, oui? Ce soir, vous mangez au restaurant, oui?*" They didn't respond so he began again. "You are the young lady from bathroom, yes? Tonight you eat out, yes?" He lowered himself to his haunches beside their table and pointed to himself. "Chef Renny. I help you, yes?"

Arty nodded and explained their dilemma. Renny shook his head and tsk tsked every few seconds. He put a finger to his lips as he opened his fabric bag, and whispered, "Come to my apartment, *oui*? I share okay?"

Before he could change his mind, Lynne waved for the check and both dancers hurried after him, following the aroma wafting from his bag as if he were a pied piper. Once they reached his apartment, the girls sat scrunched together on his sofa. In less than five minutes, the three were seated at his small table, enjoying samples from the restaurant where he worked: Caesar salad, beef bourguignon, fresh beans in garlic sauce, and a *baguette* of bread.

"You're a great cook," Arty said as she finished off the last morsel of food. "*Très magnifique.*"

Renny smiled. "I cook for you on weekends, *nes pa?*"

"Oui," Arty said. Lynne watched her stare around the room. "How will we get the food if you are not here?"

Renny handed them a key on a long red cord and smiled. "*Vous pouvez manger ici, dans mon appartement.*"

Arty started to translate, but Lynne stopped her. "I got that. We can eat in his apartment."

Lynne nodded. "*Merci*, but, how can we compensate you?"

He frowned, "Com-sate?"

Lynne pulled out her last coins and offered them to him.

Shaking his head, he looked around his apartment and disappeared into the bedroom. He stuck his head back into the living area. "You come, *oui?*"

Lynne and Arty slowly entered the room.

He stood by his bed, smiled, and pointed.

The girls backed away until they saw him tug the sheets loose. "You wash? I cook? *Non?*"

"That's reasonable," Arty said.

Renny opened his closet and set out a laundry hamper. "*Oui?*"

Both girls nodded.

After a labored conversation, they understood Renny had difficulty getting to the laundry because of his hours at the restaurant. The girls also agreed to straighten his apartment once a week. Kitsy would be on her own if she wanted a clean plate or a meal.

Lynne dumped Renny's clothes in a pile on their apartment floor and sorted it by color in the two mesh bags he provided. "Thank heavens he doesn't expect us to wash and dry his clothes. Wish I could afford to take my clothes to the laundry. Sure would save time."

Arty lounged on her bed and watched. "Maybe we could hang our clothes in Renny's closet. He's got the space, you know."

"Good idea." Lynne laughed. "When he invited us into his bedroom, I didn't know what he expected."

"Me neither. I was ready to run out of there and drag you along behind me."

"Drag me? I'd have been wa-a-ay ahead of you."

18

Thursday's rehearsal was a planned late start. Lynne sat alone at a small, round table in front of the neighborhood café and inhaled the mingled aroma of coffee, summer flowers, and warm pavement while she waited for Arty. Unable to pick up a phone and chat with friends or Noel or go for a drive or lounge in her old apartment, she felt a wave of loneliness.

Sipping her doll-sized cup of *café avec du lait*, she waited. Fireworks exploded inside her. Did the caffeine mirror the energy shot Marta felt when she took diet pills? If so, how did Marta react so calmly? Here, the walk to practices smoothed away the jitters.

She watched Parisian shop girls stroll past. Smiling young men eyed the sway of their hips and the shape of their legs in their high heels as they passed. Noel would appreciate the way their skirts ended several inches above their knees, but they were a bit too short for downtown Billings if she valued her reputation.

Since it took so long for letters to swim across the Atlantic, she doubted she'd get many before they left on tour. At a cost of twelve cents for the paper-thin blue aerogram stationary, she didn't blame them. With her birthday just a day away, she'd hoped for a card from home. Maybe there'd be time later today to check for any last minute surprises.

As their day began, Cheryl clapped for everyone's attention. "Tomorrow will be a hectic day, but it is also Lynne's nineteenth birthday!"

Clapping and loud hoots filled the room.

Cheryl pulled Lynne forward and handed her a wrapped package. "You're our first tour birthday. This is for you."

A sudden flush of heat rose through Lynne. Dancers crowded around to watch her unwrap a small box. Her hands trembled as she opened the tissue paper and removed an envelope.

"Read the card out loud, unless it's a love note," Karl said.

Everyone laughed.

Lynne swallowed hard and read, "Dear Lynne, we're missing the chance to celebrate your birthday with you. I know you're enjoying your adventure."

Tears flooded her eyes.

"Who's it from, Lynne?"

She bit her lip to stop its trembling. "It's from my dance friend, Jer."

Cheryl stepped forward and put her arm around Lynne. "Happy Birthday. I notified all the companies of our summer birthday dancers. They've sent small surprises to me to pass out on or near your birthdays. Now, let's see the gift."

Lynne smiled, then laughed as she pulled out a well-used, wadded up ace bandage and a handful of wide Band-aids with red crosses drawn on them with crayon. "These will come in handy. I'll even share!"

Everyone laughed again.

Under the joke gift, Lynne found a second envelope. She opened it and sighed. Tears flooded her eyes. She wiped them away and swallowed hard. Inside were two traveler's checks, each for twenty dollars.

"Who's it from?" Karl asked. "Must be from a boyfriend."

"No, it's from my mentor at the dance company."

Cheryl added, "That's Damien Black. He created the *An American in Paris* choreography we'll explore very soon."

"Read it aloud," Karl said.

The rest chimed in, "Yeah, read it aloud."

Lynne nodded and cleared her throat. "Lynne, hope you are enjoying your adventure. Spend these on yourself. Damien"

A hush filled the room until Cheryl clapped her hands and directed them to return to the *barres*.

For the rest of the morning, Lynne enjoyed feeling a bit special. Funny, but having the surprises from Jer and Damien meant more to her than if her parents had remembered her birthday.

༒

After *barre* and center work, Cheryl called the dancers to join her on the floor. "Before we go any further, let's discuss Friday and Saturday, or what I privately call media madness. We'll divide into two groups; everyone will dance multiple selections. We'll end with Copland's *Rodeo* 'Hoedown' to leave our guests energized.

"Expect them to drop in every hour on the hour. Performing sixteen or more of our twenty dance selections over two days will test our resiliency. We'll need stamina for all of our performances. Should be fun!"

"And exhausting," Karl said.

Everyone clapped their agreement; the guys all patted his shoulders. Despite their laughter, the strain on their faces made it obvious that asking the guys to dance in every performance without relief concerned them.

"How many guests are we expecting?" Jando asked.

"I'm hoping we'll have small groups. Regardless, we'll end each hour with interviews, photos, and a short break before we start over. I'll post the schedule. Now, let's get dancing. Later, we'll look through your costume embellishments. I'd like to know what supplemental clothing we'll have for emergency situations."

"You mean I'm expected to *share* my clothing?" Ida said; her nose wrinkled up as though she smelled dirty socks.

"Yes, but only if we run into a problem." Cheryl gazed at her watch and jumped to her feet. "Time for 'Hoedown,' everyone!"

The western-themed music began with guys moving in gallops and saunters, followed by relaxed strolls. Girls entered, tossing the hems of their long skirts side-to-side and flirting with the assembled cowboys.

When the music sprang to life, the dancing changed to leaps, square dance swings, and exaggerated sashays followed by the guys doing *pirouettes*, cartwheels, and flips. The dancers held their energy to a high level as the melody reached its crescendo. Two guys performed *grand jetés*, traveling leaps across the front of the stage. Two more performed *cabrioles*, scissoring their legs together while in the air, before they settled in next to the girls.

More solos followed with exaggerated turns, high kicks, dos-a-dos, *fouettés*, and *glissades*. After the music appeared to wind down, the dancers formed squares, and the stage once again ignited with energy. Partners competed for attention by circling, leaping, and cheering; guys lifted and spun their partners. They returned to small groups and posed in a tableau before the kettle drums boomed three loud beats at the end.

"Nice group dancing." Cheryl nodded and smiled. "Now, let's take it from the top again. We'll address the solos following our mid-afternoon break."

Lynne wiped off on her towel and looked around. In twenty minutes they'd danced "Hoedown" half a dozen times. No wonder everyone looked exhausted.

Cheryl stepped forward. "Let's go back. Guys, ramp up your actions with more spectacular kicks, leaps, and turns. Girls, use your elbows to accentuate the western dance moves. Watch Arty and Wallace."

As they danced, Cheryl commented over the music. "Notice how they lift their rib cages and upper bodies and use crisp hand movements. It creates excitement. Now, let's do it again. I know this performance will test your endurance, but I want 'Hoedown' to be our 'wow' number until we refine the *An American in Paris,* our finale choreography."

All the dancers wiped sweat from their faces onto their sleeves and prepared to dance "from the top."

∽

The girls took the Métro home and showered before heading out to relax in the neighborhood *jardin*. People of all ages spread out around the garden, resting in the shade, sitting with their feet in the ponds, or dozing on benches. Billings could use more places like this, Lynne thought. Lake Josephine was a great getaway, but here the garden parks allowed hundreds of people to find cozy pockets of space to enjoy the early evening among the trees, flowers, and ponds.

∽

Jean Paul entered their afternoon rehearsal the next day, carrying the decorated garlands. Artificial flowers and short ribbons along the half hoops made them look festive, but Lynne grimaced. If a dancer leaned the wrong direction or dipped too deeply as the lines of dancers crossed, the garlands could bump together.

Cheryl smiled. "Let's work on our crossing patterns, ladies. For now, hold them upright; no swaying side-to-side. Stay focused."

Lynne's arms began aching within the first minute. When she and Lucia danced the choreography on the ship, they'd had lots of space. Here, dancers who had not fully committed the waltz to memory struggled. Their garlands dipped, they used stutter steps to slide back into place, and some banged their garlands into others.

Cheryl stopped and restarted the rehearsal again and again. "Watch your garland hand-off to the guys. Keep your arms extended but relaxed. Watch your diagonal lines."

When the waltz rehearsal ended, the dancers set their garland aside and leaned over to catch a breath.

Cheryl waited while the dancers rested before she spoke again. "If everyone stays focused, the waltz looks graceful, even effortless. If any one of you loses your place or misses a beat, we'll look like amateurs. Relax. Gauge your crossing. This is a waltz, so keep your facial expressions soft." She checked the clock. "That's enough for now. Go home, pack your touring bag, eat a substantial dinner, and get a good night's sleep. I'll see you tomorrow at *eight-thirty* sharp."

The dancers straightened, clapped, and performed a *grande reverence* toward Cheryl, who returned their gesture with a curtsy. She smiled and waved her hands to shoo them out the door.

Lynne packed her dance tote and waited for Arty, listening to the dancers talk about the garlands. "Those hoops are a major problem. I hate them," Ida said.

Nods of agreement filled the hallway.

Cheryl locked the practice room and turned toward Ida. "I know the garlands are a pain, but they add a gracefulness to the waltz. I also know you can make it look effortless if you pay attention to your location within the group."

Ida shook her head and walked away without comment.

Cheryl frowned. "Someone needs to talk with her. We need everyone focused if it's to work."

"She's my roommate," a tiny voice said. "I'll talk to her." The dancer scurried away.

Karl and Wallace stood on the sidewalk, waiting for Lynne and Arty. Karl asked, "What took you two so long?"

"Discussion about the blasted garlands," Lynne said. "You guys are lucky to avoid them for most of the waltz."

Wallace smiled and held up his arms as though he held a garland. "If you ladies don't pass them properly, we're the ones who'll look clumsy."

Arty stopped and put her hands on her hips. "Wait just a minute, Wallace. I always hand you the garland the right way, you know."

Wallace blushed as he held up his hands in his defense. "I'm just saying, *all* the ladies need to pass them properly."

Arty huffed off ahead of the group. Wallace hurried after her. The rest walked on in silence, Lynne favoring her throbbing leg. She'd need to take good care of herself if she expected the old injury not to threaten her performances on the tour.

※

The alarm clock jangled. Lynne covered her head with her pillow. Five minutes more, just five minutes, time enough to erase the fog in her mind before she crawled off her trundle bed.

She stretched, then walked to the kitchen window to check Friday's weather. Another hot, humid day with no breeze to relieve the stickiness. She drank a glass of tap water, straightened her bedcovers, and shoved her bed under Arty's with a loud thud.

"Hey, Arty! Wake up. We've only got an hour to dress, eat, and get to rehearsals."

Arty sighed. "Coming. I had the best dream, you know. Wallace walked me to the park...we kissed...he held my hand...it was...sweet."

Lynne shook her head. "If you get moving, we'll meet him out front. Come on!"

The girls dragged their suitcases downstairs and whirled through the breakfast room. Each gobbled down a croissant, fruit, and coffee as the clock chimed eight. They snatched up their bags and exited the apartment in time to meet Wallace and Karl.

The four sauntered along the warm pavement. Wallace carried Arty's bags and his own. The look on Arty's face told the story: she thought of him as her special friend, a position Lynne had filled before.

Lynne enjoyed watching the hustle and bustle of Parisians drinking their Friday morning coffee and smoking their brown-paper-wrapped Gitane cigarettes pulled from art deco packages.

Just ahead, Arty chattered ninety miles an hour with Wallace. He laughed at whatever she'd just said. They were becoming more than occasional dance partners.

They arrived at the practice rooms and joined the other dancers reading the order of their performances. Smiles, grimaces, grumbles, and shrugs indicated each one's view of their assignments. Lynne was pleased to see her name under *Serenade* today with "Clare de Lune" and her solos tomorrow.

She headed to the dressing areas to get ready for morning warm-ups. It felt strange to be dressed to perform while doing *pliés* and *rond de jambs*, but guest rehearsal began too soon after warm-ups to change.

Cheryl gathered the dancers around. "During today's dress rehearsal, we'll be using the longer *Serenade* choreography, allowing everyone to dance. Then we'll tackle the 'Garland Waltz' again."

The rehearsal went well. As they ended, a handful of unexpected guests who had confused the invitation information arrived. Dancers hurriedly assembled chairs. Cheryl offered the early arrivals an abbreviated performance, short interviews with the dancers, and an invitation to return at two o'clock for the full program and longer interviews. Several guests shook their heads and left. A few nodded and sat down to be entertained. When the dancing ended, the troupe assembled on the floor in front of the guests. Reporters whipped out their notebooks and pens. Two photographers took informal photos.

Serenade set a relaxed tone for the dozen guests watching at two o'clock. The dancers performed in exquisite unison, recreating exact lines and gestures. When they completed the first eleven minutes, Cheryl stopped the music and moved on to share male solos since the women had danced an extra session in the morning.

At the end of each hour, Cheryl thanked the guests, passed out the troupe itinerary for July through mid-September, and walked the guests to the exit in time to invite the next group inside. When daylight faded, Cheryl turned off some of the studio lights and joined the dancers seated on the floor.

"Did you get an idea of what they thought of our program selections?" Karl said.

"They enjoyed every dance. As I suspected, the favorites were *Serenade* and your solos. That tells me the local papers will probably place their articles about us above the fold."

"What does 'above the fold' mean?" Vera Dei asked.

"Our information will appear on the top half of the newspaper. It will be *seen* by people walking by the newsstand as well as those who buy and read the papers. You've done yourselves proud! Go get rested. Be back here tomorrow at eight-thirty, and we'll begin again."

When Arty and Lynne got home, they ate the food Renny left for them in his tiny refrigerator, then washed their dance clothing, soaked their battered feet, and fell into bed.

༄

Saturday was a repeat of Friday's hectic schedule, with guests dropping in from nine in the morning until eight that evening. Cheryl skipped the "Garland Waltz" in favor of the more polished ensemble choreography of "Clare de Lune."

The piano music of "Clare de Lune" began with the women seated before they bloomed as if awakening. They rose, circled with *bourres*, their arms lifting and dropping in waves that ended with perfect, unmoving *développés en arriére,* to the back, as they awaited their partners' arrival. The music invited the dancers to bend, lift, circle, and turn as if moonlight guided their footsteps before they ended and bowed.

The guests' soft applause exploded into enthusiastic clapping as they awoke from the enchantment of Cheryl's simple choreography to ask questions before leaving for the evening.

By eight-fifteen the dancers stood alone in the room. Street sounds filtered in through the open windows. Faint laughter, clanking dishware, and occasional horn honking reminded Lynne of the world outside.

If anyone were to imagine her visit to Paris, they'd probably think she'd be out 'on the town' with friends, seeing the sights, and sitting at cafes. They'd be so, so wrong. This was so much better!

Cheryl finished packing up materials and turned to them. "That's it for the world's longest dress rehearsals. Nice job of being flexible and gracious, everyone. Now, go home, sleep, and enjoy your days off. We'll meet here Tuesday morning at nine sharp. Our dance journey is about to begin."

༄

The girls sat in Renny's apartment, picking at their food and not talking. Lynne yawned and stretched. "Ready to head to bed?"

Arty nodded. "This is an amazing beef dish, but I'm not hungry. I'm so tired I could sleep standing up. Let's pack up the extra food and leave it for the lady in 4D."

Lynne sat on the trundle, soaking her feet, while Arty dozed on her bed. Her toes burned as she dipped them into the basin of Epsom salts and warm water. How could the women be expected to share performance-quality dancing *en pointe* once or twice a day for five or six days a week on stages of unknown smoothness and with little chance to properly warm up? We just do it, she decided, as she splashed water over the toes.

Suddenly, she sat straight up. "Today is the fourth of July! We missed the hot dogs, chips, watermelon, and ice cream, plus the fireworks."

Arty yawned. "We'll get fireworks in a couple of weeks. In France they celebrate Bastille Day. Now let me sleep."

Lynne changed into her nightclothes and mumbled something about chocolate and s'mores to her unresponsive roommate. She willed her toes to stop burning and her muscles to relax so she could drift off.

꙰

Bam! Bam! Bam!

Pounding on the apartment door startled Lynne. She rushed to the door and found a small, older woman in a bathrobe, staring at her with wide eyes. The trembling lady shook her head and mumbled in French.

"Arty! Wake up! Something's wrong!"

19

"*H*urry, Arty!"

Lynne waved her hand to indicate the woman should come inside. She shook her head and didn't move.

Arty rushed to the door. "*Comment puis-je vous aider? Êtes-vous blessé ou malade?*"

The woman shook her head, then looked up at Arty. "*Je crains.*"

"Is she sick or hurt?" Lynne asked. "What's going on?"

Arty took the woman's shaking hand and brought her slowly into the apartment. "She's frightened. I asked her how we could help."

Lynne looked around the apartment. Kitsy had every chair covered with her laundry and junk. "Take her into our sleeping area. I'll make her a cup of tea."

Arty shoved Lynne's bed away and seated the woman on her rumpled bedcovers.

Lynne heard a steady stream of conversation as she heated the tea water. By the time she carried the soothing drink to the bed area, the woman looked calmer. She nodded and smiled as Lynne handed her the cup.

Arty patted the woman's hand. "Her name is Jae. She said someone was standing on her fire escape, trying to open her window. She was afraid they'd break the glass and get in. Go down and wake the manager. She'll want to call the police."

Lynne raced down the stairs barefooted and in her robe to bang on Madame Zelb's door. Five minutes later, they entered the apartment. Madame Zelb carried a large flashlight while Lynne held a heavy candlestick. They cautiously looked around. When they opened the window, they saw pry marks along the lower edge. In the beam of the light, the fire escape ladder appeared to be fully extended.

Three policemen thundered up the stairway and into Jae's apartment. For the next two hours, the fourth floor bustled with activity. Lynne and Arty kept Jae in their room until everything settled down. Madame Zelb stopped to assure her frightened tenant that the police nailed the window closed and she would install bars on the windows *"tout de suite"*.

Jae smiled as the girls walked her back to her apartment. *"Merci, je vous remercie de votre gentillesse."*

"Pas de problème," Arty said.

"What did she say?" Lynne asked as they watched Jae close her door and heard a series of locks turn.

"She thanked us for our kindness."

They crashed into bed as Kitsy returned, talking and giggling, with a male friend in tow.

༄

Lynne woke at ten the next morning, Arty soon after when pounding and drilling noises began to bounce along the hallway. "Guess the bars are going up," Arty said. "Can you imagine how frightening it would be to hear someone trying to open your window?"

"Her terrified expression sent shivers down my spine," Lynne said. "Jae is so sweet and so timid. I'm glad we've left our extra food for her like Renny suggested. She has almost nothing in her apartment."

The dancers dressed in silence. Arty slipped on her sandals and picked up her purse. "Let's go to that cute café around the corner. I feel like sitting around and maybe coming back for a nap if it doesn't get too muggy."

After a casual stroll along the tree-lined streets, they returned to the park near Le Palais to sit in the shade. They watched tourists and locals stroll, sit on benches, and share the beauty of the gardens. Bert passed, then backed up.

"Enjoying a late start, I see."

"It's our day off," Lynne said.

"I hear you had a bit of excitement last night with Jae."

"We did," Arty said. "What's her story?"

Bert settled in between them and slid his arms along the back of the bench. "It's my understanding that she's a displaced person from World War II. The Nazis confiscated her home. She was forced to live on the streets and eat whatever scraps she found. After the war she had no family left, her damaged home had to be torn down, and she lived in a camp outside Paris for five years before getting this apartment. I'm surprised she came to your door. She doesn't trust strangers."

Jae's terror haunted Lynne for the rest of day. She wondered what it felt like to be totally alone with no support, no friends to talk with, and no chance of her life changing. Lynne never wanted to be in that situation.

❦

Performing in the various neighborhoods of Paris gave the dancers a chance to visit both famous and not-so-famous sights. Their July seventh performance took place on the plaza in front of Notre-Dame Cathedral. The full-size wooden stage allowed space for them to dance a full complement of selections intermixed with local musicians, dancers, and singers. The hosts also provided guest seating and curtained-off backstage areas for preparations.

Between the afternoon and early evening performances, their local contacts provided a light lunch and a guided walk through the neighborhood, pointing out places of interest: cafés, shops, cathedrals and churches, vista points, and celebrity residences.

Their brief tour of Notre Dame included entering the church to view the famous rose window and numerous church treasures. They ended their tour by climbing the three hundred eighty-seven stone steps to the tower to peer down on their dance venue, the crowds, and the small motorboats cruising the Seine.

"This plaza is called the center of France," their guide said when they returned to ground level. "All distances are measured from this spot, so you can honestly say you're dancing in the center of France, even though geographically you're in the northern portion of the country."

❦

Lynne, Arty, Lucia, Karl, and Wallace nodded to the local dancers at their table who spoke no English. As they cleaned up to leave, Lucia let out a sigh. "I hate to say this, but I'm getting tired of croissants."

"I'm just plain tired." Karl stretched his arms above his head. "If this is a glimpse into our touring, I'll need to save a little energy for days two, three, and thirty."

"At least we're getting personalized tours," Lynne said. "I loved yesterday when we were taken in the back way to the Louvre. I plan to spend a day off looking at the paintings and sculptures,"

"Not me," yawned Arty. "I plan to sleep unless it's another blistering day, you know, and I can't get comfortable. I thought Paris had a mild climate."

"It usually does," Karl said. "I read this was to be a hot, muggy summer. Just our luck, huh?"

After evening performances ended, the dancers helped pack props before heading home to wash their clothing and treat their feet to a tub of Epsom salts in hot water.

Lynne collected postcards to send back to the states, but each evening she opted for sleep over writing. Maybe, once they began their train travels, she'd get caught up. Then she could rightfully expect mail from Marta and Noel at least.

∽

The second week of Paris neighborhoods, most of the dancers were pacing themselves for their twice-a-day performance schedule. Many stayed at the performance sites, nursing their aching bodies instead of touring local can't-be-missed sights. Lynne lasted through Wednesday, vowing to rest on Thursday afternoon.

Early that morning, they received word that their open air performances were cancelled because of the overnight storm and the continuing downpour. Neither Lynne nor Arty complained; the extra day of rest was a welcome gift to their exhausted bodies.

Lynne stood at the open window in the kitchen area, breathing in the smell of the rain. Each deep intake of the moist air calmed her more and more. She turned to Arty, who lounged on her bed. "Grab your shoes. Let's go for a walk."

"It's pouring rain, or hadn't you noticed?"

"I know. I love to walk in the rain." She slipped her feet into her sandals. "Come on! We can do the tourist stroll."

They found colorful umbrellas in a stand by the front door. The overnight deluge and a brisk wind had washed the steps and sidewalk clear of debris and dog poop. The air felt refreshed.

"This is just what I needed," Lynne said as they crossed the street and entered the neighborhood garden. "It's calm, peaceful, quiet, and... perfect for how I feel."

"I hate to admit it, but you're right. I can feel my breathing slow. Let's sit at the café and pretend we're tourists with nothing better to do before we head back."

The café they found had a deep awning that protected them from the rain. They took a seat, ordered a soft drink, and watched the parade of passersby shielded from view by their umbrellas.

"Dancing with umbrellas would make interesting and colorful choreography," Lynne said. "I can see it now—girls twirling their umbrellas and guys ducking under and then reappearing."

"Do you want to be a choreographer or something?"

Lynne paused before she answered. "I don't know what I want to be. The umbrellas look so colorful in the rain, it inspired me to think of dancing with them. But it would be more difficult than dancing with those blasted garlands, so I guess it's a bad idea. Come on, let's head back."

As they returned to their apartment floor, they saw Jae's door open. She looked startled when she first saw them. A moment later, she smiled, then quietly closed her door and set her locks.

༒

The following Monday, their day off, Lynne explored while Arty slept in. Armed with a Métro map and a coin purse of centimes, she strolled the edges of the Ile de la Cité to peruse flea market stalls and finger handmade trinkets. She crossed Pont Neuf to investigate La Samaritaine, a department store near the Louvre.

Inside the first floor entrance, she found the perfume counters and indulged her whim: to buy Evening in Paris perfume in Paris. She rationalized that Noel would appreciate it.

Fragrances floated above the perfume counter as Lynne circled, exploring the wide variety of perfumes in a rainbow-colored assortment of bottles. She spotted her intended purchase: a display of the signature cobalt blue bottles with the silver finial-shaped caps. A stylishly dressed clerk approached her. "*Puis-je vous aider?*"

"*Oui. Je voudrais* Evening in Paris perfume, *s'il vous plait.*"

The clerk nodded and picked up an atomizer, offering to spray Lynne's neck with a quick puff of fragrance.

Lynne closed her eyes and inhaled the powdery floral scent. Yes, Noel would definitely like it.

"*Voudriez-vous un parfum, eau de parfum, eau de toilette, ou eau de cologne?*"

Lynne stared at her, following her outstretched hand as she pointed to a variety of containers with a vast difference in prices; everything from a thousand francs for a tiny bottle to five francs, one dollar, for the size she'd seen in Trenton in the department store for twelve dollars.

She pointed to the least expensive bottle, the *eau de cologne*, and raised two fingers.

The clerk plucked three bottles of cologne from the shelf and wrapped each in tissue. Lynne thought she was getting a deal until the clerk asked for fifteen francs. She realized her mistake; she'd signaled incorrectly. She paid for all three, took the package, and walked toward the exit.

Back on the street, she perused scarves, ties, books, bouquets, and flea market treasures. Before she left Paris, she'd return to buy gifts, especially something for Damien. He'd given her the gift of a lifetime, regardless of what her future held.

Near the Louvre she sat in the shade and watched a steady stream of tourists enter the museum. Unable to resist the temptation to see it herself, she followed them in. The museum covered three floors of long corridors. Rooms with thirty-foot ceilings accommodated gigantic, wall-size paintings by Rubens, Michelangelo, and others. Cozy areas held small canvas pieces like the Mona Lisa. Watching the crowds and listening to their multilingual conversations fascinated her as much as viewing the masterpieces.

After a walk through the Tuileries Garden, she caught the Métro toward home, stopping at the neighborhood sweet shop before returning to Le Palais. She knocked on Jae's door, then left a little bag of lemon drops on her small table in the hall before entering Kitsy's apartment.

"Why did you buy three perfumes when you wanted two?" Arty asked when Lynne shared her purchases.

"I signaled like I do at home; I forgot to use my thumb and one finger. Do you want a bottle of *eau de cologne* or not? I'll sell it to you cheap. Only five francs."

Arty grabbed her purse and rummaged for money. "Five francs? I thought you said it was cheap."

"Okay, I'll sell it to you for four. That's less than it cost." Lynne handed her a bottle and smiled as she took Arty's money.

By nine that evening, both dancers had packed their travel bags and headed to bed. Their first tour week began in the morning in the villages around Versailles.

20

Lynne and Arty rushed down the steps and out of the apartment, luggage in tow. "We're going to miss the train," Lynne said between pants as they scurried along the sidewalk.

"We'll make it just fine," Arty assured her. "Why are you so nervous?"

"Have you considered all Cheryl told us about touring? It's a killer."

"Break it down like I did. It's not so overwhelming. When we arrive, our hosts and local guides meet and greet us. When we stay overnight, it's our usual up at seven with breakfast completed before nine. Then we have some combination of rehearsals, teaching classes, and local tours. That's not so bad, you know."

Lynne frowned. "I'm still not thrilled about days we have double performances. That means double warm-ups and double costume changes. Maybe it's because my injured leg aches at the thought of doing double performances up to six days a week."

"Look at the bright side. Our hosts organize our overnight stays in private homes or small hotels. My guess is the places we stay will be as good as or better than our tiny room at Kitsy's. We just need to show up, you know. Plus, we won't have to face a sink full of dirty dishes or clothes all over the place. Most evenings they'll provide buffets so we'll have a chance to meet local dancers and citizens. It'll be a grind, but it'll be fun."

"Arty, you have a strange view of fun." Lynne stopped, set down her bags, and shook out her arms. "My leg's hurting. That probably makes me negative today. At least I'm not acting out in front of the entire group like Ida."

"She's a real pain in the neck the way she grumbles at everything."

Lynne picked up her bags and resumed walking. "Can you believe her moaning about not having enough free time to walk around each town? When Cheryl reminded her we had a full free day most Mondays, Ida pouted like a little kid."

Arty nodded and grinned. "I liked how you put your foot in your mouth asking her what she expected."

"This is a summer dance group, not a paid tourist trip around France." Lynne said. "But I probably shouldn't have called her our most contrary member in front of the entire troupe."

"That got everyone's attention, especially Cheryl's. She didn't look pleased, you know."

Lynne winced, then grinned as she spotted the train station. "It felt good to tell her off. Now I need to make amends to Cheryl."

The early morning train to Chartres idled. Settling into their second-class seats, the dancers waited for Cheryl to share information about today's first venture outside Paris.

"Morning, everyone. Thank you for getting up early. A quick reminder: keep the tour schedule handy. It has the train station listings. Today, we've used Gare Montparnasse, but that will not be the case every time. Always, always read our travel directions *before* you leave home. We'd hate to leave any of you standing in the wrong station."

Quiet chuckles circled the troupe.

"Too bad we don't have Dick Tracy phones on our wrists," Karl shouted. "You could call us."

Cheryl smiled. "I wish. If you miss the train, we'll need to alter our program to fill in the void you create, so ple-e-ease stay up-to-date!

"Now, back to today. Chartres is over seven hundred years old. The cathedral is immense for a tiny village. Some of our local hosts are dancers; all are opening their homes to us for meals and a place to relax between performances. You are ambassadors for the United States. I'd appreciate you doing your best to be attentive listeners and appropriate guests.

"When we arrive, we'll have a guided tour, followed by lunch with our hosts. During the day you'll have a short time to explore, but save time to rest before we assemble at six-thirty. Tonight, we'll need to leave the reception before they serve dinner, so I'll provide food we can eat on the train back to Paris. For now, sit back, relax, and enjoy the scenery."

༄

The hosts welcomed the dancers and loaded up their luggage before leading them on a five-minute walk through town and up the hill to the cathedral to see the carved religious figures and three rose windows. Lynne and others climbed the ever-narrowing three hundred steps to the tower to view the tiny village, the nearby river, the covered market, and a labyrinth in the Bishop's Palace Garden.

"This is all so cool," Lynne said to Arty.

"Look at the tall houses and the way the streets wind around," someone said.

"They're called half-timbered homes," a host said. "When you walk through the village, notice the names of the streets. Before we head back, has anyone noticed a flying buttress?"

"No, but we've seen flying dancers land on their..." Karl stopped with a smirk on his face and looked around. "Sorry."

"Smart aleck," Lynne said as she passed him. "That *was* a good one, this time."

☙

Lynne, Arty, and Lucia walked around town with Wallace and Karl, looking at shops and listening as Arty translated street names to English: Change, Herbs, Milk, Fish, Golden Sun.

"These names are more fun than Mallon Street or First Avenue," Wallace said. "I read about the drawings on the street signs in my guide book. Since commoners couldn't read, they used drawings instead of words to guide them to shops."

"Aren't you a walking tour book." Arty smiled and hip-bumped him to one side.

The friends strolled toward the river and watched children toss bread to the ducks.

"When I was a little girl, I remember walking to a creek with my dad," Lynne said. "The ducks swam close to the bank and squawked until we threw our bread."

"That sounds like fun," Lucia said. "I've never fed ducks. Wish I'd saved a few bits from breakfast, although that croissant was too delicious to share."

Lynne chuckled with the others. Where had the years gone? How had she lost her connection to her dad? Maybe it wasn't too late to return to their walks and their silly moments of nonsense. She'd need to think about that.

Their midday meal was held near the performance area. Local dancers and dignitaries joined the gathering to share in the regional favorites of ham and vegetable quiches, salads, and pastries. After relaxing and talking with their host families, the dancers left to prepare for their performances. Tonight's outdoor stage allowed them to perform a medley of dances: *Serenade*, character dances from *The Nutcracker*, solos and group dances from *Sleeping Beauty*, "Clair de Lune," and "Hoedown."

Serenade was well received as were the solos. If Lynne were to judge, Lucia and Arty's duet as cygnets from *Swan Lake* garnered the most applause, followed by Vera Dei and Jando's graceful *pas de deux*. Watching dancers move in intimate partnerships always brought the audience to their feet.

After the performances ended, local performers gathered for a late meal. Once the troupe dancers had mingled for a few minutes, Cheryl spoke to the assembled group. "Thank you for inviting us to join you today and this evening. It was an honor and privilege to meet and get to know you. I'm afraid we must leave now if we want to catch the last train to Paris. *Au revoir.*"

True to her word, Cheryl rounded up dinner and kept her comments brief. Her biggest concerns involved injuries. So far only basic problems arose: turned ankles, strained calves, hyper-extended feet, and the ever-present blisters. "Not too bad for a third-class stage," she said.

※

Getting up the following morning was a chore. Arty and Lynne didn't stay up to wash out leotard and tights, which explained Cheryl's strategy of requesting they bring extras.

Both girls grabbed croissants and fresh fruit as they headed out of the apartment. Like yesterday, they hurried to the Métro with their bags, raced down several flights of stairs to their train, and jostled with other rushing passengers.

The forty-five-minute ride from Gare Lazare to Giverny lasted long enough to settle in, listen to the day's announcements, talk with seatmates, and get off the train.

The town tour began as they disembarked in Vernon and traveled the four miles to Monet's garden at Giverny. The untamed paths and gardens were reminiscent of Monet's famous paintings in which trellises, trees, roses, iris, and daisies meandered across the canvas.

Lynne heard, then saw honey bees flying from flower to flower, following the waves of color that moved from blue to purple to red to orange to yellow. She sat on a bench by the water garden, watching the breeze vibrate the kaleidoscope of colors he captured in his paintings.

"These flowers are so brilliant. How did he capture their light and color so well?" she said.

"He focused on the reflections," the guide said. "Monet saw the landscape as gently blurred images."

Lynne squinted and nodded. "Where can I buy a book that includes his paintings?"

"In Paris. We have no gift shop here yet. Now, let's walk to the walled garden near where you'll be performing this evening."

Here, as in many villages and towns, the troupe merged with local dancers to rehearse *Serenade*. Adding local dancers brought exuberant applause from the audience. By the time the troupe ended their performance, they'd won over the crowd. Young dancers, parents, local dignitaries, and reporters crowded in to speak with each dancer.

Goodbyes took longer than expected and forced them to rush to catch the train. The engine in their bus coughed, sputtered, and died well before reaching the depot. They arrived in time to see the last car fade away toward Paris.

The dancers sat on the bus while Cheryl sent the driver to call for help, which arrived an hour later as a line of cars. Each loaded up dancers and delivered them around town to any home with a spare bed.

Lynne ended up sleeping in a child's bed in a loft the size of a closet. She twisted about, trying to get comfortable, but didn't find a position that allowed for a good night's rest. Even with her head covered with a pillow, she wasn't able to block out the snoring of fellow dancers and the home owners. At least she was indoors. She thought back to the two Katies on the ship, wondering if they were sleeping under the stars, with the cows, or maybe in a campsite. She'd take almost any size bed over sleeping outside.

༄

Thursday morning, Arty and Lynne trailed behind Karl and Wallace as they boarded the local train to Versailles, the world-famous home of King Louis XIV. Last night's unexpected sleeping arrangements stirred the residents near Giverny. Their overwhelming kindness with only a few minutes notice amazed Lynne. She couldn't imagine her mother opening her home to strangers, especially foreigners, after nine o'clock in the evening.

Tired as she felt, arriving in Versailles excited her. She pinched herself as she considered her good fortune to visit the palace of the man responsible for ballet. True, he had no idea his love of dressing up and dancing would become a world-wide art form, but she for one was grateful.

A group of shiny-faced dance students and their chaperones met the train. They boarded a private bus that dropped off dancers and hosts at homes around town. The plan included time for the families to feed the dancers, take their guests on brief walking tours, and still allow time for them to relax before their late afternoon rehearsal.

Arty, Lucia, Vera Dei, and Lynne used their afternoon free time to walk along a local path in hopes of finding shade to escape the blistering heat. They followed a small stream until they came upon a collection of colorful tents and wagons.

Vera Dei smiled. "Just as I suspected. A gypsy caravan."

Except for their permanent walls, doors, and windows, colorful wheels, and elaborate detailing, the wagons resembled American covered wagons. Wooden steps led to open doorways. Fiddle music floating through the encampment reminded Lynne of Billings' summer festivals.

The vendors waved them closer to sample cooked food and to finger handcrafts, encouraging the girls to ask, *"combien?"* or "how much?"

Arty and Vera Dei bought hand-dyed purple scarves and tied them around their waists. Lynne bought earrings and a bracelet, either for herself or as gifts once she returned home; she'd decide later.

Lucia gasped and pointed. "A fortune teller!" She grabbed Lynne and Arty, pulling them along the path. "Come on. My treat."

"Wait!" Vera Dei caught up to them. "I'm part Romany, remember? Don't treat this like a joke or act disrespectful. Fortune tellers have a gift to see the future. You must listen and ask serious questions. Promise?"

The girls nodded.

"Good." Vera Dei shooed them toward the tents. "I'll wait here. My family doesn't allow me to seek my fortune from gypsies they don't personally know."

Trampled grass around the tents and the nearby wagons indicated they'd settled in several weeks ago. A hand-painted sign above one tent read 'Fortunes 40 francs'. The girls approached the purple and gold tent covered with stars and moons with an all-seeing eye design painted over the entrance.

The bright and airy interior surprised Lynne. A woman in a flowing gown of apple red and sapphire blue sat at a small table. She nodded toward the girls and beckoned for one of them to sit in her guest chair. The others she pointed toward the bench along the wall. She studied the girls as she shuffled and reshuffled her cards. *"Chacune d'entre vous voudra une lecture de l'avenir?"*

"Oui," Arty said as she turned to interpret for Lynne and Lucia. "She wants to know if we all want readings."

Lynne shook her head. What held her back? She didn't have any deep, dark secrets. Why was she feeling uncomfortable?

"Ah. Vous doute de ma compétence?"

"She said something about one of us doubting her skills."

Lynne waved her hand and stood. "That would be me. I doubt many things." She backed up. "I'll wait outside."

"No. I'm paying for you, too," Lucia said. "We'll go first. Arty can translate. It will be fun."

Lynne returned to the bench. Lucia giggled as she slid into the overstuffed, red velvet chair across from the fortune teller. Arty knelt beside the table whispering details to her.

As the reading began, Lynne watched and half-listened to the conversation, picking out occasional words.

Arty translated. "Lucia's three cards say she's a party girl with a boyfriend. She has true friends, and she's supposed to act thoughtfully."

Lynne shook her head. What a bunch of bunk. Everyone could see they were friends. The rest were just guesses. How could someone predict anything from ordinary playing cards? She thought fortune tellers used tarot cards.

Arty whispered, "Isn't this fun?"

Lynne flashed her a stage smile.

The fortune teller set the cards aside and reached for Lucia's palm.

"She says Lucia has a pioneering spirit, can expect a long life, but might be selfish. She makes life-long friends, will marry, and will have many children."

Lucia smiled as she stood, stepping aside so Arty could sit for her turn.

As the cards were read, Arty interpreted. "She said I'm a stable person, you know, but gossip is my enemy. I'm a flirt, and I should use my skills to comfort others. Am I a flirt? Really?"

Lynne laughed. "Ask Wallace. You keep making eyes at him."

The fortune teller drummed her fingers, waiting to read Arty's palm.

When Arty finished, she smiled. "That's more like it. She says I'm passionate about my career. I have unused talent; and, if I work hard, changes lie ahead."

"What kind of changes?" Lucia asked.

Arty's smile faded. "She didn't say." Arty turned back to ask her.

The fortune teller shrugged, lifting her hands and shoulders in answer.

Lynne swallowed down her nervousness and moved into the red velvet chair. She fingered the silken scarves that covered the round table and scrutinized the woman who leaned forward to stare at her. Lucia deposited the necessary coins in the fortune teller's hand.

Arty knelt next to Lynne. "Don't worry. I'll explain everything."

Lynne crossed her arms over her chest and leaned back. "Fine."

The gypsy shuffled her battered cards, then inhaled deeply with her eyes closed. When she opened them, she fanned out the deck and stared at Lynne, who sat motionless.

"She wants you to select three cards, one at a time," Arty said.

Lynne brushed one finger over the backs of the fanned out cards as she tried to decide which to select.

The fortune teller brushed her hand away. "*Non, mademoiselle! Touchez seulement trois cartes*"

Lynne grimaced as the fortune teller grabbed up and reshuffled the deck of cards. "*Ne perturbez pas les forces des cartes. Touchez une carte à la fois et remettez les moi.*"

Arty whispered, "You're disturbing the forces in the deck. Only touch one card at a time and hand it to her."

When the cards once again lay fanned out on the table, the fortune teller gestured for her to make her selections.

Lynne's hand shook as her fingers hovered above the cards.

"Dépêchez vous! Choisissez vos cartes."

"Hurry up! Make your choices, Lynne."

"I am." Lynne gritted her teeth. "I need to think." She picked up one card, but dropped it on the floor of the tent, face down.

The fortune teller gasped. *"Mon Dieu!"*

"Do I need to translate that?"

Lynne sighed. "I got it."

The fortune teller's black eyes narrowed, causing her to look fierce, almost dangerous. She pointed to the floor, gesturing for Lynne to pick up the card and place it on the table. Lynne shuddered. At that instant the gypsy resembled Madame Cosper when she became disgusted with Lynne or another dancer's antics.

The first card turned face up was a five of clubs. Arty translated: "She sees a serious injury or health problem."

"Does she mean my accident last winter, or is something coming?"

"She didn't say."

Lynne stared at the fortune teller, reminding herself that none of this was true, so why worry about what she said. Somehow, it mattered.

The second card turned face up was the two of clubs. The fortune teller frowned. Lynne waited.

Arty turned to her. "She says you'll face unexpected situations, but your future is bright."

"That's encouraging," Lynne said. "Did she say when my future would be bright?"

"No. She's waiting for you to select the last card."

21

The fortune teller blinked slowly after the last card was turned face up. She spoke in a whisper.

Arty translated. "More than one man loves you. One is older. He may be a relative who looks out for you. The other man you recently met. Both enter and exit your life at unexpected times."

Lynne sat back. A chill sliced through her body. Was the older man her father? Would they one day soon walk to the creek again to feed the ducks? Was he becoming more understanding? Or was he leaving, maybe dying soon? Was Noel the second man? Did he love her? Leave her? Forget about her?"

"What's wrong, Lynne?" Arty reached out to touch her arm.

"Is it cold in here?"

"No. It's muggy. Are you alright?"

Lynne nodded. She felt the fortune teller's stare but refused to look her direction. She stood and picked up her purse to leave.

The fortune teller shook her head, gesturing for Lynne to sit and extend her right hand. She hesitated but sat down and slowly extended her hand.

The gypsy rubbed her palm against Lynne's. When Lynne tried to pull back, the fortune teller shook her head and raised one eyebrow as she traced the lines on Lynne's palm. "Strength here... also ... allergy or maybe infection."

"I don't have allergies. Hey, she speaks English, Arty."

"Stay strong when the setback arrives."

Lynne felt a twist in her stomach. She cupped her hand slightly and pulled away. Again the woman gently pulled Lynne's hand toward her. "Heart... many cross lines... bad time... true love coming." She paused. "You wish to learn more?"

"I guess."

The gypsy traced the curved line around her thumb. "Head meets Life line. Success in life." She touched the fleshy skin that surrounded Lynne's thumb. "Mars ... plump."

"*Excusez-moi?*" Lynne said.

"*Vous êtes facilement influencée par l'amour*"

Arty laughed. "She says you're easily swayed by love, you know."

"That's an understatement."

"Heart line... broken...many loves in the past. You didn't trust them." She touched the line running up the center of her palm from her wrist to her fingers. "Fate... few breaks... you know what you want. *Nes pas?*"

Lynne shrugged. Right now she had no idea what she wanted.

The gypsy turned Lynne's hand palm down, resting it on the table. Lynne looked up to find the woman watching her. As she withdrew her hand from the table, the woman smiled and nodded.

During the walk back to their meeting place, Lynne thought about the fortune teller. "Do you guys believe what the gypsy told you?"

Arty nodded. "Even if she's wrong, it was fun to hear about my fortune, you know."

"I agree," Vera Dei said. "When I went to a fortune teller last year, she said my good fortune would continue. Here I am." She grabbed her friends' hands and began swinging them forward and back. A dreamy gaze floated across her face. "Plus, my boyfriend and I are still together. It's romantic, knowing we're destined to be a couple forever."

Lynne shook her head. "Don't you think that might be a coincidence? Maybe you made your own good luck."

Vera Dei skipped ahead, did a quick *tour jeté,* and stopped. "I like knowing that she predicted my future and that it's coming true. What about you, Lynne? Do you believe what she told you?"

"No." Lynne wondered what the gypsy meant about men leaving her. "I hope the good parts come true. Did she placed a hex on me?"

"No," Lucia said. "I've read about hexes. If she did that, she'd have to tell you."

Lynne nodded. How much of what was prophesized would be true? Did her actions determine her fortune, or could she blame someone or something else?

The girls joined their troupe for a private tour of the castle's Hall of Mirrors, state apartments, and the courtyard before heading back along the Royal Drive to the Grand Canal, their dance area. Lynne moved in a fog. Why did the fortune teller's conversation tug at her? She didn't believe the hocus pocus in the tent. The woman was a performer like herself. It was time to forget thinking about the future and focus on dancing.

༄

Friday through Sunday, the troupe danced with local entertainers. Evenings, they enjoyed the crowds that gathered to watch them near the lighted musical fountain. Sunday evening every dancer dozed on the train back to Paris. During the hour-long ride, Lynne's Versailles post cards remained blank.

On their Monday off, she woke feeling sharp pains in her previously injured leg. Why now? Probably a coincidence, she thought. Besides, how could random cards predict anything?

"Let's eat a leisurely breakfast," she said. "Then let's go to the American Embassy. Are you as curious to see who wrote to you?"

"Hardly," Arty said. "I was so busy working to earn solos this past year that I let myself drift away from my friends who aren't dancers, you know. By the time I return, they'll probably have forgotten me."

The girls sat in a public *jardin* to read their mail. Lynne smiled as she slowly sliced open the blue aerogram from Marta and read her tight, schoolgirl script. She'd filled every corner of the letter and turned her words sideways to get them all in.

> June 15
>
> Dear Lynne,
>
> The wedding was lovely. I cried for mom's happiness. I surprised her and Robert with a reception at the dance studio. Everyone came. I think she's glad I did it. We'll talk more when she gets back from their short honeymoon at Kalaloch. You must come so you can see the beach there!
>
> Lily Rose and her band reunited and performed mom's favorite songs. The students, parents, and other guests toasted my new family while our dancers buzzed around like bees. Everything looked festive. I'll share photos with you when you come for a visit.
>
> June 23
>
> (I can't believe I haven't written anything for almost ten days!)
>
> Mr. Dunbar, my elderly neighbor, is in the hospital. Since my return to Bremerton, I stop and sit beside him when he's on his

porch swing. In cool weather, I join him for a cup of tea every couple of weeks. He's lonely. I know how that feels, even though I have Steve a few hours away. I hope Mr. Dunbar recovers. I'll miss him if he doesn't.

    Mom has moved out of our family home. She likes Robert's house, but I know she'll miss her gardens. I'll miss the grape arbor, my old playhouse, and sitting in my swing late on warm summer evenings. Growing up means I've got to face Sam Faris and his mother once fall classes begin. I'm not looking forward to that. I hope he will forgive me for dating him and not wanting to get serious. I think his daughter Betty will be fine about it since I'll see her at classes every week. Sam's a great guy. Maybe you'd like to meet him, or are you still thinking about your rancher?

    Steve's career at the Portland paper is flourishing. He attacks every assignment with energy and writes great articles, if I do say so myself. I feel good about my decision to plan a future with him. Maybe by the time you get back, I'll have everything settled at the Bremerton dance studio and be able to move to Oregon. I enjoy taking the train as I imagine you're riding a few trains this summer. I picture myself riding beside you, so send those postcards. Then I'll know what I'm seeing (ha ha). You're still my #1 friend, even when you're half a world away! Marta

She smiled at Marta's newsy letter. It was about time!

    Arty poured over her two letters from home. "I guess I was wrong, you know. People remembered me after all."

"Of course they did. You're a good friend, Arty." Even with your constant addition of "you know" to every conversation, Lynne thought. She should tell Marta about that in her next letter.

She closed her eyes and drifted off, letting the warm sun in the park soak into her body. These Mondays off were precious escapes after their tightly-scheduled performances. Like the other dancers, she needed to conserve every ounce of energy to ensure she'd last the entire summer.

Lynne sat back and smiled. She sighed, curled her feet under her, and opened the last letter.

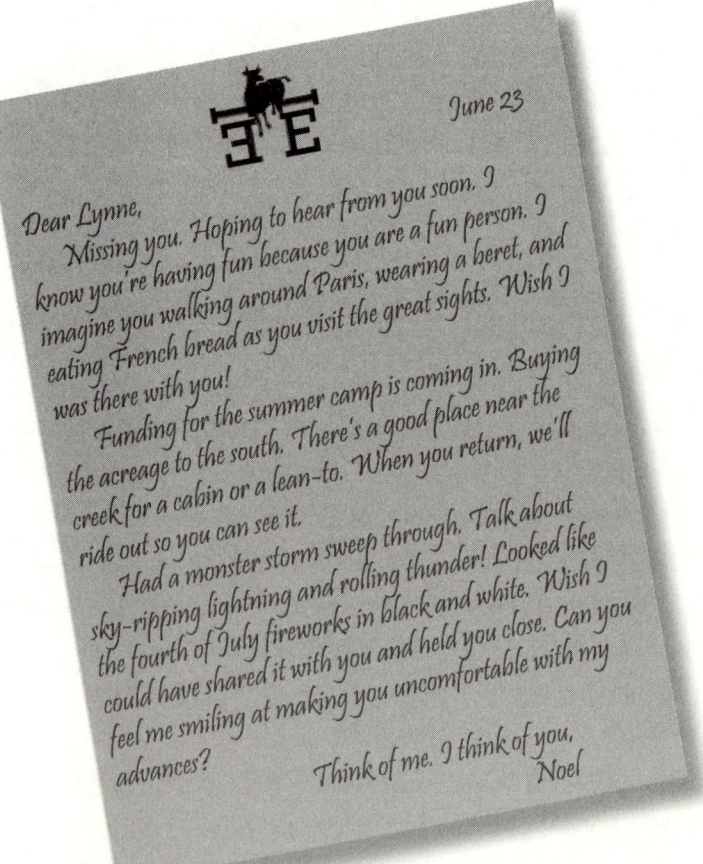

> June 23
>
> Dear Lynne,
> Missing you. Hoping to hear from you soon. I know you're having fun because you are a fun person. I imagine you walking around Paris, wearing a beret, and eating French bread as you visit the great sights. Wish I was there with you!
> Funding for the summer camp is coming in. Buying the acreage to the south. There's a good place near the creek for a cabin or a lean-to. When you return, we'll ride out so you can see it.
> Had a monster storm sweep through. Talk about sky-ripping lightning and rolling thunder! Looked like the fourth of July fireworks in black and white. Wish I could have shared it with you and held you close. Can you feel me smiling at making you uncomfortable with my advances?
>
> Think of me. I think of you.
> Noel

She closed her eyes, then reread the letter before folding it to carry in her purse.

At the neighborhood *tabac* shop, she bought three postcards showing Monet's garden. His images inspired her to move fluidly like his hands must have moved when he created his colorful, flowing paintings. His place of inspiration became hers, a memory she'd carry with her forever.

Flopping down on her trundle bed later, she listened to the subdued city noises outside the open window; the Paris work day slowed and ended, sending everyone home. She stretched, then stood to finish sorting their laundry. Somehow she'd misplaced her best black leotard. If she didn't find it, she'd need to visit the dance clothing shop across town. That was as good an excuse as any to go there.

Just then Kitsy opened her bedroom door and yawned. "You're back, *nes pas?*"

"Obviously. Did you have the day off today?"

"*Non*. I em sick." Kitsy yawned again, turned back into her room, then turned again toward Lynne, holding a dark rag with two fingers. "Iz zis yours? It was out my window."

Lynne reached for the rag—her best black leotard faded to an irregular gray, suitable only for practices. Now she was down to two usable leotards for performances.

"Thanks for bringing it in."

"*Non*. Iz not me; iz my boyfriend who find it."

Kitsy walked into her bedroom and closed the door before Lynne could say anything. Besides, confrontation took too much energy. She tossed the rag into her dance bag and sat down to write post cards. For Noel, she selected one from Versailles.

> July 27
>
> Magnificent palace. Did you know King Louis created ballet to amuse himself? I can imagine his fat body dancing in his Hall of Mirrors, where he'd see his reflection over and over and over. Lots of gardens, fountains, and courtyards. Marie Antoinette had her own chateau here on the grounds. Little good that did her!
>
> Anxious to see your summer camp plans. Doubt you'll want anything as elaborate as Versailles! Letter to follow when I have more time to write.
>
> Lynne

Marta's post card of a Monet painting looked as if it was painted from where she sat by his pond that afternoon.

> July 27
>
> Thanks for the newsy letter. Glad things are settling down. I got to wander through Monet's garden and walk around his ponds. Can you believe we danced here? We also visited Versailles. You must see it. It's too massive to imagine.
>
> Dancing more than I ever expected possible. Exhausted but enjoying everything so far.
>
> Off to northern France, then the Loire valley. Keep writing! Letter to follow as soon as my life slows down to write more.
>
> Lynne

The end of July heat blasted through the dance studio window, leaving Lynne sopping wet. Cheryl pushed them to their limits, then shoved them over the edge; but Lynne loved every minute. She felt exhausted yet stronger each day she danced.

Cheryl gathered the troupe during their break. "We're ending our rehearsals in Paris. Now we must polish *everything*, especially the waltz for the German festival. If we perform well there, we'll be invited to larger festivals, which means better stages and larger crowds in the future."

"Does it mean fewer train rides and lumpy beds?" Jando said.

The dancers laughed and nodded to each other.

"You're all pros. Wherever we dance, you'll be fine. I'm amazed at how few injuries we've had. Whatever you're doing, it's working. Let's spend our remaining practice time today reviewing Khachaturian's fabulous "Masquerade Waltz" from *Gayane*. You'll need to know it like the back of your hand."

"I love the music," Jando said. The rest nodded in agreement.

"Aram Khachaturian is becoming my favorite composer," Cheryl said. "He's the Russian who also wrote the famous 'Sabre Dance,'"

"Who's our choreographer?" Karl asked.

"I am. This is my adaptation. It's a fast-paced waltz, so keep your movements light and airy. Where there is space, we'll enter as spokes on a wheel, moving down aisles to approach the stage area. Otherwise, we'll enter diagonally. Girls may need to substitute for guys for large stages when everyone dances. Select a partner and spread out."

Cheryl clapped and counted out the steps for the series of partners entering the stage. "*Glissade, pique,* lift high, *glissade* back, *balance.* Then circle with four *pirouettes* and sweep off the stage."

Sweat poured off every body as they danced, asked questions about angles and arms, then stopped to rest.

"Next we have a series of eighteen-second solos. Girls, adjust your endings to include *chainé* or other turns carrying you off-stage. Guys, end with a flourish before you exit."

When solos ended, Cheryl frowned. "Make them showier. I need more flow, more exaggeration, more excitement. Let's go again, two at a time."

The ending reprised the partner dancing. Cheryl guided them with steady clapping and directions. The music's strong beat helped them move in near-perfect unison.

"Looks good, everyone. But I want even more extravagance in partner lifts and waltz turns."

"And this all happens in how many sweaty minutes?" Wallace said.

Cheryl grinned. "Four luxurious minutes. We'll include this in our program whenever space allows." She checked her watch. "Take your lunch break. Use the afternoon to perfect your solos. Be ready to present them to me tomorrow. I suggest you invite one or two people to critique your movements. Try to not wear out the tape."

Throughout the afternoon and early evening, Lynne practiced her solos dozens of times, playing the music in her mind and dancing in the hallway when the practice room belonged to others. She and Arty returned to Kitsy's apartment, showered, straightened up Renny's rooms, gathered and delivered his laundry to the shop, and were soon seated on a bench in the neighborhood *jardin*.

"I love this quiet part of the day," Lynne said. "Even though I'm exhausted, I feel energized. I have never worked this hard."

Arty chuckled. "I love being included in making group decisions. I wish my ballet company allowed that. It will be hard to return to being a corps dancer with no voice, you know."

"I'm already on thin ice with Madame Cosper. I may need to move to another ballet company. Cheryl's spoiled us. I'd love to find a place where I can have a say."

※

After the morning warm-up, the dancers shared their brief solos with Cheryl and the troupe. Dancers, as well as Cheryl, offered suggestions to strengthen the solos: elongate your arms, add another turn in your series, lift your *arabesque* higher, straighten your back, get more lift in your jump.

Cheryl smiled and clutched her clipboard to her chest. "I'm proud of every one of you. You've provided each other with amazing feedbacks. After our lunch break, you'll dance for me one more time. Then I'll assign the order of your solos within the music and assign cast one and two. We'll finalize the entire piece today."

"What will the girls wear?" Tu asked.

"Your colored leotard, your long wrap skirts, and pink *pointe* shoes. Guys will wear my colored vests, and you'll need a fitting. The theatrical masks will have short ribbon streamers on each side; be aware of ribbons whipping near your eyes."

On the way out for their break, Ida complained loudly. "I'd better be in cast one or Cheryl will hear from my ballet company. I wasn't sent here to come in second."

"The second cast doesn't mean we're less skilled than the first cast," Lynne said. "It means we dance the selection on the second day."

Ida whipped around in front of Lynne. "You're so stupid. Second is second. If I'm relegated to being second, I might get too sick to dance, if you get my drift."

"If you do that, you'll miss performing your solo and foul up your partner as well as our groupings," Lynne said.

"So what? I'm getting sick and tired of you and your stupid interference. I'm going back to talk with Cheryl right now. We'll see who's first and who's second!"

22

Many days, Lynne aided dancers with strains and other minor ailments. Now she sat wrapping Vera Dei's ankle.

"Keep the ace bandage on, even for performances. Cheryl's okay with that as long as it's secured properly. If your ankle doesn't feel stronger soon, you'll need to let her know so she can have a doctor check it."

Vera Dei nodded; her dark eyes clouded. "I didn't know touring would be this demanding, did you?"

"I don't think any of us knew. Everyone we meet is welcoming. But when we eat and spend overnight with them, it's exhausting."

༄

A small town came into view. Cheryl introduced the young woman who stepped onto their bus. "It gives me great happiness to introduce Monique, our Honfluer tour guide."

One more small town. One more tour of an artist's museum. One more invitation to a scenic chapel and another rose window. Lynne collected her things, put on her stage smile, and followed the local guide.

The performances in Honfleur went well, but Vera Dei wasn't dancing. The longer they traveled, the more people became casualties. Lynne knocked lightly on the wooden railing. She'd stayed strong and healthy, but it didn't hurt to cover her bases.

She and Arty reached Le Palais apartment as Sunday became Monday. They rang the office bell for Madame Zelb to let them in. Soon they'd be gone for close to a month; maybe then she'd get a full night's sleep.

Madame came to the door in glimmering party clothes. *"Ah, mesdemoiselles, vous êtes de retour. Bienvenue. Venez participer à la fête!"*

Lynne looked at Arty, who made a strange face. "They're having a party."

They followed Madame into the dining area, where a sea of young men stood drinking beer and laughing. *"Ces jeunes hommes sont en visite à Paris avant de rejoindre leu école en Italie."*

Lynne grabbed Arty's arm. "Let me try this. I think she said they're visiting on their way to school in Italy."

"Good job, Lynne. They're..."

Lynne walked into the dining room. The conversations hushed, replaced by raised eyebrows and ogles for the newest arrivals.

"Lynne?"

She recognized the voice, but she couldn't believe her ears. In the midst of the crowd stood Noel. He smiled and reached his hands toward her. The group parted. She stepped between his outstretched arms. The room erupted with cheers and cat calls.

Tears streamed down Lynne's face. Her knees gave way.

Noel grabbed her. "Hey. Don't collapse!"

She stared at his hazel eyes, then scanned his face. "I missed you." She took his hand, pulling him from the crowded room into the aging lounge across the entry hall.

"I wanted—"

"Sh-h." She stood on tiptoe to kiss him, then ran her hand along the side of his face. "It's really you. You're standing in Paris with me."

"I am." Noel kissed her and pulled her into another hug. "I couldn't wait another month to see you."

"Who's taking care of your ranch?"

"My dad and the hands. It's summer. They can handle things without me for a little while."

Lynne let out a long breath. "Wow. I mean...wow! When did you arrive? How did you know I'd be here?"

"I flew in Friday, and I'll fly out next Saturday morning. Madame Zelb told me you're doing local performances before heading out on your big tour, so I figured you'd be back tonight. I thought I'd tag along on the next one, see a performance or two, and steal you away during your free time."

"We're going out of town soon."

"That's fine." He stared at her and slowly traced his fingers along her cheek. "You look exhausted. Should I let you get some sleep? We can talk tomorrow."

Lynne shook her head. "That's not how it's going to happen." She squeezed his hand, then reached up to place her arms around his neck. "We're staying right here, right now. I'll sleep later."

Noel chuckled. "I guess I'll stand here then."

Lynne leaned against him, listening to his heart thump against her cheek, feeling him inhale and exhale. She sighed and closed her eyes. He'd come all this way to see her.

They sat down on the lumpy couch, staring at each other. Lynne's usual quick remarks escaped her. All she could do was smile and hold his hand. "Tell me about what's happening in Billings."

"It's too quiet with you gone. I've got the property development started. The lean-to had its first summer campers last week. Cook, the cows, and I miss you."

She laughed. "Good."

"I heard from a friend of mine on the patrons' committee that Madame Cosper is thinking of retiring."

Lynne sat up. "Really? Now *that* is news! Maybe going back to Billings won't be such a bad idea."

Noel pushed her to his arm's length. "Wait! You were thinking of *not* returning?"

"Of course I'm coming back. I just meant with Madame in charge, I feel like dancing there is more of an ordeal than a pleasure. Cheryl has shown me how great it feels to work with someone who appreciates everyone's efforts."

When the clock struck two, the young men from the dining room disbursed to their guest rooms. Lynne yawned. "I guess I'd better get some sleep. I have tomorrow off. Come for breakfast. Then I'll show you my favorite places in Paris."

Noel pulled her to her feet and kissed her forehead. "I'll be back for breakfast if you're sure you'll be up that early. Don't worry about showing me the sights. I've come to see you, so wherever you need to go or whatever you need to do is fine with me."

Lynne nodded and stretched on tiptoe to kiss him again before he backed out the entry door and disappeared. Maybe what the gypsy fortune teller said was coming true.

Arty opened the door to the apartment on Lynne's third knock. She yawned. "Hey. Looks like you had a special visitor."

"I did. That's Noel. I should have introduced you. He's here for the week, so you'll meet him." She yawned as she changed into her nightclothes. "Be sure I wake up for breakfast. He's joining us." She dropped her travel clothes into their laundry bag and flopped onto the trundle bed. Tired as she'd felt on arriving back in Paris, now she lay awake. Noel had flown halfway around the world just to see her.

When she woke, a shadow blocked out the usual blast of sunshine. The shadow brushed her hair off her face and kissed her forehead. "Mornin', Lynne."

She sat up and blinked. "Noel! How did you, I mean, good morning. I'm guessing I overslept."

He laughed. "Only by three hours. Arty tried to wake you, but she said you rolled over and covered your head. I'm to tell you she's gone shopping and to do the laundry and she'll see you later. Once you're wide awake, I'll take you to lunch."

After a quick shower, Lynne put on her only clean dress, the blue pin-striped shirtwaist, and slid a brush through her hair. She hurried down to meet Noel in the lounge. They walked to Renny's cafe, drank espresso, and ate croissants with their fruit plate, alternately holding hands and staring at each other.

"It's so good to see you," Lynne said. "I've planned to write more letters, but after performing I'm so exhausted I can't stay awake to write."

"I get it."

"You've caught me on our last days in Paris." Lynne reached for his hand and squeezed it. "I still can't believe you're *really* here."

They sat, smiling at each other, watching people and traffic pass. Then they took the Métro to Ile de la Cité. They walked through Notre-Dame Cathedral, climbed to view the island, and strolled to the tiny Sainte Chapelle church on their way to board a boat for a one-hour Seine River cruise.

Though the guide spoke English as well as several other languages, they cuddled in a snug hug even though the day was hot and sticky and ignored much of her descriptions.

After hours of sights and people-watching, they returned to the apartment. She changed her shoes, then grabbed Noel's hand. "I've saved the best sights for last."

Emerging from the Métro stop at Trocadero, they were met with a light breeze. Straight ahead, the Eiffle Tower stood like a giant Erector Set construction that tapered to a slender point above its crisscrossed metal beams.

"Impressive, huh?" Lynne said.

Noel squeezed her hand. "Much better in person than looking at it in a book. Let's ride to the top."

The 360-degree view didn't disappoint. Brightly lit streets dimmed as they reached for the horizon. Far below, pedestrians and traffic moved in silence, like ants seeking their next adventure.

"What do you think?" Lynne asked Noel.

"Amazing, especially seeing it with you. What's that?" he said, turning Lynne to follow his pointing finger.

"Our next stop."

At the Anvers Métro stop, they surfaced and climbed a long set of steps. The balmy night air did little to alleviate their sweating; but when they reached the plaza, they forgot their tiredness as the white onion-dome of Sacre Coeur church rose in stark contrast to the dark night sky.

"Amazing!" Noel pulled her close. "Almost as amazing as you, Miss Meadows."

Affection for this guy who'd traveled so far to see her blossomed. She gently stabbed her finger against his chest. "You're not so bad yourself."

They walked around the outside, then entered in time to hear a choir perform an acapella hymn. The soaring voices sent musical chills through Lynne. She stepped closer to Noel as they listened.

A few minutes later, they joined the star-gazing crowd seated on the steps in front of the church. Directly in front of them, the quarter moon had risen and looked as if it was tethered to the Eiffel Tower. Paris street lights twinkled like a blanket of stars surrounding the tower. Nearby, street musicians broke into the quiet with pop and classical selections. Noel and Lynne looked at each other and smiled.

"This is a perfect way to end a perfect day," he said. "Are you tired, or do you want to walk around?"

"Let's walk. Bert, our resident tour guide, suggested wandering through Montmarte to see the artists and shops. It's on our way back to the Métro."

The last moments of the evening, they held hands in the neighborhood garden. Lynne leaned her head on Noel's shoulder. "This *jardin* is where I do my thinking, especially about you."

He laughed and leaned down to kiss her hair. "So you think about me once in a while? I'm glad because you've crowded into my dreams every night since I met you."

"You mean I aced out your herds and your new property?"

"Not only did you ace them out, thinking about you interrupts my days." Noel pulled her closer. "Promise you'll come back to Billings."

Lynne smiled. "Where else would I go?"

Maybe when Leo came, she could plead to go home. Maybe he could drive around with a new friend. It was worth a try, but she doubted he'd go for it.

After planning to meet tomorrow for dinner, Noel walked her to Le Palais and kissed her good night.

Sleeping proved even more difficult than the night before. Knowing Noel was a few Métro stops away and that she'd see him over the next few days kept her mind churning. Why had it taken so long to find a guy who appreciated her *and* her career? She'd definitely been looking in the wrong places.

Lynne's wake up call was another kiss on the forehead.

Noel stood smiling down at her. "Mornin', sunshine. Ready to go?"

She stretched, "If I get a kiss every morning, maybe."

They ate breakfast together. Then Noel accompanied the dancers to rehearsals before taking off on a guy tour to visit military museums and the sewers of Paris.

Vera Dei attended rehearsal, but only to watch and walk through changes. The doctor ordered her out of pointe shoes for at least a week, leaving Lynne to dance double shifts during the Loire performances.

Midway through the afternoon session, Cheryl clapped her hands. "Let's go back to the *An American in Paris* choreography. It needs to be crisper and perkier. This is another signature piece, so show some attitude. Let's take it from the top."

Again and again, they ran through it. Something in the way Damien styled their movements created energy. Lynne wanted to figure it out, maybe share it with Marta to use with her young dancers.

As they rested before doing it once again, Cheryl approached Lynne. "What do you think? Will Damien approve our changes, or have we ruined his choreography?"

"He'll approve. I'll be sure to share your ideas with him."

"He's lucky to have you, Lynne. You set a great example of perseverance and skill for the others dancers."

"I'm guessing the ballet company didn't share their concerns about me before you offered me a position."

Cheryl smiled. "They did. I think you needed a change, maybe a break from Madame Cosper. I know how intense she can be. I began my career as a dancer for her."

Lynne stared after her as she walked off to start another section of their rehearsal. Cheryl knew Madame Cosper. Interesting.

23

Thursday's early morning train wound through the fertile Loire valley, passing streams that separated the miles of ripening crops from the castles and estates. Noel and Lynne sat amid the dancers, yet a thousand miles away in whispered conversations.

When the train slowed, Cheryl spoke. "This morning, we'll travel to the famous Chenonceau castle. This region has beautiful chateaus well worth a return visit on your own.

"Then this afternoon, we'll join the local dancers for *Serenade*. Tonight at six-thirty, we'll be driven to our evening performance with its first class stage."

Cheering and applause from the dancers filled the train car.

Noel leaned in to talk with Lynne. "Is every stop this busy?"

"Yep. It's a lot of dancing, touring, and visiting with locals. Today, though, I can't wait to wander inside a castle that I've seen in so many magazine photos."

Chateau de Chenonceau had everything she imagined a castle should have: a moat, bridges, curved stone stairways, forty-foot ceilings, candle-lit chandeliers, tapestries, paintings, coats of arms, armor, ballrooms, marble floors, and winding garden paths throughout the grounds.

Noel became as much of an attraction as the castle. She poked him in the ribs "These people aren't accustomed to a tall, handsome rancher wearing a cowboy hat. You're getting a lot of admiring glances."

He removed his hat and turned to Lynne. "The only admiring glances I notice are yours." He leaned close, kissed her cheek, and kept his hat in his hands for the rest of the tour.

*

Friday evening, after two successful performances, Noel and Lynne held hands in the Tours train station.

"I'm glad I came," he said. "I had a great time with you and your dancer friends, and I loved watching you perform."

"Which was your favorite?"

He smiled. "Any time you danced. You slip into another world. I admire your commitment and focus."

She snorted. "Me? Focused? That's a new one."

"It's true. You give yourself over to each dance. That's one of the things I love about you."

She stared at Noel. Did he say *love*? Does he love me?

"Hello? Earth calling Lynne. Where did you go?"

She tried to think of what to say, but no words made it to her lips. Just then the evening train hissed to a stop. Passengers exited and others shoved their way aboard.

Noel picked up his bag and continued to stare at her. "Lynne? Hey!"

She smiled as she stood on tiptoe to kiss him. "I'll miss you. I promise to write or at least send post cards."

He hugged her one last time and stepped toward the train. "See you in October after we both return to Billings." He disappeared into the car, took a seat at a window, and tipped his cowboy hat.

She laughed and waved, watching the train chug toward Paris.

Tomorrow he'd fly across the Atlantic and be home even before she returned to Paris. Tears slid down her face. She'd need to redirect her focus before tomorrow's performances.

༄

Her Saturday evening performance lacked its usual spark of energy and her unique finishing touches. Cheryl pulled her aside.

"What's going on? You looked wooden. Get your head into your dancing, or I'll pull your solo."

Lynne bit her lip. "I'm sorry," she said to a retreating Cheryl.

Sunday's afternoon performance started out well. Lynne danced her *Firebird* solo with ease: across the stage, side-to-side, forward and back to mid-stage. She extended every *développé* with extra flourishes, feeling the musical pulse inside her body. After her final *arabesque*, she lifted her arms and stepped back for her curtsy.

As she rose, her ankle gave way. She thrust her arms out to regain her balance, tilted to the right, and grabbed at the air. With a body-jarring jolt, she slammed onto the pavement beside the stage.

༄

Where was she? A sharp pain sliced through her head. She swallowed and tried to clear away the fog that held her captive. Antiseptic smells, hushed voices, and strange, coded messages floated around her. She swallowed again. Her mouth felt dry as a wad of cotton. She blinked several times and made a weak attempt to sit up.

A hand restrained her. "Lie still," a quiet voice said.

She moved her hands along the hard metal surface beneath her. Someone held her hand. Had Noel missed his flight?

"How are you feeling?" a voice asked. The face of Jean Paul, the dance troupe assistant, came into view.

"Like someone hit me with a club." She lifted her hand and touched the ice pack on her head. "What happened?"

"You hit your head on the edge of the stage as you fell to the pavement. We brought you to the local hospital. You may need stitches, and they may want to keep you overnight for observation. I'll stay with you for now. When you're up to talking with a nurse, I'll translate."

Lynne lay back, trying to piece together what happened. Why did she lose her balance? She'd danced dozens of times with no problem.

෨

Two hours later, she lay on a metal gurney in a small cubicle with another ice pack on her head. Familiar voices grew louder. Cheryl, Arty, and a man who must be the doctor stepped into her space. "She has a concussion and a head full of stitches. We'll x-ray her leg and arm in a few minutes to double check for fractures. We need to enter the cause of her accident."

Cheryl took Lynne's hand and held it lightly. "She stepped into a large knot hole in the outdoor stage. The festival planners are very sorry."

The doctor nodded as he made note in her chart, then excused himself to check on other patients.

"Too bad they didn't check the stage more carefully," Arty said.

"They say they did," Cheryl said. "They think the dancing jiggled the floor. Someone must have absentmindedly kicked the knot off the stage. We found it. The hole it left behind was large enough and deep enough to grab and hold your *pointe* shoe."

Arty patted Lynne's shoulder. "It wasn't your fault, you know."

"I know," Lynne said. "When will I be able to dance?"

"Patience, Lynne, patience," Cheryl said. "Lie back and relax as much as possible. Arty will stay with you. Jean Paul and I need to head back to prepare for tonight's performance." Cheryl straightened Lynne covers and patted her arm. "The doctor said broken bones or not, you'll need a minimum of a week to recover from the bruising. We're to find a doctor to remove your stitches in about ten days. I'll see you later."

"Hopefully, they'll release you to take the train back to Paris tonight," Arty said.

"Paris? Alone? Why?"

"Not alone. Angers is cancelled. A storm blew through town, you know. It damaged their outdoor stage. We're going home early."

∽

Afternoon slipped into evening. Lynne heard low voices as doctors and nurses worked on patients. Equipment beeped, drawers opened and closed, people cried and moaned. She closed her eyes and flashed back to Marta's injury almost two years before. She'd fallen through a porch railing and landed on the frozen, snow-covered ground in front of Steve's family cabin. Lynne had played the role Arty now played: a helper who can't really help.

For Marta, the injury ended her career. Lynne shuddered. Would she suffer the same outcome? They hadn't found any broken bones, but what if she strained muscles? That could take more than a couple weeks to heal. Closing her eyes, she pretended Noel was hugging her and telling her everything would be fine.

At midnight Cheryl returned to fetch Lynne and Arty for the trip back to Paris.

Lynne felt like an old granny as she moved onto the bus. Her muscles locked up between every step. She inched along, taking short breaths as the pain in her body intensified with each moment she remained on her feet.

Arty supported her as they boarded the train. The troupe watched her until she sank down in a seat. Her head ached. She felt dizzy, but she waved and smiled to those looking her direction.

Arty stood next to her, looking more like a mother than a fellow dancer. "Are you comfortable? Do you want me to fold up my jacket and make you a pillow?"

"No thanks. I'm fine."

Arty sat down across the aisle from her. "I've decided something, and there'll be no arguments. You'll sleep in the bed. I'll take the trundle."

"I'll sleep wherever you point me." Lynne bit her lip and took a shaky breath. "I may have caused my own problem, with or without that knot hole. I was distracted by Noel's leaving. I saw the hole and then forgot about it."

"We all get distracted at times, mostly when we're lost in the music, you know. I'm just glad it didn't happen during a group selection."

Lynne laughed and winced from the movement. "You're right. It could have been a huge disaster. I *do* know how it feels to knock down an entire group of dancers. It happened to me in Billings, but let's not talk about that. All I want to think about is me stretched out in a cozy bed. I plan to sleep away most of the next two days."

༺༻

As they exited their taxi in front of Le Palais, Lynne leaned heavily on Arty's outstretched arm. Her left leg ached like it did after her car accident. Hopefully, the pain and the stiffness would ease after a good night's sleep and gentle stretches.

Arty rang the entry bell. The girls waited for Madame Zelb to unlock the door.

"My body is starting to relax at just the thought of a comfortable bed."

"I know," Arty said. "Even the trundle sounds perfect."

Madame opened the door and stared at them. *"Pourquoi êtes-vous de retour?"*

"Nous avons eu un changement dans les plans" Arty said. *"Y-a-t-il un problème?"*

"Oui. Kitsy a un nouveau colocataire."

Arty gasped. "Kitsy's replaced us with a new roommate."

24

Bert came to their rescue, offering them his hide-a-bed for the night. Every time Arty shifted, Lynne woke with a start. Then Arty flung out her arm, catching her across the face. Raising her hand to protect herself, Lynne bumped her fresh stitches.

Well before dawn, she got up, took two pain pills, and sat in a chair, waiting for the summer heat to blast in the open window. Good thing the stage had been less than four feet above the pavement. Much higher and she might have broken a bone and be on her way home.

She took a sponge bath to avoid getting her stitches wet. "Eew. My hair feels like it's full of sand and grease. This is going to be a long week!"

Arty nodded and tossed their sweaty dance clothes in Bert's sink. "At least they only shaved off a small patch of your hair. Kinda like the haircut kids back home got when they had gum stuck in it, you know." She squeezed and twisted the clothes, hung them in Bert's open window, and wiped her hands. "I'm going out for food, toiletries, and to pick up our mail. You sleep. I'll check on our renting a room for tonight."

The August heat woke Lynne. She forced her body to move, but each twist or stretch made her wince in pain. Her arms felt as heavy as if she carried fifty-pound weights. Her intention of exercising to loosen her muscles faded; maybe dancing on the tour was slipping away.

Arty returned and tossed two pieces of mail on the hide-a-bed beside Lynne. "How do you rate? Noel didn't even get out of Paris before he wrote to you, not once, but twice."

Lynne smiled as she looked at the photo of the Eiffel Tower on the front of the postcard. She turned it over:

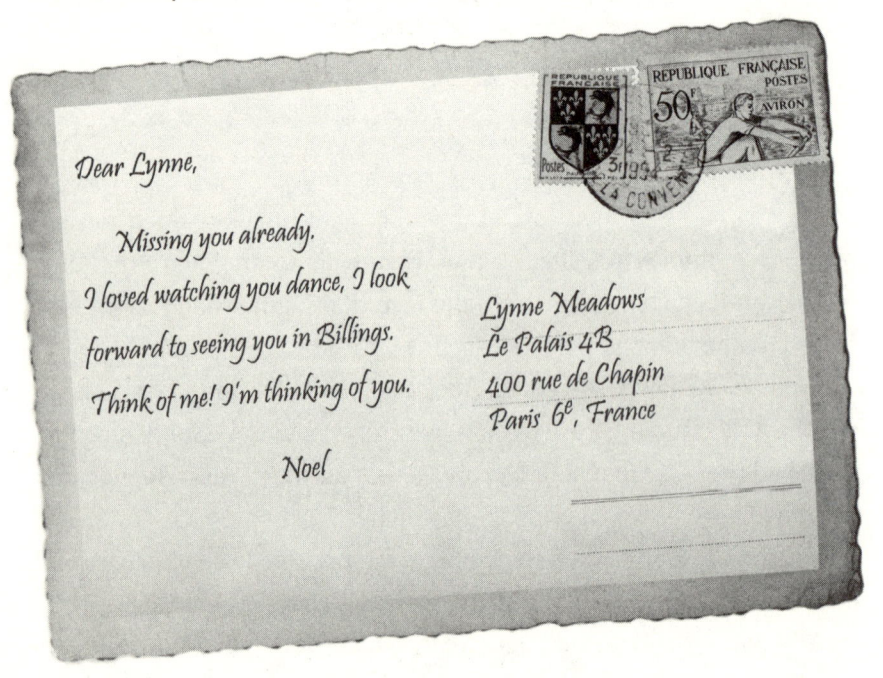

> Dear Lynne,
>
> Missing you already.
> I loved watching you dance. I look forward to seeing you in Billings. Think of me! I'm thinking of you.
>
> Noel

Lynne Meadows
Le Palais 4B
400 rue de Chapin
Paris 6ᵉ, France

"Ah-h. That's sweet. He must have written after our evening together." She opened the letter and started laughing. "Noel is such a nut! Look what he sent."

Arty leaned over Lynne's shoulder and chuckled. "Not many guys would spend fifty-cents to mail a piece of paper with the drawing of a handful of crooked hearts. Guess he wanted to be sure you knew how he felt about you. As my mom would say, he's smitten."

Lynne folded up the page and stuffed it in her purse. "Maybe. I know I am."

Wednesday morning, Arty shoved the last of her clean dance clothes into her suitcase, snapped it closed, and stood at their rented room doorway, waiting for Lynne. "Come on, we can't miss the train."

Lynne dragged herself out the door. "I wish I *could* miss the train. I'd wiggle my nose and be back home."

"Cheer up, Lynne. You'll feel better soon. It's only a month until we finish. Think about Noel waiting for you in Billings. Besides, we've got amazing sights to see. It'll be fun, you know."

Lynne shot Arty a grumpy-faced look. "Yeah. I can hardly wait. More churches, castles, markets, cobblestone streets, making nice with strangers, and dancing on odd-ball stages. Then there's Leo. You *do* remember I've scheduled an additional month with him. I'd cancel on him if I knew where he was right now."

"No, you wouldn't. That wouldn't be fair. He wouldn't walk away from you, would he?"

"At home he might. He's not too dependable. But ditching me in a foreign country would be unforgiveable."

༄

The touring and traveling days dragged when she didn't dance. To keep herself busy, she gathered post cards and hauled out the journal Noel had given her. "At least I can scribble a few lines and be grumpy all I want," she told Arty. "I'm not good at all this sitting around."

> *Fri., August 14 Bourges, France, Muggy 90°*
>
> *Stayed in a family home. Nice people. The family looks nervous having me sitting in their living room, watching the hands of the clock drag around and around. They keep trying to feed me or entertain me! I wait for the troupe performances so I can leave them in peace.*
>
> *Troupe performing 5 times, Friday to Sunday. Serenade with two dozen local dancers looked OK but lacked something besides me.*
>
> *Glad we're moving on soon!*

That Sunday on the overnight train to Lyon, Cheryl sat with Lynne. "How are you feeling?"

Lynne shrugged and exhaled. "Sore, useless."

"I thought that might be the case, so I have a job for you. I want you to act as an observer until you get your stitches out and are cleared to dance. Watch rehearsals and performances with a critical eye. Let me know what's working and what changes would improve our presentations, okay?"

"Sure. I've noticed a few places where the dancing drags."

Cheryl nodded. "Good. I need fresh eyes. Write down what you remember. Let's talk after rehearsals in Lyon."

Lynne turned to a fresh page in her journal and thought about what she'd observed.

> 1. sloppy entrances and crossings in waltzes
>
> 2. dancers complaining of being tired
>
> 3. faces look tense when dancing
>
> 4. women's arms lack extension and follow-through
>
> 5. guys' leaps are losing height and smooth transitions, especially Jando
>
> 6. Reorder the solos for a better mix of dances.

She leaned back and relaxed. It appeared she'd not be sent home like she feared. Thank heavens Cheryl looked out for her so she could continue on the tour.

༄

The train lights came on as night gave way to early morning. Before they disembarked in Lyon, Cheryl stood to speak to everyone. "Change of plans. Today is Monday, our usual day off. We'll join our local hosts and guides this morning. This afternoon, we'll have a meeting and a rehearsal."

A low groan spread through the train car.

"I know, but it can't be helped. I have concerns. Tomorrow, you have a full day off. For those of you who wish to join me, I've arranged a drive to the Alps. It's intended to inspire you."

"Are we *required* to go?" Ida said.

"No. It's optional. I'll need your decision tonight. It's a scenic drive around Annecy, then into the Alps at Chamonix, the site of the 1924 Winter Olympics. We'll return by early evening."

"I'd rather sleep than be *inspired*," Ida said in a loud whisper.

The lack of enthusiasm didn't surprise Lynne. It would be difficult for many to decide if visiting the Alps up close was worth another day on a bus. She debated what she'd do. She missed the mountains around Billings, so this trip would ease her homesickness. Maybe she'd wait to see what Arty and Lucia decided before she signed up.

The cheerful local committee met their train and boarded the private bus that drove them on a tour along the cobblestone streets. Then they took them to the breakfast room of the small hotel that had been turned into a luncheon reception complete with local food specialties and beverages. Once again, the troupe pasted on their stage smiles and chatted with local dancers and dignitaries while they ate, then headed to the added rehearsal.

༄

The dancers sat on the floor, facing Cheryl. Her usual smile was replaced by a stern set to her mouth. "You all know how special you are to me and to this tour. As emissaries of the United States, I need your best effort during *every* lesson you teach and *every* performance we share. I've asked Lynne to observe today's rehearsal and take notes. We need to find ways to repair and energize our performances."

Several dancers eyed Lynne, then moved to begin warm-ups. She sat on the sidelines and tried to look as small as possible as she made notes.

During a mid afternoon break, Cheryl and Lynne conferred before another troupe meeting. Then Cheryl shared their concerns with the group and asked for dancer input. Hands went up and ideas poured in.

"We need more rehearsal time on solos," Vera Dei said.

"Can we change the order of the program to allow us to catch our breath?" Karl asked. The rest of the guys nodded in agreement.

"Must we go on so many town tours?" Ida said. "I don't enjoy being told where to go. I'd rather explore on my own."

Nodding heads indicated consistent agreement by a majority of dancers. Lynne wrote down every idea.

Once the suggestions slowed, Cheryl spoke again. "I'm glad you're aware of what's happening. We have the rest of today and the three following days to make changes before we perform. This tour is important to me and to future troupes. I won't let us become mediocre performers. Now, get a drink of water. We'll resume practice, starting with the waltzes, and work until six tonight, then attend the banquet at seven-thirty. Yes, it's mandatory! You can rest tomorrow or choose to join me on the trip to the Alps."

At six as the dancers packed up and exited for the day, Ida cornered Lynne. "We need to talk."

"About?"

"About what you said to Cheryl. I've never received negative comments from her until today, so I imagine she's telling me what *you* said to her. What's your problem with me?"

"I didn't say a word to Cheryl. I could have, but I didn't."

Ida stepped so close Lynne saw the green flecks in her eyes. "What's *that* suppose to mean? Are you the princess of all things? Cheryl's pet? I can see how you try to butter her up."

Lynne sucked in her breath. "I haven't mentioned anything about you to Cheryl. But I'll say this. Many of us have noticed how you flap your arms like a dying duck."

Ida gasped. "Well! As for you, Miss-Know-It-All, you need to watch what you eat. Your backside is growing bigger than your mouth!" Ida grabbed her tote and marched from the practice room.

Arty leaned toward Lynne. "What bee is in her bonnet this time?"

"This time?"

"Yeah. She complains about every change in choreography to anyone who will listen, as if we have control over Cheryl's decisions."

Lynne shrugged. Engaging Ida in conversation reminded her of talking with Suzette back in Billings. In both cases she'd have a better conversation with the wall.

"So, Arty, will you join me on the trip to the mountains tomorrow? It should be a quiet break. I doubt Ida will come since she wants to wander on her own."

༄

Cheryl allowed them to choose their roommates during their three-night stay. Lynne would share the hotel room with Arty and Lucia. Thank heavens Ida would be sleeping somewhere else.

After dinner Lynne wrote post cards and entered tour comments in her journal. She'd send her last Monet post card to Mrs. B. That way she'd see it again when she returned to Billings.

Aug 17, 1959

Mrs. B.

Dancing is hectic but having a wonderful trip. Lots to see.

Love the castles and the food. Hope you've saved a room for me (mid-October).

Letter to follow if I have time.

Lynne

Marta needed to see the Chenonceau castle to remind her of their shared performance of *Sleeping Beauty*. She'd need to write as small as possible to make her thought fit.

> Marta
>   Noel came to visit and made my week! The next night I fell off a stage. I'm sidelined until I get my stitches out. I'm stiff, sore, and antsy but fine. I understand a little of how you felt when were injured.
>   Saw the Sleeping Beauty castle on this post card. More impressive in person. Wish you were here to see it.
>   Letter may follow
>   Lynne

Lynne rifled through her stash of post cards. What suited Noel? She selected a saved card of Sacre Coeur, then sat tapping her pen. She smiled as she addressed it. He'd remember their time there.

She drew an elaborate heart, added ruffles and a dangling pair of pointe shoes, but wrote no words. Then she reapplied her lipstick, kissed the card, and didn't sign it. He'd probably get ribbed about the lipstick, but it would make him smile.

That night, the exhausted dancers slipped into bed without conversations. Lynne snuggled beneath the summer-weight down comforter. She definitely needed one of these at home.

Just then, a knock on the door roused the three girls. A hotel maid turned on the light and shoved a fold-up bed into their crowded room.

She opened it, straightened the covers, and turned to speak to the person in the hall. "You come now."

The new roommate banged her bags against the beds as she settled in. "I don't see why I couldn't keep my room," she grumbled. "It wasn't my fault they gave me a single. They rousted me out of bed and brought me here to double up." She glared at the sleepy girls staring at her. "Of all the possible rooms in the hotel, I ended up with my three least favorite people in the world."

Lynne covered her head. Tonight and for two more nights, their quiet room would be shared with one of their noisiest, most inconsiderate dancers: Ida.

25

The bus to Chamonix kept the dancers glued to their windows. Wispy clouds floated across the baby blue sky, covering and uncovering the mountain peaks as if to say 'catch me if you can.' Blue-toned glaciers reminded Lynne of Monet's paintings. Maybe she'd learn to paint; it might be a good way to relax.

Stepping into the chilly mountain air, Lynne smiled and inhaled deeply. Seventy degrees felt like forty after leaving the hundred degrees of Lyon. Lucia and Arty might regret that they'd stayed behind, but she was glad they urged her to go without them.

Friday afternoon, Lynne's stitches were removed. A few snips and tugs along with quick intakes of air and she was free. Her plan: a long shower, then a talk with Cheryl. That changed when she entered her hotel room and caught Ida reading her journal.

"Can I get something for you? Maybe a different place to snoop?"

Ida smiled and tossed her the journal. "Just checking if I made your ramblings."

"I wouldn't waste ink to write anything about you. You'll never be a highlight in my life." Lynne saw Cheryl standing behind Ida and waited for Ida's next insult.

Ida put one hand on her hip and poked a finger into Lynne's shoulder. "*You* think you're so special. Cheryl treats you like her pet. That woman is crazy. I wish I'd stayed home. This is a waste of my time."

"Feel free to pack your things, Ida. We need you but not enough to put up with your nonsense. Shall I call a taxi? I'm certain you can catch a train back to Paris tonight."

Ida paled.

"Well?" Cheryl's tone left no misunderstanding of her intent. "What do you want to do?"

Ida's eyes flared. "I don't need to take this! I'm leaving!"

Cheryl watched Ida slam her clothes into her bag and storm from the room. She said nothing as she escorted the belligerent dancer down the hall. Lynne and her friends watched, closed their door, and sat in silence. A knock a few minutes later startled them.

The director stepped back into the room. "I'd appreciate if you ladies kept that conversation to yourselves. Morale is delicate right now. With Ida leaving, we'll be asking you to substitute more often. Can you help me keep things on track?" All three nodded. Cheryl excused herself.

༂

The following day, Cheryl entered the practice area wearing a stage smile. "Morning. I've toured the opera house. It has a first class stage. On a sad note, Ida had an emergency and left last night. We'll need to reorganize our two casts to cover her dances. With your help we'll carry on short-handed."

Every dancer nodded and straightened, ready for *barre* warm-ups. No one asked questions; maybe they heard Ida's loud exit.

Lynne took a deep breath and let it out slowly. She needed to return to dancing as soon as possible.

She forced a smile. Cheryl noticed the restricted turnout of her feet and the inflexibility in her hip. Not a good sign.

Serenade and the waltz practices went well. The guys shared solos. Jando made a series of turns, leaning as he landed his signature leap.

"Agh!" He toppled over and grabbed his ankle with both hands.

Every dancer stopped and looked his direction.

Cheryl hurried over. "Jando?"

He rocked from side to side; his face contorted with pain. "I landed wrong."

Jean Paul helped him out of the building and to the local hospital. When they returned late in the afternoon, everyone stopped and stared. Jando entered on crutches.

"It's a simple fracture. Three weeks or more." His voice cracked. "No... no weight." He swallowed hard and ran a hand over his face.

Cheryl bit her lip. "Let's take a break. I'll be back in a few minutes." She walked him to the other side of the room.

Panic rose in Lynne. With Ida *and* Jando out, she *had* to return as soon as possible. But knowing what she knew about how her leg felt, how could she?

The dancers stood in groups, whispering and shaking their heads. Lynne moved off by herself until Arty put her arm around her waist. "It doesn't look good for Jando, you know. I can't imagine how he's feeling."

"I can. If I can't dance my *Firebird* solo or anything rigorous, I may join him."

A few minutes later Jando and Cheryl turned back toward the group. His downcast eyes said everything. "I'm heading home. I'll miss all of you. Stay in touch." When he turned to leave, the dancers rushed to him, hugging him and wishing him well. Many turned away with tears in their eyes.

Lynne watched Cheryl walk in circles after Jando left. "It's almost three. Let's call it a day, folks. Be at the opera house at 6:30. Changes in the schedule will be posted. Lynne, stay a minute, please. Tu, please wait in the hall."

Cheryl put away their records and tapes as she spoke to Lynne. "Any pain or stiffness in your hip?"

Lynne nodded. She looked away and took a shuddering breath.

"Vera Dei will continue as your replacement. I want you as my backstage assistant, so you'll stay with the tour as you heal. Send in Tu as you leave."

Wow. Cheryl dismissed her. This wasn't the Cheryl she and the others knew and loved to please. The stress of losing two dancers and her not yet recovered had apparently taken its toll. She vowed to push herself so she could return as soon as possible.

༄

Backstage, the Lyon opera house buzzed with energy. Her fellow dancers looked tired but happy as they performed on a well-cared-for stage. Lynne struggled to hide her sadness; she'd become a stage hand instead of a dancer.

After the audience left and the last curtain closed, she strolled onto the stage and executed a slow, sweeping turn followed by a shaky *arabesque* and *balancé*. She heard clapping and turned to see Arty, Lucia and Vera Dei smiling.

"Now you can say you danced in the Lyon opera house," Lucia said.

Lynne smiled and curtsied. "I guess."

"Let's head to the after party," Vera Dei said. "I'm starving!"

The dancers stopped and stared at the stately buildings sparkling in the spotlights that accentuated their ornate exteriors. Water tumbled from a dozen urns at the center of the gigantic fountain, where a chariot drawn by four galloping horses stood guard day and night.

"I think Lyon is one of the most beautiful spots on the entire tour," Lucia said.

"I agree," Lynne said, "but mostly because of the support you're all giving me." She choked back her tears. "Thank you. I'll always remember your kindness."

༄

More days traveling, more excited guides, more town touring, more host families, more stage smiles.

"Welcome to the Burgundy region of France. Dijon is the home of the inventor of Dijon mustard. It's 85 degrees today, a bit warm, but the opera house is one of our finest attractions. Let's begin our tour there. You'll notice..."

By the last of their six performances, Lynne requested a new conversation with Cheryl on the train to Reims. "I'm ready to dance," she said. "*Serenade* will be easiest, but I feel I can also perform the waltzes."

Cheryl frowned. "Really? I'll be the judge of what I'll allow. Vera Dei and Tu are showing signs of exhaustion. I'm thinking of having them sit out performances with you."

"But you need me, don't you?"

"Yes, but not at the expense of your future career. Remember, I know Madame Cosper. If I return you broken, she'll have my hide. Now go back to your seat, rest, and make certain you're one hundred percent by the German festival."

The conversation shook Lynne. Maybe she *was* Cheryl's pet. How embarrassing. She sank down in her seat where her friends were playing Karl's game. "Your turn, Lynne," he said.

Lynne read the question aloud. "Where do I see myself in ten years?"

"Oo-oo," Lucia said. "Glad I didn't get *that* question."

Lynne bit her lip. "I'm not sure I can answer that."

Karl shook his head. "Come on. Take out a crystal ball like you gals used with the fortune teller."

Several dancers turned toward Lynne. Questions followed: "You went to a gypsy?" "Why didn't you tell us?" "What did she say?"

Lynne's shoulders tensed. Heat traveled up her neck and into her face. "It was just for fun. She didn't *tell* us things; she suggested what might happen. There was no crystal ball. She read playing cards and looked at lines on our palms."

"She predicted Lynne's boyfriend would come and that she'd have an injury," Lucia said.

Hoots and claps circled the group. Lynne slid down in her seat and turned toward the window. Why did Lucia mention the fortune teller mumbo jumbo? Knowing the troupe, they'd question and tease her about it from now until the tour ended.

26

September opened with the dancers in Reims, France, to begin their last two weeks of performing. This morning they met their guide for a short walking tour of the town. "Welcome to Reims, the town with an ancient gateway, the Porte de Mars built in 816. We also claim the invention of biscuits beginning in 1691."

A funky orange and blue car rounded the corner. The driver honked and waved to the tour guide, who waved back. "That's my friend. What do you think of his new car?"

"New?" Wallace said. "I've seen them everywhere, but I thought they were old cars."

"Nah. It's a new Deux Cheveaux. It's basic and inexpensive, but that's all you need to get around. Plus, it saves money on gas."

Lynne turned to Lucia. "I've seen them everywhere since we arrived in Paris. They remind me of wind-up tin mice like I got for Christmas when I was a child. And those headlights...they look like bug eyes."

Arty laughed. "I'd be embarrassed to own that clown car."

"I think it looks cool," Karl said. "I'd love to ride in one."

"They take tourists to the war museum and the Verdun battlefields if anyone is interested," the tour guide said.

"Count me in," Karl said. Several guys nodded approval.

After lunch the guys took off in a convoy of tiny cars while the girls wandered around the historic center before breaking into smaller groups for relaxing in sidewalk cafes or window shopping.

"I'm exhausted," Vera Dei said. "Almost too tired to window shop." She looked at Lynne and grimaced as she reached out to touch her arm. "No offense, but being your backup when you were injured was tough."

Lynne stared at Vera Dei. "I'm sorry you got pressured to be my replacement." Tears welled up. She needed to push through her pain and stiffness to give Vera Dei a rest before the remaining performances.

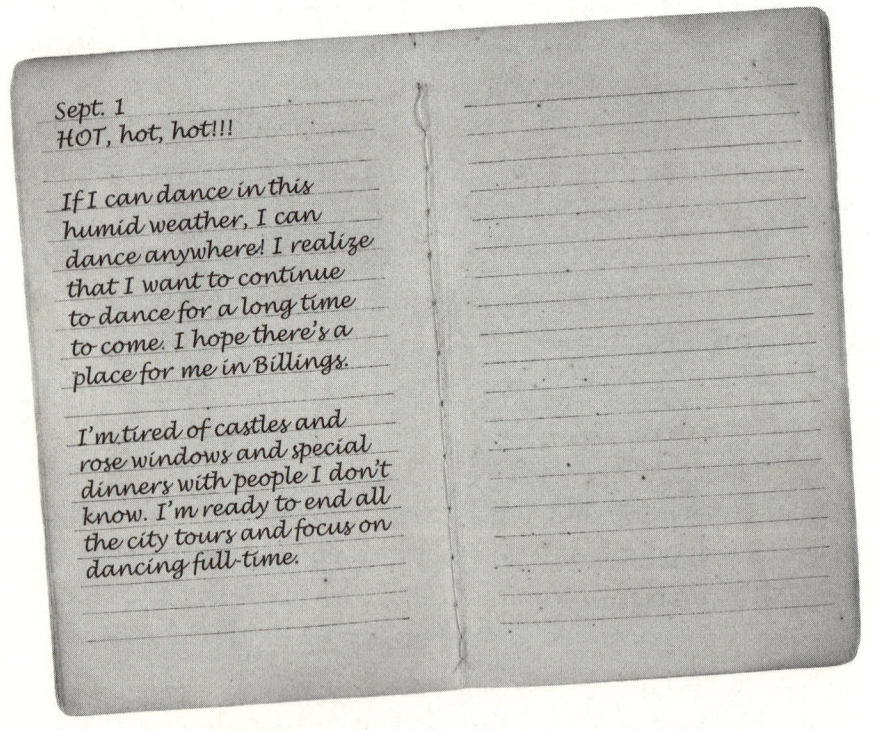

> Sept. 1
> HOT, hot, hot!!!
>
> If I can dance in this humid weather, I can dance anywhere! I realize that I want to continue to dance for a long time to come. I hope there's a place for me in Billings.
>
> I'm tired of castles and rose windows and special dinners with people I don't know. I'm ready to end all the city tours and focus on dancing full-time.

During Wednesday morning rehearsals, they ironed out smaller group dances and solos, then spent the afternoon teaching local dancers. Lynne worked with Arty leading six-, seven-, and eight-year-olds. To add a bit of fun, they handed out streamers, allowing them to create their own versions of the *Sleeping Beauty* waltz.

After the *grande reverence,* the little girls rushed to envelope them with hugs. Cheryl walked in as the students exited. "Nice job, ladies. When I stuck my head in earlier, they were laughing and excited."

"I hope it was all right that we let them be spontaneous," Arty said.

"I'd say it was a great choice. Their French instructors keep things taut. These young dancers will remember you for a long time to come."

༄

Thursday morning, they had their first glimpse of their performance space, the Theatre A L'Affiche, a lovely old building much like the small theatres in Billings but with elaborate interiors. After near-perfect performances on Friday and Saturday, they were feted with a buffet on stage.

༄

> Sept. 3   Reims
> HOT, hot, hot!!!
>
> Lovely theatre. Fancier than back home. Cheryl's getting as tired as we are.
>
> Tomorrow we head to our last stop in France. Hope the weather cools down.
>
> Yummy food and lots of guests to meet and greet..

Each person settled in to sleep, read, or talk with seatmates on the Monday morning train to Metz. Wallace passed around post cards showing old cannons, pastures that were once battlefields, and photographs of odd-looking helmets. "You girls missed a fun trip and lots of history. The war around here fifteen years ago was fierce. Whole towns were wiped out. You can still see the rubble."

"How was it riding in those tinny cars?" Vera Dei said.

"Snug," Wallace said. "I could hardly move. I had my knees pressed against my chest. Give me my big ol' Ford truck anytime."

Lynne knew about riding in snug cars. Her little Nash back home easily compared to the Deux Cheveaux. She was petite, but she looked forward to taking home a big, comfy car like Leo suggested he'd buy in Europe. And since gas was a lot cheaper back home, it wouldn't matter if her new car got fewer miles per gallon.

՞

The performance in Metz was unusual in that it began mid-week. Once again, their stage doubled as their practice area. "The magnificent Opera-Théâtre is the oldest of it's kind in France," the tour guide said. "We're proud of its long history and its elegance. Let's climb to the top tier and look down."

Lynne stared down from a box seat. The tiers surrounded and rose above the main floor audience seating. "Wow! These balconies make me feel like we should be wearing satin and lace court gowns."

Their guide laughed. "Since it was built over 200 years ago, you could have; but you'd not be able to sit in our modern plush seats with your hoops and full skirts."

"Guys were lucky," Wallace said. "They dressed a lot like us when we dance."

Karl scowled. "But they wore it *every* day. You think you'd enjoy wearing wigs, flouncy shirts, heavy brocade jackets, and heeled shoes on dates, driving around, *every* day? You're nuts!" He threw up his arms and walked into the corridor.

Wallace shouted after him. "What I meant was that maybe what we wear is intended to honor the fashion from the time ballet started."

The group on the tour stared in silence, then made their way down and onto the stage to prepare for their warm-ups.

> Sept. 7   Metz
>
> Cooler today, maybe 80
>
> Lovely performance hall. Wallace and Karl are best friends, but they're starting to argue over stupid things. It's good we're near the end of the tour.
>
> Tomorrow we have the day off. I plan to take the group walking tour and then go off on my own. I love this town!

After the optional group walking tour, Lynne returned to the market. She bought fresh fruit from a farm stall and took it to sit near the river and write a letter.

Sept. 8th

Dear Noel,

Maybe it's the canal or the rivers or the chance to wander alone, or all of them. I love Metz. It's golden buildings remind me of the fields around Billings. (I'm homesick!)

The ancient town started on an island, but now it surrounds canals and two rivers. It reminds me of Paris without the crush of tourists. Saint Stephens Cathedral claims France's largest stained glass windows. Yep. More windows!

My favorite place was the covered market with fresh food and crafts. I shopped and watched people shopping. Metz has lots of fountains with giant maidens holding their never empty pots of water. I was tempted to cool off by putting my feet in one when no one was looking, but I resisted.

I saw a section of a Roman aqueduct. Those Romans were everywhere! I'm surprised they didn't cross the Atlantic and build in the New World before anyone else got there.

Someday, I want to return to Metz, but right now, I wish I could sail or float home. Only 32 days until I get back to Billings.

Missing you.
Lynne, of course!

Their performances went without incident, especially "Clair de Lune," *An American in Paris*, and the solos. All received thunderous applause for the dancers and Cheryl. The last evening when the mayor of Metz stepped onto the stage, the audience quieted. A translator joined him.

"It is my distinct pleasure to present Miss Cheryl Menkins with the key to the city. We invite her, along with her young American dancers, to return to teach and perform whenever possible."

The audience stood to applaud; the dancers joined them

When the curtain closed for the last time, hugs from the dancers encircled Cheryl.

"Thanks, guys, this means a lot." She wiped away tears, then shooed them to the foyer to mingle with audience members and city officials.

Lynne stood to one side, watching the interactions. She felt a tap on her hand and looked down. A young girl smiled up at her. "You sign, *oui*?" The tiny, bun-headed dancer handed Lynne a program and a pen. Lynne nodded, wrote a short note, and signed her name with a flourish. The young girl curtsied and walked to another dancer.

Sept. 11th
Cooled today to 80

Our French performances ended last night. Everyone feels relieved. We're more than ready to head back to Paris.

Truth be told, I'm beginning to see the intoxication of being a prima ballerina. I could get used to plum roles, dancing with famous partners, and traveling to perform in other cities with all expenses paid. Being the princess of all things might be worth the effort. I need to get healthy, practice until I collapse, and learn to keep my thoughts to myself if I want to make it happen.

a five-hour trip and the last stop on their tour. After their arrival, Lynne stared out the bus window as they drove through town to their hotel. Many thoroughfare intersections sported streamers and banners: Willkomen, Bienvenue, Welkom, Velkomst, Fàilte Välkomna, Benwenuto, and Welcome. Shop windows invited everyone to stop and admire their displays and tribute to the waltz festival.

"Now this is more like it," Karl said. "A little appreciation for what we do. About time, I'd say."

"This festival is a huge deal," Cheryl said. "It's beginning its fiftieth year. People travel from great distances, much like Americans flock to sporting events."

"Wish they'd flock to see us dance back home, you know," Arty said.

"Maybe someday," Cheryl said. "But don't hold your breath."

Their hotel welcomed them with complementary floral arrangements and fruit baskets in their rooms. After a quick freshening up, the dancers were whisked away to a local school, followed by a visit to a dance studio to meet with locals and photographers. Frankfurt vibrated with festive eagerness.

Each day of rehearsals ended with banquets and mingling with a host of international dance groups. During Friday evening's performance, the German Chancellor, his cabinet, and their families would attend. Their city guide pointed out the government seal that hung prominently in front of the Chancellor's box in the center of the first balcony.

"That's as close as we'll get to royalty." Karl said.

꼬

Lynne and Wallace stood at the back of one wide aisle, awaiting their special entrance for Khachaturian's "Masquerade Waltz."

"How do you feel, Lynne?" he whispered.

"Like I swallowed a bag of Mexican jumping beans. How about you?"

Wallace rubbed his hands on his tights. "My hands are slippery with sweat. Do you think the audience will like this entrance?"

"Others liked our surprise of entering along the aisles. I just worry about the live orchestra remembering to play the opening section twice so we have time to step onto the stage gracefully."

"I want you to know I've enjoyed partnering with you, even though I started out squeezing you like toothpaste."

"I remember. If you ever want to move to another company, you should apply to the Intermountain in Billings. The girls would like dancing with you."

"Really? I might do that if Arty's company doesn't have openings."

"You two are cute together. I hope it works out, Wallace, but keep Billings in mind."

The waltz before them ended. Wallace straightened as he took Lynne's hand in his. On cue, they both smiled. He pulled her into their first waltzing turn down the aisle as other American dancers entered down other aisles as well as across the stage.

Lynne let the sweeping turns seep into her dancing. Her energy rose with every special flourish, elevating her moves to near-perfection.

After the performance, the dancers remained backstage to mingle with the other groups. Lynne reappeared and sauntered over to stand with Lucia.

"Where have you been? We're about ready to board the bus."

Lynne pursed her lips as she handed Lucia several used programs. "Collecting. Take a few of the programs I found. We danced for the Chancellor of Germany! I doubt any of us will dance for such a prestigious guest anytime soon."

By special request, the American troupe performed an additional Sunday afternoon program in a medium-size performance hall. The requested program included *Serenade, Rodeo's* "Hoedown," Damien's *An American in Paris,* and their showiest solos, including Lynne's "Firebird."

"Okay, dancers," Cheryl said with a sly smile on her face. "We've got a sellout crowd from a tiny mention in the festival flyer. It's not the giant performance center or for bigwigs, but we sold eight hundred tickets. We've danced far beyond our projected fifty performances in eighty days. I know you're tired, but let's give them our best."

After the last curtain closed, photographers took group shots of them, asking for poses in their various dance costumes. The local ex-pat newspaper promised to print an article on Cheryl and the tour as well as the special performance.

Lynne wrapped her knees as soon as the media people left. The excessive number of performances took a toll on her body and her energy. She'd finished the tour with Cheryl's help. The ones who'd danced every performance without complaining were her new dance heroes. She'd need to build her stamina as well as figure a way to handle her ongoing problems with Madame Cosper. But today, and for the next month, she'd relax and enjoy a leisurely tour with Leo. Once back in Billings, she'd take back her career.

Before heading to bed, she packed for their morning train back to Paris. Her bags were filled to capacity with little purchases and gifts for friends as well as programs and flyers from across their tour. After her stop in Paris, she'd stow her dance bag in Leo's car, her car, until she caught the ship back home. No more dragging two bags in and out of homes and hotels. Everything would settle down, become easier.

Sept. 13   75° all week
Frankfurt, Germany

No touring, just dancing. Long days but we were treated like royalty; performed for dignitaries as well as visitors and locals.

Cheryl looked relieved that we made it. I fell in love once again with ballet. This time, forever.

27

As the train headed toward Paris, Cheryl stood to share details one last time. Karl spoke before she had a chance. "Three cheers for Cheryl, our fearless choreographer and instigator!"

Cheryl blushed and curtsied when the dancers stood, cheered, and clapped. "We did it, didn't we? You've been great. I'd take you with me again if I could. Now, get some well-deserved rest."

Lynne sighed. They'd met and exceeded their obligations, overcome obstacles, and experienced more challenges than they dreamed possible. Sure, they'd *say* they'd stay in contact, but would they really? She doubted it as she focused on writing to her friends.

> Mrs. B.,
>
> Photo shows Frankfurt the end of a wonderful but exhausting experience!
>
> I'm crossing my fingers you've saved a room for me.
>
> Lynne

> Dear Marta,
>
> The photo shows our last stop, Frankfurt's massive waltz festival. Every bone and muscle in my body aches more than any Nutcracker tour you and I shared. I'm tired but glad I made the trip.
>
> We're heading back to Paris. I'll try to send post cards on vacation with Leo. Probably no letter to follow.
>
> Lynne

Next, she opened her blue aerogram paper and reread what she wrote last week:

> Sept. 7
>
> Dear Noel,
>
> Still thinking about Metz. Typical old town but with charm I'll always remember. It takes third place after Paris and our day trip to the Alps.
>
> 1 rehearsal, 3 performances, and a train trip to the waltz festival in Frankfurt. I feel like a horse ready to turn back to the barn and race home. My feet need a break!

She clicked her pen over and over as she thought of what she'd add to the letter. Should she tell him how much she missed him? What if he no longer missed her, or worse, if he'd moved on? Best to keep her comments casual, just in case.

> Sept. 14
>
> Dear Noel,
>
> I'm back! Frankfurt was a hectic, massive festival. Danced mostly waltzes. My blisters appreciate a rest from pointe shoes.
>
> Arty is leaving for Italy in two days. We vowed to stay in contact. After this experience, I know I want to dance until my body gives up. I hope Intermountain Ballet Company wants me back.
>
> One month until I return to Billings. I'm excited to visit French, Spanish, and Portuguese villages. Don't expect many more post cards or letters. I'll carry them home and share their stories in person. I hope you'll remember me until then.
>
> Getting my new European car. Don't know what it will be, but I'll look so classy you may not recognize me!
>
> Anxious to find letters from you waiting for me in Paris.
>
> Thinking of you!
> Lynne

She sealed the letter and leaned back to rest until the Paris skyline came into view. Everyone bustled around, chattering as they assembled their belongings. She'd come full circle. Mission completed.

Cheryl stood and clapped for their attention. "Meet me at the practice rooms tonight at eight o'clock. Feel free to dress up; It's time to celebrate a fantastic trip!"

☙

Arty and Lynne returned to Le Palais, where they'd booked one night in a tourist room on the second floor. The room was basic: twin beds, a dresser, and one chair. Arty flopped down on one bed and closed her eyes. She yawned. "I'm so ready to go home. I wish I hadn't over-planned. Wake me in time to get ready for tonight."

Lynne nodded. "I over-planned too. Uncle Leo told me he'd be here the day after our return from the tour—that's tomorrow—to start our month-long adventure. I want to go home to Billings. Maybe I can talk him into shortening it."

☙

Laughter spilled out of the practice rooms, and the girls found their dancer friends dressed in party clothes. They'd seen everyone's outfits before, but tonight their faces sparkled as brightly as their clothes. Lynne laughed when she saw Karl in a Scottish kilt with a blue shirt and knee-high green stockings. He was the center of attention, his favorite place.

Caterers carried in platters of finger food: cheese and bread trays and artistically cut veggies. Two buffet tables held covered warming trays. A tall cone of cream puffs decorated with edible flowers and swirls of thin, lattice icing sat on a small, round table. Each table had a rose-colored linen cloth and a bouquet of white roses.

"Wow!" Lynne said. "Cheryl went all out. Arty, take pictures for me."

Arty began snapping photos of the room, the dancers, and Cheryl. "She's really something, you know. I'd love to be her assistant."

"Ask her. Maybe Jean Paul is ready to move on. Your French has really improved."

Arty stared at Lynne. "Do you really think. Maybe I *will* ask her."

Dinner was served amid laughter and jokes. When the meal ended, the dancers helped clear away the food platters and dishes. Servers returned with bowls of ice cream topped with chocolate sauce and whipped cream, then invited all to dismantle the cream puff tower.

Once everyone was seated again, Cheryl stood and tapped her water glass. "This has been a magical group and a magical trip. Even though we lost Jando and Ida, had injuries, and suffered a bus breakdown, you've stayed surprisingly healthy and engaged. Your dedication and your skill level gave me great confidence that my selecting each of you was the right choice. Thank you from the bottom of my heart."

"And from the bottom of our worn out shoes," Karl shouted.

Everyone laughed and applauded.

"I have good news and great news. First, Jando expects a full recovery. Second, the international dance art sponsors will continue to fund this project for at least two more summers."

More cheers and applause filled the room.

"Best of all is my great news. We came in under our projected budget. That means your bonuses will be slightly larger than anticipated."

More applause erupted. The dancers stood to honor Cheryl and their good fortune.

"If anyone needs help arranging their trip home, contact me. I'll be in Paris for another week. I wish I could invite you back a second summer, but the rules are clear: no repeats. We want to spread this opportunity to as many dancers as possible. I'm certain your experiences in France will enhance your positions in your dance companies."

She wiped away a tear that slid down her face. "I appreciate each and every one of you."

Before Cheryl could sit down, Karl stood and walked toward her. "We have a presentation to share with you, Cheryl, so sit back and let us be in charge."

Small groups stepped forward and shared jibes at themselves and others: mangled suitcases, scheduling errors, mismatched costumes, waltz garlands tangled together, and racing for trains. They hinted at troupe romances, dancers eating too much, and fortune teller predictions, all in good fun.

When the tributes and jokes ended, Karl stood again. "We want to thank you for working us beyond the last ounce of our endurance and providing endless train rides, strange meals, and mind-staggering hours of dancing." He handed her a large box with a huge black bow.

Cheryl opened the box and started laughing as she drew out a handful of broken pointe shoes, holey tights, and dingy towels. "What on earth am I suppose to do with these?"

"Maybe your next group will need a few spares," he said.

"Frame them," shouted Wallace.

Cheryl laughed with the dancers.

Karl handed her one last gift. "Maybe this is a better souvenir." She opened the present: a framed group photo signed by each dancer.

Everyone stood and clapped. Many wiped away tears.

"When was this taken? I don't remember doing this."

Karl pointed to Wallace. "That first week we met for rehearsals, Wallace asked a photographer from where he was staying to take it. We hope you'll remember us; we'll always remember you and our experience."

Last-minute good-byes brought more tears. Lucia grabbed Lynne. "I'm so glad we met. I enjoyed our time together on the ship. I promise I'll write, and you promised you'd write too."

Lynne tightened her arms around Lucia. "I will! Good luck in Italy and the rest of your time in Europe."

Vera Dei hugged her next. "I hope you will enjoy a long career. Come visit me in Florida. I promise no gypsy fortune telling."

Lynne wiped aside another tear and laughed. "Or come visit me. I'll show you our mountains and prairies."

Karl and Wallace hung back, waiting for Lynne and Arty to finish hugging their friends.

"You two are the crying-est pair," Karl said. "You'd think we'll never see each other again."

"I doubt we will." More tears streamed down Lynne's face. "We say we'll stay in touch, but I don't think it will happen."

"I, for one, will see Arty," Wallace said. "We've made plans to meet during our winter break, right Arty?"

She nodded and blushed.

"You never know," Karl said. "Once I become a soloist, I plan to visit your dance companies and demand you be my partner for my *pas de deux*." He executed a deep bow.

The guys hugged Lynne and Arty, then shoved each other out of the way as they left, looking back to be certain the girls followed their antics.

Cheryl put her arms around both girls. "This is good-bye. I'm so glad to have met and worked with you. You're both amazing dancers and leaders. Arty, I'd love to have you as my assistant when Jean Paul moves on, so make sure I have a current address for you. Lynne, don't let Madame Cosper's brusqueness defeat you. She knows you're talented; she'll find a place for you with Intermountain."

As they left the practice room, a hollowness built up inside Lynne. "I can't believe it's over. I doubt we'll ever duplicate the family feeling of this group."

"I know," Arty said. "This summer already seems like a dream." She sat down on the entry steps. "Let's open our bonus envelopes. Maybe that will cheer us up."

The girls ripped into their envelopes. Arty laughed. "Wow! This is enough money to splurge a little. I'm going shopping first thing tomorrow!"

Lynne smiled. The bonus would help stretch her finances through her re-audition back home. But money took second place to the memory of living and dancing the summer troupe experience.

༄

The next morning, Lynne wandered off alone to sort through her feelings. She strolled through the bookstore, bought a book that contained photos of Monet paintings, and relived memories of her time in his garden through its pages. She also bought a ballet figurine that reminded her of Arty *en pointe* with her arms reaching skyward.

Before returning to the apartment, she made one final trek to the American Embassy to gather the mail. During the heat of summer, she'd have stopped on a park bench to read it. Today, the brisk wind and threat of rain sent her inside Le Palais instead.

Marta's letter said Steve found her a small apartment near her future dance studio job and his small house. She'd move in over winter break and live there until they got married next June. The dance studio had a great new ballet teacher, and the financial partnership with her women's group was a perfect fit.

Noel's two letters updated her on the summer camp and his financing for the kids' campsite, thanks to her suggestion. He reminded her several times that he missed her and ended each letter with strings of x's and o's, saying he longed for the real thing when she returned.

༄

Saying good-by to Arty at noon brought more tears.

"I promise to write, you know. We can't let our friendship end after all this time together. Maybe we can visit each other during breaks." Arty picked up her suitcases.

"I'll make it a priority. Send me your ballet programs. I'll expect to see you using your proper name, Artemesia. It suits you."

The door closed. Lynne stared at it, then sat in the lounge to wait for Leo. She thought of the troupe. Why was this experience different than back home, where she'd isolated herself from the *corps* dancers? Was it too late to build new connections so she wasn't seen in the same light as Suzette or Ida? She'd find a way to change.

After tucking away a few last minute purchases, she reread the letters from home. In all those weeks away, across an ocean and in a foreign country, her folks hadn't sent a single post card or letter. Had they been too busy? Did they write off her trip as her being selfish and not supporting the family? Should she spend part of her bonus and call home? No. Trenton was no longer 'home.' She'd let Leo fill them in. He'd probably hold court at another buffet her mom would provide for his friends.

Her thoughts flashed back to the fortune teller. The gypsy got some things right, the accident and Noel's unexpected visit. Thank goodness she hadn't experienced the predicted setbacks.

She checked the clock in the lounge. Two-thirty. Leo was late. She began pacing the entry. By seven that evening when he hadn't shown up, Madame sat down beside her and patted her hand. "You waiting more, yes?"

"Yes. I don't know where he could be."

Madame shook her head and signaled for Lynne to follow her into the dining room. She handed her tablecloths and gestured for her to spread them onto the tables. *"Si vous m'aidez vous pourrez rester pour le dîner?"*

"*Oui, merci.*" Lynne prepared the tables. It appeared she'd earn dinner before Leo arrived. Unfortunately, the tourist rooms were full, so she'd have no place to sleep. If she left to find a room elsewhere, how would Leo find her? Perhaps she could sleep in the lounge after everyone headed upstairs.

ତ

The sofa in the lounge was long enough for her to stretch out, but she felt as if she'd slept on a lumpy pile of dirty clothes. By six the next morning, when the tenants gathered for breakfast, Madame invited her to join in, after which Lynne helped clean up.

Morning turned to afternoon. What if he never came? Anger began to replace her worry. Had he forgotten about her or decided to let her fend for herself? Her bonus wouldn't cover the cost of the ship.

When the doorbell rang, Madame Zelb hurried to answer. Her uncle's excited voice filled the entry. "I'm Leo Turner. I've come to fetch my niece, Lynne Meadows."

Madame leaned against the open door, her voice almost cooing as she smoothed her hair and spoke to Leo in a sultry mix of English and French as Lynne walked up.

"Uncle Leo! Where have you been? You were coming yesterday."

"Ah, Lynnie. It's vacation. I'm here, aren't I? What's the rush?" He stepped inside and turned to Madame. "I'm sure this lovely woman took excellent care of you."

Madame preened and smiled. "Of course, *Monsieur* Turner."

He bowed and kissed her extended hand. "I'm Leo to my friends, but you may call me 'charmed to meet you,' Madame."

Lynne picked up her suitcases and started for the door.

Leo stopped her. "What's the rush, Lynnie? Let's take this beautiful lady to coffee before we leave."

Madame smiled and raised her hand to suggest she'd be right back. She returned wearing an exquisite shawl. "Ready?" she said in near-perfect English. She led them out the door and down the block.

Lynne stashed her bags in the lounge and caught up to them just as Leo held the chair for Madame and sat next to her. Lynne pulled a chair from the nearby table and sat down to watch him converse in the only language he spoke: English.

No worries. Most of the conversation between them involved sly smiles and hand touching. Lynne turned away to watch passersby. She had to give him credit; no matter where he went, he knew how to flatter a woman without speaking her language.

An hour later, Madame stood and extended her hand to Leo. He leaped to his feet, kissed it, and waved as she left. Lynne followed her back to Le Palais, grabbed her suitcases, and said goodbye.

When she reached the sidewalk, Leo stood beside a new, powder-blue BMW. She nearly cried. Wait until Jer saw this! He'd *finally* stop teasing her.

She stepped into the street, waiting for him to open the trunk. He didn't. "Uncle Leo? The trunk? We need to get moving to miss the afternoon traffic."

His brow furrowed. He began backing down the block.

"Uncle Leo?"

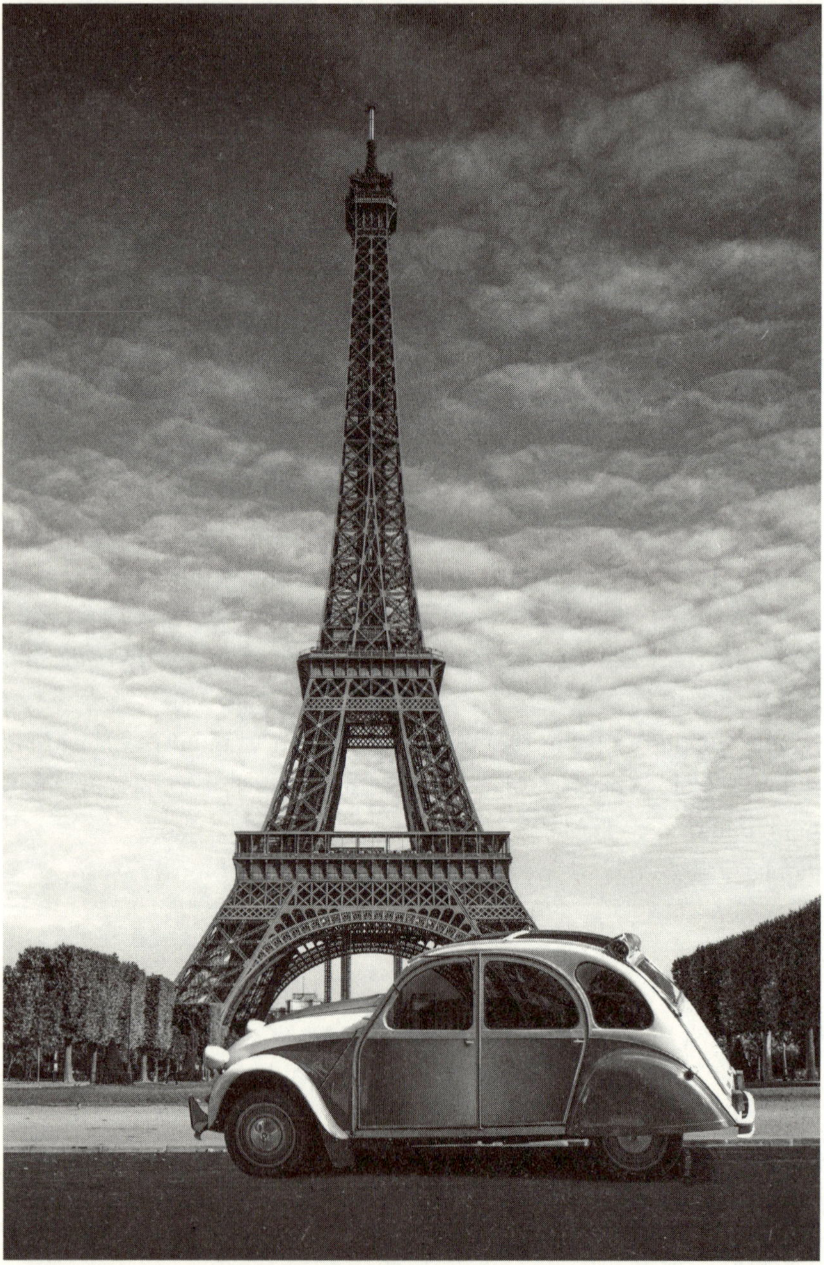

28

Leo stepped to the side of a tinny Deux Cheveaux and smiled. "What do you think? Cute, huh? I got it for next to nothing. They say it gets sixty miles to the gallon, so it will save us *tons* of money for play time."

Lynne let her suitcases drop to the sidewalk. Her mouth fell open. What had he done? Her excitement faded as she walked around the car. Shaped like a poor cousin to a Volkswagen bug, it was one of those ridiculous little cars the boys rode in on the dance tour, with odd-shaped windows and an orange and yellow paint job. It screamed clown car, especially the bug-eyed headlights.

"I thought you were getting a BMW or a Porsche. What happened?"

"Money. This little beauty is used and only cost five hundred American dollars. It's a stick shift, so we'll get better mileage. With a bargain car like this, we can afford to fly home."

"*You* drove it here?"

Leo laughed. "No. I paid my new friend, Frank, to do that. He's waiting to drive us out of Paris traffic." He waved to a middle-aged man sitting on a nearby bench. Frank nodded and extinguished his cigarette. "Once we get out of heavy traffic, he'll give you a driving lesson. Looks simple enough. Your friends will be excited to see you driving this around town. It's a real eye-catcher."

Lynne stared at Leo. Eye catcher? More like a laugh catcher.

He opened the orange-painted trunk, then reached for her bags. "Shall we get moving? After your driving lesson, we'll need to skedaddle and find a place for tonight."

The tiny trunk was empty.

"Where are your bags?"

"In the back seat."

Lynne nodded but stayed rooted to the sidewalk.

"Come on. Shake a leg, Lynnie. Times a wastin'. Hop in the back."

As she opened the back door, her foot slid across something soft and slippery. Great. Another completed cycle. Her first and her last souvenir from a Paris sidewalk—dog poop.

She sat on the edge of the sidewalk to scrape off her shoe. Frank's and Leo's noses crinkled as they watched and waited for her to finish.

After rearranging Leo's pile of bags, she shoved her way into the back seat, then looked for a handle. "How do I open the window?"

"Back seat windows don't open. But check out mine." Leo pushed the base out and shoved it up against the top one half of the window, where it was held in place by a special clip. "Clever, huh?"

She didn't comment.

Frank started the car and pulled the knob on the thin metal shaft to put the car in gear. He pulled into traffic.

Honk! Honk! Honk!

Frank shoved his hand out his open window and gestured to the irritated driver, who'd stopped almost against the rear bumper, then drove on. The engine sounded like a motorcycle in low gear and blocked any conversation between the back and front seats.

After long minutes of dodging cars and driving through narrow streets, they reached the outskirts of Paris. Frank stopped on a wide shoulder and signaled for Lynne to take his place. He took Leo's seat.

Gestures became the language for the driving lesson. Frank fiddled with each of the instruments on the dashboard and adjusted the gearshift. *"Une, deux, trois, quatre. Comprende?"*

Lynne nodded and started the car. She jerked her hand off the gear shift when she heard loud, grinding sounds. "Oops." She tried again. The car jumped forward and died.

The third time, she felt a change in the tinny vibrations. The car crept forward. She released the clutch; the car bounced down the street.

"Magnifique!" Frank motioned for her to stop and let him out. He waved to a car behind them and hurried to climb in the passenger seat. The car turned back toward Paris and shot away.

Stunned at being left to figure out the toy car on her own, she watched Leo climb back in the front seat, close his eyes, and appear to take a nap.

For the next few minutes, she practiced shifting gears. Sweat ran down her sides as she fumbled with the odd gearshift and drove at a snail's pace down side streets. When they came to a dead end, she ground the gears until she found reverse, turned the car around, and shut off the engine to rest.

Leo sat up. He checked his watch. "It's getting late. We need to get a move on."

Lynne bit her lip to keep from saying what was on her mind. A sign to a secondary road hung on a nearby corner, directing them away from Paris. She held the steering wheel in a death grip and turned. Next stop, somewhere northwest of Paris, assuming they found more route signs.

Saturday afternoon traffic was light since they'd left the city. At Evreux they stopped for gas and took the time to roll back the roof.

Leo laughed. "I like this little car. With a little work we can make it air conditioned."

The 'little work' meant they stood on either side of the car, released the canopy latches, and rolled it back like a jelly roll without the delicious filling.

Leo bounced in his seat. "How do you like these springs? Comfy, huh, for a stick shift? Remember, it has four gears. You can shift up when you get to thirty."

Lynne bit her lip again. It wouldn't do any good to remind him she drove stick shifts all the time, just not a Deux Cheveaux. She settled in, listening to the wind-up-toy sound of the engine and Leo jabbering about his adventures and his marvelous car find. Only time would tell if the car was worthy of being a member of the Citroen family.

"Is this car legal in the states? It's got an exposed drive column and the windows fold open. Aren't there standards a car needs to meet at home?"

Leo laughed. "It will be fine. I have a friend who can make any modifications we'll need."

"We? You said the car would be mine."

"I did? Hm-m. I thought we could share it when we get back to Jersey."

Lynne slowed and pulled onto the shoulder of the roadway, causing those following her to honk and gesture. "Uncle Leo, I'm not going back to Jersey. I'm returning to Billings. How can we share the car?"

"I guess that won't work, will it? In that case, I'll keep it. You can drive it when we both visit your parents." Leo leaned back and closed his eyes. "Don't worry, we'll get it worked out."

Her grip on the wheel tightened. She counted to ten several times, waiting for her anger to seep away. He'd purchased her ticket on the ship and arranged for the practice room, so she tried to be grateful. At least she wouldn't be driving this misfit car once she got home; she'd be driving her turquoise Nash, a misfit she knew and now missed.

Leo faced the sunshine and snored as if everything moved in perfect order. She shoved down her frustration, put the car into gear, and got back on the road. She should have known he'd find a way to weasel out of his commitment. One day very soon, she'd need to talk with him.

∽

They found an inexpensive bed and breakfast along D-12 near the village of Ryes. The owners had created a tiny cafe with three tables and a small bar. Tonight's *plat de jour*: a salmon quiche and garden salad with a *brioche* roll.

As they waited for their food to arrive, they discussed destinations. They agreed on the French Atlantic coastline. After that, Lynne wanted to explore Portugal and Spain as they'd already planned. Leo suggested they visit the Mediterranean side of Italy first, where they could meet up with his new friends near Florence and spend a week or two with them before driving north to the Germany beer and wine festivals.

"I'm doing all the driving. I should have some say. We need to stick to our original plan, or you can let me out right now."

"Keep your voice down, Lynnie. People are looking at us." Leo ran his hand through his thinning hair and sighed. "Alright. We'll follow our original itinerary, but I plan to enjoy those beer festivals next month, with or without you."

By the time they'd eaten, they'd ironed out their route through Spain and Portugal. Score one for her. Time would tell whether he was more reasonable than she'd given him credit for.

Out her window she saw a lighted path that led to a lawn swing. Grabbing her jacket, she walked out to sit and think for a few minutes. Random images and conversations with her parents, Noel, Marta, Jer, Aunt Vivian, Cheryl, and Madame Cosper floated past. Some brought smiles; others made her frown. So many people she wanted to please; so many mistakes she'd made with each of them.

She stood so suddenly the swing hit the backs of her knees. Why was she worrying about the past? She needed to look forward, change what she could, and live with the rest. Hopefully, Leo would change as well.

～

The next morning, she pulled onto a gravel roadway and stopped. The sudden clattering of rocks on the undercarriage of the car roused Leo. "Where are we?"

"At the Omaha Beach Cemetery. Let's look around. I've heard we'll still be able to see signs of the World War II landing."

Gentle waves rolled onto the Atlantic shoreline. Leftover landing craft from fifteen years ago lay half buried in the golden sand. Neither of them spoke for several moments.

"The world went mad in the 1940s," Leo finally said. "The battles along these beaches were horrible." They stared at row after row of white crosses. "We thought, we hoped, it would be the last war. But trouble around the world just keeps coming."

They walked to the edge of the bluff. "Were you in the war, Uncle Leo?"

"Oh, no. I was well past the draft age. My best friend, Owen, lost his son on this beach. He'd named the boy after both of us. Leo Owen planned to go into business with his dad and me after the war. The three of us were going to open a car dealership with a first class service department. The boy was a crackerjack mechanic, his dad was a great finance man, and I thought I could sell a car to anyone walking in the door. When the boy died here, Owen and I didn't have the heart to do it without him." He sniffed and looked away.

"I'm sorry."

He turned back toward the car. "Let's head on. We've got a lot of places to visit."

The low tide at Mont St. Michel allowed them access to the island. Lynne felt a calm spread through her as they climbed the steps and entered the small town that surrounded the crowning jewel of the island, the abbey.

"This is a perfect slice of French history," she said. "A small town, a church, ramparts, and a market place gathered onto one small island."

Leo laughed. "You sound like a tour guide."

"I met enough of them to be one. We visited lots of places with lots of rose windows and ancient history, but this place beats them all." She took a deep breath. "Let's walk around the walls. Just so you know, I plan to dance along the beach and get sand between my toes before we leave."

After an hour on the beach, the tide began to return. They headed south, driving through Rennes, then on to Nantes for a last glimpse of the Loire River where it flowed into the Atlantic Ocean. Afterward, they bought picnic supplies and pulled off the roadway to eat before continuing on to Bordeaux.

Their overnight lodging took them to a rustic hotel near downtown. It included two small rooms, a bathroom down the hall, and dinner at a tiny cafe serving quiches, salads, and carafes of *vin ordinaire*, inexpensive wines from local wineries.

Leo consumed every drop of the wine while she drank water. The more he drank, the chattier he became. He stayed behind to visit with English tourists while she headed to bed. At three times her age, he had more energy than she did. Maybe if she napped like he did, she'd be able to keep up with him.

A sharp rap on her room door startled her. "Who is it?"

"It's Leo. Let me in for a minute."

She glanced at the clock. "What's wrong?"

"Nothing. I want to tell you what I found out after you left."

"Right now? It's one in the morning."

"Let me in, Lynnie. It's important." She opened the door and staggered back to bed. He plopped down in the room's single chair. His animated talking wiped away any sleep she'd gotten.

"There's a wine fest at St. Emilion, a short distance up the river. The town's ancient, with lots of ruins and an old church that's not to be missed. You can explore them while I do the wine tour. Wake me at nine. We'll eat breakfast, then caravan the twenty miles with my new friends."

"Okay." She yawned and let him out. She'd agreed to a change in plans so she could get some sleep. In the morning they'd need to talk about his promise that they'd decide on changes *together*.

29

Their side trip followed the Dordogne River for several miles, then veered north to St. Emilion. When the caravan stopped, Leo jumped from the car and waved as he hurried to join his new friends. "Back in a couple of hours," he called out over his shoulder.

She watched him disappear into a small bus filled with yapping tourists on their way to a wine tasting. A pop of smoke filled the air, followed by a rattling engine as the bus chugged away. Her temper rose faster than an oven on broil. Since he'd slept the entire drive, there'd been no opportunity to talk about what she'd do or where they'd meet or how far they'd travel tonight. Now she stood in a tiny village surrounded by vineyards and weathered walls with hours of free time and no idea of where to venture.

When Leo returned late that afternoon, they drove south to Dax, a small town where they found no vacancies. Continuing on as dusk approached, they located a small inn that provided beds and breakfasts but no evening meals.

Leo rubbed his hands together. "I'm hungry, what say we drive on to Biarritz to eat and gamble for a few hours?"

Lynne shook her head. "The only way I'm getting back on the road is to drive to San Sebastian. And I'm not giving you driving lessons tonight."

Leo shrugged and left. She thought he'd gone to his room, but the next morning as she ate breakfast, he strolled in with two strangers in tow. "Mornin', Lynnie. Boy, you missed a great evening, right, Phyllis?"

The woman nodded and giggled like a teenager. "I'll say. Leo won big! Show her your wad of bills."

Leo's wallet bulged with money and barely fit in his jacket pocket. "Can't even get this in my pants." He laughed. "Might need a purse to hold my winnings."

The man with her reached out to take her hand. "Come on, hon. We need to get back to our hotel." He offered Leo his hand. "Nice to have met you. See you on the Portuguese beaches?"

"That's the plan. Lynnie and I will be there in about a week, give or take a few days. I've got your address here." He patted another jacket pocket.

Leo sat down as the hostess brought him a breakfast plate and coffee. "Nice folks. Met them while I was walking into town, looking for a taxi. Saved a bundle hitching a ride with them. Only cost me a couple of drinks."

She watched him attack his food. It appeared he'd not eaten dinner. "Will you be ready to go in an hour or so?"

He checked his watch and took a long swig of coffee. "Give me two hours to catch a nap. I'll meet you down here at eleven-thirty."

She wandered the tiny town and returned to their inn by noon. When she didn't see Leo in the entry, she went to his room and knocked. "Hey! Uncle Leo? Time to get going."

He stuck his head out the door. "Give me ten minutes." Slam.

Lynne felt her patience unravel. Their afternoon drive would provide plenty of time to give him a chunk of her anger. She had no intention of letting this turn into his playtime in Europe.

After they loaded up the car, she turned to Leo. "How could you promise total strangers where we'll be in a week? We've got to plan our stops together. But we haven't because every time you get in the car, you fall asleep."

"I know. I'm sorry. Let's talk now." He opened the glove box and unfolded a map of western Europe. "If we hug the Spanish coast to Biarritz or San Sebastian, then turn south to Burgos, we'll see a lot of the Spanish countryside before we drop down into Portugal. Is that okay with you?"

"That's fine, but I want us to sit down each evening or morning and plan our next stop. I have a few places I want to see, and you can't keep running off so I have no idea where you've gone."

"My, my, I didn't realize you were so much like your mother, planning every inch of your life."

"I'm nothing like my mother! You're handling the money, so I need to know how to reach you if there's an emergency. And since you're navigating, you need to stay awake to alert me of turns in our route. I need you to include *my* stops, okay?"

He pulled back and saluted briskly. "Got it, Boss."

She opened her mouth to reply, but stopped. No need to get touchy. That appeared to be Leo's way to handle things.

He stared at her, smiled, and continued. "Take this road straight into San Sebastian. Let's take a break at the beach. Okay? Now, may I take a nap?"

She nodded as they pulled away from the inn and headed west. Finally, he'd listened.

Just to make a point that *she* needed to be heard and part of the planning, she took an extra-long walk on the beaches after their arrival. Even if it started to rain, she'd make him wait on her for a change.

The sky matched the sea's Wedgewood blue. A few clouds hung like horsetails. With the chance of rain at zero, she scanned the beach and decided to follow it's near-perfect curve to the north and explore a knoll of land. She expected she'd return to find Leo pacing. It would serve him right, always rushing away without thinking of her feelings or interests.

She watched him stretch out on a bench along the promenade as she began her walk. The dust-colored sand felt good under her bare feet. Here she was, walking barefoot along the chilly shore in Spain in September. She tied her sweater around her waist and picked up her pace. If she wanted to reach that knoll and get back before evening, she'd need to hustle.

Surprised and disappointed to find Leo asleep on the bench where she'd left him hours ago, she frowned. So much for making him wait. "Uncle Leo, wake up! We need to get back on the road if we're going to find a place to stay."

He sat up, stretched, and yawned. "Guess I was tired." He leaned over and slipped on his shoes. "I needed that nap. How far did you walk?"

"To the far point."

He reached for his jacket and looked puzzled. "Did you take the money from my jacket?

"No, why would I?"

"I just wondered." He shook open his jacket and ran his hands through each pocket. "My money's missing."

"Where was your jacket?"

"I used it as a pillow, but then it must have slipped off the bench. I found it on the ground."

Leo patted each of his pants pockets. "I still have my passport, but my wallet and my gambling money are gone. I've been robbed."

Within the hour they found a local police officer, tried to explain the theft, and were answered with a sad shrug that implied nothing could be done. They returned to sit in the car and discuss their next step.

"How much money do you have, Lynnie?"

"Maybe forty francs. I put the rest in our fund. Where's that envelope?"

Leo looked away. "I used it as seed money for the casinos."

She gasped.

"Now, before you get all excited, I did earn it back, probably four times over."

"A lot of good that does us. It's all gone, Uncle Leo. We need gas, food, and places to stay. My forty francs won't get us far."

He nodded. "I know. In the morning we'll find a place where we can wire your folks."

"Don't expect them to help us. They're buried in dad's hospital bills. You'll need to get a hold of your friends or your bank."

"What about your bank, Lynnie?"

She counted to ten before she answered. "I have exactly fifty dollars in my account. I need that to rent a room when I get back to Billings. I'm on leave from the dance company, remember? They aren't paying me a cent until the end of the month when I return to dancing."

He slumped in the car seat. "What about your friends? That guy you're dating?"

Her eyebrows shot up. She opened her mouth in surprise. "You expect me to contact a guy I've just started dating and ask for money?"

"Why not? If he cares about you, he'll wire it."

"Maybe you could contact your gambling buddies, Phyllis and her husband."

Leo shook his head. "I borrowed money from them to keep my winning streak alive. I haven't paid them back yet."

"Why not?"

"It slipped my mind."

Lynne opened her car door, climbed out, and slammed it closed with so much force Leo jumped. "*You* caused the problem," she said. "*You* need to solve it! I'm going for a walk. Stay with the car! We don't need it stolen as well."

Angry and hungry, she walked along the promenade and back through town. Tiny eateries stuffed with people standing around talking as they ate bite-size samples of food made her even hungrier. Her mouth watered. Should she treat herself? No, then she'd be selfish like Leo. If he couldn't come up with funds, she'd need to contact Noel. She prayed he would figure it out by morning.

She returned to the car to find him sleeping. Slipping behind the wheel, she drove out of town and found a small inn that included dinner and breakfast in the cost of their room. "Eat hearty, " she said. "This may be our last cozy night as well as our last meals for awhile."

He nodded, but didn't meet her glance.

༄

By mid-morning, they returned to San Sebastian and found a bank that did international transactions. Noon in Spain was seven in the morning back home in Jersey; the five-hour time lag meant their day would be spent waiting for the bank to open and then holding their breath that they'd make contact before the local bank closed for the day.

At one, the banks closed for their two-hour siesta break. Three o'clock, no news. By four-thirty local time, Leo's bank wired three hundred dollars, closing his account. Then they drove to Burgos, Spain, after Lynne insisted they forgo another coastal town with a casino.

Conversation was non-existent as the car chugged uphill onto the Spanish plain. At times she knew she could have walked faster than the tiny car moved along the steep, twisting road. Every time she was forced to stop to let cars with greater horsepower pass them or to cool down the engine of their tinny vehicle, she became angrier.

Finally, they found a studio with twin beds and a guest bathroom down the hall. Dinner consisted of a brief and inexpensive stop at a tapa shop. Their bite-sized snacks were mouthfuls of savory meats atop bread, vegetable-filled giant pasta shells, and meat and cheese roll-ups like the ones she'd passed on her walk in San Sebastian.

The next morning, the car wheezed like a tired old man as their route continued its climb. The ocean vistas and breezes were replaced by miles of harvested fields and hot, dry air. By the time they reached Salamanca, Lynne's shirt was soaked with perspiration. They found a parking place and separated to search for a room.

When they met an hour later, she hadn't found anything reasonable. Leo found a cheap room up three flights of stairs that overlooked the Grand Square in the center of town. From the tiny patio, they looked down on hundreds of cafe umbrellas along the outer edges of the square.

"Looks like a beach in the middle of a castle courtyard," he said.

"I can't begin to count the number of people wandering every which way. This must be something special during pageants and celebrations."

"It would be a great place to hold a party," Leo said. "With all the students starting classes, the manager told me it'll stay busy every night until they head home in late spring."

The manager's comment had been an understatement. As the hushed sounds of people eating and talking ended, raucous singing and caterwauling began. Each time the square quieted and Lynne drifted back to sleep, another band of students entered and began a new, off-tune musical serenade. By dawn she'd slept a matter of minutes instead of hours. Leo, on the other hand, appeared to have slept through every solo, duet, and mournful explosion of voices.

She yawned and closed her eyes for a quick nap just as a steady stream of large trucks entered the square to discharge their daily food deliveries. Brakes squeaked, truck roll-up doors opened with thuds, chains clattered, and excited voices carried on early morning conversations that funneled up the walls of the square and into their room. She covered her head, then gave up. Surely they'd find a place to take a break and nap as they crossed the mountains to enter Portugal.

After a quick breakfast of bread and coffee purchased in the square, they rethought their next stop. "I think we need to head toward Lisbon," Lynne said.

Leo made a sad face. "I'd hoped to visit Porto, take in the wineries. My friends said it's quite a tasty stop."

"Can we afford a big town and have money to get back to the ship? No! Small towns along the coast in Portugal are inexpensive." She leaned in. "We may need to skip Italy."

Leo sighed and looked around the square. He rubbed his hand over his face and gave her what she knew as his needy look. "How about we turn back now and head to Italy?"

"No! I told you I wanted to visit the Portuguese coastline. Why should I give up the one special destination I wanted outside of France? You've had your wine tasting and gambling stops while I've done all the driving."

He rolled his eyes as he finished his coffee, then slumped down and gave Lynne another needy look she'd seen him use on her family.

"All right," he said. "But if I can get a loan from my friends, we're putting Italy back on our list. Think of all the art, the ancient history, the architecture we'll miss if we skip Italy. I promised your family I'd show you the best of Europe. Now you want to disappoint them?"

Lynne bit her lip and straightened. "I'm the one who's disappointed. You *promised* you'd give me the car if I did all the driving. I've kept my part of the bargain. You've handed me a gutless car that drives like a wind-up toy, and then you told me I can't have it."

Leo stood and looked down at her. "I didn't know you were such an ingrate. Maybe we should turn back today."

Lynne shoved her chair back with such force it tipped over. "Don't make me the villain. Now pick up your bags and let's get on the road. I'm going to Lisbon." She grabbed her bags and walked toward the car.

The early part of the drive over the mountains into Portugal was a repeat of their slow ascent onto the Spanish plain. Leo made a show of placing their combined funds into a pouch, which he handed to her. "I understand now that you're right about a few things. I've been selfish. You take care of our money for the rest of the trip. I found a couple of traveler's checks in my pants pocket, so that will help. If we need more funds, maybe you can contact your friend and ask him to send us a little as a cushion."

Lynne nodded. Her insides uncoiled as Leo slid down in his seat and went to sleep.

※

The drive into Portugal dropped out of the mountains. They stopped in Coimbra for gas and food for a picnic lunch, then ate in the shade along a river.

"This is nice. It's cooler than Salamanca," he said.

"Less crowded too. I heard there are Roman ruins nearby. Let's stop for a few minutes. Both the car and I could use a break."

He shrugged. "If you'd like. I guess I owe you a few stops since I've been bossy. I'm used to being by myself, making my own rules, and doing what I please. I'm sorry, Lynnie."

She looked at him. Was he feeding her what he thought she wanted to hear? His face looked sincere. Maybe he'd made a change. She hoped so.

※

Fifty miles later, Lynne stopped at a crossroads and pointed to the signpost. "Nazaré. This is the town Cheryl mentioned. She stayed here years ago. It's a fishing community right on the Atlantic. Let's see if we can get a room."

The road into town offered a wide view of the ocean. Whitewashed buildings lined narrow streets. After looking around, they found a room above a village bakery.

Leo's charm didn't do its magic on the bakery and apartment owner. Their traveler's checks were met with scowls and head shakes. "These are the same as dollars," Leo pleaded.

"*Apenas dólares, apenas dólares.*" She shook her head and crossed her arms.

"She means she'll only take Portuguese dollars." The English came from a young, college student who came to their rescue. After they explained their predicament, he reassured the owner the travelers checks were as good as cash. In the end, she took them on the condition they'd stay two nights and buy bread and food from her shop.

After they carried their bags and bread upstairs, Lynne walked to the door. "I'm off to investigate the beach."

"I'll come with you," Leo said.

"Did you notice all the petticoats that baker wore?" he said as they walked along the street. "Her skirt looked like those puffy square dance outfits back home. And back at the corner, did you see the woman wearing all black? I bet we wouldn't see that in a big city."

Lynne nodded. "Cheryl said it was unique. I already appreciate the slower pace."

They rounded the next corner, stopped, and stared.

30

"Look! Those oxen are backing carts into the ocean." Lynne said.

Leo nodded. "That must be the way the fishermen haul their small boats from the water. Let's walk closer."

The oxen stood half submerged in the waves as handfuls of men aligned each incoming boat with its cart and guided each ox from the water. Women rushed to unload baskets of tiny fish, spread them on racks, and set them out to dry along the beach.

On closer investigation, they found the fish were the size of popsicle sticks. The women smiled as Lynne and Leo stood nearby. They offered them a taste of the fish; both politely refused and walked on to buy food before Sunday's expected closure of all businesses, excluding restaurants they couldn't afford.

The next morning, a cacophony of church bells woke Lynne. She fixed coffee in their economy kitchen and sat down to watch the parade of families walking to church along the narrow streets. Today she'd write postcards and wander the beach. What Leo chose to do was none of her concern. As long as she had the money pouch, she'd make certain they'd spend their meager funds wisely.

When Lynne dumped out her suitcase to reorganize her clothing, the small journal Noel had given her fell out. "So much for keeping my daily log since Paris," she muttered to herself. It must have been her stress at driving that distracted her from writing each evening. That, and Leo's loss of their money.

She flipped through the empty pages, leaving one blank page for each of the twelve days she'd missed. She decided to enter today's observations before writing her final letters of the trip.

> Sept. 27, 1959
>
> Nazaré, Portugal
> Sunny, 70°
>
> Ladies in colorful layers of skirts. Fishing boats hauled out by oxen. Golden sand beaches. Counting our money closely. We'll get to my most desired stop, the end of the world, very soon!
>
> Glad I have control of our money since Leo doesn't grasp the fact that we're living on fumes after his winnings were stolen in San Sebastian, Spain. I've calculated we can make it on three dollars a day, including gas.
>
> Not starving, but not enjoying special food either.

Sept. 27

Marta,

You'd love Salamanca, Spain, if you were a college student. It's a noisy, busy town with golden stone walls and tall buildings. It felt warm like Billings in the fall.

The mountains between Spain and Portugal are like the Rockies with narrow, curvy roads and pine forests. I was excited to get to the coast and see Roman ruins.

Our current village, Nazaré, is a small, quiet port. Like most places, the people walk everywhere. They carry their possessions in cloth bags or baskets.

The next stop is Lisbon before we head to the southern coast of Portugal. I'll be on the ocean playing, so this is my last letter (plus I'm not mailing new postcards either. I need to save money for food and gas and places to stay. I'll explain when I see you)

Miss you, I have days of stories to share.
Lynne

Sept. 27

Dear Noel,

On the road with Leo is a challenge, but we're seeing interesting sights. I especially love the small towns and villages.

Recently, we've been to an expensive beach in San Sebastian, Spain, and the college town of Salamanca, also in Spain. We chugged through the mountains that separate Spain and Portugal. Now we're in Nazaré, a fishing village near Lisbon. From here we'll head south to my final destination choice, Sagres, on the southern most tip of Europe. Cool, huh?

No letters to follow, but I'll bring back post cards and let you read that journal you gave me. Yes, I'm using it. You may find a few pages of grumbling, but it will be too late to give me a lecture about that. See you in a few weeks. Thanks for all your letters. They brightened my days.

Thinking of you,

Lynne

That evening, they sat at a cafe near the beach and planned their next week of travels. Monday, they'd drive the sixty miles to Lisbon, walk around the sights, and drive out to see Sintra, Lynne's idea. Tuesday, they'd drive to Cascais, a small nearby town for gambling, Leo's idea. He'd be allowed ten dollars to play for as long as he could make it last. Wednesday, they'd end September by driving south along the coast for one hundred fifty miles to Lagos and Sagres, the last stops on Lynne's wish list.

"So we're agreed?" Lynne asked. "You can plan our last days, as long as we get back to Le Havre in time to meet the ship."

Leo frowned. "We'll miss most of Italy even if you drive long days. If you called your friends and borrowed money, we could stay longer and see more sights: Florence's art, Rome's Colosseum, Naples, and Venice."

"I can't, Leo. None of my friends have money to spare. We didn't realize the distances and how long the driving would take. I know you want me to give up my trip to the south of Portugal, but I won't. You're getting time at a casino near Lisbon. Come back another time without me and spend your time wherever you wish."

৯

Their next day Leo pouted as they toured Lisbon and Sintra. He snapped out of his mood after his time at the casino in Cascais, where he won twenty dollars. He even kept up the conversation along the road to Sagres.

When they stopped and got out of the car, he stretched and walked around. "This is certainly off the tourist path. Must have two dozen residents. Where's the nearest town?"

"Cheryl said Portimão is less than forty miles. Let's take today to relax. I'm exhausted from driving. After we see Henry Hudson's mariner's school, I'll drive there. You can explore all day and into the evening."

Lynne began to unwind as she watched the waves crashing against the point and blowing skyward with towering force. She sighed. To the west was home, less than two weeks and five thousand miles away. She could hardly wait.

The sunny drive east to the town of Portimão wandered through hills and along the coast. Lynne parked the car. "I'll check back here at five and then at seven. Have fun!" She walked off toward the waterfront; Leo walked toward the shops in town, whistling with his hand in his pocket.

⁓

Day three in Sagres, Lynne returned from the beach, ready for a quick nap before it was time to drive on. She loved the town and wished they were staying longer, but Leo wanted to get underway. In response to another of his 'looks,' she'd promised him she'd drive where he wanted for the rest of their trip.

At her room, she found a note sticking out beneath the door. That's funny, she thought as she opened the paper. Why would someone leave her a note?

> Dear Lynnie,
>
> I've left to drive to Monte Carlo with my new friends. I know you'll be fine on your own.
>
> Leo
>
> P.S. I borrowed money from our fund. I'm sure, like me, you held back a few dollars you didn't tell me about.

She gasped and sank to the floor in the hallway. He *borrowed* the money? Was he kidding? How dare he suggest she'd held out on him! Their fund had less than two hundred fifty dollars, including two traveler's checks.

She pulled herself up and raced to his room. She knocked. "Uncle Leo! Open the door. Leo!"

No answer. She knocked louder.

She saw the maid pushing her cart toward her.

"*Excusé moi.* I need to get into my uncle's room."

The maid's eyebrows knitted together. She tipped her head.

"*Parle Anglais?*"

The maid shrugged.

How stupid. Why was she speaking French to a Portuguese woman? She gestured toward the door to Leo's room.

The maid straightened, moved in front of Leo's door, and crossed her arms over her chest.

"Please," Lynne cried. "I must get inside this room! Leo left me!"

Neighboring doors opened. People leaned out and stared.

"Does anyone speak English?" she shouted.

The doors closed.

She stared at the maid, who stared back and didn't move away from door. Lynne started down the hall. When the maid unlocked the door to Leo's room, she dashed past her, opening drawers and looking under the bed. Nothing.

The maid screamed and batted at her with her long-handled broom. Faces appeared at the door. The hotel manager arrived, yelling in Portuguese. He tried pushing Lynne back into the hallway, but she gripped the door frame with all her strength.

"My uncle was in this room. He left me an envelope. I have to find it!"

Two men helped the manager drag Lynne into the hall. They blocked her re-entry into Leo's room.

Tears clouded her eyes as she stepped into her room and pulled out her suitcase to pack her belongings. The manager never took his eyes off her. As she picked up her purse, she spotted an envelope behind the door.

She grabbed it before he could intercept her. Inside it were the last traveler's checks and a handful of mixed currency. She counted about thirty dollars. Picking up her suitcase, she lifted her chin and walked from the room.

The hotel manager followed her toward the reception desk. Suddenly, he raced around her, blocking her exit from the building. He waved a paper in her face.

She stared at him and shrugged. He shook the paper again.

Then it struck her. Leo hadn't paid the bill. No wonder the manager acted frantic.

She opened her purse and counted out the coins. The manager grabbed them and held out his hand for more.

She handed him a ten-dollar traveler's check. Again, his head shook. He called to the woman behind the reception counter, who raced out the door.

Lynne sat down in the entry. Blasted traveler's checks. Small town merchants were skeptical of the funny money. The ten she'd given him was worth more than what was owed, but he wouldn't know that until he cashed it. By then she'd probably be in jail.

A local policeman arrived in a tiny car. He gave her a menacing look and motioned for her to stay seated. She began to shake. Why didn't she see this coming? Leo had acted strange last night when he spoke of his new friends who traveled in style.

The police officer signaled for her to grab her bag and get into his car. They drove to a small, whitewashed building up the hill from the beach. She followed him inside, hoping someone spoke English.

The hotel manager arrived. Conversations flew. People stared at her like she was a criminal. The room quieted as a young woman entered and walked to the counter.

The woman turned toward Lynne and shook her hand. "My name ez Zetta. I am college student. I study English. I hep you."

Lynne explained the situation with Leo, about the traveler's check, and the fact it was worth more than needed to pay the bill. Zetta listened and shared the information. Heads nodded. Anger subsided. She was free to go.

The manager exited the police station after Lynne. Using sign language he offered her a ride back to his hotel. She nodded. She needed to get the car.

At the hotel he signaled for her to return inside, then hurried behind the counter, opened a metal box, and handed her two U.S. passports: hers and Leo's. He shrugged with a shy smile and disappeared into the back room.

Lynne looked at the passports. Leo wasn't as clever as he thought he was because she now had *his* passport. Should she give it back to the hotel manager? Keep it with her? Turn it in to the local police? She'd drive to the station and leave it there.

She picked up her bag and walked to the parking area behind the hotel. Her body began to relax. She stopped and turned slowly in a full circle. *Where* was the car? Had somebody stolen it?

Tears streamed down her face. She sank to the ground. How could she survive without money or a car to travel the more than 1,000 miles back to Le Havre to board the ship?

"You American, yes?" Lynne followed the sound of the voice. A young girl sat on the branch of a large tree overlooking the parking area.

Lynne nodded. "You speak English."

"Little bit."

Lynne wiped her face and plastered on a stage smile. "My name is Lynne. Do you know Zetta?"

The little girl nodded and hopped down from the branch. "You come?"

Lynne picked up her suitcase and followed the young girl to a nearby *taverna*. They entered a small kitchen in the back. A woman cutting vegetables looked up and chattered with the child. Eying Lynne as she listened, she started toward her, knife in hand. Lynne backed away. The woman frowned, then smiled as she laid down the knife.

"Sit, please. Coffee?"

Lynne nodded.

The woman poured sludge-thick coffee into two small cups and signaled for Lynne to sit on the bench behind a small table in the corner. She and the young girl slid in beside her, never taking their eyes off Lynne.

"You have problem, yes?"

"I have problem. Do you know Zetta?"

The woman nodded.

Tears trickled down Lynne's cheeks. "My uncle left me here with little money and now…now the car is missing. I want to go home but…" She gasped. Her dance bag! The return ticket was in her dance bag, along with gifts for the people back home, in the trunk of the tinny car. She thought she might throw up…or faint.

The woman patted her hands and smiled. "We hep you." She spoke to the young girl, who disappeared out the door.

Soon, the local police officer arrived, followed by Zetta and a string of curious residents. The woman directed everyone into the dining area. She poured more cups of coffee and set out a basket of warm bread.

Zetta shared details about Leo, the money, and the missing car. A collective gasp and much head bobbing followed. Voices shouted and fingers wagged toward the hotel next door.

Zetta explained. "We talk wiz Tonio, okay? You stay more days, okay?"

"No," Lynne said. "I don't have money to stay. I need to get to an American Embassy. Where is the nearest office?"

Zetta shrugged. "I do not know American Bassie. You go to Lisboa. Big city. More offices to hep you."

"How far is Lisbon? My car was stolen. Or…or Leo drove off in it."

The young woman spoke to the group. Lynne heard Leo's name.

One woman pointed toward the road. Another nodded. The policeman demonstrated a person driving in a bouncing motion. Everyone laughed except Lynne.

"People saw heem go," Zetta said. "He drive so funny."

She pasted on a stage smile. "Is there a train I can take to Lisbon?"

"No train, just bus. Or we drive you."

Tears again flooded Lynne's eyes. "Where can I catch the bus?"

Zetta turned to speak with the crowd of citizens, then spoke to Lynne. "Today no bus. You catch tomorrow to Lisboa." She patted Lynne's arm. "Tonight you stay wiz me. Come. I show you."

Zetta lived in a one room apartment over the village laundry. The space was tidy, the daybed made up with a worn but clean quilt. Lynne sat down on one end while Zetta fussed at a small counter, making tea.

"I hep get bus tomorrow. Now we have tea. You tell me about you."

Lynne explained her dance trip as simply as possible. Zetta nodded and smiled. Not a good sign—that's what Lynne did when she pretended to understand what was spoken throughout her dance tour.

Zetta pushed her small table aside. "You dance much? You show me? I learn."

Lynne shared basic ballet moves. Zetta's appeared confused. When she switched to showing her ballroom steps, Zetta's face lit up.

৯

After thanking Zetta for her hospitality and reluctantly accepting several coins the woman pressed into her hand, Lynne boarded the bus. She carried Zetta's address in her purse and promised to write. The two women exchanged waves until the bus turned onto the main road and headed north to Lisbon.

Stops in every small town along the way collected people heading to the city. The three-hour drive that she'd made from Lisbon to Sagres took the bus all day to complete.

They crossed the Tagus River and stopped at a terminal in the midst of downtown. Lynne got directions and walked several blocks to the American Embassy office. Lines of U.S. travelers gathered their mail and asked questions When it was her turn, she asked about her best and cheapest way to reach Paris.

The woman behind the desk said, "The cheapest and slowest way is by bus. Fastest would be the train. It costs much more." She wrote down the information. Lynne would need twice as much money as she had to buy even a bus ticket.

"Can I call home from here? And is there a charge?"

The woman frowned. "You'll need to go to the post office to make a trans-Atlantic call. It's pricey but faster than sending a letter. We can wire a message for you. That costs..." She turned away to check. "...thirty dollars. Expect it to take a day or two for a response."

Lynne half smiled. "Thanks."

"Good luck," the woman called to her.

Half an hour later, she stood in another line in the post office. The mix of languages and the hubbub frazzled her nerves. She paid her money and sat in a small booth, waiting for her call to be connected. Ten dollars for five minutes still shocked her. That left her with a handful of coins.

The phone at her parents' house rang and rang. As Lynne started to hang up, she heard her mother's voice. "Hello."

"Hi, Mom. How are you and Dad?"

"We're fine. Your dad's back to work. Where are you and Leo?"

She sniffed back her tears. "That's my problem. I have no idea where he's gone. He drove off without me to meet up with his rich friends."

"What did you do, Lynnie? Why did Leo leave you?"

31

"Mom. Listen. I need your help. This is an expensive call. Leo took most of our travel money. I spent the little he left me to travel all day on a bus to call you. Could you wire me $70?"

"Lynne! We don't have that kind of money. Call one of your friends."

Her stomach churned. "How can I call anyone else? I used my last money to call you. Please, Mom, I need the money so I can get home."

"Oh, Lynne. We knew this would happen. I was telling Vivian just the other day that we expected to hear from you. We knew you'd make a mess of the trip. Poor Leo. Where did you leave him?"

"Mom, I *didn't* leave him. He left me."

༄

Lynne hung up and dragged her bag outside. If she allowed herself to start crying, she'd never stop. "This is a test," she said aloud. "Think, self, think."

Even if she gathered enough money, who could she call? Not Marta. She and her mom were buying the dance studio. Jer lived paycheck to paycheck. His girlfriend was a student. Besides, she didn't know their phone numbers.

Should she call Noel? She hated asking him for money, but who else could help her? Then she remembered he'd said he'd be out of town until the middle of the month.

A thorough search of her purse produced a handful of French coins and four Spanish dollars. That made a little more than eleven dollars in assorted monies from three countries, at best a mixed value in Portugal. But if she returned to the American Embassy office, she could ask to exchange her mishmash of coins. Maybe someone would have an idea about how she could get a message home.

At the embassy she begged, and a friendly receptionist exchanged her money. She now had enough to make one international call. The counter person handed her the maps of Portugal and Spain that she requested and suggested she contact anyone she could think of and ask them to make calls for her.

"There's no one left to call," she said.

The woman handed her a paper with a phone number and an address. "The closest youth hostel is near the train station. Perhaps they can help you."

Lynne walked away, trying to think of ways to get back to Montana. One thought stopped her mid-stride. The entertainment director from the ship had mentioned she could earn money on the return trip to New York if she taught classes. That could pay help pay her crossing fare. Or maybe he could find a way to help her replace the missing ticket. She quickened her pace. The sooner she headed toward Paris and on to Le Havre, the better.

The walk to the youth hostel took twenty minutes. Flags of several nations, including the stars and stripes, hung from the front of the tall, skinny building. Throngs of teens and early twenty-aged students lounged on the steps, speaking a variety of languages, smoking, and people-watching. Her arrival turned heads, or was it her appearance? No one there carried a suitcase. No one wore summer sandals in October. No one looked as lost as she felt.

She smiled as she wound her way through the unmoving bodies, feeling their eyes follow her to the entry. Inside, she approached a battered desk and waited for someone to appear.

"Ring the bell," directed a young woman. "The manager's out back."

"Thanks," Lynne said. "How did you know I spoke English?"

The girl smiled and pointed down. "Your shoes. American shoes look different." The girl stuck out her hand. "I'm Bev from Colorado."

Lynne tried to return her smile. "Hi. I'm Lynne."

A young man appeared from the back room. "Posso te ajudar?" When she didn't respond, he switched languages: "¿Puedo ayudarlo? Puis-je vous aider? May I help you?"

"I need a room for the night."

"We have only dormitories, men separate from women. It's sixty cents a night, and we expect you to help in the hostel. Any questions?"

Lynne shook her head. "Can I work extra jobs instead of paying for bed and a meal? I only have a few dollars to my name and no way to get money until I reach Paris."

He frowned. "I see." He sucked in his lips and called to the back room, *"Ella, me ajudar. Temos uma jovem mulher em perigo."* To Lynne he said, "One moment. Let me see what we can do."

He disappeared into a back room for several minutes, then returned with a woman he introduced as his wife. "If you want to stay one night, you can work for your room. If you wish to stay longer we will do our best. We serve no food since our guests buy and fix their own meals."

"I'll do any job you have."

"The kitchen is always in need of cleaning. The stove and mopping the floor around the always-hungry students. There is laundry and ironing on the back porch. You'll not have time to tour Lisbon."

Cinderella time, Lynne thought, but she smiled. "That's fine. I've seen Lisbon. I appreciate any jobs and help you can give me."

The woman nodded. "Let's stow your belongings so you can get started. Perhaps you can beg a bit of food from the students while they cook."

Beg? she thought. Now I need to beg? "I'm ready to get started. Do you have gloves I can use?"

She spent the rest of the afternoon working. Her back ached from bending over the ironing board; her knees ached from working on all fours to clean around the constant stream of students cooking in the kitchen. But it meant a free night's lodging.

As she finished, a new crowd of students entered the kitchen to prepare their meals. Lynne moved to the entry and sat down to catch her breath. The innkeeper approached her. "You did a good job cleaning. It needed to be done weeks ago. Please come with me."

She followed him into the innkeeper's quarters, where his wife had set out a tray of sandwiches, a plate of cookies, and a pot of tea with three cups. "Please join us for a light meal," he said.

They listened with great interest to her story, the man translating for his wife. He suggested hitchhiking. "Talk with Sven, the tall blonde who wears that crazy hat with strings hanging down. He's hiking the continent." He paused, then continued. "I'll call my friend who drives trucks to Spain. Perhaps he can give you a lift. The weather changes quickly this time of year. You don't want to be stranded crossing the mountains."

Lynne found Sven in the back yard, surrounded by a circle of young women vying for his attention. When the group broke up, she approached him. "Do you speak English?"

"Yes."

"The innkeeper said you are hitchhiking. I've never done that, but I need to now. Any suggestions are appreciated."

Sven nodded and took the map she held out to him.

"Hitching is legal where you want to go, but the shortest route is not always best. I suggest this way." He traced a path with his finger. "Pick roadsides with wide shoulders so cars and trucks can pull off. Travel by way of Guarda, and hitch a ride before you get to the mountains. Produce trucks are good choices because they travel quickly to deliver their loads. For a woman, cars with women drivers or families are a good idea. Always ask how far they are going."

She made mental notes of his suggestions. "Do I need to pay people for a ride?"

"No, but always thank them."

Lynne nodded. "What about my suitcase?"

Sven held up his finger for her to wait. He disappeared upstairs and returned with a length of rope. "Keep your hands free. Make a sling to carry your suitcase on your back. Write your destination in big, fat letters on a piece of paper. Fasten it onto your bag so people know where you're headed."

"Wow. You know all the tricks."

"One last thing, get a tarp or raincoat so you'll have a cover if you get caught out overnight."

Lynne shuddered at the thought of spending the night outside. Roughing it had never been a part of her lifestyle.

Bev from Colorado and three English-speaking friends joined her in the back yard, and she repeated her story. When she mentioned returning home by ship, they helped her locate and call the ship offices.

"Hal sails on the ship that leaves from Le Havre in eight days," she reported a few minutes later. "Since he knows me, he'll do what he can to help."

"That's great!" Bev said.

"There are no cabins available, only crew quarters, but it's a way home. Plus, they'll refund part of my ticket."

The waiting group nodded and smiled.

Bev handed Lynne a worn neck scarf. "While you were on the telephone, we did a little work ourselves."

Lynne opened the scarf and gasped. It held handfuls of coins.

"We asked students to give us what they could to help you. It isn't much, but you'll have money for emergencies."

"I don't know what to say. This is...amazing. Thank you." Lynne attempted to brush away the tears in her eyes, but they kept coming. The assembled students watched her, then patted her on the back as they went their separate ways, except for Bev.

"Good luck, Lynne. We hope you make it to the ship in time." She slipped a paper into Lynne's hand. "Write to me. Tell me how your adventure works out. I'll write back, I promise."

Lynne sat on the back steps alone for several minutes, wishing she could do something to repay the funds students donated for her journey. She could hardly believe they'd pitched in while her family would not.

The hostel manager confirmed his friend would take her if she could get to the truckers' warehouse before five in the morning. "He must leave early. He has a twelve-hour drive."

Lynne heaved a sigh of relief. She'd have a ride across the mountains and into Spain. After showering, she headed to her assigned bunk and tried to sleep. Her mind raced. Thanks to the students, she could afford small meals or a couple of nights in a hostel, but she needed to keep money for a call home, just in case. She'd dismissed the two Katy's as strange girls. She should have listened to their stories about hitchhiking.

> Oct. 4 Lisbon
> 65° and windy
>
> Strangers are better than family right now. I have around $13 to get me back to Paris and only 8 days to get beyond there to catch the ship in Le Havre.
>
> I have no idea if I can travel that far that fast, but I have no choice but to try. Not dressed for this weather!

Lynne arrived at the warehouse before dawn. Suddenly, the roll-up door opened. Trucks started their engines and exited in a serpentine, leaving an exhaust plume hanging in the air.

She stood to one side, waiting for the innkeeper's friend to pick her up. An ancient truck stopped beside her. The driver signaled for her to hop in. She hoisted herself up into the cab and reached out to shake the driver's hand.

He nodded as they chugged onto the city streets. She leaned against the passenger door and pulled her arms inside her sweater.

The truck lurched to a stop, waking Lynne. She'd slept long enough for the darkness to give way to morning clouds with bursts of sunlight. A roadside sign read "Guarda 40 km." She was on the path Sven had suggested. Soon they'd be crossing the mountains and entering Spain.

The driver got out and opened the hood. He tinkered for several minutes, got back in the cab, and tried to restarted the engine; it choked to life. He made repeated stops as the road climbed through the mountains that reminded her of home. Thinking of all that had happened over the past few months, she had an epiphany. 'Home' now meant Billings.

༄

The driver stopped in a small town and unloaded several crates. When he finished, he signaled for her to get out, gesturing that he was turning south while she wanted to travel north toward Salamanca.

It was close to dusk as she watched the truck lumber away, too late to hitch any further. By her estimate she'd come about 500 kilometers or about 300 miles. Salamanca lay a short distance ahead.

If she could travel that far every day, she'd make her ship connection in seven days. What if she had to walk most of the way? She'd make sixteen to twenty miles on level ground. That meant more than seventy days to cover the remaining fourteen hundred miles.

She shuddered. Being on the road through winter, wearing summer clothes and sandals, would never work. Her only hope was catching long rides every day.

Salamanca's Grand Square buzzed with activity after dark. People strolled or sat inside numerous small restaurants. With no clue to the location of the youth hostel, she approached the hotel overlooking the giant courtyard where they'd stayed on their drive.

The manager shook his head. No money, no bed. She nodded. As she walked through the wide open square, she spotted a bakery closing. The baker removed the last of the breads and turned toward her back room.

Lynne knocked on her door and held out several Portuguese coins as she pointed to the bread.

The baker looked at the coins and shook her head. Lynne joined her hands in supplication with a pathetic expression. The woman unlocked the door. She took a few coins, handed Lynne four hard rolls and a loaf of dark bread, and signaled for her to leave.

Lynne backed out of the bakery, smiling and bowing her head. Once she reached the sidewalk, she rounded the corner of the square, collapsed against the building, and began to cry. So this was what it was like to live on the street.

As she ate one dry bun, a handful of students passed. "Can you point me toward the youth hostel?"

She paid her fifty cents for a bed and shared her bread with fellow vagabonds in exchange for a cup of soup and a handful of raw veggies. Talk over the welcome meal offered more hitching advice.

Oct. 5 Salamanca, Spain
65° cool & cloudy

Ride to here in a ratty truck like Dad's. Hostel dorm near empty this time of year. No heat but I'm inside. My job tonight: wash dishes and mop the kitchen.

Heard the Burgos hostel is closed. Was my next stop. Some hitchers say it wasn't safe anyway. Not sure what I'll do tomorrow if I get that far.

Dare I think I could get further by tomorrow evening?

Miles to Paris: about 900
Days to the ship: 7

Spent: Hostel 50¢
Food: 35¢
Started with $13.40
Money left: $12.55

32

Well before dawn, Lynne closed her suitcase and walked to the bridge. The rain overnight cooled the air, but walking at a brisk pace kept her warm. If it started to rain again, she'd be in trouble; she didn't have the money to buy the raincoat or tarp Sven had suggested.

Trucks and a few cars passed. When a bus approached, she flagged it down. "Burgos? How much?"

"*Dois dólares*," the driver replied.

She shook her head and backed away. Two dollars was too much to spend if she could catch a ride for free. Spending her call money wasn't an option. She sat on the bridge abutment with her thumb out for the next hour, then started walking.

The mist became a drizzle that destroyed her sign but not her determination. She walked faster. Near a small village a car slowed. A family squeezed her into the backseat with their three kids who stared at her for several minutes before they returned to their bickering. An hour later, they dropped her near a river, where they turned off the main road. She waved, then walked on, thinking about bickering with her brothers in the back seat of their family car. She couldn't remember now what had been so special about being the one who got to lie on the ledge in the back window, but it always caused a fight. Of course, her brothers won.

A series of short rides took her to Burgos in time to buy day-old bread, an apple, and a bottle of milk. She wandered through alleys, found a plastic dry-cleaning bag, and wrapped it around herself. At home she'd have tossed it in the garbage; today it became an extra layer against the drizzle. A damp stone bench behind a quiet church offered her a place to rest, eat, and write her journal entry.

> Oct. 6   Burgos, Spain
> Steady rain all day
>
> My sandals are soaking wet and starting to fall apart. My sweater isn't warm enough to keep away my shivering even when I walk fast. I need to find a second-hand store.
>
> Sleeping like a hobo on church steps is embarrassing, especially if they find me and force me to move on. I miss the most uncomfortable beds from the tour.
>
> Miles to Paris: 650
>
> Days to make the ship: 6
>
> Spent:
> 50¢ on food
> Money left: $12.05

> October 7 Vitoria, Spain
>
> Rainy
>
> Slow progress. Walked a dozen miles and got short rides into town to about 60 miles beyond Burgos.
>
> At a second-hand store I tried to sell the stuff in my suitcase. They only wanted my dressy clothes. I bought sturdy but ugly boots, wool socks, a jacket with a hood, and a holey tarp. No backpacks for sale. Kind people pick up hitchers. Stingy people run shops.
>
> Miles to Paris: 590
>
> Days to the ship: 5
>
> Spent:
> $1 hostel, 50¢ tarp,
> $1.50 clothes
> Money left: $9.05

After a bowl of soup and a hunk of bread, included in her stay at the hostel, she sat on her bunk. No other hitchers arrived, and the people who ran the place spoke little English. Once again she was alone. At least she got to sleep inside.

Her thoughts unraveled like the rope around her suitcase. She cried and jammed a corner of her jacket into her mouth to muffle her sobs. What had she done that was so bad she deserved to be left behind? Why did her mom blame her for Leo leaving? "Not only do I come in a poor second to *my* siblings, I rank below *her* selfish, lying brother," she muttered in a fit of self-pity. Picking up her boots, she threw them across the room. Her suitcase followed. The lock broke, spilling out her remaining clothes.

The hostel's manager appeared in the doorway as she sat on the floor collecting her clothes, tears streaming down her cheeks. He stared at her with raised eyebrows. She glared at him until he left, then returned to shoving her clothes back into her suitcase. Wiping away her tears with the back of her hand, she retied the rope backpack-style so her suitcase would stay closed, then lay on her bunk, waiting to fall asleep.

The next two days, the miles passed slowly as she approached San Sebastian. Her back no longer ached, but her legs felt as heavy as when she danced double performances on the tour. The used boots allowed her feet to slide around, and new blisters formed with each step. When she stopped to investigate, she shuddered. As she peeled off her socks, she exposed raw skin on the tops of her toes. A search through her purse produced one lone band aid, a remnant from her car accident in Billings. She laughed, then cried, thinking about how messed up her life felt. Wrapping her worst blister, she slipped on a pair of thin anklets and stuffed the toes of the boots with the remaining socks from her suitcase.

"Ah, much better," she mumbled to herself. "Life would be even better if I had a friend to keep me company." She laughed aloud. "I'd even welcome Suzette or Ida."

Talking and singing entertained her, but they interfered with her breathing, so she ran music from warm-ups and choreography through her head. She smiled to herself once she realized she'd selected music that matched the tempo of her best walking stride.

As dusk arrived with no hostel or *pensione* in sight, she took shelter in a lean-to that looked like a bus-waiting area. No food, no blanket, just her holey tarp. The overnight rain pelted the roof and blew inside to the bench where she'd stretched out. At least she was partially out of the downpour. She hoped the Katies were as well.

The rain continued the next day, but no cars stopped to offer rides. As the daylight faded, she saw the sign for a bed and breakfast. She walked along a rutted road until she arrived at a farm house. She knocked on the side door and waited. An elderly man opened it and looked at her with a furrowed brow.

"May I sleep in your shed?" She pointed to the structure. "I can pay." She held out a small handful of coins.

He looked confused and called into the house; another gentleman came to the door. They chattered and looked curiously at her.

She repeated her request and pointed to the shed, then held out the coins again.

They turned to one another, nodded, and took her coins. She backed away toward the shed.

The inside space was a mess of equipment, so she hung up the rakes and shovels, then rearranged two bales of straw to make a cozy corner. She sat on the bales, about to write in her journal. When the door opened, she jumped up and reached for the pitchfork hanging near her.

Both men stood in the doorway, staring at her. She set down the pitchfork and smiled. They smiled and closed the door to the shed.

Minutes later, they returned with a blanket and a bowl of hot soup.

Tears filled her eyes. *"Merci."*

Tonight she'd skip her journal and enjoy the hot chicken soup while she had enough light to see what she was given. Once she set the empty bowl aside, she pulled the blanket around her, curled up against the straw, and cried herself to sleep.

The next morning, as she left, she saw a cloth bag next to the shed door. Inside she found a feast: two pieces of cooked chicken, an apple, a piece of cheese, a square of cake, and her coins. She smiled and looked toward the house. Two faces looked out the kitchen window. She lifted the bag and waved. They waved back.

Wintry winds buffeted the curved bay of San Sebastian. The last time here, she'd strolled the beach while Leo slept and his money was stolen. Oh, how she wished she was on the other side of the Atlantic.

Nightfall found her in the warmth of an actual home that had one room set aside for hitchhikers. In the summer all eight bunks crammed into the tight space were no doubt filled; but this late in the season, she was the only boarder. The woman allowed her to work as part of her stay, so she helped feed the cows and chickens. Noel had taught her well. The woman nodded her approval and added dessert to her evening meal. Lynne took a warm shower, wrote in her journal, then fell onto the bed.

Oct. 11

San Sebastian, Spain
Cloudy and rainy again

The last few days are a blur. Walking in the rain for so long, I almost gave up. Then I thought, how can I quit? Where would I go if I quit? I just kept walking, hoping for the rain to stop and that I'd pass farmers markets where I could buy even one bun. Not much luck with that! When I needed water, all I had to do was tip my head back. Really!

Last night everything changed. I stayed dry in a shed. Two old guys gave me food. In the morning I got a ride to the town's hostel. Decided to stay so I could get a shower and try to dry my clothes. Wish I had time to wash them. They smell yucky as Roquefort cheese.

The beach is empty. No sun means no tourists. I ate the leftovers from my bag of food by the bay, then wandered the streets of town, looking in windows of tapa shops.

> Deserted. Thank heavens this hostel room is almost warm enough to keep my teeth from chattering. If I ever hitchhike on purpose, I'll carry a sleeping bag!
>
> Today I'd hoped to reach Le Havre but I'm not even close to Paris! Too sad to cry, too tired to have a hissy fit. I need to find some way to cross the stormy Atlantic.
>
> Miles to Paris: 500
>
> Days to the ship: 1
>
> Spent:
> Hostel $1, Food last 3 days $1
> Money left: $7.05

Heavy traffic hurried along the roadway the next morning. The tinny cars made her wonder whether Leo had found his passport at the police station where she'd left it. She doubted he got himself across any country borders with his charm. Some day she'd hear his tale of woe. But she wouldn't share her hitching stories with him or her family. Never!

During the next few hours, cars stopped to give her rides. According to the mileage signposts, she traveled close to a hundred miles further into France. She stopped at a hostel in a small village near Bordeaux. Much to her delight, the manager spoke English.

"I know someone driving toward Paris this afternoon," said the hostel manager. "Let me make a call."

Shortly, a small car arrived, driven by an older woman with long, gray hair. The hostel manager introduced them. "This is Madame Sarfo. She speaks no English, but she drives to Poiters every Tuesday."

Madame Sarfo nodded.

Lynne shook hands with her, noticing her fingers felt as smooth as a *pointe* shoe satin, like her grandmother's. Madame drove north into the countryside near Poiters where she pulled off the road and pointed to a farmhouse. *"Ici? Pensione, oui?"*

Lynne stepped from the car with her suitcase. *"Merci, Madame."* She stood to watch the car disappear over a rise in the road. As she walked toward the farmhouse, she hoped Madame understood she was broke rather than expecting she could pay for cozy overnight accommodations.

Oct. 12
Near Poiters, France
Chilly

I had a ride to a hostel that was really a farmhouse. The owner let me sleep in a loft and gave me a meal since I helped in the kitchen. Hearing her radio play ballet music brought tears to my eyes, but the promise of a shower and breakfast makes me smile.

Miles to Paris: 140

Days to make Paris: 0
but I tried!

Spent: $1 bed & breakfast
Money left: $6.05

The next morning, her sixty-mile trek toward Tours began with four hours of walking before she caught a ride that dropped her near the tourist information center. The older woman who manned the office stared at Lynne as she entered.

Lynne smiled. "I'm looking for people who danced in the summer performances last month. I'd like to meet with them, if possible." She stopped when the woman's face screwed up into a frown. Her clothes. She forgot how scruffy she looked. She started again.

"I'm a dancer. My ride ditched me in Portugal. I'm hitchhiking back to Paris. I thought maybe one of the dancers I'd met last month might help me find a free place to stay."

The woman nodded and picked up the phone. Twenty minutes later, a woman entered the office and exchanged nods with the worker. "Vous avez dansé ici en Août, oui?"

"*Oui. Americains à Paris,*" Lynne said.

The woman who arrived led Lynne to her car and drove her several miles, chattering in French all the way. Lynne smiled and nodded.

They stopped at a small home in the countryside with a handful of cars parked out front. Lynne was greeted by a roomful of young dancers and their parents. She was shown to a small bedroom with a bathroom down the hall. The homeowner handed her a fluffy towel and a fresh bar of lavender-scented, French-milled soap.

Lynne emerged in her cleanest clothes and with her hair pulled into a tidy ponytail. She was placed at the head of the table and saw that everyone sat looking her direction. Were they waiting for her like she'd waited for Madame Zelb in Paris? Maybe. She nodded. Immediately, the plates of breads and cheeses and bowls of hot squash soup were sent around the table. Tears rose in her eyes; they'd waited for her. Even though she wore ratty clothing and frumpy socks, she was their guest of honor.

As they ate, the dancers peppered her with questions in a mix of French and English. She did her best to answer, noticing their amused expressions at her fragmented French. When she laughed at herself, they joined in, putting her at ease.

Later the homeowner shoved back the living room furniture. The young dancers shared several routines and invited Lynne to join them. She quickly slipped off her itchy socks and took a deep breath as she let herself sway and dance barefoot to snippets from *Sleeping Beauty*, the *Nutcracker* and *Giselle*. After an hour everyone stopped, too exhausted to continue.

The group disbanded, but not before Lynne invited everyone to visit her in Montana. "I'll find a place for each of you to stay. I hope you will come to visit."

After the guests left, the hostess handed Lynne a second fresh towel and motioned toward the bathroom, indicating she was welcome to take another shower if she wished. She patted Lynne's arm and departed. "*Bon Nuit*."

The evening of dancing, laughter and companionship, and the second shower made her feel cared for. She scrubbed her hair and fell into a cozy bed with sheets, a blanket, and a quilt, knowing she'd sleep well for one of the few times since she'd left Sagres.

In the morning a car arrived to drive her Orléans. She was handed a paid train ticket for Paris and a cloth bag with a packed lunch.

Tears overwhelmed her. She hugged the hostess and promised to write and send Intermountain Ballet performance programs for the young dancers she met last night.

As the Orléans train slid away from the depot, Lynne waved to her ride, then leaned back and closed her eyes. She'd made a trek of over fifteen hundred miles on her own with help from caring strangers. Soon she'd be in Paris. She smiled and took out her journal.

Oct. 14 Orléans, France

drizzly outside / sunny inside myself

  Last few days a handful of strangers took me in and cared for me. Last night I showered twice, ate, danced, and laughed. I've missed any chance to take the ship home with Hal as my mentor, but I'm okay. Now I'm riding on a train to Paris, thanks to the kindness and a few dollars from French dancers and their families. Somehow it will all work out.

Miles to Paris: 100 but doesn't matter anymore

Money spent: $0
Money left: $6.05

33

Lynne exited the Métro and took a slow, deep breath. It smelled different in the fall with the muggy heat gone, replaced by a breeze and the aroma of wet autumn leaves, but it was still Paris.

"Welcome home, Lynne. Why, thank you. It's good to be back!" Her loud declaration drew stares from a few, but most Parisians who passed her this late evening appeared not to notice.

She climbed the stairs to street level and headed to Le Palais, her former home away from home, hoping to find a friendly face and a bed for the night. Tomorrow, she'd work out how to get back to Billings.

Since she had no money left for rent, she waited until the door opened to sneak inside and up the stairs to Kitsy's room. The hallway was quiet. She slid off her second-hand jacket and used it like a cushion outside Kitsy's door. It probably would be a three-hour wait, but she wasn't in a rush any longer.

Footsteps in the hallway woke her. Renny looked down at her. "*Mon Cherie*! You arz bak. Kitsy no live here now."

"Where did she go?"

"To live wiz boyfriend. Now a man live here."

Lynne felt her insides drop. She did a quick recovery and stood up. "May I stay with you, *s'il vous plaît*?"

He shook his head. "Now girl friend stay wiz me." He backed away and knocked on Jae's door. Was he deserting her, just like that?

Locks clicked and the door opened. Jae smiled as Renny handed her a bag of food. They spoke quietly for a few moments; he turned to Lynne.

"She say you stay wiz her. One or two night, okay?"

Lynne nodded and stepped into the apartment. Jae signaled for her to sit on a small sofa and for Renny to join her as she began a long conversation with him.

"She thanks your kindness to her and welcomes you. She wants to say she is shy."

"I know. Bert shared her story with us."

At the mention of Bert's name, Jae smiled and spoke again with Renny. "She say he kind like you. We wonder why you dress so different today."

Lynne explained about Uncle Leo, her long trek, and her current lack of funds. Tears spilled down her cheeks as she told them how much she wanted to go home.

When Renny stood up to leave, he reached into his pocket and pulled out several coins. He put them in Lynne's hand. She shook her head.

"We are friends, *oui*?"

"*Oui*."

"You take."

She blinked away her tears and gave him a quick hug. "*Merci beaucoup*."

Jae latched the four locks behind him, then handed Lynne a soft wool blanket, pointed to the sofa, tucked her in, turned down the lights, and disappeared into her bedroom. Lynne smiled. Tomorrow, she would figure out how to get back home. Tonight, she closed her eyes, grateful for dear friends and this warm place to sleep.

Thursday morning dawned cloudy and windy. Lynne walked to the post office to make her call. Earlier she'd exchanged her remaining coins from Spain and Portugal and, with the money Renny had given her, she could make one transatlantic call and take the Métro to Le Palais.

The call went through quickly, but not before her palms became sweaty and her body became jittery. What if no one answered?

"Hello?"

"Noel. It's Lynne." She choked back her tears. "I kinda need your help. Leo left me. I made it back to Paris, but I missed the ship by several days. I don't have any money or any way to get back to the states."

"My lord, Lynne. What happened? Are you okay?"

"I'm fine. I hate to ask you, but could you loan me the money to come home? I might be able to catch a freighter to New York. I have my train ticket, so I can get back to Billings. I promise I'll repay you as soon as I get my job back." She crossed her fingers...*if* she got her job back. "I'll explain everything when I get there."

"Is there a way I can call you back?"

"Not easily. Could you spare two hundred dollars so I can catch a freighter home?"

Noel was silent for a few seconds.

Lynne's heart raced. Her expensive call time was ticking away. Was he trying to avoid helping her? Maybe he'd moved on in his life and wanted to brush her aside.

"Give me overnight, Lynne. I'll book you a seat on a Pan Am flight. Call back tomorrow to get the details. I'll pick you up in Billings."

She started crying. "I can't call you back. This call took all my money."

"Let me think about this a minute."

Seconds ticked by. Her call time was running out.

"I'll schedule you a flight as soon as possible. Then I'll call Le Palais and leave a message with Madame Zelb with the day and time. Does that work?"

"Oh, yes! Thanks. I just need to get to New York. I'll call as soon as I get home, okay?"

"Not a problem. I miss you. You're sure you're okay?"

"I am now. I'll wait to get your message from Madame. Thanks for bailing me out. I'll see you soon, and I promise to pay you back." She hung up and sat quietly while her heart calmed.

After she checked for mail at the American Express office and found nothing, she walked back to Le Palais. As she entered the foyer, she met Madame Zelb. Through their mixture of fractured French, occasional English, and sign language, she explained her presence and the anticipated phone call to Madame's phone. The surprised proprietor nodded her cooperation and gave her a hug. Lynne would miss these people more than she had ever imagined when she applied to be part of the ballet tour.

୨୦

That evening she sat with Jae and ate the food Renny brought upstairs. They listened to records and went to bed early. Once again she slept soundly, moving through a series of dreams about hiking, dancing, and facing Madame Cosper while wearing her boots and wooly socks.

The call the next morning from Pan Am confirmed her ticket to New York leaving late that evening. Thanks to Noel, she could finally go home.

That afternoon Jae stood by her window, cranking in her clothesline. She handed Lynne the clothes they'd washed last night.

"*Merci.*" Lynne shook out her blue-pinstriped shirtwaist dress. She slipped it on and smoothed the skirt. The cigarette burn was mended.

She pointed to the tiny stitches with each stripe perfectly matched and looked at Jae. "*Vous?*"

"*Oui.*" Jae blushed and smiled.

Tears tumbled from Lynne's eyes. Why was she so emotional over a mended skirt? She reached out and hugged the elderly lady, who returned the embrace.

Once her suitcase was packed she handed it to Jae. "*Je voudrais... vous donne ...donner...ma ...suitcase.*"

Jae stared, then nodded. She rushed to find her purse and pressed ten francs into Lynne's hand.

"*Non.* Too much!" She squeezed her fingers closer together.

Jae nodded, fished around in her purse, and handed her five more *francs*.

Lynne laughed and handed back the ten francs. Both women smiled.

༄

The flight was half full as Lynne stepped onto the plane and handed her ticket to a stewardess. The young woman escorted her to a window seat in the fourth row.

Lynne looked around. "This must be wrong."

"No, Miss Meadows, your seat assignment is here, in first class. May I bring you a blanket and a beverage?"

Lynne nodded and sat down. It felt good to be spoiled after months of frenzied choreography and performances, the pain of her fall and recovery, and being left almost penniless to travel through three foreign countries where she didn't speak the language. Despite it all, she had survived, made new friends, and was going home.

The overnight flight was quiet after dinner was served on a real plate with real silverware and free wine if she'd wanted it. She leaned back her seat and slept until the intercom announcement they'd be landing shortly. At the airport, she exchanged her last francs for dollars, then took a taxi to Penn Station. She called Noel, then boarded the train home.

༄

She yawned as she placed the promised collect call to Noel from Great Falls. No answer. She walked outside, while waiting for her connecting train to Billings to arrive. After another unsuccessful attempt to reach Noel, she resigned herself to walking to Mrs. B.'s boarding house.

༄

The conductor announced their approach to Billings as the train passed the oil refineries. She pulled out her comb and lipstick as she'd done so many times in Europe, determined to look 'put together,' as Cheryl called it. She doubted the people of Billings would notice or care.

The train rolled to a stop. She stood in the aisle and moved to the exit, dreading the cold blast of air waiting for her outside. She buttoned her jacket, straightened her shoulders, and stepped onto the platform. That's when she heard, "Lynne Meadows to the ticket counter, Lynne Meadows."

Noel stood next to the entry door, his nose buried in his coat, his cowboy hat pulled low. He'd come. She waved and rushed toward him. He pushed back his hat and opened his arms just before she slammed into him and pressed herself snugly against his chest.

"Wow!" He coughed. "Welcome home."

She felt his heartbeat through his coat. "How did you know I'd arrive early?"

"I didn't, but I've met every train since yesterday, just in case you caught an earlier one." He kissed her hair.

Tears trailed down her cheeks. She stood on tiptoe and kissed him.

"Let's get out of this wind," he said as he grabbed her hand.

Inside, they stood in a silent embrace and kissed. "Hi," she said.

"I've missed you, Lynne Meadows. Are you hungry or thirsty? Want to stop somewhere after we grab your bags?"

"I don't have any bags. What you see is all that made the trip home."

"All I need is the pretty girl I left in France." Noel eased her away from him and frowned. "You've lost a lot of weight. Are you okay?"

"I'll be fine once you take me to the Dude Ranch. It was a favorite hangout for Marta and me. I'd love one of their big, sloppy burgers, plus a huge plate of fries."

Noel laughed. "Anything you want, darlin'."

They talked, ate, and talked some more. His eyes grew wide and misty as she related how Leo abandoned her and she had to hitch rides back to Paris. He chastised her gently for not calling him sooner. "I'd have been heartbroken if anything happened to you."

She was almost afraid to believe him after her family—the people who were supposed to love her most—had turned their backs on her. Then she remembered all the strangers who had helped her along the way. Maybe family wasn't always determined by blood.

Noel checked his watch. "It's five o'clock; where are we headed? Do you have a place to stay?"

"I need to call Mrs. B.'s boarding house. That's where Marta lived when she danced in Billings. I hope she saved me a room."

He started his truck. "I have a better idea. I think you should take a couple days off and then ease back into Billings. We have tons of space at the ranch. You'd have an entire wing of the house to yourself. You can sleep in, make calls, do whenever you want. What do you think?"

"I think it sounds great, but I have no clothes."

He laughed. "Billings has stores. We'll pick up what you need."

"You do remember I'm penniless."

"I can spare a few dollars."

She smiled to herself. Coming home had never felt so good.

※

The sun shone in the bedroom where Lynne spent that night. The clock beside the bed read ten-thirty. Where was she? What day was it? The telltale painting of a cowboy roping a horse made her smile. Noel's ranch.

She took her second shower since arriving, enjoying the leisure of unlimited hot water without worrying about how many coins she'd need to keep it warm. After she slipped on her new jeans, striped cotton blouse, and thick, plum-colored sweater, she found Noel working in his office.

"Good morning."

He looked up from his paperwork and smiled. "Mornin'. How did you sleep?" He stood and walked to hug her.

"Like a baby."

"Good. Hungry? Want to call anyone?"

"Always hungry and yes, I need to call Mrs. B."

The rest of the day while Noel worked, she dozed, walked around the house, investigated rooms, and met the ranch hands until time to visit with Mrs. B.

Now she stood with Noel on the boarding house porch, waiting for someone to answer their knock. They stood in a tight hug until the door opened and Lynne saw Mrs. B.'s friendly face.

"Ah, Lynne! You made it. Welcome home!" Mrs. B. grabbed her and hugged her. "Come in, come in."

She led them into the dining room, where the boarders sat eating apple pie and drinking coffee. Mrs. B. gestured toward two empty chairs. "Please join us. May I offer you dessert and coffee?"

"Coffee," Lynne and Noel said in unison and laughed.

For the next half hour, Shorty, James, and Faith, the new woman living in the downstairs room, spoke with Lynne about her dancing and traveling through Europe.

"I'm not certain where I stand with the ballet company," Lynne said. "I'm calling tomorrow to speak with Madame Cosper."

Mrs. B.'s expression sobered. She reached for Lynne's hand. "Anna Cosper had a stroke. She's in Billings General."

Lynne gasped. "How is she doing? Is she allowed visitors?"

"I understand she's recovering slowly. As far as visitors go, I suggest you call Damien tomorrow."

Just then Carol, the perpetual boarder, walked in. She stopped and stared. "You?" Carol turned to Mrs. B. "What is *she* doing here?"

Mrs. B. smiled. "Lynne is our newest boarder. She's taking Marta's old room tomorrow."

"Is she also using the basement to practice?"

Mrs. B. turned to Lynne. "If she wishes. It just needs a little cleaning up. You do remember you have boxes stowed down there?"

Lynne smiled and looked at Carol. "Yes. I plan to use the space evenings after classes." She watched Carol roll her eyes and leave the dining area. "Where were we? Oh yes, I was telling you about my hitchhiking experience."

Later that evening she returned to Noel's ranch to pack her belongings in a small bag Noel loaned her. She felt bittersweet about leaving, but it wouldn't be proper to stay longer. Word of an extended stay would no doubt seep back to the ballet company, putting her morals into question before she had a chance to prove her worth as a dancer.

Losing the chance to see Noel every day left a sad spot inside her. She needed to think about something else, like dealing with Carol. Wait until she told Marta about Carol still living at the boarding house and working as a shop girl instead of the business office manager she'd blathered on and on about last year.

The news about Madame worried her. Even though they'd had their differences, she wished the woman a full recovery. Tomorrow, she'd call Damien and talk with him about Madame and about regaining a position with the company. After she moved into the boarding house, she'd update Marta on everything, or as much as she could afford, considering the cost of long distance rates.

34

Lynne drove her turquoise Nash to the ballet company for her meeting with Damien. She smiled as she drove alone, in her own car, on familiar streets. She felt as if she'd never left, that her past five months were part dream, part nightmare instead of a life-changing experience.

She entered through the dancer's side door. Nothing had changed since she'd left: the smell of sweat and rosin, instructions shouted over music that started and stopped. Only the music was different.

She moved quietly past the practice rooms and up the stairs to the ballet office, knowing she was early, a new habit she hoped would impress Damien. He'd dismiss classes any minute for their lunch break, so she'd know the company decision very soon.

His voice carried up the stairway before she saw him. "Check with the theatre. I'll be down in a few minutes."

She straightened as he approached. His smile reassured her that she remained in his good graces.

"Lynne! Welcome back! I hope you are feeling well. You look a bit gaunt. Dieting or hard work?"

"Dancing over fifty performances, traveling, and walking long distances tend to wear off any excess."

He invited her into the office and closed the door. "Before you ask, Madame is improving. She's out of urgent care and may have visitors soon. We're all relieved. As you can imagine, our prep for our upcoming performances has taken a back seat."

"I'm glad Madame will be fine."

"She's not going to be fine. She's experiencing partial paralysis, but we hope she recovers her mobility."

"May I see her and bring Marta along?"

Damien nodded. "I'll put you on the list for later next week when she'll be up to having company. Now, on to you. How was your dance experience? Cheryl sent me a note that you were especially helpful. She mentioned your injury but said your help with my choreography and support of the other dancers proved invaluable. I'm impressed."

"Enough to offer me a contract to the end of this year?"

"Absolutely. I don't think we need you to re-audition either. Return for warm-ups and rehearsals, starting tomorrow. That will allow me to cover you for our remaining seven months of the season. Sound okay?"

"Perfect. Thank you." Lynne turned to leave but stopped and turned back to face him. "Thanks for supporting me for the summer troupe. I learned a lot. Cheryl was a great mentor."

"I remember Anna mentioning she was a strong dancer. She wasn't soloist material, but she's proven to be an excellent teacher."

"I'm hoping I'll prove to you that I'll make a dependable soloist. Is there room for one more?"

Damien grinned. "I think a space will open up, if your attitude has permanently changed since last spring. Cheryl's report suggests that's the case."

The boarding house dinner dishes were cleared away and everyone moved on to their evening activities when Mrs. B. handed Lynne the key to her room, Marta's old room.

"I'm surprised it's still available. I thought it would be taken by now."

"No, dear, the college finished new dormitories. Students like being close to their activities and classes. Plus, that large apartment complex west of town opened in August. These days, more and more people want their own space."

"Well, I love it here and I'm glad you had room for me. I do have one problem: money. I won't see a paycheck until the end of November. I have a little savings, but not enough to cover my rent."

Mrs. B. smiled. "Lynne, I've known you for more than two years. You'll pay me as soon as you can. In the meantime, take some time to settle in; make the room yours. I had James and Shorty bring your boxes up from the basement. They're stacked in the closet. Let me know if I can do anything to help you. I'll bring up a pot of tea in a few minutes. A hot drink always makes a task easier."

Lynne finished unpacking her last box just as Mrs. B. arrived carrying a tray with a small teapot, two cups and a plate of cookies. "I thought you might be ready for a snack." She set the tray on the dresser by the window and plopped down in the rocking chair. "Almost done, I see."

Lynne sat on the bed with her legs folded in front of her. "I'd tossed out so much before I left that I only have the bare essentials." She paused. "After living out of a suitcase for months, I want a less cluttered life."

Mrs. B. nodded and reached into her apron pocket. She handed Lynne two letters. "Marta sent these here for you. I suggest you open the top envelope first.

> Elle Selbryth and Robert Marsden
> announce their private family wedding ceremony
> Sunday, July 12, 1959
> at the Marsden home
> Bremerton, Washington
>
> You are cordially invited to attend their
> Reception Celebration
> Sunday, July 12, 1959
>
> Drop-in between
> 4:00 - 7:00 PM
> Holland Dance Studio
> Burwell at Montgomery
> Bremerton, Washington

Lynne smiled. "Did you go to the wedding?"

Mrs. B. shook her head. "I couldn't get away. I sent a leather-covered photo album from you and me. Elle loved it and said to thank you when I saw you. And, no, you can't pay for half of it."

"Thanks. So, ah, Carol hasn't changed?"

"Yes and no. She gave up on college and took a job she thinks is beneath her dignity. It's made her more sour than ever. If she gives you trouble, let me know."

"Don't worry. I can handle Carol."

After Mrs. B. left and Lynne finished putting her belongings away, she opened the second letter.

August 20, 1959

Dear Lynne,

 The news I sent to you in June boomeranged back to me. I'm resending it, this time to Mrs. B. I knew you left your boxes in her basement, so you'd return to claim them after your French adventure.

 Also, I thought you might move into her boarding house if you're staying in Billings.

 From your post cards and letters, I sense you're having a great experience. Bet you were exhausted by the end of the season! Once you settle in, I'll expect a call so you can share the nitty-gritty details with me.

 Mom and Robert's ceremony was beautiful. His garden was in full bloom. Mom carried a bouquet of his Peace roses. She wore a lovely beige dress she made last year but had never worn.

 The reception at the dance studio was great fun. We celebrated owning the building as well as their marriage. Tons of dancers and their families came. We ran out of food, but no one cared. It was a lovely summer day, like I imagine you enjoyed across France.

 By the time you get this, we'll be well into our fall classes. Call me. I want to see and hear all about _everything!_

STOP!!

You need to sit down before you read the Bremerton Sun Announcements for June, 1959. I think you'll be pleasantly surprised. At least I hope you will. I am.

(*Seattle Times* reprinted from *Portland News Tribune* article)

Mrs. Robert Marsden of Bremerton, Washington announces the engagement of her daughter, Marta Selbryth to Steven Mason, son of Diane and Neal Mason of Billings, Montana.

The future bride is a former dancer with the Intermountain Ballet Company and is the current co-owner of the Holland Dance Studio in Bremerton, Washington.

The future groom is a recent graduate of Rocky Mountain College in Billings, Montana, and a reporter for the Portland News Tribune.

A June 1960 wedding is planned in Bremerton, Washington. The couple will make their home in Portland, Oregon.

I expect you to be my maid of honor.
Marta (almost Mason!)

Lynne thought, all that time Marta spent deciding where her heart felt most comfortable, with Steve or Sam, I could have told her if she'd asked me. She fell for Steve early on. She didn't know it, but I did. I wonder what she'd have decided for me if she'd met all the guys I dated before Noel? Would she have warned me off? What if I'd met Noel first?

Lynne continued reading the letter.

> That's all for now, except to tell you I love Steve with all my heart. I see him most weekends and on holidays. He drives up or I take the train to Portland. Someday soon I need my own car! (when I have the $$ to spare). Bet you love having a new car! I'm jealous.
>
> Steve's rented a small house near where he works. I planted a tiny veggie garden that he's kept growing fairly well. Of course, now the only things still growing are the squash and pumpkins. I really need to learn how to cook like my mom to make the garden count! Only got until next June to learn so many things before I become Mrs. Steve Mason. I'm excited, scared, and happy all at once!
>
> Call me as soon as you get this. Good luck with whatever you decide about dancing and Noel and life!
>
> Love,
> Marta

Lynne slid the letter in the bedside table and poured a second cup of tea. Hm-m. Peppermint tasted good on a chilly evening. While she drank her tea, she surveyed the way Marta arranged the room. Should she rearrange it? Make it her unique space? Nah. This worked.

She walked to her dresser and picked up the picture of her and Marta taken during their first year with the ballet company. She looked in the mirror, then back to the photo. Marta looked the same as when she'd seen her last December. But she herself looked different. Was it her makeup? Her hair?

Suddenly, she laughed until tears streaked down her face. A deep calm settled over her. It wasn't her face or the way she did her hair. She'd changed inside. What she saw now was a woman instead of a girl.

She walked to the phone in the hall alcove and called Marta collect. No answer.

୧

Butterflies raced through Lynne as she parked, locked her car, and entered the ballet company, ready to rejoin warm-ups. She found her locker with her name still on it, a good sign they expected her to return. As she slipped on her ballet slippers, she heard a familiar, grating voice and looked up to see Suzette.

"So, they kicked you out of the troupe, huh? I'm not surprised."

Lynne lifted her chin and smiled. "No, the season ended last month. I took the last few weeks to travel around Europe. Now I'm back and ready to resume dancing."

"Well, don't expect us to put you on a pedestal or anything. You're no better than we are. In fact, I'm about to make soloist. I doubt there'll be room for you since I see you're wearing ballet slippers instead of *pointe* shoes."

"We danced well over fifty performances during our tour. I'm starting out slowly, but I expect to be ready for upcoming auditions." She walked out of the dressing room picturing Suzette as a hairy bug. She stopped. A slimy slug was more appropriate.

Before class began, she chatted with the dancers she knew and was introduced to the new members. They asked about her summer just as Damien walked into the practice room. "I'll tell you what. Once my dance bag reaches me, I'll invite you over to see our dance programs. We can talk about some of the dancers I met."

Lynne felt stiff as warm-ups moved from the *barre* to center work. She'd not used her dance muscles for a month, but there was no way she'd share that with Suzette or anyone else. She straightened and resumed practice.

Each evening over the next week, she practiced choreography from *Sleeping Beauty,* the program for the upcoming October performances. At dinner one evening, the boarders asked her about the production.

"It's the first time we're doing the full ballet. Even though I know much of it, they have blocked out the dancing without me because I wasn't here for rehearsals."

Carol pointed her fork toward Lynne. "I'm sick of that slow, fairy music twittering over and over. And that wedding music! First it's slow, then loud, then full of violin solos. Why do you practice when you aren't dancing in any of the shows?"

Lynne stared at her and smiled. Carol must know the ballet and was actually listening to their conversation. "It's for muscle memory. When the ballet is performed in future years, I'll remember Damien's adaptations of the choreography and be prepared to dance in the production."

Carol shook her head. "That sounds just plain stupid." She returned to her usual head-down-and-eat position, leaving the rest of the table staring at the top of her head.

After dinner, when she'd finished practicing, Lynne tried again to reach Marta. Maybe she'd need to send her a post card from Billings. She'd done that when she left back in June.

∽

Her weekend with Noel began with an early Saturday dinner at his ranch, after which he started a fire in the fireplace and pulled her to join him on a nearby sofa.

"We could go to a movie or out for something to drink. I bet you didn't see many movies while you were gone."

"You're right. No movies and no Green River sodas. But it feels good just to sit here and talk or watch one of your western shows. Besides, then we can get cozy." She leaned over, rested her head on his shoulder, and closed her eyes.

He kissed her hair. "Plus, I have you all to myself."

❧

By the time *Sleeping Beauty* performances ended, Lynne knew the corps dances and the major solos. She prepared as a backup dancer, but wasn't needed. Instead, she was relegated to helping back stage and watching the company dancers perform without her.

Jer exited the theatre the same time as Lynne. "How was it, watching us dance?"

"It was fine, but my feet itched to be out there with you. Having *The Nutcracker* up next is a bit of a letdown. I love the ballet, but I dread living out of a suitcase so soon after my months doing that in Europe."

He laughed. "So that's how it's going to be. Every time we tour, you're going to complain like Suzette about how awful your life was touring in Europe?"

"That's not what I meant. I'm anxious to learn new choreography, like the *corps* dances in *Firebird* that's coming up in January."

Jer tapped her head. "Hello! Anyone in there? Read the schedule. We'll be working on *Firebird* as well as *The Nutcracker*, so you'll get your wish." He backed away toward his car. "I expect you to give Suzette lots of competition for solos!"

Lynne smiled as she walked on, but one large hurdle still lay ahead. She'd finally reached Marta, who would arrive in two days. It was time to visit Madame Cosper.

35

Lynne grabbed Marta in a bear hug. Tears and laughter melted away their long months of separation.

"Let me look at you." Marta held Lynne at arms length. "Something's different. Have you changed your hair? Fallen in love? Lost weight?"

"All of the above. It looks like you've changed as well. I think your engagement brings out the smiles in your eyes." Lynne hugged Marta again. "I've thought about you and missed you so much."

They spent the entire day holed up, talking in Lynne's room, only emerging for dinner conversation with Mrs. B., James, and Shorty. Once Carol saw Marta seated at the table, she stopped in the doorway and left the boarding house muttering, "I can't deal with two of them!"

When she and Marta returned upstairs, Lynne shared her travel journal. Marta closed the cover, she reached out, and hugged Lynne. "I can't imagine how I'd handle all those setbacks. Some days must have felt like weeks. How did you keep going?"

"What choice did I have? Besides, I knew *someone* would help me."

"I'd have found a way if you'd called."

"I know. I thought of contacting you, but your plate is full. I got back, didn't I?"

"So when do I meet your Noel? You can't tell me how wonderful he is and not introduce us."

"We'll drive out to his ranch tomorrow afternoon. He's fixing us his Saturday special: a chuck wagon meal. Actually, Cook does most of the work. Noel just lights the barbecue and makes his special sauce."

⁂

Lynne watched Marta, who watched Noel standing at the barbecue, stirring his concoction. The day turned sunny, but they needed jackets and blankets if they planned to tough-out the wind and remain outside until the chuck wagon meal was finished and brought inside.

Marta carried on a steady conversation with Noel about the ranch and the herd, then changed the subject. "What's your version of meeting Lynne?"

Lynne looked up, her eyes wide with surprise. "Marta! I told you how we met."

Noel turned to Lynne. "I don't think I ever told you *my* version." His eyes twinkled as he looked from her to Marta. "Now's a good time to share it. So, Marta, I went to the ballet to represent our family and to speak with the directors and a few patrons. When I'd done my duty, I looked for a quick escape. I stepped into a small room by an exit and saw Lynne. She looked a little lonely and probably wanted to be left alone, but something told me I should get to know her."

"Really?" Lynne stood with her hands on her hips. "You thought I looked lonely? I was tired and biding my time until it was okay to leave."

"Sh-h! It's my story! I walked over, sat down, and watched her out of the corner of my eye. She was watching me as well and—"

"I was not! I think you're making this up to entertain Marta."

"Her side glances invited me to get to know her, and here we are, five months later." He looked at Lynne and winked. "She can fill in the details she wants to share." He pulled the meat from the barbecue and handed the platter to Lynne. Then he picked up his sauce, held the door to the kitchen open, and ushered them to the dining table.

∾

On the drive back to the boarding house, Marta chuckled. "I think you two are a perfect match. He likes you as you are; plus, he appreciates and supports your career. He loves to tease you and rile you up. I'm sure you counter every move he makes, right?"

Lynne grinned. "I do. He's easygoing and kind. Regardless of which story you believe, I'm glad we met. The fortune teller was right when she mentioned the almost-loves in my past and that I now know what I want. Noel makes me feel content; he makes me feel important."

∾

Sunday morning, Marta and Lynne met Damien at the ballet company and shared a brief but pleasant conversation.

"Soon I'll move to Portland," Marta said, "and I'll continue to teach dance. I'm getting married next June, so I'll also pursue a new chapter in my life."

Damien smiled. "Good for you. I'm glad to hear you've found a way to share your love of dancing. Are you ready to begin solo tryouts, Lynne?"

"Me? I thought I'd missed them. Suzette said..." Lynne stopped and chuckled. "She implied she'd gotten the position. I guess I need to read the bulletin board for myself."

Damien nodded his head. "Yes, you should. I'd share more if I could. I suggest you listen to the dancers' gossip. You'll get the latest on Miss

Suzette's antics as well as her future." As they prepared to leave to visit Madame, he added, "Early afternoon is the best time of day for your visit. I'm certain she'll be as glad to see both of you as I've been."

༄

The convalescent center was more inviting than a sterile hospital room. Lynne and Marta checked in and were directed to Madame's room at the end of the hallway. Hand rails and framed art trailed along the walls. Many people in wheelchairs sat in doorways, watching the comings and goings of visitors.

They knocked on Madame's closed door and heard a faint, "Come."

Madame sat in a wheelchair looking out a window onto a courtyard. She turned as they entered. "Oh." Her lopsided smile faded as though she expected someone else.

They entered and handed Madame a bouquet of yellow roses with baby's breath. She reached out for them, then dropped her shaking arm and struggled to point. "There. Put in water."

The air in the room felt used up. Lynne wondered if she could stand here and breathe without fainting. Did Marta feel the same way?

Marta filled a waiting vase with water while Lynne shifted from one foot to the other.

"Well?" Madame said as she stared at them.

"We wanted to stop in and see how you were feeling," Lynne said. "We're sorry you've been ill."

"I'm not...ill. I...had...a stroke. You've...seen...now... go...re...port... to... others."

"Madame, we're not here to report back to anyone," Lynne said. "We're here because we care about you. Marta took the train here just to see you."

"I really want you to have a speedy recovery," Marta said. "Is there anything we can do for you?"

A tear slid down Madame's cheek. She attempted to wipe it away with her shaky arm, but dropped her hand and her head. Slowly she looked up at them. "My... career...ended. Like...yours."

"My career isn't over," Lynne blurted out. "I've returned to the company and am preparing to try out as a soloist."

"And my dancing hasn't ended either, Madame Cosper," Marta reached out to touch Madame's shoulder. "I teach others to dance. I find it satisfying and—"

Madame pulled away from Marta's touch. "Both...of... you...," she shook her head, "disappoint...like...my...daugh…ters."

෴

Twenty long minutes later, Lynne and Marta walked to Lynne's car. They sat in the parking lot in silence for several minutes, then drove to the Bison Cafe for a cup of tea.

Lynne wadded up her napkin and tossed it away from her. "I'm shocked that Madame lost so much of her speech and that her hands tremble."

Marta nodded. "It is shocking, almost as much as when she compared us to her two daughters and how we disappointed her. I didn't know she had children."

"Neither did I," Lynne said. "But a lot of what she said is true. I *was* often late, and I was constantly putting my foot in my mouth. You *were* shy. You did take chances, like the hiking afternoon with Steve. But she can't blame you for breaking your ankle. That was an accident. It sounds like her daughter Valaria's broken leg was serious, but Madame blames her for it not healing properly. Maybe when they spend some time together over the next few months, they'll reconcile."

Marta laughed. "Not if she calls both of them cripples. Why doesn't she see that she still has a lot to share? She could consult or create choreography. Even though she's grumpy, she's extremely talented."

The waitress returned with hot water and laid their bill on the table. Marta grabbed it off the table. "My treat! You let me invade your weekend as well as your room. If you're the hothead Madame seems to think you are, I'll expect you to wrestle me to the floor over the bill."

Lynne laughed. "I may be a hothead and have dated a lot of guys like her second daughter, but I'm not married and living in Canada. Hitchhiking was as close I ever plan to get to living in the backwoods and pumping water for my family. I wonder who kept Madame so well informed about my life. Somebody must have; she knew a lot."

Marta reached across the table to pat Lynne's hands. "You handled her angry words well. Better than I'd have done."

Lynne shrugged. "Standing there, taking in her insults and listening to her rant about my dating misadventures, made me feel naked, exposed. I wonder if she thought I was Natia."

"I don't know. When she said she knew we'd tell the local newspaper about her condition and destroy her reputation, I nearly fainted."

Lynne stood and grabbed her purse. "Like we'd betray her to anyone or make the dance company look bad. Neither of us wants that."

"Madame's disappointments explain a lot of her bitterness. I'm glad she's wrong about you and me. How could she not see how happy we are? I hope she doesn't unload on her daughters like she did on us."

Lynne stopped on the sidewalk next to her car and turned toward Marta. "If Madame was disappointed in us, she saw our potential. She knew we were strong dancers. When you got hurt and when I acted like a thorn in her life, she may have felt betrayed. She did let me go to

France." Lynne paused. "Maybe she's not an ogre; maybe she really cares about us."

Marta hugged Lynne. "I think you're right! Now promise me you'll stay upbeat and crazy, and this new, thoughtful you won't become bitter like Madame. If that happens, I'll never speak to you again."

※

Sunday evening, Lynne drove Marta to her train. The distance from her friend grew wider and wider as they approached the depot. "We need to be better about staying in touch. I need to know you're okay, and I need you to tell me I'm okay too."

Marta nodded and placed her hand on Lynne's arm. "And I need *you* to keep me upbeat when I'm losing focus. Keep me in the loop about how Noel works out. I really like him. You're a good match."

The PA announced the incoming train. "Passengers traveling west to Bozeman, Missoula, Spokane, and Seattle, prepare to board."

Lynne and Marta looked at each other, smiled, and wiped away their tears. "Write, promise?" they said in unison.

Marta nodded. "I'll get you the gaudiest bridesmaid dress I can find."

Lynne laughed. "That's exactly what I'd expect from you. Let's go back to talking on Sunday evenings."

※

The train disappeared from view, and Lynne once again felt a loss from Marta's leaving. This time she had a special friend to console her, even if he didn't know he was expected to fill that role in her life.

Back in her boarding house room, Lynne looked for stationery. Not finding any, she pulled out a battered, blank post card of downtown Billings.

Dear Mom and Dad,

    I'm back home in Billings. When you see Leo, ask him to ship my second suitcase to 1616 Yellowstone Avenue.

    You're welcome to come for a visit. I won't be returning to Trenton anytime soon.

L.

Our real success in life will be determined by how well we deal with adversity; whether we run from it or race up to it; whether we shrink or grow from it; whether we surrender to it or triumph over it.

What we become depends on our decisions.

—*Life's Greatest Lessons: 20 Things That Matter*
Hal Urban

Glossary of Ballet Terms

arabesque: one leg lifted and held behind the body

balancé: a dancer's waltz step

battement: beating one ankle with the other foot pointed

bourré: tiny steps made while circling or gliding across the floor

chaîné: 2-step linked turns

changement: changing feet positions in the air before landing

chassé: a gliding gallop where one foot chases the other

derrière: toward the back or your backside

développé: to gradually unfold a leg

dos-a-dos: square dancing step; partners circle each other back-to-back

fish dive: a male dancer holds a female and angles her head and arms gracefully toward the stage while her legs slant upward

grand jeté: a split-legged jump

grand reverence: a bow to the instructor to show respect

jeté: a brushing jump from one foot to the other with pointed toes

pas de deux: a dance for two people, usually a male and a female

pirouette: turns on one leg with the other bent

plié: bending the knees over the feet

port de bras: graceful arm movement from one position to another

relevé: to rise onto the ball of the foot or onto pointe

rond de jambe: a half circle drawn with the foot

tour jeté: a dramatic turning jump that circles the floor

Chat, Comment, and Connect with the Author

Book clubs and schools are invited to participate in FREE virtual discussions with Paddy Eger.

Chat:
Invite Paddy to chat with your group via the web or phone.

Comment:
Ask thought-provoking questions or give Paddy feedback.

Connect:
Find Paddy at a local book talk or meet and greet. Visit her blog and website for dates, times, and locations or to set up your group's virtual discussion. For excerpts, author interviews, news, and future releases, visit PaddyEger.com

About the Author

Paddy Eger is the multi-award winning author of *84 Ribbons* and *When the Music Stops—Dance On*, the first two books in her ballet trilogy. The books follow Marta, a young professional dancer, through her year with a ballet company and afterward as she heads home to put her life back together. The third book follows her life and her best friend, Lynne's, as both young women lay out their careers and step into adulthood.

As a former dancer, Paddy shares her love of music and dance as well as choreography and travel through her young adult novels. "It's important to look at the struggles as well as the successes the characters experience so they are well-rounded and human."

Non-fiction is another interest Paddy shares with people who work with students. Her *Educating America* book and materials share easy-to-use ideas to involve students as well as classroom assistants.

In her free time, Paddy writes in other genres, reads, helps in classrooms, and travels. She and her family live in western Washington, but consider the world their home base.

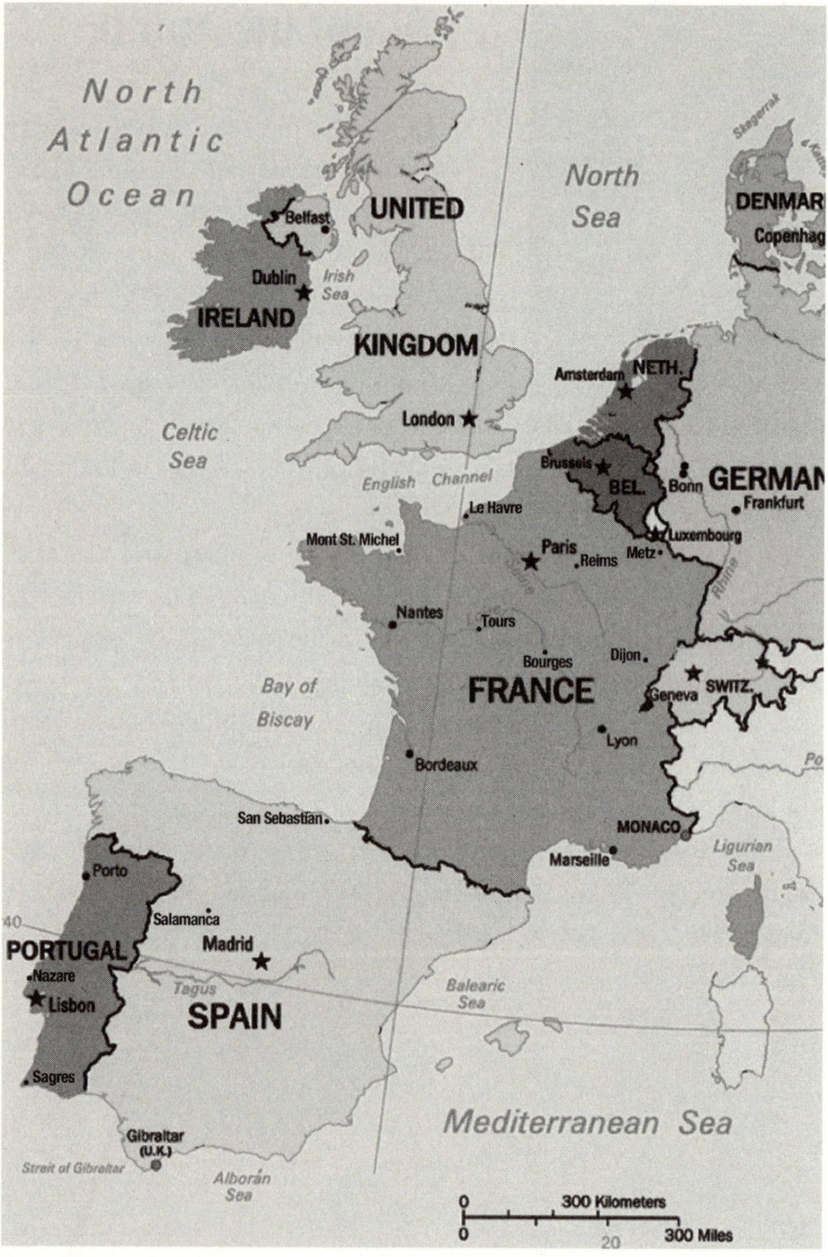

North Atlantic Ocean
UNITED KINGDOM
North Sea
Skagerrak
DENMARK
Copenhagen
Belfast
Dublin
Irish Sea
IRELAND
NETH.
Amsterdam
London
Celtic Sea
English Channel
Brussels
BEL.
Bonn
GERMANY
Frankfurt
Luxembourg
Le Havre
Mont St. Michel
Paris
Reims
Metz
Rhine
Seine
Nantes
Tours
Bourges
Dijon
SWITZ.
Geneva
Bay of Biscay
FRANCE
Lyon
Bordeaux
San Sebastian
MONACO
Ligurian Sea
Marseille
Porto
Salamanca
PORTUGAL
Madrid
Nazare
Lisbon
Tagus
SPAIN
Balearic Sea
Sagres
Mediterranean Sea
Gibraltar (U.K.)
Strait of Gibraltar
Alborán Sea
40
20
0
300 Kilometers
0
300 Miles

General Reader's Guide

How would you characterize Lynne's personality?

What problems does Lynne face:
    while dancing with the Intermountain Ballet?
    with her family?
    dating Noel?
How effective are her efforts to make changes?

**What traits serve her well throughout her adventure?
Which created problems?**

Characters in stories interact and affect each other in positive and negative ways.

How do the characters in *Letters to Follow* impact Lynne's decisions?

Lynne faces several challenges on her dance adventure. In your opinion which events created the most difficulty? Why do you believe that to be true?

Lynne forms various 'families' over the course of the story. How does each affect her life and her decisions?

If you read the trilogy, how would you compare the way Marta and Lynne grow and change? How each approached problems?

Hopefully the online music and dance suggestions enhanced your enjoyment of the story. Which segments pique your interest in the attending a live ballet performance?

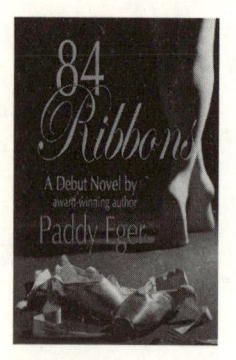

84 Ribbons

"A pure coming-of-age tale with moments of quiet drama *84 Ribbons* is about thriving despite the imperfections of life." YA Foresight, *Foreword Reviews*, Spring 2014. *DanceSpirit* Magazine's Pick of the Month, April 2014. "Any young dancer will find herself in Marta's story", Newbery Honor Author, Kirby Larson, *Hattie Big Sky*.

When the Music Stops—Dance On

Step into Marta's world

In the multi-award-winning second book, Marta struggles to regain her ability to dance and support herself at the same time stepping into adulthood amid unexpected challenges. Will she find a deep well of strength to meet her life-changing situations head-on?

Coming Soon from Paddy Eger

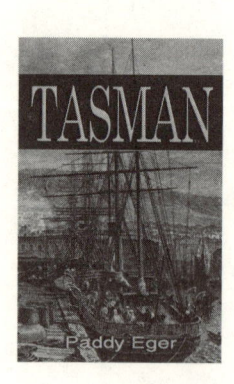

Tasman

In 1850, sixteen year-old Irish lad, Ean McCloud, steps off the boat, his legs in iron shackles, and steps into serving a three-year sentence at the Port Arthur Penal Colony in Tasmania. Falsely convicted, he must now survive the brutal conditions, the backbreaking labor, and time in the silent prison—a place that breaks men's souls. Follow Ean's adventures as he seeks not only to survive but to escape!